SPLICED

JON McGORAN

HOLIDAY HOUSE · NEW YORK

Printed and Bound in December 2018 at Berryville Graphics, Berryville, VA, USA.
www.holidayhouse.com
3   5   7   9   10   8   6   4   2
Library of Congress Cataloging-in-Publication Data

Names: McGoran, Jon, author.
Title: Spliced / by Jon McGoran.
Description: First edition. | New York : Holiday House,
[2017] | Summary: "Sixteen-year-old Jimi Corcoran and
Del, her genetically altered best friend, fight for survival in
a near-future society that is redefining
what it means to be human"— Provided by publisher.
Identifiers: LCCN 2016058466 | ISBN 9780823438556 (hardcover)
Subjects: | CYAC: Genetic engineering—Fiction.
Survival—Fiction. | Toleration—Fiction. | Best friends—Fiction.
Friendship—Fiction. | Science fiction.
Classification: LCC PZ7.1.M43523 Spl 2017 | DDC [Fic]—dc23
LC record available at https://lccn.loc.gov/2016058466
ISBN 978-0-8234-4234-8 (paperback)

To people deciding who they want to be,
and to Earth for everyone

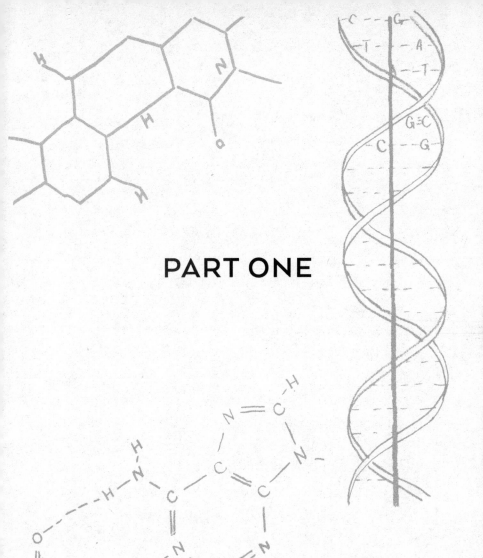

PART ONE

ONE

I awoke with a start to the sound of yelling and the sight of spaceships doing battle above my bed.

It wasn't the first time this had happened. If I left the Holovid set to automatic, it turned off when I fell asleep but started playing again as soon as I woke up. I waved it off and looked at the clock.

Six fifty-six.

The yelling was coming from next door. Nothing new there, either. But in the two weeks my mom and Kevin had been gone, I'd gotten used to our house being extra quiet. When there was noise, I really heard it.

My alarm was set for seven, and I closed my eyes, determined to enjoy those last few minutes in spite of the ruckus. Then I heard a crash.

I jumped out of bed, yanked on a bathrobe over my thin tank top, and looked out my window as Del came half running, half falling down his back steps. His momentum took him across the stretch of grass that separated our houses. I was almost down the stairs when he started banging on the back door.

He didn't stop until he saw me through the small panes of glass. His face always got red when he was angry, but this morning it was redder than usual. Especially the hand-shaped mark that took up the whole left side.

I opened the door, and he flew past me, stomping around the kitchen table twice before he uttered a word.

"I *hate* Stan," he finally said, his face twisting with emotion.

This was not news.

Lots of kids say they hate their parents, but Stan—Del's dad—was truly bad, mean in a crazy-strict kind of way. He'd always been a jerk, but he'd gotten more vicious over the last few years. Sometimes when he'd bring his patrol car home, I'd look at the TO SERVE AND PROTECT written on the side and wonder if it was supposed to be ironic or just plain sarcastic.

I poured us two glasses of orange juice. It was kind of a ritual between us, something my mom started doing when we were younger and Del would come over upset about something.

I put the glasses on the table and sat in front of one of them. Del circled the kitchen a few more times, eyes burning with rage, before settling in front of the other.

I took stock of him while he seethed, and it struck me how different he looked compared to just a few months ago, maybe even a few weeks ago. Lately my mom wouldn't shut up about how much we were both changing, how quickly we were growing up. It was annoying, the way she went on about it, but looking at Del that morning, I could sort of see what she meant.

He wasn't anywhere close to physically intimidating Stan. But he was tall—almost six feet now—and getting more solid, more muscular. He still had that Del vulnerability, but skinny had turned to slender. Below his prominent cheekbones, his jawline looked stronger, too, but that could have been because it was clenched so hard. This morning, his unruly dark hair could pass for tousled.

It occurred to me that objectively speaking, Del was sort of hot. But he'd be the last person on earth to own it, which was one of the many reasons I liked him.

I waited until he sipped some juice before I asked, "You okay?"

His eyes were still burning, but then they rolled, annoyed. He started laughing. I did, too. I had meant it seriously, but we both knew it was a ridiculous question.

"Yeah, Jimi," he said. "I'm just great."

We'd come a long way since the first few times Del's dad had gone off on him. Back when we were little, Stan scared the living crap out of us. These days, the whole situation was more depressing than scary. It wasn't the end of the world; it's just how the world *was*. Or at least Del's corner of it.

It would have been nice if he had more people in that corner with him. But besides me, Del didn't have any real friends, and Stan was his only family. His mom had committed suicide a few years ago, after the last big flu outbreak, a year after the one that killed my dad. Del didn't like to talk about it. Stan had been a mess ever since.

"You got any bagels?" Del asked.

"Yeah." I reached behind me and grabbed the bag out of the fridge. As I tossed it onto the table, Del gave me a funny look.

"What?" I said.

He cocked an eyebrow. "Moons and stars?"

He was smirking but blushing, too, and at first I had no idea what he was talking about. Then I realized my robe had come open.

"Don't be an idiot."

"What? It's a pretty shirt. What there is of it."

"I didn't have time to get dressed because some wacko was banging on my door. Besides, you've seen me in tank tops a million times."

"Well, the moons-and-stars one is especially cute."

I rolled my eyes at him, but the way he had been looking at me was messing with my head. The morning had already gotten off to a sucky start. I didn't need things getting awkward, too. "I have to get ready," I said, standing up and tying my robe tight.

Del cleared his throat and pulled a bagel out of the bag. "Do you want one?" he asked as he started hacking at it with a knife, sprinkling poppy seeds everywhere.

"Sure," I called back as I ran up the stairs.

———

I tend to shower pretty quickly, but for some reason, knowing Del was downstairs, and after the way he'd been looking at me, I finished up even faster than usual. We'd been friends forever—we'd probably even been in the tub together at some point—but things were different now.

It occurred to me as I rinsed off that maybe my mom's daily comments about us growing up weren't so much about the physical changes. Those were pretty obvious, and every kid who'd taken fifth-grade health class knew they were coming. Maybe it was more about who we were becoming as people.

I was out of the shower before the mirror had fogged, and I paused in front of it. My mom told me—constantly—that I was pretty. But she said it in this wistful way that made me wonder if she was really talking about how much I looked like my dad: the small curve at the end of my nose, the faint freckles, the light hair, the brown eyes. People said all the time that I looked like him. I never used to see it, but lately even I had been struck by the resemblance.

I put on jeans and a light sweater, tied back my damp hair, rubbed some moisturizer on my face, and ran back downstairs.

Del had a bagel waiting for me—hacked, toasted, and buttered—on a plate.

"Thanks." I took a giant bite, then looked up at the clock. "Yikes. We need to go."

Del looked over my shoulder and out the window. "Crap."

"What?"

"Stan's car's still there. He hasn't left for the station yet."

"So?"

"So, I need my bag."

My stomach sank. I looked at the clock again. "Okay," I said, steering him toward the door with my hand on his back. "Just get in and get out. Fast and quiet. He won't even know you're there."

TWO

The shouting started up again as soon as Del slipped back inside his house. As I wolfed down the rest of my breakfast and headed out the door, I could make out Stan's voice now and again saying "disgrace" or "heathen."

I tried not to roll my eyes. Stan loved the word *heathen*. He used to be a normal guy who went to church once a week like lots of people did. But then Del's mom died, and it was like, once a week just wasn't enough. So he found another church—a different kind of church, called the Church of the Eternal Truth. It was pretty intense—like, I think they spent a lot of time talking about who was going to hell—and Stan got into it big-time. He volunteered for all sorts of things there. Sometimes I wondered if he spent so much time there because he was afraid to be home with Del. If so, the feeling was mutual.

Standing outside in the almost-chill of early autumn, I could hear them going back and forth—not the words anymore, just their voices, taking turns trying to hurt each other.

The mail drone flew past our houses, and I looked at my watch. It was almost 7:30. I hated running late, and we were really pushing it. The drone stopped down the street and left a package on the Merricks' porch, then it shot off into the sky and disappeared.

I was starting to get seriously antsy when I heard two noises—the screech of Del's screen door as he finally came out and the hum of the school bus cruising past our stop, right on schedule.

We ran to the end of the block and got there just in time to watch the bus disappear around the next corner.

I scowled at Del.

"Sorry," he said with a shrug. "What can I say? My dad's a jerk."

I stifled a growl and started speed walking. I could hear him coming up behind me. "Let's just ditch," he called.

I turned to look at him, trying to read his face. He had a mischievous twinkle in his eye and a half smile. He had one earbud in his ear, the other clipped to his shirt. If we'd made the bus, we'd probably be sharing a song by now, something he'd found on some weird playlist I'd never heard of.

I'd never ditched school in my life. But for a moment, the expression on Del's face had me thinking about it—wondering what the day would look like, what we would do. What it would feel like to let loose a little.

Del seemed to sense my resistance wavering. "Come on," he said. "We deserve a mental health day."

I laughed. "You need a mental health *month*, at least. Maybe a year. But I can't ditch." I turned away and kept walking. "Besides, we have a test."

"Oh, come on. That class is a joke." Honors calculus was the one class Del was better in than I was. I got mostly As, but for me, calc was work.

Del came up beside me. "We can just take a makeup."

I turned and looked at him again, trying not to let him know how seriously I was considering it. He bobbed an eyebrow at me, and we walked that way for a few seconds, neither of us looking where we were going.

I turned away first. "I can't ditch," I said again. "And neither can you. It's not like we're a shoe-in for Temple U, or anywhere else. We can't afford to be screwing around. Not junior year. And you know what my mom would do if she found out."

He stayed quiet, sulking. Okay by me, I thought. *I* should be the one sulking, since he was the one who'd made me miss the bus. Luckily, since our bus route was so long and convoluted, walking wouldn't get us to school much later than usual. If I'd *really* been worried, I could have just run and gotten there in no time. I probably would have enjoyed it. But Del was no athlete. And annoyed as I was, I didn't want to leave him behind.

We hopped fences and snuck through backyards, cutting diagonally through our neighborhood. Oakton was a decent neighborhood on the northwest edge of Philadelphia, not far from Broad Street, which bisected the city going north and south. My mom thought we were a little too close to the zurbs, but there were lots of trees and grass, and it was better than a lot of other neighborhoods in the city. My dad used to say it reminded him of how the zurbs used to be, but with electricity and stuff that you could only get in the city now.

We'd walked about a block without saying anything when Del got over himself and broke his silence. "Okay, I was going to save this for after school, but check this out," he said, stepping closer.

He rolled up his sleeve to show a massive chameleon freshly tattooed onto the inside of his right forearm. Its tail was coiled in a tight spiral that perfectly hid the scar at its center, where Stan had held a lit cigarette several months earlier. Del had made me promise not to tell anyone about it, and I still wondered if I should have.

"A tattoo?" I said. "Seriously? When did you get that?"

He laughed. I didn't. He knew I didn't like tattoos. I couldn't believe he had gotten it without telling me. Then again, he probably knew I would have tried to talk him out of it.

"Last night, while Stan was at his Bible study meeting. There's a parlor by the Avenue that does them cheap. Pretty cool, right? It looks just like Sydney."

Sydney was Del's nine-inch pet tiger salamander. He'd wanted to get a chameleon, but Stan wouldn't let him. Technically, he didn't let him get a salamander, either—Del just went and got it.

"You do know that's a chameleon, and that Sydney's a salamander, right?"

Del shrugged. "Artistic license. Besides, I think it captures Sydney's spirit."

Sydney was cute, as amphibians go, and Del loved him more than a salamander should really be loved. It was like an obsession.

I shook my head. "What is it with you and that salamander?"

He looked at me with mock indignation. "Are you serious? You mean apart from the fact that salamanders are the only animals that can regenerate limbs? Salamanders are *awesome*. And Sydney is the best one there is."

I couldn't help but smile. "Okay, I'll admit, Sydney *is* pretty cool, for a lizard."

"Sydney's an amphibian," Del said, correcting me.

"Yeah, yeah, I know. So is that why your dad's so angry?" I asked, pointing at the tattoo.

He rolled down his sleeve as we turned onto Devon Street. "Are you kidding? Stan hasn't seen this. He'd go nuts."

I was going to ask Del if *he* was the one who'd gone nuts, doing something he knew was going to set his father off.

Instead, I stopped in my tracks and said, "Oh no."

Our chances of getting to school on time suddenly looked an awful lot slimmer.

THREE

The red plastic fence spanned the entire road, sidewalk to sidewalk. A sign attached to it said DEVON STREET BRIDGE CLOSED. I ran up and peered over it.

The bridge wasn't just closed; it was gone. Empty space yawned where it used to be. I looked right and left, up and down the rails that stretched each way into the distance.

"When did this happen?"

The mail drone flew over our heads, effortlessly crossing the void where the bridge once stood. It seemed to be rubbing it in.

Del stepped up next to me and said, "Huh."

The tracks were sandwiched between two tall fences. Together, they stretched into the distance. To the right I could see the Forrest Avenue Bridge, a mile away. To the left was the old McAllister Street Bridge, a quarter that distance. But outside the city. In the zurbs.

Del spat into the ravine, watching the little white dot as it arced up into the air and landed on the dusty rocks between the two sets of tracks.

I punched him in the arm.

"Ouch," he said, kind of laughing, but not completely.

"What are we going to do now?" I demanded.

He hooked his fingers into the construction fence and gave it a little shake. Before I could tell him we were *not* going to climb the fences, a soft whispering sound grabbed our attention, and we both looked down at the tracks. The sound grew for a second, then exploded into a roar as a long, silver Lev train flashed below us. It was moving so fast you couldn't see the gaps between the train cars—just an uninterrupted silver blur. Trash and freshly fallen leaves whipped around violently as the train tore through the air.

A shorter train going the other way appeared on the other track, startling us both.

Then they were gone, replaced by the drizzly sound of the debris settling back to the ground.

"We could ditch," Del said.

I punched him again.

"Stop it," he said, rubbing his arm.

"Damn it, Del, for the last time, I can't ditch! And I can't be late, either. I barely managed to talk my mom into letting me stay on my own. You know she said if I screw up I'll have to stay with Aunt Trudy."

Trudy was my eccentric aunt—my dad's sister. She ran an art gallery in the city, but lived out in the zurbs, in an area called Perkins Park. She seemed nice enough, but I hardly knew her. She'd moved out to the West Coast when I was little, and I'd met her exactly twice since then: once for a few hours at my dad's funeral, and once a year ago after she moved back east and my mom invited her over for what may have been the most awkward dinner of my life.

Aunt Trudy was the only family we had. When Mom agreed to let me stay in the house alone while she was doing college visits with Kevin, she made it clear that if she later decided it wasn't working out, I'd end up staying with Aunt Trudy. My mom wasn't known for bluffing.

I glared at Del and kicked the fence.

"It's not my fault we're late," Del said defensively. "You know how my dad is."

"Yeah, and I know how you are, too."

"What do you mean by that?" he said, his voice rising.

"I *mean*, just because he's an abusive jerk who's always looking for a fight, doesn't mean you always have to give him one."

He glared back at me.

"I'm serious, Del," I said, softening my voice. "You're not going to change him. Sometimes you have to just walk away and let him be his miserable self."

He turned and started walking away from me instead.

"Del!" I called after him. I felt bad, even though what I'd said was true. I started to follow him, but when he got to the corner, he turned right instead of left. Toward the McAllister Street Bridge. The one outside the city.

"Uh, Del?" I called after him, running to catch up. "Where are you going?"

"You said it yourself. You can't be late. This way is fastest."

"Well, yeah," I said, hurrying to keep up with him. "But it's outside the city."

"It's not the edge of the world," he said with a sharp laugh. "You're not going to sail off the edge, for God's sake."

I didn't like the way he was taunting me, and I really didn't like the fact that it was working. I'd been outside the city, plenty of times. We used to go all the time when I was little. But the zurbs had gotten weirder since then. I wasn't scared. I just didn't like it.

On the last block before North Avenue, the northern edge of the city, the houses turned ratty. Some had beat-up cars out front, old gasoline models retrofitted with electric motors. Half a block from the Avenue, the Super-E utility lines came out of the ground in huge gray pipes that rose onto metal structures taller than the nearby houses. The Super-E lines didn't cross the Avenue. That's where the city ended, and so did the reach of the city's electricity. The lines made a faint, high-pitched hum, but it was mostly drowned out by the whine of the cars whooshing past us on the Avenue.

The blur of cars looked a lot like the Levline, except instead of silver it was all different colors blending together. The Avenue wasn't technically a Smart-route, since it had traffic lights and pedestrian crossings. But your car had to be in autodrive to be on it, or else you could get major fines.

The sound of the traffic grew louder as we approached, then it fell away altogether as the crossing light turned green.

I stopped walking, but Del didn't. The numbers on the pedestrian light were counting down. Soon it would turn red, and it would be at least five minutes before it turned green again.

Where I was standing, on the city side of the Avenue, the sidewalk was trashy and unkempt, but the other side was a hundred times worse—there was twice as much litter, and the concrete was cracked and split and overgrown with weeds. The houses lining the far side of the Avenue were vacant and covered with vines.

"You're going to be late," Del called over his shoulder, taunting me again. He was halfway to the other side. The light clicked to yellow.

I ran after him, across six lanes. We both stepped onto the curb just as the light clicked to red.

Del grinned down at me.

"Now what?" I said, shouting over the sudden rush of cars accelerating behind us.

He shrugged and started walking down the road. "We cross the McAllister Street Bridge, and we go to school."

A block off the Avenue, the traffic sounds faded away to an unsettling quiet. The houses were more and more run-down the farther we walked. Dark, vacant windows stared down at us.

Two blocks from the Avenue, the street was pocked with sinkholes. Some of the houses were completely hidden by foliage. Some had been torn down, with the debris piled into what used to be the basements and half-covered with dirt. The rest had been left to fall down on their own, and many were well on their way. One had a tree growing through the second-floor window. The window wasn't even broken; someone had left it open, and now a tree was growing through it.

I would never have let on to Del that I was the slightest bit nervous, but as we walked, I could feel imaginary eyes watching my every step.

It wasn't until the next block that I discovered they were real.

FOUR

Chimeras.

Three of them. Two were on the front steps and one was in the driveway of a big old stone mansion that looked like it had been converted into apartments before being abandoned altogether.

None of them moved a muscle as they watched us. It creeped me out that we might have just as easily walked right past and never noticed them.

The two on the steps had bird splices. Beige feathers covered their heads instead of hair. Their huge black eyes stared at us, unblinking, above noses that were large but somehow graceful, with a pronounced curve. They looked exotic—maybe even beautiful. But they were also unsettling.

They wore jeans and T-shirts. The one on the left had a green stone set in her pierced nose. Apart from that they could have been twins. If they'd gotten their splices from the same batch, I guess in a way they were.

The one in the driveway, wearing khakis and a maroon jacket, had some kind of cat splice. His ears were pointy, his nose flat, and he had a thin sheen of striped fur on his face, more tabby than tiger. His upper lip was slightly puffed out. His eyes were different, too; they were still human in shape, but the pupils seemed elongated.

I realized I'd seen him before, in the city, getting kicked out of Genaro's Deli. Genaro was a cranky old guy, and a big-time chimera-hater. He had signs all over his deli saying HUMANS ONLY and ANIMALS MUST WAIT OUTSIDE. I'd heard that chimeras sometimes went there just to provoke him.

The cat was staring at me, but I couldn't tell if he recognized me.

"Jesus," I whispered involuntarily as we passed.

"Chimeras," Del said softly.

"Don't stare," I said, quickening my step.

"They're so cool," he said, stopping to look back at them.

"They're not cool," I said. "They're creepy. What are they thinking, doing that to themselves?" I stopped and looked back, too, and the cat chimera in the driveway narrowed his eyes. Maybe he sensed my disapproval, or maybe he did recognize me from the neighborhood.

There was a movement at the doorway, and I noticed a fourth chimera, looking out from the shadows inside the house. He stooped as he came through the doorway and out onto the porch.

I couldn't tell what he was spliced with—maybe a dog or a wolf—but his face was striking. His skin looked smooth and fair, but tanned from the sun. His ears were slightly pointed and his nose was wide, ending in a flat triangle. He had a prominent mouth, full lips, and a strong jawline. His hair was kind of awesome, chestnut brown, peaking down into his forehead and spiked up as it swept backward. But his most arresting feature was his eyes—large and wide set, they were a deep, soulful brown; calm but wary, and radiating intelligence.

He was also massive—probably close to seven feet tall, and solidly muscled, like he was part mastiff and part landmass. Come to think of it, he may actually have *been* part mastiff.

The whole effect was not entirely unattractive, if you were into that sort of thing.

I'd never seen him before, but I got the sense that maybe he recognized us.

The two bird chimeras on the steps looked up at him with a quick, jerky, simultaneous movement. Then their heads snapped back in unison to stare at us.

"What's up, Del?" said a voice, sudden and surprisingly close.

I turned to discover yet another chimera, leaning against a tree right near us. He had pale brown eyes in a face that narrowed to a point, with a faint coat of fur, reddish brown on the top half and white along his jaw, chin, and neck. He might have been part fox. I was still trying to figure it out when I heard Del responding, "What's up, Sly?"

I looked at Del as it sank in that he knew this chimera. Then the big guy in the doorway said something to his friends. His words were too soft for me to hear—just a low rumble that I felt in my chest—but the bird chimeras rose together in response and hurried inside. I turned to see that the cat in the driveway was gone, and so was Sly. The big dog chimera stared at me another moment, then stepped back through the doorway and disappeared into the shadows.

FIVE

We were half a block beyond the chimera house when I laid into Del.

"How did that chimera know your name?" I demanded.

He shrugged, like it was no big deal. "What do you mean?"

I glanced back over my shoulder, then gave him a stern look. He knew what I meant.

"I know some chimeras," he said, shrugging again. "They're cool."

"They're depressing," I snapped.

"You've never seen one before, have you?"

"I've seen plenty of them," I said. Chimeras had been a thing for at least fifteen years, after the bio-hackers started mixing with the body-mods to see what would happen. But people who actually got spliced had stayed pretty much underground until the last five or ten years. And up until two minutes ago, I'd only met or seen up close a dozen or so, including that cat from Genaro's Deli.

The only chimeras I actually knew were pals of Nina Tanaka, who'd been one of my best friends until seventh grade, when she moved into a giant house on a much nicer block and started hanging out with the rich kids over there. One of her chimera friends had a single cheetah spot on her shoulder and the other had three tiny parakeet feathers in her earlobe.

It wasn't illegal to get spliced. But it was illegal for anyone other than a doctor to give someone a splice—and since the American Medical Association had made it clear that any doctor caught giving someone a splice would lose their license, there weren't a lot of medical professionals willing to risk it.

Some countries were more chill about splicing and it was legal and regulated, sometimes even promoted by the tourism board as a reason to visit. Nina's friends had probably gotten spliced at some posh spa in Belize or Switzerland, or someplace else where one-percenters could pay big bucks for a licensed doctor to give them a targeted splice and come out with a tiny, discreet—and very fashionable—alteration.

The guys we had just encountered had probably gotten spliced by a "genie," some weirdo in a basement or a garage somewhere. It was a hell of a lot cheaper, but they took their chances and got what they got.

"Splicing is stupid, Del," I said. "It creeps me out, and so does the fact that you think it's cool. Mixing animal genes into your DNA just to get some feathers or a tail or whatever? It's nuts."

"It's not nuts." He laughed, but his voice sounded hot.

"You know they use a live virus, right? They load the splice into a virus and infect you with it. That's how they do it. They make you sick."

"Doctors use the same technique to treat all sorts of things. It's how Syngenius does their genetic enhancements, and they're totally legit."

I rolled my eyes. Syngenius did synthetic gene alterations for all sorts of physical traits. More hair here, less hair there. Brown eyes with green flecks, green eyes with brown flecks. Instead of splicing in new genes, they edited your existing genes. It was super expensive but getting more popular with the people who could afford it.

"Well, I'm not nuts about Syngenius, either," I said.

"Of course you're not, Jimi. You get squeamish about tattoos, for God's sake."

"That's right, and splicing is a thousand times worse! You saw the same health vids I did, about people's bodies rejecting splices and having bad reactions, their immune systems going haywire, their organs becoming malformed, infections, all that stuff! And even if everything goes right, what about the future? What about college?"

He laughed. "Not everybody is destined to go to college."

Del's grades had been tanking lately and he had been dropping hints that maybe college wasn't for him—hints I tried to ignore, because I didn't know where that left me. For years we'd had a plan: we were going to stay in Philly and go to Temple University, *together*.

Once again, I changed the subject.

"Never mind about college," I said. "What kind of jobs are they going to get? Remember that article we had to read for Mr. Martinez? Kids who get spliced are *way* more likely to end up unemployed. What kind of future is that?"

Mr. Martinez was our US History teacher. I think I liked him a little more than Del did.

Del turned to look back at the chimera house. "An awesome future."

"Squatting in some abandoned house outside the city? That looks awesome to you?"

"Compared to working at a bank every day, or something like that? Hell, yeah!"

"Who says you have to work in a bank?" I rolled my eyes again. "You're being ridiculous."

"No, I'm not," he said, looking right at me, his eyes fired with intensity. "There's plenty of ways to make a living where you don't have to sell your soul. Those guys have the right idea." He pointed back at the chimeras' squat house. "You don't think every miserable drone working at a big-box store or sitting around in some crappy cubicle had said at some point they would never end up like that? Well, these chimeras made sure of it. They burned the ships behind them. That's awesome."

"It's not just jobs. What if they decide they want a family? Can you even have kids if you're a chimera?"

"Of course you can have kids."

"What if they come out as some horrible genetic jumble?"

"That's not how it works, and you know it, Jimi—or did you miss *that* part of the health class vid? It's somatic. The gene splices don't affect the genes you pass on."

He said *somatic* like it was his vocabulary word of the week, but he was right. I was surprised he remembered—and that I'd forgotten. "Well, you'd have to be crazy to become a chimera these days, anyway," I said. "So many people hate them."

"Crazy people hate them."

Del's dad was one of those crazy people, even more than Mr. Genaro. But I thought I probably shouldn't mention that. Instead I lowered my voice and tried a different approach. "I don't know if you've been paying attention, but those crazy people are trying to pass laws against chimeras. Starting right here, Del. Did you know that? Have you heard of the Genetic Heritage Act? It's already passed the Pennsylvania state legislature. If the governor signs GHA into law, chimeras would legally be considered nonhuman."

"First of all, of course I know that. Everyone does. Second, it doesn't say they would be legally non*human*, it says they would be legally non*persons*, and third, there's no chance in hell it's going to become law. But if it did and I were spliced, I'd just go somewhere else. Somewhere less screwed up."

It bugged the hell out of me that he was technically right about there being a distinction between *human* and *person*, especially since I knew that he had no idea what that distinction was. *Human* was a biological and social concept. Legally it had no meaning. But legally, a *person* was someone with rights and protections, compared to a *nonperson,* which had all the rights of a cinder block or an apple. I almost called him on it but I wanted to hear more about his crazy plans.

" 'Go somewhere else'? And where exactly would that be? You know they're pushing GHA laws in, like, thirty-something states."

"And they're going to fail everywhere," he said smugly. "But if they succeeded, I'd just go to Chimerica."

I laughed. "There's no such place as Chimerica."

"Sure there is. I know chimeras who have friends that have gone there."

"Del." I tried not to roll my eyes again but failed. "Chimerica is a make-believe fairyland invented by people who want to pretend their kids or brothers or sisters or friends who were dumb enough to get spliced didn't die from it. Or die from living in a squat with no food or medical care because they can't get a job."

I may have laid it on a little thick, but that didn't make it any less true. I'd heard kids at school talking about some mysterious, secret, safe place that only chimeras knew about, the same way kids talked about UFOs and alien abductions. With all this Genetic Heritage Act crap in the news, Chimerica was a trending topic. In a way, I got it—if someone I cared about had ruined their life by getting spliced, I'd want to believe in a magical safe haven for them, too. Especially now. But really, the whole idea was ridiculous.

Del seemed entirely unfazed by what I'd said. "Then you can't come."

I felt a cold anger at him—for being so immature and condescending, and for making the future sound so bleak. But I also felt scared, and that made me even angrier.

"Just shut up," I said, picking up my pace as we crossed the McAllister Street Bridge. Doubling back toward the city, we passed through a neighborhood that seemed to be inhabited—smoke rising from chimneys, cars that were junked up but looked like they still ran. But after we crossed back into Philadelphia, the streets were oddly deserted. The fact that we weren't speaking to each other might have made them seem even more so.

We got to school before the end of homeroom, but we had to sign in late anyway. I gave Del a glare to let him know I was still annoyed, and we went our separate ways.

We passed each other in the hallway between classes a couple of times, but we didn't speak. We didn't even make eye contact during our calculus test. And when Del missed the bus after school, I went ahead and got on it. I wasn't going to let him make me late twice in the same day. Besides, I needed to be home when my mom called to check up on me.

SIX

Coming home to the empty house, I felt the usual mixture of loneliness on one hand and relief on the other.

Sure, I loved my family, but generally I was glad they weren't around. My brother, Kevin, was a hotshot athlete, the star center for the varsity basketball team, among other things. He was a senior, and my mom was taking him on a four-week US tour, visiting all the big colleges that wanted him to come play for them.

"This year is about Kevin," she had said when she told me she was taking time off from her job as a marketing consultant to shop him around.

I understood. His college ball career was about to take off, and he would probably make a lot of money someday. But I still had to laugh—because when was there a year that *wasn't* about Kevin?

Still, every day at four thirty, my mom called to make sure I wasn't burning the place down, to make her feel like she was a good parent, and to remind me that if I screwed up, I would have to stay with Aunt Trudy.

The call came right on time, a video call on the landline. When I was younger I had a personal web phone, but that was before the Cyber Wars. Then Russia and China and North Korea and everyone else—including the US—thought it would be a really good idea to send all these super viruses and killer malware at each other. The wars were brief and ended in a tie, pretty much, but they succeeded in making the Internet and the old cellular systems a useless tangle of garbage that collapsed under its own weight. Now mobile phones are for rich people, the Secure Web is for even richer people, and the richest people of all have networked computer implants in their skulls. Everyone else is out of luck.

"Hey, Mom," I said.

"Hey, Champ," she said unironically. "How was school?"

"Good."

"What kind of homework do you have?"

I went through the list of classes and assignments, getting more and more depressed as I realized how much my evening was going to suck.

"Well, that doesn't sound so bad," she said when I was finished. Like she hadn't been listening.

"Nope, not too bad."

She took a deep breath and seemed to hold it. At this point in the conversation, she either told me how my brother was doing or she paused, waiting for me to ask.

"How's Kevin doing?" I asked.

She smiled. "He's doing great. Working hard so he doesn't fall behind on his schoolwork and impressing the heck out of all the coaches."

"Yay." Maybe I didn't put enough into it, because her smile faltered. Since I'd gone to the trouble of asking and all, I beefed up my own smile so she didn't launch into one of her "Kevin" talks. I was in no mood for a "Kevin" talk.

She took a few minutes to tell me about some of Kevin's most spectacular plays of the day, and when she could tell I'd had enough, she paused, trying to think of something else to talk about. As always, she failed.

"Okay, then," she said with a wise nod. "You're doing okay, right?" She never asked me how I was doing without letting me know what the answer was supposed to be.

"Doing fine, Mom."

"Great. We'll be home before you know it. And we'll get back on track with those driving lessons, right?"

"Sounds good."

"Love you, Jimi."

"Love you too, Mom."

▬ ▬ ▬

The next few hours were peanut butter crackers followed by homework. I had been hoping to go for a run, but by the time I finished my homework, I was tired and it was late. I was making some mac and cheese with ham and peas for dinner when the shouting started up next door. Apparently, Del had come home. It began with a quick back-and-forth followed by a door slamming deep inside the house—too brief to be the end of it.

I found myself wishing I'd been more forceful with Del when I'd said he shouldn't push back so much with his dad. Stan was getting crazier by the day, and I didn't blame Del for sticking up for himself, but usually the way he did it made things worse.

Even before Del's mom died, Del and Stan hadn't known what to make of each other, but when we were younger and Stan was still working as a chemical engineer, he was always at the office. He got fired after Del's mom died and he kept missing work. She was gone and Stan was unemployed and the two of them were stuck in that house. It was awful.

Then Stan got temporary work setting up illegal gas drills and liquefied coal wells out in the sticks. He'd be out of town for a week or two at a time and during the school year, he'd leave Del with us, which was cool. But in the summer, he would drag Del along, and that was even worse than when they were home.

Stan loved the work, partly because he got to go hunting while he was out there—even though there wasn't really anything wild left to hunt. Del was miserable, though, being dragged off to all these little towns where he didn't know anybody. He got a hard enough time from our classmates in the city, what with his amphibian fixation and his weird music. But some of those small-town kids would just tease him mercilessly.

He hated the hunting part, too. When he'd come home he'd entertain me with impersonations of Stan tiptoeing through the woods with his rifle. It was more Elmer Fudd than anything else, but I would laugh my butt off.

Stan didn't think it was funny at all. He wasn't supposed to see Del's impressions, but a couple times he caught us, and then nobody would be laughing.

Del was relieved when Stan got the job as a cop in the zurbs, but at that point, they were already at each other's throats.

By the time my mac and cheese was ready, Del and Stan were going back and forth again, louder and harsher than before. It reminded me of two gunfighters in an old Western movie, one going *bang, bang, bang,* then the other one going *pow, pow, pow.* Except the gunfight quickly escalated from six-shooters to machine guns, then bazookas and heavy artillery.

There was an ominous pause in the shouting and my shoulders tensed. In my mind I heard the cartoon whistle of a bomb falling from the sky, about to explode. What I actually heard was a jumble of sounds—furniture sliding, glass falling but not breaking, silverware hitting the floor.

Then I heard a scream.

SEVEN

I ran to the phone to call the police. Then I stopped, realizing how futile that would be. Stan might work out in the zurbs, but he was still police. Del was a troubled kid whom the other cops would never officially believe, even if they knew he was telling the truth. Besides, they would figure he probably did something to deserve it.

For the first time since she'd left, I wanted my mom.

I was weighing whether I should call her when Del's screen door screeched and slammed. Then there he was, running across the grass toward my house. His face was wet and he had a dish towel wrapped around his left arm. There was blood on his shirt. I opened the door just as he got there. He didn't slow down as he came in. Instead of running past me, though, he pushed into me, throwing his right arm around me, burying his face in my hair and sobbing.

I hugged him back, whispering "It's okay" in his ear. I pulled him inside, far enough that I could kick the door closed, then I reached out and locked it. Just in case.

After a minute I pulled back and looked at his face.

"What happened?" I asked quietly.

His head was still down, but his eyes looked up at me, the tears replaced by a haunted look, full of pain and smoldering with anger.

"Stan killed Sydney."

"He *what*?"

"He said he was done having a serpent in the house. He said something like, 'Let's see if he can regenerate *this*.' Then he stomped on him and flushed him down the toilet."

I put my hand over my mouth. "Oh Del." Then I noticed blood seeping through the towel wrapped around his arm. "What happened to your arm?"

He kept his eyes locked on mine as he gingerly unwound the fabric, wincing as he pulled away the last bit. The tattoo was in bloody tatters.

I looked up at him. "He did this to you?"

"With a cheese grater," he said, his voice croaky. His face was like stone except for a twitch in his eye. "He said it was blasphemy."

I put my arm back around him and pulled him tight. It was clear that Stan had gone off the deep end. This situation was out of control.

Eventually Del put his hand on my shoulder and stepped back, until he was at arm's length. His eyes met mine, and the weird thing was, he looked like he felt sorry for me. And it wasn't just sympathy, there was a tiny hint of condescension as well. Like he'd learned some truth about life I wasn't yet ready for. Like he was suddenly older and wiser than me.

Then it vanished as a hint of a smile pulled at the corner of his mouth. "You making mac and cheese?"

I nodded. "You hungry?"

He shook his head. "Not right now."

"I should clean that," I said, looking at his arm.

He shrugged, like it didn't matter, but his eyes looked afraid. I couldn't blame him. It was going to hurt.

━━ ━━ ━━

We sat in the living room—him on the sofa, me on the floor, the reading lamp shining directly on his arm.

I gingerly peeled away the towel again, and before anything else, I doused his arm with numbing spray. A lot of numbing spray. I gently cleaned it with damp gauze, then gave it more numbing spray, just in case.

Three sets of gouges crisscrossed his arm, obliterating most of the tattoo. All that remained was the coiled tail. I shuddered, wondering what kind of man would do that to his own son, again and again.

I guess the spray worked, or maybe Del was tougher than I thought, because he kept it together the whole time. As I finished bandaging his arm, I noticed he was looking down at me with an odd smile.

"What?" I asked.

"Thanks," he said softly.

His smile lingered. He looked like he wanted to say something important. Or do something.

His hand rested on my shoulder. I could feel its warmth spreading through my body. But I also felt awkward and self-conscious, and my head was spinning over what had just happened.

"We should eat something," I said, looking down as I finished taping his bandage.

"Okay," he said, and the moment dissipated.

— —— —

Del might have said he wasn't hungry, but he ate with gusto, holding his fork like a little kid and shoveling it in. "This is really good," he said, his mouth full of food.

When we were done, we sat on the sofa with the Holovid on, but neither of us was really watching it. Del flicked through the channels absentmindedly and for some reason stopped on the local news, which was generally stupid and always depressing.

They led with the weather, then reported that the year was on a pace to break another record for global temperatures and sea level rise, the twenty-ninth time in the last forty years. They seemed almost excited about it, like they had a streak going and they wanted to see how long it would last.

After the weather was a story about a big Humans for Humanity march tomorrow. H4H was the anti-chimera group pushing GHA. They'd been around for years, long before splicing became a thing. Mr. Martinez told us H4H was originally started to oppose efforts by groups that were fighting to win legal rights, or *personhood,* for animals—meaning that animals had *some* kind of rights, so there was a distinction between, say, a chimpanzee and a brick, and limits to the messed-up things people could do to animals. The H4Hers tried to make it sound like these groups were trying to give animals the same rights as people, which they weren't, and everyone knew it. So it was an obscure fight, and H4H remained an obscure group. Then, about ten years ago, when splicing really started to become a thing, this bazillionaire named Howard Wells took over and transformed H4H into an anti-chimera group—and a pro–Howard Wells group.

Not that Wells needed the publicity. He was already a household name. He'd founded a bunch of big companies, and the first one, WellPharm, was one of the biggest drug manufacturers in the country. But he really got famous when he got into tech. He created Well-Plant, which made super-expensive high-tech implants that securely streamed music, data, voice, and text; recorded video; and performed high-level computing, like the Secure Web on steroids, all inside your skull. Very cool stuff, if you could afford it.

Also very creepy, if you asked me.

It was Wells who came up with the idea for GHA, which said that once someone got spliced, once their DNA was anything less than one hundred point zero zero zero zero percent human, they were no longer legally a person.

That was crazy. I mean, if I squinted really hard, I could kind of see where Wells and H4H were coming from—splice in enough animal genes and at some point, maybe someone *wasn't* entirely human anymore—but saying that anybody who had any kind of splice is no longer a person? Saying they deserved to be discriminated against? That was just wrong. I might have thought splicing was idiotic, but I didn't hate chimeras.

The H4Hers really, really did, though. They blamed chimeras for *everything* that was wrong with the world—crime, unemployment, disease, and more—all totally made up and based on nothing.

The whole GHA thing was so out there that no one took it seriously at first. But late this past summer, against all predictions, Wells's buddies got it passed in the Pennsylvania state house. Suddenly, bills just like GHA were being introduced all over—and H4H was a big deal across the country. So was Wells.

He seemed to be enjoying the notoriety. His face was everywhere— tanned and handsome, with his signature shiny black WellPlant embedded over his left eye. He was already a hugely successful businessman, but the pundits were speculating that as the leader of H4H, Wells seemed to have set his sights on something else. A lot of people thought he was going to run for governor, or even president.

The Holovid cut to a packed church basement where people were making signs and singing songs. The reporter, a young woman in a purple dress, was pressing her earpiece tightly against her head as she stood next to a guy in a white H4H shirt and a matching hat.

"I'm reporting live from Church of the Eternal Truth, where Humans for Humanity is gearing up for tomorrow's march. With me is Philadelphia H4H chapter president Gus Joyner. Mr. Joyner, can you tell us why tomorrow's rally is so important to you?"

Joyner was nodding the whole time she was talking, like he couldn't wait to say his piece. He looked intelligent enough, but his eyes had an odd gleam. "We're going to show the governor, and the whole world, that we are not going to rest until we have saved humanity from the ungodly taint of chimeras ruining our way of life." He pronounced *chimeras* with a *sh* sound instead of a *k* sound.

"I believe they're called *kimeras*," the reporter said, correcting him.

Joyner scowled at her and pulled the microphone back. "These *mixies* are thieves and vandals. They spread disease. Look at the flu that killed millions, right at the same time this whole splicing thing began."

This time the reporter pulled the microphone back, looking into the camera with a forced smile. "Of course, we all know that scientists have proven the virus from the flu pandemic originated decades before the splicing phenomenon began, so there is absolutely no connection between the two."

Joyner put his face next to hers and shouted, "And they're a burden on taxpayers and they're an abomination before God!"

"Man, that guy's really off the rails," Del said as the guy kept going.

"Yup," I said. "But look at that crowd. There's a lot of people out there who feel the same way he does."

When they finally cut back to the studio, the anchor segued to a report on the status of the Genetic Heritage Act along with a holo-clip of Howard Wells appearing at the state capitol with a bunch of his H4H pals from the legislature.

Del was getting worked up watching it, especially when the anchorwoman explained that while it was highly unlikely he would sign it, the governor could receive the GHA legislation as early as that week.

I took the remote away from him and changed the channel until I found an old Batman movie that was just starting. Del gave me a dubious look, but we watched the movie in silence, letting it calm us both down.

Halfway into it, I turned to him and asked, "What are you going to do?"

Del rubbed the bridge of his nose and sighed. "I'll think of something," he said. "Next year I'll be eighteen, and I can move out. It's not so far away." He glanced in the direction of his house, his father. His eyes flared hot for a moment. Then they came back to meet mine. "I'll be fine."

I glanced at his arm, then looked back at the Holovid.

The way his dad was getting, I couldn't see Del lasting another year in that house. But I didn't have any other ideas, either. It wasn't like Stan would let him just move in with us, even if that were an option.

Del leaned forward to take off his boots. When he sat back, he was right up next to me. Touching.

I could feel the heat coming off him. We sat there, eyes ahead, pretending to watch the movie. He rested his hand on mine, and I let him.

EIGHT

I woke up slowly with a feeling of warmth and security that was slowly penetrated by the strangely distant sound of my alarm. With a jolt, I realized that it was morning and I was in the wrong place. Del's arm was around me, and my head was on his chest. The clock on the mantel said seven twenty. I jumped up with a yelp. *"Crap!"*

Del jumped up, too, startled and confused.

"We fell asleep," I said, pointing at the clock.

He raised a hand to rub his eyes, but winced at the pain, then looked at his arm, at the bandage around it. He stared at me for a second, thinking, then looked down at the bloodstain on the front of his shirt. "I need a clean shirt," he said.

We both looked out the window. Stan's car was gone. I was surprised he hadn't come over at some point, banging on the door and demanding Del come home. Maybe he was freaked out about what he'd done, figured he needed to cool off or give Del time to get over it.

"Okay, go get one," I said. "I'm going to brush my teeth. We can still make the bus."

Del half smiled, like maybe he was relieved but disappointed. Then he nodded. "I'll meet you at the bus stop. But if I'm late, don't wait for me."

I cocked my head at him. "We've got time," I said. "Just hurry up and grab your stuff."

I brushed my teeth, splashed water on my face, tied back my hair, and changed into fresh clothes. Four minutes later I was standing on the grass between our houses, looking at my watch and waiting for Del to come out. He didn't. I waited. And I worried.

The mail drone zipped by, high overhead. No packages for the Merricks today. I heard the bus approaching, then passing by.

As soon as it was gone, the back door opened and Del poked his head out, rolling his eyes as he spotted me.

"I told you not to wait for me," he said.

"What are you up to?"

He laughed, shambling down the steps. He had on a long-sleeved flannel shirt, covering the bandage. He wasn't carrying his schoolbag.

"Traveling light, huh?" I said.

"I don't need my stuff today."

I nodded, not buying it and hoping my expression said as much.

He came up next to me and said, "Let's go," then kept walking past me.

As I turned to walk alongside him, he put his arm around my shoulders. "Thanks for taking care of me last night."

I looked at him, trying to read his face and not getting anything. "Of course."

At the end of the block, he turned left.

I paused. "Bridge is out, remember?" I said.

"I know. McAllister Street's still quicker." He turned around, walking backward away from me, watching to see what I would do.

I let out a sigh and followed him.

We crossed North Avenue, out of the city, walking in silence. Del seemed strangely excited, happy even. I wondered if he was in shock from the trauma of what his dad had done to him. But as we approached the chimera house, his demeanor turned serious and his pace slowed. He paused, looking around.

I was starting to suspect he had intentionally missed the bus so he could come this way and see the chimeras again. But before I could say anything about it, a police car came skidding around the corner. It roared toward us with its old-fashioned lights flashing on top, like something from an old movie. Then it screeched to a halt right next to us.

NINE

I had assumed it was Stan, coming for Del, but I didn't recognize the cop that got out. His badge said OFFICER CANTRELL. He had a scar across the side of his nose, and a quarter-inch black glass disk over his right eyebrow, a WellPlant. I did a double take at that—it was strange to see a cop with an expensive computer implant like that, especially a cop working out in the zurbs.

He scowled as he rushed past us toward the front door of the chimera house. He had a stun gun in one hand and a shock baton in the other. "Officer Cantrell, Montgomery County Police!" he barked, pounding on the door with the butt of the stun gun. "Open up!"

Instead of waiting for a response, he ran alongside the porch and jumped over the railing, disappearing around the side of the house. I wondered what those chimeras had done.

Del turned to look at me, his face churning with a mix of emotions I couldn't identify. Then he grabbed me by the shoulders and kissed me full on the lips.

It was deep and intense, and everything around me fell away as I kissed him back. Then it ended and I stood there, light-headed and tingling, wondering if this was where we'd been headed all along, knowing in that instant our entire relationship, a friendship that was older than I could remember, would never be the same.

By the time I came to my senses, Del was thirty yards away, running along the sidewalk to get a better angle so he could see what was happening.

"Del!" I called in a loud whisper. "Get back here!"

He ignored me and I started to run after him, but I was distracted when the side door flew open just as Cantrell ran up to it.

One of the bird chimeras burst through. Cantrell took two steps after her, then reached out with the shock baton. There was a faint crackling sound, and the chimera crumpled into a ball.

I gasped at the sudden violence. Cantrell prodded her again and again, making her convulse on the ground.

The other bird chimera ran through the door, followed by the fox, Sly. They tried to slip past on either side of him, but Cantrell reached out with his baton and tripped the other bird chimera.

Before she could get up, he was on her, pressing the baton into her midsection and holding it there as she squirmed and shuddered and made strange warbling noises.

"Stop it!" I yelled. "You'll kill her!"

He finally pulled the baton away, but only when he spotted Sly running toward a shallow stream that fed into a storm drain and charged after him.

The first bird was up on her hands and knees, but the second one wasn't moving. I ran over to her and saw her mouth frothing. The way she was lying on the slope, her head was lower than her body. I was afraid she was going to choke. I grabbed her arms and dragged her around so that her head was elevated. She was surprisingly light. I was wondering what to do next when she coughed and opened her eyes, deep black orbs that seemed wide and innocent.

She looked up at me and smiled.

We were both startled as Cantrell yelled, "Freeze!"

Sly was zigzagging through the trees toward the stream. Cantrell was standing with his legs braced wide and his stun gun out in front of him.

Del was running toward him. I didn't know what he planned to do, but before I could call out, the cat chimera appeared from behind another tree, twenty feet away. His arm was cocked, a rock the size of a baseball in his hand. Then he whipped it forward.

The rock flew like a bullet, a straight line with almost no arc. It hit

Cantrell square in the back of the head, and he collapsed, sprawling across the top of the retaining wall that ran along the creek.

For a moment, the only sound was the rustle of feet shuffling through the grass and fallen leaves. Sly stopped and turned, then started creeping back. The cat stepped forward, tentatively, his nose twitching.

Sly looked over at him and smiled. "Hell of a throw, Ryan."

Del walked over to the cop, then crouched down for a closer look. My stomach lurched when I saw the look on Del's face—the same, still expression I'd seen after Stan shredded his arm.

"Del," I called out, but he ignored me. Then I realized he was holding the cop's shock baton. *"Del!"* I called again, louder, starting toward him.

He turned his head halfway toward me and said, "Run." Then he jammed the baton against Cantrell's neck, holding it there while the cop's body trembled and shook.

"Del! *No!*" I screamed.

He finally pulled the baton away, but then pressed his foot against Cantrell's midsection and rolled him off the wall and into the stream.

The cop landed with a splash and a thud, hitting both the shallow water and the rocks below.

The chimeras scattered, terrified, running in every direction. At the same moment, I heard sirens, seemingly coming from everywhere.

Del turned and looked at me, his face laughing and crying and somehow strangely blank, all at the same time. He mouthed the word *run,* and then that's what he did.

I looked back at the cop, Cantrell, lying facedown in the water, a thin ribbon of red curling away from his head. I wanted to run, too, but I couldn't let the man die. I couldn't let Del become a murderer.

I thought I could get over there, flip him over, and still get away before things went horribly wrong.

I scrambled into the water, heaved Cantrell onto his back, and started to run away. Even then I might have had time to escape, but he coughed and his head flopped to the side, half-submerged, his mouth blowing bloody bubbles in the water.

I paused, defeated, and went back, crouching in the water and pulling him out on the other side of the creek. He let out a soft groan and a gurgle. Then he coughed, spewing water across my shoes.

He was alive.

I dug in my toes to run again, but it was already too late.

Three cops were closing in on me. If I thought for a second maybe I could still get away, that ended when I saw their faces and their guns. I glanced down at the bloody figure at my feet, and I knew there was nothing they wanted more than an excuse to shoot me.

"Freeze," the closest one said. His face was red, his eyes flickering back and forth between me and his fallen comrade. He said it so softly, I wondered if he was hoping I wouldn't do as he said.

I thought about Del's dad, about what he would do if he were one of these cops.

As the other cops shouted out a barrage of contradictory commands, I put up my hands and knelt down on the ground. And I prepared for my life to turn to crap.

TEN

The walls were cracked, the ceiling was water-stained, and the corners of the old-fashioned fluorescent lights were piled deep with dead bugs. I wondered if the police interview rooms in the city were any nicer.

I'd been sitting there in Montgomery County's eastern police division for two hours. It had been an hour since anybody had spoken to me, which gave me plenty of time to think about everything that had happened—the police, the chimeras, the interrogation. All of it was scary as hell. And in between every other thought, I wondered about Del and that kiss.

It had been electrifying, for sure, but I didn't know what it meant, and I didn't know how I felt about it.

Frankly, I was surprised to still be alive and contemplating anything. When those cops had surrounded me, pointing their guns and yelling different instructions—hands behind your head, hands in the air, hands where I can see them—all red-faced and screaming, fingers on their triggers, I thought I was a goner. They were pretty rough about cuffing me and yanking me to my feet as they read me my rights.

When I said I hadn't done anything, one of them pointed his gun right in my face and told me to shut up.

I shut up.

The cop I'd pulled out of the creek had groaned again as they led me away. I turned to look back at him, but they shoved me and told me to keep walking.

When we got to the station—a big, run-down brick building—they put me in this room and grilled me: Who was I, why had I been at that house, how did I know those chimeras? After the first half hour, they calmed down and their questions changed focus. They wanted to know about Del.

Instead I told them my name. I repeated that I hadn't done anything and added that I hadn't seen anything. And I told them I wanted a lawyer so many times, they finally left me alone.

After an hour of nothing, the door opened again and a different cop walked in. He had two cups of water and he put one down in front of me.

"I want a lawyer," I told him.

"I'm not here to listen," he said, sitting in the chair across from me. "I'm here to talk."

I stared back at him blankly, waiting for the lecture.

"I saw the video from the patrol car. I know you fished Officer Cantrell out of the creek." He raised his cup. "Thanks."

I nodded and held up my hands, jangling the chain connecting them. "Do you think you could find the guy who put these on me, and get him to take them off?"

He looked amused and said, "We all have the same key." He pulled a key ring out of his pocket, reached over, and unlocked the cuffs.

My wrists had little red lines on them. I rubbed one, then the other.

"It doesn't look like you actually did anything wrong," he said. "But that doesn't mean you're not in trouble. Those chimera friends of yours are bad news. They've done some bad things."

"Like what?"

"Theft, vandalism. They break into houses and start fires for heat, but when those fires get out of control, they can burn down whole neighborhoods." He leaned closer. "You city kids think the zurbs are some kind of wasteland, but people do live out here."

"That's why those chimeras were being arrested?"

"Just look at them," he said, sitting back. "They've got *bad decisions* written all over them."

On that, we absolutely agreed. But he hadn't answered my question. I stayed quiet.

"And your friend Del Grainger. He's bad news waiting to happen as well." He paused. "You're sure you didn't see anything?"

"Nothing," I said. "I saw the officer in the water and I helped him."

"So, you didn't call Del by name, and he didn't tell you to run?"

I went quiet again.

"That's okay. I saw enough on the video." He lowered his voice. "I know Del's father, and I know he's bad news, too. Since he's police, there's a good chance this will all be handled internally, lucky for Del. But he's not always going to be so lucky. So you need to be a little bit smarter about who you're hanging out with, okay?" Then he stood up. "You can go now."

I was about to ask if they were going to take me back to where they picked me up, or take me to school. But then he opened the door and I saw my mom standing there, and I realized my troubles were just beginning.

ELEVEN

eally, Jimi?" That was all my mom could say at first. She'd said it three times now. Maybe she was waiting for an answer, but I didn't have one to give her.

"I didn't do anything," I finally said.

She whipped her head around to glare at me. "Of course you did something! We're at the police station, for God's sake. I don't have time for nonsense like this, Jimi, and neither do you. You need to grow up. Lucky for you, Kevin and I were at University of Maryland and not halfway across the damned country."

We were walking across the parking lot to the car. I could see Kevin sitting in the passenger seat, shaking his head. While my mom was turned facing me, he raised his middle finger. When she turned back around, I flipped it back at him. I let her get a few paces in front of me. I figured the worst that could happen was she would drive off without me, which wouldn't have been so bad.

Instead, she started up the car and sat waiting for me. I slid into the backseat, unable to tell which was clenched tighter: her jaw or her hands on the steering wheel. As we drove off, Kevin turned to look back at me, still shaking his head and trying not to laugh.

We drove in silence. Kevin turned on the radio, but my mom turned it off.

The police station was just a few miles west of the chimera house. We zigzagged through the zurbs to North Avenue. We were just turning onto Broad Street, back into the city, when my mom said, "Oh, what now?"

Up ahead, the street was blocked by a big crowd of people with signs and banners.

One of the signs had big block letters. Even from afar, it was easy to read: HUMANS FOR HUMANITY.

My mom growled. "Oh, great. Not these idiots."

It was the march they'd been talking about on the news. I slid down in my seat and groaned. The last thing I wanted was to be stuck in that car any longer than I had to be, especially if it was because of those people.

As we got closer, Mom honked her horn, but the marchers just turned and looked at her with pious condescension, like they pitied us for not being out there marching with them. I was relieved to have her anger focused on them instead of me. It didn't last long.

"See?" she said, turning in her seat. "This is part of the reason I don't want you hanging out with chimeras."

"I wasn't *hanging out with chimeras*," I snapped. As if I ever would. "And what, you agree with these people now?" I said, trying to turn it around. "You think chimeras shouldn't have rights as people?"

The marchers were waving signs that said HUMANS ARE MADE IN GOD'S IMAGE and CHIMERAS AREN'T PEOPLE. A lot of them were carrying printed placards saying PRESERVE OUR GENETIC HERITAGE or SUPPORT THE GENETIC HERITAGE ACT! or GHA ALL THE WAY! Their faces all radiated the same zeal.

"Don't be ridiculous," Mom snapped back. "You know that's not what I mean. I'm saying the whole chimera thing is terrible and stupid and tragic, and in addition to all the reasons we've talked about in the past, now *these* people are out there." She waved her hand at the passing crowd. "People who hate chimeras. And as wrong as it is, they're winning the political battles. Everyone says the governor will never sign GHA into law, but they said the legislature wouldn't pass it, either."

She pointed a finger in my face. "I'd ground you for life if I thought you were even thinking about getting spliced. It ruins lives and tears families apart. I don't want you hanging out with chimeras because I don't want you around when these marching morons start to act on their hatred."

"I don't know what the chimeras' problem is anyway," Kevin

said loudly. "If a bunch of idiots want to get spliced so they're not completely human, I say let 'em. But how can they whine about a law that *says*, 'Yeah, you're not completely human?' How can they even get upset about that?"

I let out an exasperated sigh, irritated that Kevin's stupidity was forcing me to defend the chimeras. "It's not about being human, or whether they are or aren't or how much. It's about taking away their rights as people. They're two totally separate things."

He screwed up his face and let out a sarcastic snort. "Oh, yeah, humans and people, totally different. Always have been." I could tell from the gleam in his eye that he knew he was being an ass. He was doing it to wind me up, and he was getting a huge kick out of how well it was working.

"Don't be such a tool," I said.

"The two of you, stop it!" Mom said, rubbing her temples.

The marchers kept coming, and my mom put the car in reverse. But when she looked in the rearview mirror, she swore. I turned to see at least half a dozen cars behind us.

We were stuck. And the crowd in front of us was growing instead of shrinking. There must have been a few thousand people that had passed by already.

"Hey, look! That's Howard Wells!" Kevin said. "My poli-sci teacher thinks he could be the next president."

Wells was surrounded by big bodyguards in suits and dark shades, and the whole entourage was being mobbed by video news crews, but he still stood out. In person he was as movie-star handsome as he looked on the Holovid. Early sixties, with a deep tan, white teeth, and a suit that reeked of expensive. As he waved to the marchers and onlookers, the sun glinted off the black glass of the WellPlant above his eyebrow.

My mom made a strangled noise in her throat and shook her head. "That man is a twit."

I was pretty sure Howard Wells was not a twit, but I knew what she meant.

After Wells passed, the crowd of marchers thinned out. That's when Kevin sat bolt upright in his seat, pointing. "Holy crap," he said. "Is that Stan Grainger?"

Sure enough, there was Del's dad, bringing up the rear. He was holding one end of a banner with the H4H logo and the words THERE'S NO PLACE IN HEAVEN FOR ABOMINATIONS.

My mom tutted and sighed. "If he spent less time on this H4H stuff and more time worrying about his son . . ."

I was afraid she was going to pull over and try to talk to him, maybe tell him about what had happened that morning, but mercifully, she didn't.

As Stan marched past, Kevin laughed. "What a bonehead."

Finally, the road cleared, and as soon as the cops waved us on, my mom drove through the intersection and sped off.

We seemed to be taking a strange route home, but between the rally and everything else that had happened that morning, I was too distracted to pay much attention. I didn't realize until we pulled up in front of it that we'd actually been heading to school.

As she opened her door, Mom clearly sensed my surprise. "Surely you didn't think a stunt like this was going to get you a day off, did you?"

I didn't say anything. I just got out and walked past her toward the building. Behind me, I could hear Kevin saying, "Can I stay here?"

When we got inside, we had to wait behind some freshman being signed in by his mom. Standing there with my own mom, I felt mortified, like I was a little kid, too.

The woman in front of us took forever signing in her son, and when she was finally done, she closed the book instead of leaving it open.

My mom stepped up and flicked through the pages. She found

today's page, but something seemed to catch her eye, and she flicked back to yesterday's. She turned to me with a glare. "You were late yesterday, too?" She closed her eyes, like she was summoning strength.

"I—"

"Go to class," she said, cutting me off.

The secretary behind the counter looked on sympathetically, and it annoyed me that it was sympathy for my mom, not me.

"But—"

"I said, go to class," she snapped. "We'll discuss this when you get home."

TWELVE

It was twelve thirty by the time I got to class, but the day still seemed to drag on forever. At lunch I sat at a table alone, going over the events of the morning in my head. I didn't really have any close friends apart from Del, but there were people I was friendly with and ate with sometimes. None of them came to sit with me. Maybe I was putting out a vibe. That was fine with me.

Del never showed up.

I was pretty sure he'd gotten away—it definitely seemed like all the cops had been focused on me—but I didn't know where he'd gone.

The rest of the day was a blur. Predictably, everyone was talking about the rally and whether GHA was really going to become a law. Every teacher made at least some mention of it, even in math class. In US History, it took up the whole period.

"How many of you can tell me what the Genetic Heritage Act means?" Mr. Martinez asked once everyone was seated.

Most of the hands in the class went up. I kept mine down. I felt like I'd been answering enough questions, and I was preoccupied with Del's empty desk.

"Well, you're all ahead of the game," he said, "because I don't even think the people who wrote it could actually tell you what it means."

"It means mixies aren't people," said Greg Borden, bonehead in training.

Martinez nodded slowly. "Not crazy about that term, but you're right in a way. What does that mean, though?"

Greg just looked back at him.

"If chimeras aren't people, can they vote?" Martinez asked.

"No." Greg sat back with his arms folded.

"Can they work?"

Greg thought for a moment. "No."

Someone else called out, "Who'd hire them, anyway?" Half the class laughed, but Mr. Martinez ignored the remark.

"Can they be sued? Do they have to pay taxes? Can they owe you money? Do they have to obey the laws of the land? Can they be arrested?"

Greg furrowed his brow, looking even dumber than usual. Martinez raised an eyebrow, waiting, letting him know he was going to have to answer.

"I don't know," he finally said.

"Don't feel bad," Martinez said. "Neither do the folks who wrote the law, or the politicians supporting it. There is an absolute lack of clarity on some of the most basic elements of what the law asserts, not to mention subtleties like what happens to chimeras from other states when they come to Pennsylvania."

He paused and looked at the class, studying our faces. "Ladies and gentlemen, there is a technical term for this kind of law." He turned and wrote on the Holoboard: HALF-ASSED.

I really did like Mr. Martinez.

About half the kids in the room laughed, but the others, the ones who'd been laughing about not hiring chimeras, squirmed in their seats. I suddenly realized they were probably H4Hers.

Half the class. That blew me away.

A lot of the kids were still talking about the march on the bus after school. That was no surprise—it was a big deal. What did surprise me was how many of them seemed to be in favor of GHA. I may not have had a ton of friends, but these were people I knew. Or people I thought I knew.

When I got home, my heart sank at the sight of my mom's car parked on the charging pad in the driveway. A tiny, unreasonable part of me had hoped she'd be gone, letting me off with a warning.

When I got inside she was sitting at the kitchen table with a cup of coffee and the phone.

The house was silent. It felt even quieter than when I was alone.

"Where's Kevin?" I asked.

"At Malik's."

Malik was his best friend, also on the basketball team. I nodded, waiting for it. I didn't have to wait long.

"So what the hell, Jimi?" she asked, pinching the bridge of her nose. "What are you doing?"

"Mom, I'm not doing anything. Del had another fight with his dad, and we were late—"

"Del and his dad have nothing to do with you being on time for school."

"—so we had to walk. The bridge on Devon Street is out, so we had to go around it, to the bridge over on McAllister—"

"Out in the zurbs?"

"We were passing by these chimeras' house—"

"A squat. They were squatting. That's not their house."

"—then this cop car drives up. He bangs on the door and starts shocking all the chimeras as they run out." I told her the rest of the story, without names, to protect the innocent. But I told her about pulling the cop out of the creek, and then getting arrested.

She let out a sad sigh, then leaned forward and cupped my chin. "You are so much like your father." Then she sat back. "I trust that you mean well, Jimi. But that was a situation you shouldn't have been in. One I shouldn't have let you be in." She let out another sigh. "Kevin and I will be done visiting colleges in a couple weeks. Until then, you'll be staying with Aunt Trudy."

"*No!*"

"It's just for a little while. And it's not a punishment. It's a consequence. There are always consequences. And frankly, this is a consequence for me, too. This is what we should have been doing the whole time you've been on your own."

"*Mom!*"

"Trust me. It'll be better. You'll actually have *more* freedom. You won't have to be home for when I call every day, and Trudy can drive you places. Maybe she can even give you some more driving lessons."

"I don't even *know* her. She's out in the zurbs! You can't—"

"It's a done deal, Jimi. I called her this afternoon. We're going over there after school tomorrow to get you settled, and then Kevin and I will head out again. North Carolina, this time."

"Mom—"

"I really am sorry, sweetie. But we'll be back before you know it."

I wanted to throw something, to break something, but instead I left the room and went outside. I half thought she'd come after me, afraid I was running away. But she didn't. She knew I wasn't.

I ran to the Graingers' and banged on the back door, something I hadn't done in a while.

I was angry at Del for getting me into this mess, but mostly I wanted to cry on his shoulder and tell him how unfair it was that I had to go stay with Aunt Trudy. I was going to miss him while I was there, and my eyes surprised me by welling up. Then I thought about that kiss, and I banged on the door again, harder.

When Stan opened the door, I pulled myself together. "Hi, Mr. Grainger."

He looked down at me, his eyes narrow, his face looking withered.

"Del's not here," he said. In the living room behind him, I could see a full ashtray with a cigarette burning and a couple of beer cans on the coffee table. He had newspapers spread out across the floor with his hunting rifles laid across them. A chill went through me, until I saw they were disassembled.

The smell of gun oil brought me back to when Del and I were little, watching Stan clean his guns before his hunting trips, and listening to his crazy stories about how one day he was going to Africa to hunt wild, exotic animals. Even then there was hardly anything wild left to hunt. Now there was virtually nothing—a thought that brought my eyes back to the rifles, and brought the chill back with a vengeance.

"Do you know when he'll be home?" I asked.

"No. Do *you*? From what I hear you were with him this morning when he disappeared."

"He's not back?"

I didn't think it was possible for Stan's face to harden any more, but it turned to granite. "He stole a thousand dollars out of my dresser. If he's smart, he won't *be* back. That money was going to the Church of the Eternal Truth. He stole from God."

"Oh."

"Yeah, 'oh.' You see him, you tell him enough's enough. This time, there's going to be consequences." Parents apparently loved that word, but coming from Del's dad, it sounded sinister.

He gave me a long look, then stepped back inside the house and closed the door.

I hurried back to my house, turning the facts over in my head. Del was missing. And he had stolen money from his dad. So he was up to something. Maybe he was thinking about taking off, getting out of there. But a thousand dollars wasn't going to get him very far. And really, it wasn't like he had anyplace to go. I needed to find him.

Back inside, I went upstairs, threw on some running tights, and put on my running shoes. My mom was at the bottom of the steps when I came down, looking like she wanted to talk.

"I'm going out," I said, slipping past her and out the back door.

I loved to run. I tried the track team once, just to make my mom happy, but it was like taking something pure and ruining it with a bunch of unnecessary complications. Normally, I ran to clear my head, but today, I ran to find Del. I pictured the look on his face as he was about to shock that cop, as he heaved him into the stream and left him for dead. I had to find him, to make sure that he was okay and wasn't about to screw up even worse.

Genaro's Deli was six blocks from my house, so I was barely warmed up by the time I got there. Two kids from school were in the parking lot, failing to do simple skateboard tricks and applauding each time they got close.

"Hey," I said as I walked up.

They looked at me and nodded.

"Jimi, right?" one of them said.

I nodded, looking around to see if anyone else was nearby. "What are you guys up to?"

They both shrugged. I was thinking maybe this was a stupid idea. Before I could ask if they'd seen Del, the door opened and I heard raised voices. Two chimeras were backing out, and I recognized them from that morning—Sly, the fox chimera that Del knew, and the cat chimera, Ryan.

"Yeah, 'no animals,' " Sly said with a sharp laugh. He slapped his own butt. "Well, you can kiss this animal's behind."

Ryan was laughing, too. He was holding a blue sports drink, and as the door closed slowly behind them, he twisted off the cap and flicked it back into the store.

Sly was still shaking his head. He stopped when he saw me. "You're Del's friend, right?"

"Have you seen him?"

Ryan moved off to the side, watching me.

Sly grinned. "That was a crazy morning back there, wasn't it?"

The two skateboarders sidestepped us and went into the store. I couldn't tell if they were creeped out by the chimeras or by me. I fought the urge to follow them.

Instead, I said, "Sure was. Have you seen Del? He's gone missing."

Sly laughed. "He hasn't gone missing. He's just gone."

"What do you mean?"

"He didn't tell you? I thought you two were friends."

Ryan snorted at that.

"Where is he?"

Sly shrugged. "He had enough of that crazy-assed father of his."

"Where *is* he?"

"Went to see a genie."

"What do you mean?"

"He's getting spliced."

"*What?*"

They both laughed. "Come on, it ain't so bad," Sly said. "Look at me."

"*Where is he?*" I grabbed Sly by the collar and gave him a shake. He thought that was hilarious, but he made sure I saw his sharp teeth as he laughed.

Ryan put a small hand on my shoulder. "Easy there," he said.

"Yeah, calm down. Don't damage the jacket. It's not easy finding clothes that fit this good once you get spliced."

I let go but I was seething. Between my anger at Del and the way they were toying with me, I could feel my frustration about to explode. I took a deep breath and let it out. "Look," I said, trying to sound as calm as I could. "I'm just trying to find my friend."

A look passed between them and Sly said, "Yeah, okay. Last I heard, he was over on Adelaide Street, at McAllister, across from the house we were at this morning." He looked at the watch on his tiny little wrist. The strap had extra holes punched in it and a couple inches of extra leather were flapping around, but it was still loose on him. He shook his head. "You're probably too late."

"Too late for . . ."

He held out his arms and smiled, like, *Too late for this*. Then he looked at my face and started laughing again.

The anger and frustration threatened to boil over. I wanted to lash out, to hit him in his stupid fox face.

Instead, I turned and started running for the zurbs.

THIRTEEN

S ly had said I was too late, but until I knew for sure, I had to try and stop Del. I couldn't believe he would actually get himself spliced . . . and yet, it was absolutely like him: stupid and self-destructive and immature and melodramatic. I was angry and afraid, and as I ran toward the edge of the city, I felt tears streaming down my face, down my neck, soaking into the front of my shirt.

I couldn't believe how badly things had fallen apart in twenty-four hours. I'd never felt so alone in my life.

The neighborhood streets were empty. When I was little, they had seemed like they were always filled with kids, with friends of mine. Del next door. Nina Tanaka up the block. Tiny Leo Byron in the corner house. Looking back, our little group hadn't lasted long. Leo, the youngest and the smallest, was my first close friend—and the first to leave. His parents moved across the city and we never saw him again. Nina only moved a few blocks, but she may as well have been on the moon, for all we talked now.

It had sucked losing them both. But there had always been Del.

Now he was leaving, too.

The thought made me kick up my pace to a sprint. I was half a block from the Avenue when the crossing light up ahead turned green. If I missed it, I'd have to wait five minutes for the next one. I couldn't bear the thought of that, so I found yet a little more speed.

I was halfway across the intersection when the light turned red. The cars surged forward, then halted, their horns bleating as their sensors stopped them from running me over. As soon as I stepped onto the sidewalk, the cars shot forward, swirling grit and debris behind me.

It was getting late. With no streetlights, and with the trees closing out the sky overhead, the road in front of me was already dark. I looked back at the Avenue, at the blur of traffic separating me from the city. Then I turned and ran into the shadows.

— — —

This was the third time I'd come this way in just a couple days. But alone and with night falling, it was scarier than before.

By the end of the first block, my eyes had adjusted to the darkness. The trees opened up a bit, letting in the last bit of light from the fading sky.

I turned up Adelaide Street and ran past the creek where the cop had almost drowned that morning. I couldn't believe it was the same day.

Up ahead, I saw a dim light in one of the houses. It was one of eight or ten small stone townhouses, raised above the street on concrete steps that were cracked and crooked from tree roots and storm water. I hurried toward it and ran up the steps to the front door.

I paused for one deep breath and knocked lightly, then again, harder. The sound echoed through the deserted streets. I looked over my shoulder at the other houses behind me, with their dark and broken windows.

Then I turned back to the door right in front of me. The light I'd seen from down the block somehow seemed even dimmer up close, a pale wash spilling into the front room from deeper within.

I put my hand on the doorknob and gave it a twist. The door swung inward and I opened my mouth to call out hello but only managed a dry croak.

The front room was littered with fast-food wrappers and other trash. I tried to step around it, but the paper rustled under my feet and the floorboards creaked loudly. My heart was almost as loud, pounding in my chest.

I cleared my throat and tried again. "Hello?"

I jumped as the trash rustled, on its own this time. Then I heard a loud squeak and realized it was a rat.

Creeping into the living room, I could see that the light was coming from the kitchen.

"Hello?" I called again, louder. There was no answer. To my right, the stairs ascended into shadows. As I went through to the dining room, I could see a chemlight stick on a windowsill in the kitchen. A torn net curtain stirred in the breeze coming through a cracked window, making the light dance around.

"Del?" I called out, taking another step toward the kitchen.

Empty plastic bottles littered the countertop. The sink was full of dirty beakers, and plastic bags and tubing with traces of liquid tinged with red, like something mixed with blood.

I had just stepped into the kitchen when a raspy voice behind me said, "What are you doing here?"

I jumped and turned. A figure stood in the shadows of the living room, some sort of chimera. I didn't know if it had followed me in or come down the stairs. I hadn't heard a thing. Squinting, I could make out its shape, but I couldn't quite tell what it had been spliced with. For a horrible instant I thought it was Del, but I knew it wasn't. This one seemed somehow ancient.

"I'm looking for my friend," I told him, trying hard to keep my voice steady.

He moved closer, tall and broad, but stooped to one side. His skin was patchy, but in the dim light I couldn't tell if it was scales or fur or something else. "Del? He's not here," he said, stepping forward again. His face was hideous and covered with growths. It got worse when he smiled. "He was here. But he's gone."

"Did he get . . . spliced?"

"Not here."

"Do you know where he went?"

"Nah." He took another step toward me. "My name's Simon," he said. "I could be your friend."

"No, I better go." I stepped backward, away from him, further into the kitchen. The back door had a two-by-four nailed across it. I was trapped. Simon seemed to know it, too. His smile grew, and he licked his bumpy lips with a bumpy tongue.

"But you just got here." He was already blocking the doorway to the dining room, inching closer, looming over me. I scanned the counter for a knife, a weapon of any kind. There was nothing.

Most of the drawers were open, and even in the murky light I could see they were empty. The one right next to me was closed, and I realized my one dim hope was that there was something in it I could use as a weapon. I reached out to yank open the drawer, but Simon slammed it with the back of his fist, splintering the wood. I jumped to my right to slip around him, but he stepped in front of me, laughing.

"Come here, little one," he rasped softly, looking down at me, blocking the light.

Then a large hand clamped onto the back of his neck, and he vanished.

I heard a crash as he landed hard in the dining room. I couldn't move at first; I was just trying to catch my breath. I heard scrambling coming from the other room, then that raspy voice muttering curses, countered by a low, rumbling growl. There was a heavy, muffled thud followed by quiet. A moment later a different massive figure stood in the doorway. It was one of the chimeras from the squat that first morning, the dog or wolf, the one who seemed to be in charge.

"Are you okay?" he said, his voice so deep I could feel it in my chest again.

I nodded.

"I'm Rex," he said.

"Jimi."

He nodded, then stepped out of the way. "Let's get out of here."

———

"He'll be fine," Rex said as he led me back through the dining room. I was staring at Simon, lying in a heap on the floor. "He'll have a headache when he wakes up. That's all."

I started to shake as we stepped through the front door. There'd been a moment when I didn't think I'd make it back out. A breeze picked up, and I realized I was soaked with sweat. I turned to Rex. "Thanks," I said. "For in there."

He nodded. "What were you doing?"

"Looking for a friend."

"Del," he said.

I looked up at him and nodded. "Do you know where he is?"

He shook his head.

"Someone told me he was going to get spliced around here," I told him.

"And you were trying to stop him?"

I nodded. "No offense."

He shrugged. "It's not for everyone. Let's get you back to the city."

"No," I said, shaking my head. The panic from being threatened by Simon was still subsiding, but having seen the squalor and the horror of what could happen, the panic about finding Del returned ten times worse. "I have to find Del."

Rex took a deep breath and looked down at me as he slowly let it out. "I can look around, see if I can find him."

"Really?" I studied his face in the moonlight. It still didn't seem entirely human. But it was close. Standing this near to him, I saw in his eyes a strength and compassion I hadn't noticed before. I didn't know him, and he was one of them, but I felt I could trust him.

He nodded. "But you have to promise me you won't do anything stupid like go into a house like that on your own again. Maybe Simon was messing with you, but probably not."

"Okay, understood. So where are we going?"

"I'm going to ask around. You're going to go home."

"No, I need to find Del. Now, before it's too late."

"You need to go home. So when I find him, I can find you."

"Where are you going to look?"

"I know people you don't know."

"Why can't I come with you?"

He sighed. "Because you just can't."

"But you don't even know where I live!"

He smiled. "Like I said, I'll find you."

"But I'll be at school tomorrow, and then I'm going to stay with my aunt in Perkins Park. I don't even know where."

"Hardly anyone lives in Perkins Park anymore. I'll find you. As soon as I know anything."

"Del hasn't thought this through—"

He held up a hand. "That's a conversation you can have with him."

I nodded reluctantly.

He gestured toward the Avenue, then we both started walking. I felt a lot safer with him towering over me than I had on my own.

"I heard what you did this morning," he said as we approached the Avenue. "With Ruth. And with that cop. You saved them both."

I guessed Ruth was the bird chimera. "Well, I don't know—"

"I should have been there," he said, his voice solemn.

We walked the last twenty yards without speaking. When we got to the Avenue I turned and said, "Well, thanks again—"

But he was already gone.

FOURTEEN

I was a little old for imaginary friends, but as I stood there on the wedge of concrete between the darkened zurb streets and the blurred wall of speeding traffic, I wondered if I had a new one.

Something about Rex's presence had made me trust him, but now that he was gone, that trust was wearing off. Maybe it was because I knew he couldn't trust me. Despite what I'd told him, I had every intention to keep looking for Del. The only problem, I realized, was that I had no idea where else to look.

I wondered if I should tell Stan what was going on. But then what? He had already disowned Del, and after what he had done over a stupid tattoo, I couldn't imagine what he'd do if he knew Del was getting a splice.

I racked my brain, trying to think of any kind of lead, but there was nothing. Only Rex.

The traffic stopped as the crossing light turned green. I looked around one last time. Then I ran home, trying to keep ahead of all the images of the horrible things that could be happening to Del. I didn't slow down until I burst through the back door and into the kitchen, slamming into the jarringly normal scene of my mom cooking dinner.

She looked at me suspiciously. "Long run," she said, dicing celery for some chicken dish she liked to make.

I hated cooked celery.

"Yeah," I said, extra sullen. It was bad enough she was sending me to live with Aunt Trudy—now she was feeding me cooked celery.

I slipped through the kitchen, and by the time she said, "You know, I'm only—" I was heading up the stairs.

When I was safely in my room, I put on my headphones and opened my biology textbook. Then I took out a notebook and pretended to study while I tried to come up with a list of places Del could be, people who might know where he was, things I could do to find him.

My mom knocked on the door, like I knew she would. I ignored her, and when she opened the door I lifted one headphone and looked up at her, annoyed.

She looked like she wanted to say something, but I wasn't in the mood to help her get it out. "Dinner's in ten," she said finally.

I nodded and let the headphone clamp back onto my ear.

Then I looked down at my notebook. Apart from a few hundred little dots from where I'd been tapping the pen, the only mark on the page was the word *Rex*. I added the words *Sly, Ryan, Ruth,* and after a long pause, *Simon*. I didn't expect help from any of them—definitely not Simon—but those names were the only leads I had.

Kevin opened my bedroom door without knocking, his eyes narrowing as I quickly flipped the notebook closed.

"Food time," he said.

When I got downstairs, I was relieved to discover that Malik was eating with us. Malik was almost as much of a meathead as Kevin, but the two of them talking nonstop took the pressure off my mom and me.

They ate twice as fast as I did, but three times as much. They were on their fourth helpings when I declared I was finished and asked to be excused. My plate was empty apart from the discarded celery. I was determined to get out of the room before I was stuck in there alone with my mom.

"Sure, honey," she said, looking at me with a pained expression that I found gratifying. "You need to get your stuff ready for tomorrow," she added quietly.

Kevin and Malik stared at me, mumbling and snickering. I felt a momentary, overwhelming hatred for them, and then the mortifying threat of tears.

As I turned to go, my mom said, "There's a suitcase in the—"

"I have a suitcase," I said.

"It's just a couple weeks," she called after me.

When I got to my room, I closed the door and sat with my back against it. And I let the tears come. When they finally stopped, I felt like all the energy had been drained out of me and replaced with sadness. I couldn't find my suitcase, but I had a couple totes and a duffel bag. They would do.

As I dug them out from under my bed, I tried to recall what I could of Aunt Trudy. I mostly had vague impressions of her from when I was younger. She had seemed nice, although a little goofy. I remember her trying to cheer me up after my dad's funeral, back at the house, after Del and Nina had left. She cornered me in the back room and we talked about my dad for a bit. Then she insisted we talk about something else, asking me what toys and movies I liked. Somehow, she got me to laugh, just for a minute. Then she was out of the picture again, until she moved back to Pennsylvania a year ago and came over for that awful dinner. I couldn't quite put my finger on what had made it so awkward, but I took a guilty pleasure in wondering if maybe my Mom just had that effect on people.

I packed up my school stuff, then moved on to clothes. Once I had all the practical stuff taken care of, I grabbed my favorite blanket. It was a microthermal soft fleece my dad had gotten me when we lost power for a week and had to camp out in the living room. He taught us a card game called Casino, and I remember playing for hours and hours wrapped in that blanket, feeling safe and warm while laughing at my dad's stupid jokes.

Next, I took the bobblehead snowman Del had given me a few Christmases ago. And finally, I grabbed the family photo from when I was seven that I kept on my dresser.

I took a long look at it. Things had changed so much since then. My mom had been young and easygoing and happy. Kevin had been rambunctious instead of obnoxious. I was laughing in the photo—I laughed a lot back then. And my dad was so . . . alive. Six months later, he'd be gone.

A lot of people died that flu season. It was the last of the bad ones, but far from the worst. Ten years earlier there were a few that killed way more people. It was kind of weird when the subject of the flu epidemic came up in school, with everyone turning to look at the kids who'd lost someone. Part of me always wanted to hide under my desk when it happened, but part of me also wanted to stand on my desk and shout about what a great guy my dad had been.

It was hard to think about the epidemic objectively, but our teachers talked about it all the time, trying to get us to understand how much it had changed everything, in addition to taking away people we loved.

The worst of the outbreaks hit right when the seasonal storms were getting especially bad—torrents of rain in the spring, summer, and fall; tons of snow and ice in the winter. Everyone was running out of power, and the storms were bringing down more and more of the old utility lines every week. Fortunately, there was already a huge program in place to install super-expensive, super-efficient power transmission lines, the Super-E. I could vaguely remember utility workers digging up streets all around Philadelphia to get us connected.

The plan was to wire major cities across the country, and then get the zurbs squared away. But suddenly, there was no money left to do it.

Everyone was broke after the flu epidemic, and the real estate market crashed all over because there were so many houses available from people who died. But on top of that, all the rain and the rising water levels meant that a lot of the low-lying zurbs were constantly flooded. With the Super-E installation stalled at the edge of the city, the people who could afford it started just walking away from their homes in the zurbs and buying houses in the city, where there was not only electricity but working pumps to keep the flooding down.

As home prices rose in urban areas, they dropped even further in the zurbs. Suddenly, houses there were truly worthless. People abandoned whole neighborhoods.

Mr. Martinez said there was never an actual policy decision to cut off the zurbs, to leave them off the Super-E grid, but by the time they had the money to consider expanding the grid, the zurbs were pretty much empty. It just didn't make sense. Some people did stay behind, making a go of it with solar and stuff, but they still couldn't sell their houses. Even the ones in good shape were surrounded by so many empties, nobody wanted them. Aunt Trudy probably paid next to nothing for her place in Perkins Park.

I remembered my parents driving us through the zurbs when I was still pretty young. Things hadn't gotten horrible yet. There were grownups washing their cars and gardening, and kids playing football and skateboarding in the streets. Hard to imagine that was the same place I had been walking through with Del.

I pictured Del, first as the little kid who used to come to the beach with us, then as the boy who that very morning had rewired my brain with a kiss. Now, just hours later, he was an emotionally damaged missing person, out there chasing a terrible mistake while I lay in my bed, unable to do anything to help him. Unable to do anything but hope that Rex could come through for me again, hope that he would find Del, hope that I could somehow save Del from his own self-destructive tendencies. I wondered if I'd ever see either one of them again.

I heaved a big sigh, then lay back on my bed and fell asleep, still holding the picture.

I awoke to my mom gently taking off my shoes. She smiled sadly when I opened my eyes. She tucked me into bed, and I let her. Then I went to sleep for real.

FIFTEEN

The next day, as I waited for the bus, I was half hoping Del would show up, too. When the bus arrived and he still hadn't, the anxiety I had been holding at bay came over me in a wave. I didn't want to get on, but I didn't know what else to do.

I was supposed to be waiting to hear from Rex, waiting for some kind of lead. But what if I never heard anything? What if he couldn't find me at Aunt Trudy's? What if Rex was as gone as Del?

I found an empty seat and put my forehead against the window. As we drove, I realized the bus was taking the longer detour around the missing bridge, staying inside the city. A figure on the sidewalk caught my eye. It was a chimera, and he seemed to be in bad shape. He was dirty and disheveled. His coat was in tatters. He looked part bird or maybe some kind of reptile. His body and face were oddly asymmetrical. He looked older, too. I wondered if he was one of the early ones, or if he'd been older when he got spliced. Or if his splice had just made him that way.

It would be bad enough if Del became a chimera, but what if he ended up like *that*? Things *did* go wrong. All the time. It was still unusual to see chimeras walking around, and in less than twenty-four hours, I'd seen Simon and this guy, two chimeras with messed-up splices. Just like in all the cautionary tales. And even if Del didn't actually end up getting spliced, there were a lot of shady things that could still happen. I'd heard stories of people getting rolled, robbed, left for dead, all sorts of stuff, by real genies and by scam artists pretending to be genies.

I craned my neck to watch the chimera as we drove by and came up with the best plan I could. Rex seemed truly willing to help me, but I hadn't heard from him. So I'd give him today. If he didn't make contact, I'd sneak away from Aunt Trudy's. Try to find Sly and Ryan. See if they'd heard anything since our little encounter yesterday. And if I couldn't find them, well, I'd just keep looking on my own.

I felt better having a plan, but it made the day drag on even more. It didn't help that the kids and the teachers all seemed to be looking at me funny and acting weird. After lunch the vice principal sent for me. Generally speaking, Mr. Sciorra wasn't so bad. He tried to be intimidating—and as the school's disciplinarian, he was supposed to be—but he wasn't fooling anyone.

"Dymphna Corcoran," he said when I walked in. He appeared to be showing off that he knew my full name, even though he had my file right there in front of him.

"Jimi," I corrected him.

He motioned to the chair in front of his desk and I sat down. "That's quite a name. Dymphna."

"She was an ancient Irish saint." The patron saint of the mentally ill, but I kept that part to myself. "Everyone calls me Jimi."

He nodded and studied the file, like he was looking for where it said to call me Jimi. Eventually, he shrugged and closed it. "How are you doing, Jimi?"

I shrugged. "Okay."

"We're aware of what happened yesterday. Sounds pretty intense."

"I guess."

"The police are doing everything they can to find Del, and the chimeras that got away." He was looking at me closely. I didn't say anything.

"Chimeras are bad news, you know that, right?"

I shrugged.

"I'm not just talking about the type of kids who would decide to go to a genie and get spliced with some garage-quality animal DNA. I'm talking about the end result. Those kids are changed, and not for the better. Sometimes for the much worse. They're part wild animal, you know. They're dangerous and unpredictable."

I nodded, but I made it plain it was an *I hear you and I understand* nod, and not an *I agree with you* nod.

He let out a sigh. "Plus, I'm not one of them, but there are a lot of people out there who hate chimeras. You know that, right? They're trying to have chimeras declared nonpeople, since they are not one hundred percent human. Right or wrong, that's going to cause problems for chimeras."

"Sure is. Seems kind of harsh, doesn't it?"

"Maybe so," he conceded.

"Why is it okay to have a WellPlant inserted into your head, but it's not okay to have new genes spliced into your existing genes?" The question had been bugging me, but I don't know why I asked him—I certainly didn't expect any kind of intelligent answer.

He closed his eyes, but I could see him rolling them. "The two are totally different. Totally different. Anyway, I'm just saying, it's getting more dangerous just to be near those kids. Not that you should want to be near them, anyway. Do you get where I'm coming from?"

"Yeah, I feel you."

He looked down at his desk, trying to hide a satisfied smile, oblivious to the fact that I was mocking him.

Then he looked up and asked abruptly, "Where's Del?"

I wondered if he thought that was some sort of interrogation technique, like he was going to trip me up and I would blurt it out.

"I don't know," I answered.

"No idea?"

"I went looking for him last night, but I couldn't find him."

"Looking for him where?"

I shrugged. "A house outside the city. Someone said he was there, but he wasn't."

"In the zurbs? You be careful out there."

I snorted.

"That's funny?"

"I'm going to be living in the zurbs." I could feel him tense up, and I almost laughed, thinking it would be hilarious if my mom got me kicked out of school by shipping me out of the district. "Just for a couple of weeks," I added.

"Outside the city?"

"With my aunt. While my mom takes Kevin to look at schools."

"Ahh, Kevin," he said. As if that explained it. "Yes, he has a bright future, that boy. Quite a talent."

Right, I thought. I didn't say anything at first, but after a moment I cleared my throat and Sciorra came down from his Kevin high.

"Well," he said, "if your living situation changes for more than a few days, the office needs to be informed. And what will be your temporary address?"

"I have no idea."

"Right. I'll have to get that from your mother," he said, scribbling a note to himself in his book. With that out of the way, he gave me what I assumed was supposed to be a meaningful gaze. "Jimi, you do understand that Del is in trouble, don't you?"

I didn't say anything.

"He stole from his father. He assaulted a police officer. That's not minor stuff. It's serious. You need to stay away from him. And if you see him, you need to tell someone. Your mom or your aunt or a teacher. Or me."

I didn't know if I would ever see Del again, but if I did, I was sure I wasn't going to tell Sciorra about it.

"Absolutely," I said.

SIXTEEN

I spent the rest of the day tuning out my biology and English classes by successfully imagining Del in all sorts of terrible situations and unsuccessfully trying to imagine ways of getting him out of them. When school was finally over, I was walking out the door and noticed Nina Tanaka staring at me with a concerned look. We hadn't spoken in months. Years if you didn't count "Hey" or "How's it going?"

This time she came over and put her hand on my arm. "You doing okay?" she asked.

"I'm fine," I snapped. I was touched by her concern but embarrassed that people were obviously talking about me. Plus, Nina used to be friends with Del, too, and I couldn't help thinking that maybe if I hadn't been Del's only friend, he wouldn't have been in this mess. Still, I regretted my tone. I hadn't meant to come off so harsh.

Nina stepped back. "Okay, sorry. Um . . . have a good weekend."

"You, too," I said, trying too late and too halfheartedly to sound friendly. I started to apologize, but she was already gone.

I hadn't realized it was Friday. I was relieved not to have school tomorrow, but knowing I wasn't going home and staying there made everything that much worse.

I sat alone on the bus, the way I always did if I wasn't with Del. The other kids seemed to be making more of an effort than usual to keep their distance. Maybe they'd seen me snap at Nina.

They had never really known what to make of Del. Or me either, I guess, since I hung out with him constantly. But I was easier to ignore. Del was a weirdo. He cemented that reputation in third grade when he brought in a worm for show-and-tell, and he took it out on the bus and kissed it. The other kids—even Nina—screamed so loud, the driver almost lost control of the bus.

I smiled at the memory. Then I felt guilty for smiling while he was out there, in trouble, possibly in danger. Then I felt guiltier, because deep down, what worried me most wasn't actually the danger. It was that if it all went fine, Del would be different once he got spliced. I'd lose my best friend. And then things really would never be the same.

———

My mom was sitting on the front steps, waiting for me, when I got home. She gave me an apologetic smile and I gave her a tight, noncommittal one back, letting her know I didn't totally hate her but I was still angry. When I went inside I was assaulted by the smell of freshly baked cookies. It pissed me off, the way she thought she could play me like that. What also pissed me off was the fact that it actually did make me feel better.

I grabbed a stack and sat at the kitchen table. She came in and sat next to me. I gave her one of my cookies and she put her hand on the back of my neck and pulled me in for a hug. The feeling of her arms around me made me want to cry, but I'd been crying a lot. I was determined not to start up again.

I knew what was going to happen when I pulled away. But I pulled away anyway.

She stood up and sniffed. "I guess we better get going."

I nodded and got up, too.

"Give me your house key," she said quietly.

"What?" I assumed I hadn't heard her right.

"Give me your house key." She put out her hand. "I'm going to give it to Trudy while you're staying there."

"Why don't you give her the spare? I'll run over to Mrs. Edwards's and get it." Mrs. Edwards was the nice old lady on the block who kept everyone's spare key.

"Mrs. Edwards is going to be keeping an eye on the house and bringing in the mail. But that's neither here nor there. I want to give Trudy *your* key."

It took a second to sink in. She wasn't just giving Aunt Trudy a key. She was taking mine away.

"You're locking me out of my own house? What if I need to get something?"

"Trudy will let you in."

"Are you serious?"

She didn't answer, just stood there with her hand out, waiting.

I don't know if I'd ever been so angry before in my life. My fingers trembled as I pried the key off my keychain. I wanted to throw it at her. Instead, I tossed it onto the kitchen table and ran out to the car. I heard the key bounce once before it hit the floor.

I sat in the backseat while Kevin brought out my bags. He and my mom got in the front without looking at me, and we drove off.

SEVENTEEN

When my dad and my grandparents were still alive, there would be these big family get-togethers, for holidays and things. Maybe it was because I had been so little, or maybe my memory built them up, but there always seemed to be more people at those gatherings than my family actually had.

But right before my grandparents died, family relations went south. Nobody told me exactly what everyone was arguing about, but now I realized it was probably money, or where Grandma and Grandpa should be living and who should take care of them. At the time, all I knew was that my grandparents had suddenly gone from "jolly"-old to "out-of-it"-old, and the rest of the family seemed to be falling apart around them.

Then they died and Aunt Trudy moved away. I didn't see her again until my dad's funeral a few years later, where she and my mom spoke about two words to each other. My mom tried to mend fences by inviting her over for dinner last year, but she only tried once.

Apart from whatever other issues she had with Aunt Trudy, Mom clearly just didn't know what to make of her decision to live outside the city, off the grid and away from everything. Now that she was driving me there, however, she tried to make Aunt Trudy's situation sound great.

"It's right by the Levline, just two stops from your school. She's got all the solar power you could want and fresh vegetables growing out back."

Kevin snickered at the ridiculousness of it, earning a smack on the arm from my mom and a smidgen of respect from me, which he would undoubtedly squander at any moment by being a boneheaded jerkface again.

"She's an artist, but she's also a homesteader," my mom said, as if Aunt Trudy were a rustic romantic. "That takes a lot of courage."

Kevin snorted. "You told me last week she was nuts to be living out there."

"Kevin!" she said, flashing him a glare.

"What? You did! You said that's why you didn't want Jimi staying out there in the first place, because of that and what happened—"

My mom silenced him with a look, but in the awkward quiet that followed, I realized two things: My mom had let me stay on my own not because she trusted me, but because she was afraid of me being out in the zurbs. And that fear stemmed from something that happened a long time ago.

We had gone on a daytrip to visit the Davidsons, who were family friends. Mr. Davidson had worked with my dad, but he got laid off. They sold their house in Oakton and moved out to the zurbs, a place called Rockland that was already a little sketchy, flooding-wise, and where the houses were getting cheaper by the second.

We had a full van heading out. The Davidsons' sons, Trent and Tristan, were more Kevin's friends than mine, so Mrs. Davidson told my mom I was welcome to bring some friends of my own. Nina's folks wouldn't let her go. Leo's parents weren't crazy about it either, but ultimately they said okay, as long as Leo brought his water bottle and inhaler. Del's mom was already struggling at that point, and Stan was happy to have Del out of his hair.

My mom made me wear this knee-length party dress that Mrs. Davidson had sent for my birthday. I liked it okay, but I remember thinking, *Don't blame me if it gets messed up.*

We sat around the Davidsons' house with the grown-ups for a while, eating pretzels, making faces at each other, and pretending not to notice the mildewy smell that permeated the entire neighborhood. When we were being enough of a pain, the grown-ups said we could play at the rec center around the block.

It was lame: a rusted-out playground in one corner and across from it an overgrown baseball diamond with a dilapidated dugout. Kevin and Trevor and Tristan ditched us as soon as we got there to go throw rocks at the slide.

Del and Leo and I started playing tag on top of the dugout, running back and forth on the roof and laughing like idiots, when out of nowhere, this huge hand reached up from underneath and grabbed my ankle.

I fell over hard, shocked at first, and then scared as the hand started dragging me over the edge. I was halfway off the roof before Leo grabbed my wrists and started pulling me back. Then Del began pulling, too. I could feel the rusty metal on the edge of the roof cutting into the backs of my knees.

Suddenly, the big hand let go of my ankle and we all went sprawling. Before we could get to our feet, three guys, sixteen or seventeen years old, climbed up onto the roof. They were snickering and mumbling, like they were on drugs or something.

"What are you little shits doing here?" said the biggest one. I was pretty sure he was the one who had grabbed me.

"We didn't know you were down there," Leo said. "We didn't mean to bother you."

Del shouldered Leo aside. "We're allowed to be up here. Why don't you just . . . go to hell!"

The big kids thought that was hilarious. When they stopped laughing, the biggest one took a step forward and looked down at me, a strange smile on his face. "That's a pretty dress," he said. Then he turned back to Del. "You can't be up here unless we say so. People think they can come out here, do whatever they want. Like this place don't count anymore." He forced a laugh, then stopped. "Well in this park, we do whatever *we* want. Got it?"

I still didn't know what was going on, but I knew it was time to get out of there. I shot to my feet and tried to run, but he grabbed my head, palmed it like a basketball, and pushed me down. This time my head hit the roof, hard.

The next thing I knew, I was in the back of an ambulance with ice on my head. A couple of paramedics were cleaning the scrapes on my legs and taking my blood pressure. My parents were looking on, Mom silently crying and Dad trying not to. I kept asking about Del and Leo, but everybody kept shushing me and telling me everything was okay.

When we got to the hospital, a nice doctor examined me while Mom held my hand. I had a bump on my head and cuts on the backs of my knees. Other than that, and the fact that the whole ordeal was scary as hell, I was fine.

When I got home, Del was waiting for me on our back steps. He had a bandage above his eye, and I couldn't help but think how heroic he looked.

I sat down with him and asked him what had happened. Del's recap was short. After I blacked out, he had drawn the big kids away from me, goaded them into chasing him and Leo. They both got roughed up, then the big kids bolted when Kevin and the Davidson boys saw what was happening and ran over yelling.

Del and I went inside the house and told my mom we wanted to see Leo.

"They took him to the hospital, too, sweetie. He'll be okay, but they're keeping him a little longer for observation. Mr. and Mrs. Byron just want to make absolutely sure."

I wasn't too surprised—Leo's folks had always been protective, but until that week, I didn't realize just how protective. When Leo got out of the hospital two days later, his parents sent him straight to his grandparents' for the rest of the summer.

It was weird not having Leo around. Del and Nina and I missed our foursome and looked forward to him coming back. But one day, toward the end of August, a moving van showed up in front of the

Byrons' house, packed up all their stuff, and left. Mr. and Mrs. Byron left with it.

I was stunned, but my parents didn't seem surprised. One of the neighbors said she heard the Byrons had moved into one of the big new towers on the other side of the city. I pestered my parents mercilessly for a while to find out which one. But they said we needed to respect the Byrons' privacy.

I now recognized that Leo's parents had probably been furious at mine for letting him get hurt out in the zurbs. It hadn't been their fault, really—they obviously didn't know just how dangerous Rockland had gotten, and sometimes stuff just happens—but I didn't think the Byrons ever spoke to my parents after that. And none of us ever saw Leo again.

Over the years I realized what could have happened to me if Del hadn't drawn away those kids who'd been harassing us that day. And what an incredible friend he was. I'd always tried to be there for Del because of that, apart from anything else.

But now, thanks to my mom, I was going to be stuck at my aunt Trudy's house when he needed me most.

EIGHTEEN

As we turned off the Avenue to leave the city, my mom took manual control of the car. Autodrive could be a risky proposition on the crumbling roads of the zurbs. The street we were on curved along a creek, past the Perkins Park Levline station and a couple of acres of parking spots enclosed by a ten-foot security fence. We turned onto another street and descended into a vine-covered flood zone, the street lined with big old stone houses decaying into the mud.

A handful of squirrels skittered about, and there were probably rats in the houses. My dad told me that when he was a kid, there were deer and raccoons and possums and skunks and even foxes and coyotes around here, but they were pretty much gone now—poisoned by one thing or another.

Finally, we came to a fence like the one at the Levline station, surrounding neat rows of crops. Halfway up the block, there was a gate with a security panel. As we pulled up, the gate swung inward. We drove onto a dirt driveway that curved around to a small, dusty-looking ranch house. The front porch dangled with wind chimes and whirligigs. An old Volvo was parked on the charging pad.

The front door opened and Aunt Trudy came out, drying her hands on a dish towel. She looked pretty much how I remembered her from a year ago, but somehow more normal. She wore jeans and a loose white blouse, and her long, curly blond hair was losing the fight with gray. She waved as we pulled up. I raised my hand in response and put it back on my lap.

Mom gave me a smile that seemed mostly fake. Then she got out of the car and it turned *all* fake.

Aunt Trudy was grinning—mostly real, I think—and I found myself smiling back.

"Hi, Diane," she said to my mom, then she turned to me and said, "Oh, my God," putting her hands on my shoulders like she was trying to get a physical sense of me, make sure I was real. "Look what a year has done—you're a grown woman!" Mom's eye twitched at that one. "And so pretty, just like your mom. And Kevin, look at you!"

"Hi, Trudy," Mom said. "Thanks."

Aunt Trudy turned to my mom and went in for a hug, but my mom leaned forward for an awkward cheek-to-cheek air kiss.

"I brought some cookies," Mom said, holding out the plastic container, giving it a little shake.

Aunt Trudy turned around and motioned toward the house. "Well, come on in and let's have some."

Her house was decent. Not too neat or too messy, a bit jumbled, filled with strange, cool objects—artwork and gadgets and wooden toys and stuff.

Kevin sat in the armchair. Mom and I sat on the sofa. Aunt Trudy put the cookies on the table in front of us and brought in a chair from the dining room. My mom declined when Aunt Trudy offered coffee or tea.

The next half hour was a blur of predictable awkwardness. I stayed pretty quiet, freaked out by the whole situation. I guess they were freaked out, too. They seemed to be trying to have a conversation without actually saying anything, like they were playing one of those games where you have to tell a story but you can't use certain words. Except in this case, the list of forbidden words seemed to be half the English language.

Kevin caught my eye and gave me a "this is really weird" look. I was glad to have an ally there, however briefly.

The conversation inevitably turned to him, and when it did he was swept up in the euphoria of people talking about how great he was and how bright his future was.

But there really is only so much you can say about Kevin, even if you say it all twice. When we had each eaten our fill of cookies, my mom put her hand on my knee and gave me that sad smile again, the one that made me sad, too. And angry.

"We'd better get going," she said, almost a whisper.

I nodded, determined not to make it easier on her.

"Kevin, help your sister get her bags from the car," she said.

Aunt Trudy looked on with a crooked half smile, like it was cute. Like she didn't have the slightest idea how awful this was for me.

Kevin and I went out to the car, but when we got out there, instead of opening the trunk, he leaned against it. "So, I guess this kind of sucks, huh?"

I rolled my eyes. "You think?"

"She seems nice."

"Sure."

He punched me in the shoulder, a little too hard for a "cheer up" punch, but then he said, "Cheer up. We'll be back in a couple weeks. And this time next year, I'll be gone. Then you can have Mom all to yourself."

He saw something in my expression that made him laugh. "That's right," he said. "You think it's been easy having everything focused on me while you're flying under the radar, doing whatever the hell it is you're doing? Well, soon, it's going to be just you and Mom."

"Crap." This hadn't actually occurred to me.

He put his hand on my shoulder and squeezed. "Ah, I'm just messing with you." He turned and started opening the trunk. "You'll be fine." Then he stopped and looked over his shoulder. "But you do need to be more careful about hanging out with weirdos like Del freaking Grainger."

NINETEEN

Aunt Trudy and I stood on the porch and watched my mom and Kevin drive away. Then she turned to me and said softly, "It's going to be okay. You know that, right?"

The way she said it made me believe her, and that made me more suspicious than anything else. I nodded and she smiled.

"What say we put your stuff up in your room?"

"Okay."

We grabbed my bags and I followed her down a long hallway. "That's my room," she said, pointing at the doorway to our left. It was spacious and nice, with pale lavender walls and wood flooring and furniture. "You're in here," she said, leading me up a half flight of steps and through an open doorway. We stepped into a large, airy room with bookcases, a vaulted ceiling, a skylight, and sliding glass doors that opened onto a deck set about ten feet off the ground. In the yard below, there were half a dozen garden patches; a few were covered with hay, the others were planted with tomatoes, peppers, and greens. Some looked fresh and green, while some were browning and leggy and definitely past their prime. The yard was surrounded by dense brush and trees.

"Wow," I said, before I could stop myself.

"You like it? Oh, good." She put the bags down and looked around appreciatively. "I love this room."

We stood there for a moment.

"Okay, kiddo, I'll go get dinner started and let you get settled in." She smiled sympathetically. "Unfortunately, I'll be working a lot this weekend. Not much of a host, I'm afraid. I need to set up an exhibit, so I'll be leaving at seven tomorrow and won't be home until around midnight. I'll be gone a few hours on Sunday, too. But the rest of the time I'll be here."

"Oh, that's too bad. I mean, about the weekend." I tried to keep the relief and excitement out of my voice. I'd been trying to figure how I would get out of there to search for Del, wondering if I should just run or try to be sneaky about it. I knew the clock was still ticking, but this changed things. If I waited until she went to work, I could just walk out the front door.

"Will you be okay on your own for a bit?" Aunt Trudy asked.

"Oh, sure," I said. "I have a lot of homework to do." That was true. Not that I was going to do it. Del would be proud, I thought, and it occurred to me that he was turning out to be a bad influence even when he wasn't around.

"Okay. Well, you do your thing, and I'll call you when dinner's ready."

I looked at the books on the shelves and pulled out a few. Some Tolkien, and one of the later Rot & Ruin books. I opened *The Hobbit*, which was an old favorite, but a few chapters in I found I couldn't remember who was who or what was going on. Worse, I realized I no longer cared.

I could feel the minutes ticking by. Even with Del getting farther and farther away from me, I could also feel my head getting heavy. The events of the past couple days seemed to break over me like a wave. I fought to stay awake, trying to force my brain to come up with a plan of action.

I failed on both accounts.

It was dark when I awoke to Aunt Trudy tapping on the door.

"Dinner's ready, okay, kiddo?"

It took a moment to remember where I was. Then it all came back to me. "Okay, I'll be out in a second," I called.

Dinner was vegetables over rice and a salad. I was still full of cookies, but it smelled good.

Aunt Trudy looked at me over the table with a sympathetic smile. "You okay?"

I nodded. "Tired, I guess."

"You've been through a lot the last few days."

I let out a soft laugh. I sure had.

"Your mom told me what happened with the police," she said, spooning rice onto my plate. "That must have been scary. It was brave what you did, staying behind and saving that cop."

I nodded and put some rice and veggies in my mouth. "This is really good," I said, sounding more surprised than I had intended.

"I grew it all out back," she said. "Except the rice and the ginger."

"That's pretty cool," I said. "But . . . this is all so weird."

"What, the ginger?"

"No," I said, smiling in spite of myself. "Being out in the zurbs. I mean, it seems nice around here—your garden and all the trees and stuff. But some parts are a mess. It's weird how the zurbs got the way they are."

She nodded. "It's very, very weird. It's amazing how quickly the world can change. How things can fall apart." She sat back. "What do they tell you about it in school?"

"The basics, I guess. The flu pandemic and the energy shortages."

"A lot of it was the weather, too."

"Yeah. The storms, right?"

She nodded. "They got so bad, the old-fashioned power lines couldn't hold up. And in the winter, with the ice and snow . . . People would lose electricity for days, weeks, months even. I remember one winter, they rebuilt the power lines three times, but they kept coming down, again and again. That summer they rebuilt and reinforced it all, and we got this early snowstorm, a blizzard, the day before Halloween—it was a fluke even for now, and it just took out everything. It was spooky, no lights at all except for all these candlelit jack-o'-lanterns in the snow. I think that was the tipping point, you know? When people first started really abandoning the zurbs. Some of the small towns managed to survive by building solar arrays and wind farms and stuff. And some set up coal wells and gas drills, even though they were illegal, and even though they knew it was making things worse."

"My friend Del's dad did that for a while. Building illegal coal wells out in the sticks, before he became a cop."

"Nice," she said sarcastically, shaking her head. I thought about Stan, dragging Del along with him as he went out building those things, knowing they were illegal, knowing how bad they were for the environment. "Anyway, some places got by okay, out there on their own. Others just . . . didn't."

She looked at my face and must have seen something there, because she immediately changed the subject. "So, how about Kevin? That must be exciting, that he's going to be a big college basketball star."

I made an effort to nod. She was sweet, trying to stay away from anything controversial, trying to make this easy for me. But the last thing I wanted to talk about was Kevin, and I was tired of answering questions. I had a few questions of my own. And I was still mad enough at my mom that I felt bold enough to ask them.

"So how come you and my mom aren't closer?"

I had to give her credit, she didn't look shocked or jump down my throat or anything. She just bit the inside of her cheek, and after a few seconds, she said, "We used to be. When you were little."

"What happened?"

"I don't know, Jimi. Families are weird."

I almost laughed, but I stayed quiet instead, waiting for her to continue. She wasn't getting off that easy.

She took a deep breath. "Did you know you have another aunt?"

"Excuse me?"

She nodded. "You're named after her, actually."

This time, I did laugh. "I'm named after some weird old Irish saint."

"Your *aunt Dymphna* is named after a weird old Irish saint. You're named after your aunt—my sister. She didn't like the name any more than you do. Her friends called her Dee."

For a moment I thought maybe Aunt Trudy was crazy after all. But the look on her face was serious. And very sane.

"Are you kidding me? How come I never knew about her?" My smoldering anger at my mom flared up again, hot and bright.

Aunt Trudy paused again, like she was trying to decide how much to tell. "It's a long story. And stupid really—just one of those family arguments that people never got over. . . . Dee was the oldest. She was a brilliant academic, I can't even remember how many degrees she had, but more important to her, she was an activist, always going to protests about the environment and things like that, hanging out with people my parents—your grandparents—didn't approve of. She moved away." She glanced up at me and then down at the table. "Far away. And it broke your grandparents' hearts."

"Where did she move?"

She paused. "All over. China, India. Europe. She especially loved Ireland, in spite of how she felt about her name. Anyway, our parents hated the fact that she traveled so much, and frankly, a lot of the choices she was making. That meant your father was angry at her, too. He loved your grandparents. I mean, we all did, but he was especially protective of them. Personally, I felt like, if that's where Dee's path lay, she had to follow it. Maybe I was wrong, but that's how it seemed to me. Your grandma was already sick, but when Dee . . . left . . . for good . . . it took the fight out of her, out of both of them. She got worse and worse. Then when your granddad died unexpectedly, it was too much for your grandma."

Aunt Trudy shook her head, her eyes welling with tears. "It was a bad time. Dymphna couldn't make it back for your grandmother's funeral. Your father was furious at her, and at me, too. At the world. He was in so much pain. The whole family fell apart. Your mother tried to smooth things between him and me, but it was too soon."

Tears rolled down her face, and I realized my face was wet, too.

"In time, we would have gotten past it, but I got a job in San Diego. Then your dad got sick, and he died, too." Her voice was almost a whisper. "Your mother was devastated. We all were."

She grabbed a few tissues and handed the box to me. When we'd blown our noses and wiped our eyes, she went on.

"Your mom and I have always exchanged Christmas cards, but that was about it." She reached across the table to squeeze my hand. "She always included a photo of you and Kevin."

I was having a hard time taking it all in. "Where's Dymphna now?"

Aunt Trudy shook her head. "She was in Ireland, last we heard from her. But she stopped keeping in touch after your dad died."

We were quiet for a moment, Aunt Trudy overwhelmed by memories and me by revelations. Then she gently clapped her hands together. "Anyway, last year, I was offered a job running an art gallery here in Philadelphia, and I took it. And I'm really glad to be so much closer to you and Kevin and your mom. I hope we can all work on seeing each other more often. Even after your stay here is over."

We spent the next few minutes in a comfortable silence, finishing our food. When dinner was over, Aunt Trudy asked if I wanted to watch a movie or eat some ice cream.

"No, I'm good," I told her as I helped her clear the table. "I'll probably just do some homework and go to bed." Even after my nap, I was still tired, but mostly I just wanted to be alone to think about things.

"Okay, kiddo," she said. "Well, if I don't see you before tomorrow, there's plenty of food in the fridge, and the Levline is just a couple blocks away." She handed me a Levpass. "Your mom left you this, so you can get around if I'm not here."

"Thanks," I said, slipping it into my pocket.

"Will you be okay?"

"I'll be fine."

"Will I see you before I go?"

"If you're leaving at seven, I don't think so." I gave her a smile and said good night, then I went upstairs before she could ask any more questions.

Back in my room, I flopped on the bed, clothes and all, turned off the light, and closed my eyes. My head was spinning from everything Aunt Trudy had told me, on top of everything else. I concentrated on the present and visualized myself not just finding Del, but saving him. I pictured him grateful, and maybe, finally, happy.

TWENTY

I woke with a start in darkness and looked at the clock. It was eleven thirty. The wind was blowing the trees around. I felt vulnerable, alone in a strange room, an unfamiliar house, outside the city.

I heard a loud creak and froze. It sounded like floorboards. I told myself it was Aunt Trudy, but she was snoring in her room. I told myself it was just the unfamiliar house settling, but I knew it wasn't.

I jumped when I heard it again. I couldn't tell where it was coming from. Moonlight poured through the sliding doors leading to the deck, illuminating the middle of the bedroom floor. The only place to hide was behind the drapes hanging bunched on either side of them. I leaped out of bed, halfway across the room, and wrapped myself in the fabric. My heart pounded as I peeked at the doorknob, waiting for it to start turning in the darkness. Seconds ticked by, and I had almost transitioned from terrified to sheepish when something tapped the glass right behind my head.

I spun and fell, taking the drapes and their hardware down with me in a helpless, tangled heap. The figure on the deck outside was huge, its shadow fully engulfing me on the floor. I was about to scream when the figure lifted a finger to its lips.

It was Rex.

The relief I felt was mixed with more than a little anger that he had damn near caused me to pee myself. I flailed my way out of the mass of fabric and slid open the door.

"Hi," he said.

"You scared the crap out of me," I said in a terse whisper. I paused for a moment, tilting my head back to confirm that Aunt Trudy was still snoring. "How did you find me?" I demanded.

"I said I would."

"Yeah, but how?"

"Because I'm good like that. Listen. I got a lead on your friend." He was trying to whisper, his voice rumbling in his chest.

"Oh my God. You found Del? Is he okay?"

"I don't know. They said he's at a house in a place called Tyson's Point."

"Where's Tyson's Point?" I asked.

"In the zurbs. A few miles farther out."

"Can we go there? Right now?"

He nodded, then motioned with his head for me to follow him. He leaned back and flipped over the railing. I ran out onto the deck and looked down at him, standing there in the darkness looking up at me.

"I can't do that," I said, keeping my voice down.

"I'll catch you."

I didn't want to be difficult, but I was totally not doing that. Instead, I put on my jacket and hiking boots and climbed over the railing. It was so dark I couldn't see the ground below me. It seemed far away. Too far. I couldn't will my hands to let go.

I lowered myself as far as I could, but my feet were still dangling. I hung there, trying to let go, and after a few seconds I felt Rex's hands on my waist—large and strong—and a firm but gentle pressure as he took my weight.

I let go and he lowered me to the ground.

I turned to look up at him, embarrassed. "Thanks," I said, my voice strangely hoarse.

His eyes twinkled in the dim light and he smiled. "Let's go." Then he turned and trotted off into the trees.

Hurrying to follow him, I looked over my shoulder at Aunt Trudy's house. I felt bad sneaking out on her, but I'd be back before she knew I was gone, I told myself. Then the trees swallowed me up.

For a moment I thought Rex had gone on without me. But then I put out a hand in the darkness and it landed on his chest. I snatched it back immediately.

"Sorry," I said.

"It's okay," he said. "The trees will thin out in a minute. Here, hold my hand."

His massive hand was warm and dry as it enveloped mine.

He led me down into a shallow gulley that smelled of mud, then back up the other side. The trees parted and moonlight shone on the tall grass.

He let go of my hand. "You okay?" he asked.

I nodded. "Yeah, I'm good."

He pointed up ahead. "We have to get over the fence. How are you at fence climbing?"

When I was younger, I'd been an enthusiast, but it had been a little while. "Great," I said.

He didn't raise an eyebrow, but I was getting better at reading his expressions. He had doubts.

"Let's go," I said quickly, before he could voice them.

TWENTY-ONE

The base of the fence was twenty feet away from where we stood. The top was probably another fifteen feet, straight up.

As we approached, Rex paused and looked at me. This time he actually did raise an eyebrow, and then an arm, gesturing for me to go first. Annoyed by his lack of faith, I hooked my fingers into the links, dug in with the toes of my boots, and started climbing.

The first ten feet wasn't bad, but then it got tougher. I was two feet from the top when my foot slipped.

I'm not going to say I wasn't a little scared, but I still had everything under control. My other foot stayed where it was and my hands kept their grip. Even so, the fence suddenly shook violently and then Rex was there next to me, one hand grasping the fence and the other hand on the small of my back, barely touching me but ready to catch me if I fell.

"I got it," I told him.

He stayed where he was as I climbed the rest of the way, then over the top. Frankly, fifteen feet off the ground, I would have felt better having him there with me, but now I really had something to prove. I met his gaze through the chain links as I climbed down the other side. Once I was on the ground, he flipped over the top and landed on his feet with a soft thud right next to me.

"Big fence," he said, his eyes flashing in the darkness.

"Very big fence," I agreed.

We crept through some more dense woods and out a rusted gate and onto a wide deteriorating street I didn't recognize. Rex turned to the left, and I followed along.

"How do you know Del's in Tyson's Point?"

"I've been asking around." He looked at me. "Like I said I would."

"Has he already been spliced?"

"I don't know."

We walked in silence. The street was badly cracked and dark except for spots of moonlight. Through the dense trees that lined the road, I caught glimpses of houses being swallowed up in the kudzu and mile-a-minute vines.

It was a lot like the zurbs where Del and I had first encountered Rex and his friends. Some houses were almost whole, and others were almost reduced to rubble. Same thing with the streets—some looked like streets in the city, others were little more than asphalt stepping-stones through a forest of trees and weeds.

Twice we passed enclaves that seemed to be functioning neighborhoods—clusters of nice houses with solar roofs on top, orderly rows of garden plots, and warm candlelight inside. I knew plenty of towns managed to operate with their own wind or solar power and everything, but I hadn't thought of anyone living out in the zurbs between them, at least not anyone but chimeras and criminals. And Aunt Trudy.

Maybe Tyson's Point wouldn't be so bad.

After another twenty minutes or so, we cut through a damp, empty neighborhood of small brick townhouses, most of them tinged with green at the bottom from mold or moss or algae. The place seemed vaguely familiar. A couple of blocks in, we came to a deep gully gouged diagonally across the street. A small creek ran along the bottom, its banks littered with chunks of asphalt and the remains of houses that had collapsed into it. We climbed down to cross it and I paused at the bottom. Looking both ways, I could see it extending off in each direction, cutting a jagged line through the neighborhood.

We climbed out the other side, and Rex quickened his pace. I hurried to keep up with him, walking alongside a rusted-out fence. Through it, in the moonlight, I could see an old playing field, now more swamp than anything else. The baseball diamond was completely gone, but remnants of a batting cage and dugout were still there.

A faded sign on the fence said ROCKLAND REC CENTER.

I gasped at the realization that this was the park where Del and Leo and I had been attacked so many years ago. Rockland had been bad then—now this was what was left of it.

Rex looked at me strangely, his eyes narrow and intense. "You okay?" he asked.

"It's nothing," I said, quickening my pace even more so that he had to speed up to keep up with me. In the back of my mind, I wondered what had become of the Davidsons. "Are we almost there?"

"About a mile."

The streets grew wider and the houses became bigger and more spread out. To the east I saw a flicker of light as a Levline train zipped across a bridge in the distance.

Fifteen minutes later we came to a street flanked by two low, curved walls of fake stone that had crumbled to reveal powdery concrete underneath. There were faint lines and marks on the wall, where letters had once been attached to it. Squinting, I could make out the words: *Tyson's Point.*

"Is this it?" I whispered.

He nodded, angling toward it.

The street was lined with houses and driveways spaced every hundred feet or so. Most of the yards were overtaken with brush and vines, but there were gaps where some of the lawns were just high grass.

Rex pointed them out. "Weed killer," he said. "You can tell which houses used the heavy-duty chemicals right up until the end."

It was interesting, I guess, but I really just wanted to get to Del. The street curved around, but Rex went straight, up onto the buckled sidewalk and across one of the weed-killer lawns.

We crossed between two darkened houses. They were both halfway collapsed, but I couldn't shake the feeling we were trespassing. As we shuffled through a thick layer of fallen leaves, Rex put his hand on my shoulder and gently guided me off to the side. "Careful," he said He tossed a stick right where I had been about to walk. The ground wobbled and the branch disappeared for a moment, then surfaced, glistening wet in the moonlight. "Swimming pools," he said. "Empty or full, they can get you either way."

As we kept walking, I looked back. The leaves on the water settled down and looked once again just like dry land.

The next street over was a cul-de-sac, and at the end of it there was a house, mostly intact, with lights flickering in the windows.

"Is that where Del is?" I whispered.

"We'll see," he said as we stepped onto the front path. "Stay close."

TWENTY-TWO

Two dog chimeras came through the front door of the house and positioned themselves on either side of it, like guards. Physically, there were obvious similarities to Rex—the structure of their noses, the jutting jaw and mouth—but the vibe they gave off couldn't have been more different. Their eyes were cold and black, their faces hard. I wondered how much of the disparity between them and Rex was due to differences in their splices and how much of it was due to differences in who they had been to start out with. Rex ignored them as he walked up and grabbed the doorknob, but one of the guards growled at him. The other one looked down at me and lifted his lips to show big, sharp teeth.

Rex snarled with a sudden ferocity that shocked me, first at the one who had growled at him, then at the other one. They both stepped back, off balance.

Not a word was spoken in the exchange. Maybe words weren't important in that kind of competition—for chimeras or regular people, for that matter—or maybe they actually had used their words, in some dog-chimera kind of way.

Rex loomed over them, staring them down as he held open the door. I ducked under his arm and went inside.

My hands were shaking—from that exchange, from anxiety about whether we'd find Del, and from apprehension about what state he would be in.

The inside was dim—just two candles on a wooden crate—but we'd been walking in darkness so long I could see fine. I immediately wished I couldn't.

In one corner was a low-tech lab setup—battery-powered hot plate, beakers and a test tube rack, a couple of pipettes and syringes. A guy who looked about twenty with a shaved head and a goatee sat on a cushion, his face devoid of expression. An IV tube ran from his arm to a bag hanging from a nail in the wall. I stared at it for a second—the IV was feeding him the spliced virus, infecting him with some foreign gene.

In another corner a girl my age was sitting on a mattress, crying. A chimera with cat ears and tabby stripes sat with her, talking to her soothingly.

It all seemed horribly wrong. The vibe of the place was decay and ruin. I'd seen Del make some bad decisions, self-destructive ones, but this was worse than I'd even imagined.

Rex had been noble and helpful and great, but he was part of this, too. He'd made this same decision. He was part of this world.

The cat chimera looked up, and I saw it was Ryan. He gave me a smile that was surprisingly gentle and nodded at me. I nodded back, but I didn't smile. He seemed like he was being nice to that girl, caring for her, but he was also encouraging her to go through with this terrible mistake. I wondered if someone was doing the same thing with Del, talking him through it, convincing him to take the plunge.

I followed Rex past the stairs, into what had probably been the dining room.

Several rolled-up rugs were stacked against one of the walls, like a makeshift sofa. Three chimeras were sitting on them, smoking in the light of a lantern. They looked up when we walked in. The one in the middle said, "Rex. What's up, dog?"

Rex tipped his head. "Malcolm."

Malcolm was small and twitchy, almost squirrely, but vaguely predatory as well. He looked like a rat, beady eyes and a narrow face, but he was thin and wiry, like a mongoose or a ferret. He got to his feet in a single fluid motion and looked at me like he was sizing me up. "Someone wants to join our ranks?"

I stepped back and suppressed a shudder at the thought.

Rex shook his head. "We're looking for a friend."

Malcolm's eyes narrowed. "Looking why?"

The air was suddenly tense. The other two chimeras got to their feet, too. They were bigger than Malcolm, more formidable. They both had pointy faces with wide black-and-white streaks emanating from their snouts. Badgers, I thought.

Rex held up his hands, palms out. "Just want to talk to him."

"What's this friend's name?" Malcolm asked.

Rex turned to me.

"Del," I said quietly. Then I cleared my throat. "Del Grainger."

Malcolm smiled and let out a soft laugh. The other two relaxed as well. "Yeah, you can talk to Del. He's upstairs in the front room."

My heart jumped, but as I wheeled around toward the stairs, Malcolm called after us, "If you're here to talk him out of it, you're too late. He's up there sweating out the change. We spliced him this morning."

TWENTY-THREE

I ran upstairs to the darkened second floor, Rex pounding up the steps behind me. I'd heard about the sweating out. Chimeras reacted differently to their splices, depending on the animal they were spliced with, the genes inserted, and the individuals themselves, as well as the skill of the genie. Most of the changes took place in the first twenty-four hours after the splice, and that's when it hurt the most. In health class, after the "Things Can Go Wrong" speech about all the kids who die from bad splices, they focused on how much it hurts as your bones and your organs and your skin stretch and change and rearrange.

As I rounded the banister at the top of the steps, I heard a sound from the front room, a cross between a groan and a whimper. Then I heard my own voice whispering, "Del?" as I sprinted down the hallway.

The room was dark, but in the moonlight through the dusty window, I could see him.

It was Del, lying under a thin blanket on the floor, trembling, his skin glistening with sweat. Rex came up behind me, lighting up the room with a flashlight, and I gasped.

Del's skin was a sickly green and his forehead was swollen and bruised. His lips—the lips that had kissed me—were cracked and bleeding.

I knelt beside him. "Jesus, Del," I whispered. "What have you done?"

His eyes fluttered open but didn't focus.

"He won't be able to answer you for a few hours yet," said a voice behind me. I turned and saw Malcolm standing at Rex's elbow, smoking a cigarette.

"What did you do?" I demanded.

He shrugged. "I just helped. The question is, what did he do? And the answer is, same thing I did." He hooked a thumb at Rex. "Same thing big dog did." Then he laughed, a cruel, wheezy cackle. "Course, I never done a salamander splice before, but I always wanted to try a lizard, so there you go."

"A salamander?" I looked back at Del and put a hand on his swollen face. It was damp and cool. The texture was strange, rubbery.

Like Sydney.

He started coughing, and his body shuddered as a convulsion ran through him. His mouth stretched wide in a noiseless scream, the cracks deepening in his lips, fresh blood welling up in them.

"Del!" I cried.

Malcolm laughed again. "He'll be fine. It's all part of it. Just give him a few hours."

I looked over at Rex, and he nodded. "That's how it happens."

I tried not to think about how Del had permanently changed himself, how the friend I had known my whole life was never coming back. I tried not to think of how angry I was, how lonely I felt. Right now, my only concern had to be for Del's well-being. "And this lasts twenty-four hours?"

Rex scratched behind his neck. "Sometimes a little longer."

Malcolm snickered again and shook his head. "I told him, go mammal and you'll get through it quicker. Less chance of complications, too. But he insisted." He shrugged. "I told him same as I told you, I never done a lizard, but he wouldn't let it go."

"It's an amphibian," I said.

"Whatever," he said. "At least he'll have a good sweating-out story. Bragging rights, you know what I mean?"

I didn't answer and as he walked away, I looked back at Rex. "I'm going to stay with him."

Rex stared at me wordlessly for a moment, then nodded. "Okay. I'll be back soon." Then he was gone, too.

I sat against the wall with Del's head on my lap. The feel of his skin was unsettling, but I brushed the damp hair from his face and patted it dry with my sleeve.

He shifted and his arm flopped out from under the covers. His bandages had been changed, but they were bunched up, exposing the wound where his father had scraped the skin off. It looked better than I expected: healing well with no signs of infection. I adjusted the bandage and tucked his arm back under the covers.

After a few minutes, the trembling stopped and his breathing slowed. His eyes opened briefly, and he looked up at me. This time there was recognition. He gave a soft sigh of a laugh and a hint of a smile. Then he closed his eyes and slept.

I sat there for a long time, just me and him. I pictured him as a little kid, running around in the sunshine with me and Leo and Nina. Back when Del's mom and my dad were still alive. It seemed so unbelievably, irretrievably long ago. Tears streamed down my face as I was overcome with sadness, mourning the loss of it all.

TWENTY-FOUR

I let myself weep long enough to feel I'd gotten some small part of it out of my system. As I was pulling myself together, I heard a quiet voice say, "Are you okay?"

I looked up and saw a bird chimera standing at the door, a girl, looking at me with big dark eyes. I didn't say anything, and she looked away, a nervous, jerky movement. But she came into the room anyway.

"He'll be all right, you know," she said, one hand absentmindedly smoothing the beige feathers on her head. "We all go through it." She turned her back to me and the room lit up from a lantern she had brought. She turned back around with a reassuring smile and I saw it was Ruth, the girl the cop had shocked so badly.

The stark light exaggerated the otherworldliness of her face, the texture of the feathers that covered her head, the shadows cast by the arc of her beak-like nose. Her large black eyes flashed with some kind of light from within. She was strange, all right, but she had an innate sweetness.

She sat next to me on the floor and put two bottles of water between us. "Keep him hydrated," she said. "You too."

"Thanks." I realized I was parched. I opened one of the bottles and drank half of it.

"There's more downstairs," she said. She turned to look at me again. "I'm Ruth."

"Jimi," I said.

Her head tilted to the side.

"You helped me before," she said. "Back at the other house, with the cop."

I nodded.

"Thanks."

I nodded again.

She fumbled in her bag and held something out to me. It was a small button, a black pattern against a white background, the heads of three stylized animals radiating from the center—a lion, a ram, and a snake. "This is for you," she said.

"What is it?"

"It's a gift. In mythology, chimeras were part ram, part lion, and part snake."

"I know, the ancient Greeks."

"Exactly." She looked down with a shy shrug. "So you're, like, an honorary chimera."

"Thanks," I said, putting it on my shirt. Honorary was fine.

Del coughed, a dry hacking sound.

"He sounds thirsty," she said. She opened the other bottle, and dribbled some water between his lips. He didn't quite wake up, but he reached up and grabbed the bottle with one hand and guzzled it down. When it was empty, he coughed again. Then his arm went slack and he was asleep once more.

"Guess he was," I said.

For the next half hour, we sat there in silence. Thoughts buzzed through my head. What would Del be like when this was over, not just physically, but as a person? Would we still be friends? Where would he live? What would his dad do? And what would happen to me?

I was already in trouble. I wondered how much worse it could get.

Part of me wished Ruth would leave me alone, but part of me was really glad to have her there, especially when Del went through another rough stretch. It started with a twitch running across his face. Then he began coughing and convulsing. His limbs shook violently. Horrible clicking, grinding noises came from deep within his body. It was difficult to watch, difficult to be near. It could have been my imagination, but when he settled back down, his forehead seemed to be bulging more than before. I wondered if it was swelling or if that's just how it was now. The cuts at either corner of his mouth had gotten deeper.

Ruth smiled down at him, warm and sympathetic, and I was ashamed that what I felt was revulsion and sorrow and anger that he had done this to himself. But I couldn't help it. This was crazy.

She put her hand on my arm. I was relieved that it looked normal. "You should take a break," she said. "I can be here with him."

"No, I'm okay," I replied.

I did want to get out of there, desperately, but I didn't want to tell her that. I looked down at Del. "He's still sweating," I said. "Okay if I open a window?"

Ruth looked up at me. "Sure," she said, her sympathy directed as much toward me as toward Del. "That would be great."

I wrestled it open and cool air flowed in, making me realize just how stuffy the room had been. I put my head through the window and breathed deeply. When I pulled myself back inside, Ruth looked up at me again. "He needs more water."

"I'll get it," I said quickly. "Where is it?"

"On the kitchen table."

I nodded and glanced at Del, then went downstairs.

The guy with the goatee was asleep in the living room, still hooked up to an IV. The girl who had been crying was gone. The dining room was empty, but there was a candle burning on the kitchen table and a case of water next to it. I went in and grabbed two bottles. Two eyes flashed in the darkness, and a voice said, "Jimi, right?"

It was Ryan, standing by the back door. "How's Del doing?"

"Um . . . okay, I think. I don't know."

"He'll be fine, you know. In a couple hours he'll be laughing about it, geeking out over his new self."

He smiled, but I couldn't smile back. "Right."

"I'm going to get some air," he said, opening the door. "You look like you could use some too."

I shook my head and held up the water. "No thanks. I should bring these up."

He gave me a gentle smile, like he understood. Then he slipped outside.

TWENTY-FIVE

Back upstairs, Del was wheezing loudly, and I felt an intense pang of guilt for having left his side.

"Is he okay?" I asked, my heart pounding. What I meant was, *Is he dying?*

"He's fine," Ruth said soothingly. She took one of the water bottles and put it to his lips, but he turned away.

I sat on the floor and put my palms against my eyes.

"Are *you* okay?" she asked as she put the cap back on the bottle.

"Yes, I'm okay," I said, more defensively than I intended. "Sorry. I just don't know why Del would do this to himself."

She moved over next to me. "It's a big decision."

I laughed and shook my head. "Yes, it is. And I don't think he's thought it through. This changes everything."

"Maybe he wanted to change everything. Not you, maybe, but everything else. I talked with him while he was waiting to see the genie. He told me about his dad, showed me his arm. He needed to get away."

"I know, but this?"

She gave me a patient smile to let me know she wasn't taking offense but could have.

"Sorry. I didn't mean it like that," I said. "But how's he going to live? How's he going to get a job?"

"We manage okay. There's jobs. Some people actually do hire us. Some of us grow food, some do landscaping. I clean houses some-times. My best friend is a barista at New Ground Coffee Shop."

"What about college?"

"College isn't for everyone." There was that line again. I wanted to tell her about how Del and I planned to go to school together, but it sounded somehow childish even before I said it. I switched tactics. "You know they're trying to pass a law, right? If the governor signs it, anyone whose DNA isn't one hundred percent human won't legally be a person."

Ruth nodded solemnly. "I do know. And why would *humans* do that? It makes you wonder, what's so great about being one hundred percent human anyway?" She shook her head, her voice getting louder. "You look at what humans do to each other, what they do to chimeras and to animals and to the planet. Chimeras are people, Jimi, regardless of any law, but for some of us, 'human' just isn't a club we want to be a part of."

"Not all humans are like that," I said, feeling defensive.

She smiled, almost patronizingly. "Well, I sure hope not."

I thought about my frightening encounter with Simon, but before I could point out that chimeras weren't all sweetness and light, either, Rex came up the stairs with a bundle under his arm. "I brought some crackers and some extra blankets," he said. "I have to go out."

Ruth took the bundle from him. "What's going on out there?"

He shook his head. "Probably nothing. Ryan seems to have wandered off."

Ruth's eyes flashed with fear. "Poachers?"

"I doubt it. He went for a walk after talking that girl out of getting spliced."

I was taken aback. I thought he'd been trying to talk her into it. Rex gave me a small smile that lingered, just a second. I wondered if he could tell what I'd been thinking.

"I just want to make sure he didn't fall in a swimming pool or anything," he said. "I'll get Del something to help with the fever, okay?"

"Thanks," I said.

"Be careful," Ruth said.

"Of course," he said. Then he turned to me. "You okay?"

I nodded.

He nodded back and left.

A few seconds later, I looked out the window and saw him loping across the lawns in the moonlight, his bulk moving improbably fast.

"What was that about?" I asked as he disappeared into the shadows. "Poachers?"

"That's what we call them. Chimeras go missing," she said sadly. "Abducted."

"By who?"

"By 'one hundred percent humans,' I imagine," she said with a wry smile. "Although it's a mystery which ones."

"Are you serious? Why?"

"Who knows?" she said. "I don't like to think about it. They do it to each other, too, so I guess it shouldn't come as a surprise. Abductions have been around forever, right? Especially kids. They used to put the victims' pictures on milk cartons, in the olden days."

"Have you told the police?"

She laughed, covering her mouth, embarrassed to be laughing at me so openly but incredulous that I could be so naïve.

"I'm sure they already know," she said.

I could feel my face going hot. I'd seen with my own eyes how the police treated chimeras. I couldn't see Officer Cantrell rushing to help if a chimera went missing.

She opened the crackers and passed them to me. "Luckily, we have Rex," she said. "He makes sure nothing bad happens. Rex is really good. I don't know what we'd do without him."

"Have you known him long?"

"A few years, I guess. Since right after I changed. It seems like forever."

I put a cracker in my mouth. It was stale, but I was starving. I passed the box back to Ruth and for a few minutes we were quiet except for the crunching.

"So, why did you?" I asked quietly. "Get spliced, I mean."

She studied my face as if trying to decide if I really wanted to know or I just wanted to judge her. She shrugged, as if maybe it didn't matter.

"Partly what I said before," she said. She had a far-off look, like she was remembering something from a long time ago. "I wanted to protest what humanity has done to the natural world, to do what I could not to be complicit, and to show my allegiance to the animals we're wiping out. But people have all sorts of reasons. For some it's just a fashion thing, others are trying preserve at least a part of a species that's endangered or extinct. I've always been fascinated by birds. I've always wanted to fly." She laughed. "I still can't, of course. But it's pretty cool being part bird. I get to see the world differently, I think, being a chimera. It gives me a broader view of how everything is connected."

"Do you ever wish you hadn't gotten spliced?"

She shrugged. "Sometimes, I guess. Not much. I have a good life. I have good friends, like Rex and Pell."

"Is that who you were sitting with on the porch the other day?"

She nodded, smiling. "Yeah. Pell's my bestie. Birds of a feather, you know?"

I nodded like I knew. But I didn't, really. Not anymore. My closest friend—my *only* friend—was lying on the floor changing from someone I didn't know as well as I thought into someone I barely knew at all.

Ruth leaned her head back, still smiling, and slowly closed her eyes. Her mouth fell open and she started making a soft whistling sound as she breathed. She was asleep.

Sitting there beside her, I vaguely wondered what would happen if Aunt Trudy checked on me before she left and realized I wasn't there. But as my own exhaustion hit me, I felt a strange calm. So what if my mom grounded me for months? If Del was gone, I'd have no one to hang out with anyway. And if I couldn't get my driver's license, I'd just deal with it. I hadn't come all this way just to leave Del like this. I needed to stay with him and make sure he was okay.

Ruth turned in her sleep, and her head sagged over, her soft feathers resting on my shoulder. Up close, they were quite beautiful, but they were so nonhuman that for a brief moment I felt a twinge of something like revulsion, as if deep down my brain still didn't know what my reaction should be. But she was so sweet and so caring, my heart knew my reaction shouldn't be that.

She smiled in her sleep. And as I felt my eyes closing, I smiled too.

TWENTY-SIX

When I awoke, bright sunlight was streaming in through the open window. Del was lying next to me on the floor, tangled in the covers. He should have been better by now, but he looked worse. His skin had gone from sickly green to a blotchy gray. His eyes and his nose were crusty and dry. His lips had scabbed over, which I hoped was a good sign, but they looked terrible.

Ruth was standing by the door, looking upset. The feathers on her head seemed ruffled, disheveled.

I looked back at Del and my heart seized up. "Is he—"

"He's alive," she said harshly, "but he's not doing great. Here," she said, shoving a paper bag at me. "Rex got this for him. To help with the pain and the fever."

Her voice sounded different, and her nose was pierced with a tiny green stud.

I suddenly realized it wasn't Ruth I was talking to. It was Pell.

"Wait. Where's Ruth?" I asked. "What's wrong?"

Pell's shoulders heaved as she choked back a sob. "Ruth's gone."

"What do you mean?" I said, scrambling to my feet.

"She went outside last night to get some air, and she disappeared. While you were *sleeping*. While Rex was out getting Children's goddamn Tylenol, worrying about you and your friend instead of protecting Ruth from poachers."

I was taken aback by the force of her anger.

"Well, I'm really sorry about Ruth," I said, and I was. "But I'm trying to save my friend's life, and look at him!" I pointed at Del. "I'm sure a little Children's Tylenol will fix him *right* up."

She blinked rapidly, surprised, like she'd been so wrapped up in her own fury and fear that it hadn't crossed her mind that I might be anxious too.

"You chimeras think it's a joke," I continued, "that it's no big deal people are dying from these splices—"

" 'You chimeras'?" she repeated. "You sound like an H4Her. Are you sure you don't mean 'You mixies'?"

"—you tell people they can live this carefree life, not a worry in the world—"

"No worries except for poachers and people like you," she shot back, "who think they're more important than some disgusting mixies."

"—and when things go wrong, you have no idea how to fix it. Children's *Tylenol*?" I said. "Are you kidding me?"

We both turned at the sound of heavy footsteps rushing up the stairs. Rex rounded the top of the stairs and came down the hallway toward us. His eyes looked burdened and his forehead was creased.

He met Pell's gaze and she started crying again, and as he came into the room, he put an arm around her. He looked down at Del. "How's he doing?" he asked.

"Look at him," I said. "He's dying!"

Rex rubbed his chin, studying him. "It could be a bad splice. Something might have gone wrong."

"Do you think so?" I said, sarcastic and shrill.

Rex took a step back. "Did you get the Tylenol?"

I wanted to throw the bag at him. "Yes, I got the Tylenol!" I took a deep breath, pointing at Del. "Do you really think Tylenol is going to fix that?"

"It'll help with the fever," he said.

"He needs a doctor!" I shouted. "Where's Malcolm? He did this. He needs to fix it."

"Malcolm's gone, but even if he were here, there's nothing he could do."

"Then we need to get Del to a hospital!"

"A hospital won't help him," he said.

"What do you mean?"

"They won't even try. Not for chimeras," Pell said bitterly.

"Why? Because chimera biology is so different?"

Pell laughed. "Because they don't have to."

"Insurance companies don't have to cover us, so they don't," Rex said. "Hospitals and doctors say their liability isn't covered. Nothing says they have to treat us, so mostly they don't. The best they'll do is monitor him until he dies."

I was stunned. Not only did these chimeras let Del do this to himself, now they were telling me we couldn't even take him to a hospital. Del coughed again, his breathing growing more ragged. Tears filled my eyes, but I willed them to stop. "So then, what do we do? There must be something we can do."

Rex felt Del's pulse and looked into his eyes. He seemed so sure of himself, but more and more I was realizing none of them had any idea what they were doing.

He stood and let out a sigh. "Look," he said softly. "Nobody talked Del into doing this, not even Malcolm. It was a decision Del made on his own. But there might be something we can do to help him."

"What? Tell me!"

Rex ignored me and turned to Pell. "I'll find them," he told her, his voice burning with determination. "But first, we need to clear out of here, in case the poachers come back for more."

Pell started crying again, but she nodded and left the room. Downstairs, I could hear the others packing up.

Rex turned to me. "And we'll take care of Del too."

"How?" I asked.

"We can take him to a fixer."

"A what?"

He looked away from me before he continued. "First twenty-four to forty-eight hours, before a splice really takes hold, it can be undone. Fixers are people who can reverse a bad splice. Change him back, if it's not too late."

A wave of relief crashed over me at the thought that this horrible mistake could still be undone. Del might be angry, but he'd get over it. And if reversing the splice would save his life, how could he argue with that? I felt a sudden, intense optimism, a sense that things could be salvaged, that Del could be saved, that maybe the craziness that had taken over the world in the last couple days wasn't a done deal.

But as the news sank in, I realized I was angry as hell. "Why didn't you tell me this before?" I asked, my voice loud and hot.

"This isn't a choice to be taken lightly."

"If it can save his life it is!"

"And that's why I'm telling you about it now. But Del chose to get spliced, whether you agree with it or not. It was his decision. He paid for his splice, both in money and in the pain he's been sweating through. If I had told you about the fixer last night, you would have wanted to bring him there immediately. And if you deny it, you're lying."

I opened my mouth to protest but thought better of it. "Okay, whatever. So let's get him there now."

"It's not that simple. We need a way to get him there, which won't be easy. And we need a way to pay for it. Do you have a driver's license?"

"I have a permit, and I know how to drive."

His face said he took that as a no. "How much money do you have?"

"On me? Forty bucks."

He frowned. "How much can you get your hands on?"

"I have another forty at my aunt's. And sixty more at my house, but I can't get in there."

He frowned even more.

"Why?" I asked. "How much does it cost?"

"A lot more than that. Maybe a thousand. There's a guy who owes me a favor, but . . . We're still going to need some money."

I could feel the shiny, happy future fading away as quickly as it had come into being. "We can get the money from his dad," I said with absolute confidence, hoping Rex would believe me, and hoping that would make it real.

Rex screwed up his nose. "His father who hates chimeras? The one who did that to his arm?"

"Yes," I said. "If he hates chimeras so much, he'd do whatever it takes to make sure his only son doesn't become one, right?"

The logic sounded good. But Stan Grainger wasn't a logical person. I had a hard time picturing him doing anything good for Del. But Del was his son, goddamn it—Stan had to step up. Besides, it was the only solution I could think of.

Rex furrowed his brow. "Maybe," he said. For someone who was usually hard to read, he was making it pretty plain he didn't like the idea. "You wait here. I'll be back as soon as I can."

"Where are you going?"

"I'm going to get the others squared away, and figure out how to get Del out of here and where to take him. Then we'll think about how to get the money."

— — —

I stayed in the room with Del, keeping out of the way as the others packed up to go. It didn't take them long. I got the impression they were used to relocating.

Fifteen minutes later the sounds of activity inside the house had been replaced by hushed voices outside. I looked out to see everyone standing on the front lawn.

I didn't see Pell out there. When I turned away from the window, she was at the bedroom doorway, leaning against the frame. Her eyes were red.

"Sorry," she said. "About before."

"Me too," I said. "It's okay."

"It's not," she said. "None of this is your fault. I know you had nothing to do with it. I'm just scared, you know? For Ruth."

I nodded.

"Where'd you get that?" she said, pointing at my shirt.

I looked down at the chimera pin. "Ruth gave it to me."

Pell smiled. "She must have liked you. Likes you, I mean. She likes you." She sniffed and put a hand over her face.

I got up and hugged her narrow shoulders. "She'll be okay." I could feel her trembling.

"I know," she said, pulling back and wiping her eyes on her sleeve. "I know she will." She said it deliberately, as if she was trying to convince herself. "It's just hard right now. I'll see you soon, okay?" she said, reaching up and patting my cheek. Then she pointed at Del. "And he'll be fine too. You'll see."

"I know," I said, trying to convince myself as well, suddenly choking back tears.

Then she turned and left. I watched through the window as she joined the group out front, each of them carrying a duffel or a backpack. When they got to the street, Pell turned and looked back, waved up at me in the window. I waved back. Then they disappeared around the corner.

TWENTY-SEVEN

Sitting there alone with Del, I could hear the house creaking and groaning around me. When I was little and heard noises at night, my dad would tell me it was just the house settling. But this house wasn't settling. It was falling apart, along with everything else.

I dripped a double dose of Tylenol into Del's mouth, followed by a little water.

He didn't seem to get any worse after that, but he wasn't getting better, either. As the hours went by, that was almost as bad.

I couldn't stop looking at his face. It was barely recognizable, but I couldn't tell how much of the change was permanent and how much was swelling and bruising that might heal.

After six hours I gave him another dose of Tylenol, feeling more and more anxious about how much time had passed since his splice. He tossed and turned the whole time, at one point throwing off his covers entirely. His body looked longer and more sinewy than before.

I rearranged the covers over his body and sat there, willing Rex to return as soon as possible and watching a patch of sunlight from the window slide across the floor before disappearing entirely in the late afternoon.

I was thinking about going to look for some food in the kitchen when the house creaked again, differently this time. It was the sound of floorboards. I sat there, silently listening. Soon I could make out one set of footsteps. Then two. Maybe more. I heard snickering.

The steps creaked.

Crap, I thought. *They're coming upstairs*.

Del was helpless, lying on the floor, making me even more vulnerable than I would have been on my own. The bedroom closet was open, and there was a metal clothing rod leaning in the corner. It was the closest thing to a weapon I had. I crept into the closet, grabbed the rod, and pulled the door partway closed.

As the footsteps moved closer in the hallway, Del stirred and let out a soft groan, the first sound he had made in hours.

Good timing, Del, I thought.

When the door to the room opened, I shrank back, watching through the gap.

There were three of them. I was relieved at first to see they were my age. Then I saw their faces. They looked mean.

"Holy crap," the biggest one said, snickering. He wore a two-tone jock jacket with the name DIETRICH across the back. "Look at this freak."

They stood over Del's unconscious body.

"Is it even alive?" one of the others said.

Dietrich put his foot against Del's ribs and gave a push. "What's it even mixed with?" he asked, his face screwed up in disgust as he kicked a little harder. Del groaned again.

The other two exchanged uncertain glances.

Dietrich kicked Del again, even harder. He turned to the other two. "Come on, don't let me have all the fun."

I didn't know what to do.

The other two stood there for a moment. Then one of them stepped forward and raised a foot behind him, tensing like he was about to deliver a brutal kick.

"Stop!" I yelled, stepping out from the closet. I held the rod behind my leg.

They jumped, startled, then Dietrich's mouth spread into an unpleasant grin. The other two looked even more nervous than before.

"Would you look at that? It's a goddamned mixie-lover," Dietrich said, coming at me with his fist cocked.

I didn't hesitate. I swung the rod as hard as I could. It connected with the side of his head, ringing like a bell. But the angle wasn't great and the rod kind of ricocheted off his skull. He staggered back but didn't go down.

His friends stared at him, their eyes round, like they were afraid of what he would do next.

"That. Hurt," he said through gritted teeth. If his face looked mean before, now it was downright evil. A trickle of blood rolled down his cheek.

"Good," I said, with more bravado than I felt. My hands started to shake, a tremor that threatened to spread throughout my body. But I widened my stance and braced my legs.

"Dietrich, man, let's just go," said one of his friends.

"Screw that," Dietrich said, and he lunged at me.

I swung the bar again, with everything I had. This time it connected squarely against his jaw. He stumbled back against the opposite wall, the bottom half of his face strangely misshapen. Blood spurted from his mouth and nose. He cupped one hand around his chin. It moved like a wet bag full of gravel. Then his eyes rolled up and he passed out, sliding down the wall to the floor. If I hadn't been so scared, I might have thrown up.

"Holy crap!" one of his friends yelled. They backpedaled toward the door. One of them said to me, "Now you're going to get it." They ran down the steps and out the door, and then it was just me and Del and jackass crumpled on the floor.

TWENTY-EIGHT

Five minutes later I heard the front door bang open and heavy footsteps thundering up the stairs. I tightened my grip on the closet rod, bracing myself to fight off whoever those guys had gotten to come back and avenge their asshole friend.

But it wasn't one of them. It was Rex.

He skidded to a stop when he entered the room. His eyes went from Del to Dietrich on the floor, then to me.

He looked stricken. "Are you okay?" he asked.

I nodded.

He reached up to touch my face. I flinched, but I let him. He wiped my cheek and his hand came away wet with tears and blood. "Did he hurt you?"

I shook my head. "It's not my blood."

He looked down at the guy on the floor. "You did that?"

I nodded. "With the closet rod. There were two others. They ran away. Do you think they were the poachers?"

He shook his head. "Probably just some lunkheads. But maybe dangerous lunkheads." He took his eyes off Dietrich to meet mine. "Chimeras have to deal with that type all the time. And this whole GHA thing is only going to make it worse."

"They said they were coming back."

He nodded. "I bet." He checked Del's pulse again, looked in his eyes. Then he checked Dietrich.

"He's breathing okay," I said. "But I think I broke his jaw. He . . . wouldn't stay back."

"He'll be fine until his friends come back. We need to get out of here, though."

He wrapped Del up in his blanket and hoisted him, cradling him like a small child in one arm.

Del stirred. His eyes flickered open, just for a second, and his arm flopped out from under the cover.

I gasped at the sight of it.

"What is it?"

"His arm. It's almost healed." The wound was almost gone, just a few scabs and some faint streaks of pink against the greenish skin.

Rex grabbed the closet rod and ducked through the doorway. "Guess the injury wasn't as bad as we thought."

"I guess not," I said, but I knew it had been. I wondered if the healing had something to do with the splice.

I followed Rex down through the darkened first floor and out the front door. Daylight was fading fast.

I hadn't really thought about how we would transport Del. But somehow I hadn't been expecting an old Volkswagen Beetle. When Rex opened the door, I saw the driver's seat had been torn from its mountings and wedged against the backseat.

"Is this yours?" I asked.

"A friend lets me use it. We're the same size. Well, almost the same size."

He tossed the closet rod over his head in a casual hook shot. It spun lazily through the air, then plunged into the swimming pool next door with barely a ripple. He laid Del on the backseat and folded himself through the door, filling the space behind the steering wheel. When he had squeezed inside, he pulled the door closed and started the motor.

He looked out the window and said, "Let's go."

━━ ━━ ━━

I started to tell Rex where Del's house was, but he seemed to know where he was going. He was a surprisingly decent driver, effortlessly navigating the chewed-up zurb streets. As dire as the situation was,

I was struck by the comical sight, this huge dog chimera hunched over the wheel. I looked at him and smiled, wondering if he was fighting the urge to stick his head out the window and let his tongue flap in the wind.

He turned and saw me looking at him.

"What?"

"Nothing." I figured I should keep that thought to myself.

I focused instead on Stan Grainger, wondering how I was possibly going to hit him up for money. It was my plan. I'd put it out there. And it still made sense, but the optimism I'd summoned when I first suggested it was long gone.

As we approached the Avenue, the lights of the city seemed garishly bright after the darkness of the zurbs. Tyson's Point had felt like some faraway place, but by car, it was just ten minutes from the city.

My unease grew as we turned onto the Avenue, and even more, minutes later, when we arrived on my block.

Rex pulled over in front of my darkened house, and I felt a wave of sadness. I'd be back there in a couple weeks—if I didn't end up in jail or a boarding school somewhere—but at that moment it felt like I no longer lived there. Worse, it looked like no one else did, either, like the house I grew up in was as abandoned as the crumbling wrecks in the forgotten zurbs outside the city.

And even if I did end up back there, safe and sound, it would be different. Deep down, I knew it. Del wouldn't be there. He couldn't be. Even if he got out of this unscathed and unspliced, even if he didn't go to jail for stealing from his dad or assaulting that cop, he couldn't just move back in with crazy, mean, abusive Stan. That part of his life— that part of my life—was over.

"You okay?" Rex asked, staring at me.

I nodded and wiped my eyes. We got out of the car and stood there for a moment, looking at Del's house, then at mine.

"That's your house," Rex said. "And that's Del's, right?"

I nodded, vaguely wondering if his splice gave him some kind of homing powers.

We both looked back at Del, still unconscious, his face gray and swollen, crusty and bleeding. But still alive. As Rex hauled him out of the car and up onto his feet, his eyelids fluttered and he groaned. I licked the sleeve of my shirt and dabbed his face, cleaning it up a little. As I pulled his arm over my shoulder, his head lolled back. He seemed to be trying to help us, trying to stand, but he was mostly limp.

Rex grabbed his other arm and ducked down to put it over his shoulder.

"You can't come with us," I said. "Del's dad hates chimeras."

Rex let out an angry sigh. "Yeah, well, the feeling is mutual." He slid his shoulder out from under Del's arm and stepped back. I took a few shuffling steps, almost toppling over twice as Del's weight shifted.

Rex watched for a moment, then came over and picked Del up and carried him to the Graingers' front walk. I ran after him.

"Thanks," I whispered. "Now go wait in the car."

I paused to watch him go—and to gather my strength. When Rex was back in the car, I shuffled up to the front door with Del.

I felt vulnerable, exposed, and increasingly frightened. I rang the bell as soon as I got to the front door, afraid that if I paused I wouldn't do it at all.

The door opened and there was Stan, holding a can of beer, silhouetted in the light coming from inside.

He looked at me and grunted. "What do you want?" I don't think he recognized Del at first. Then he leaned forward and squinted. "Jesus Christ, what the hell is that?"

"It's Del, Mr. Grainger. He needs your help."

"My help? I don't think so."

"He made a mistake, Mr. Grainger, but it's not too late to fix it."

"A mistake?" He started laughing, a wobbly bark that sounded like it was going to fall apart at any second. "He knew what he was doing. It was an affront to God and an affront to me. He wanted to be forsaken. Now he's forsaken."

"He needs a thousand dollars to undo the splice and change back. To get him back to you, just like he was before."

"Just like he was, huh? You mean a thieving, blaspheming, would-be cop-killer?"

Del was getting heavier by the second, and I worried I was going to drop him. I took a deep breath and looked into Stan's eyes, searching for something to grab on to, something to make him feel, to make him human. "Del's mother—" I began, but he cut me off.

"His mother . . ." he repeated. He started to laugh again; then his eyes looked distant for a second, distracted, like the clouds had momentarily parted or he thought he'd seen something far away. Then it was gone. His eyes focused, looking right at me. His bottom lip quivered. It was wet and so were his eyes. "She didn't bring him into this world so he could defile himself. Defile the only thing left of her."

"She wouldn't abandon him now. You know she wouldn't."

He looked thoughtful for a moment. Then his eyes turned cold and hard, like they'd been flash frozen. "She already abandoned him. Abandoned us both."

"If you don't help him, he's going to die!"

Stan's eyes glowed in his face, like they were lit from inside. "My son's already dead. As for this 'thing,' if this was my jurisdiction, I'd arrest him myself. As it is, I'm calling it in as soon as I close this door. You might want to be gone before they show up."

"He's your son, Mr. Grainger! He—"

"No!" he snapped. "I don't know what that thing is, but it's not my son. I got no son. Now get off my property."

TWENTY-NINE

As soon as Stan slammed the door, Rex was out of the car and hurrying over to help me. What little strength Del might have had was gone now. He was completely limp.

"That looked like it went pretty well," Rex said, carrying Del back to the car. "What did he say?"

I could feel the rage boiling inside me. "He's calling the police."

Rex grunted at that. "Well, we need to get going then."

We laid Del out in the backseat. His mouth was bleeding again.

"Where?" I asked.

Rex didn't answer; we just got into the car and drove.

"That man is a monster," I said. "I think he's truly evil."

Rex's jaw was grinding, the muscles in the side of his head working up and down. "He's running out of time," he said, looking over his shoulder at Del. "Forty-eight hours is an absolute maximum for a fix, not a given time frame. Especially with a splice that's gone wrong, twenty-four is ideal. We're closing on thirty-six."

I'd been so angry at Stan for saying no, the reality of what it actually meant was only now sinking in. The window for saving Del was closing. "What are we going to do?"

Rex didn't answer right away, but after a few seconds, the car lurched forward as he pushed down on the accelerator. Five minutes later, we pulled up next to Genaro's Deli. The parking lot was half-empty, but Rex parked on the street, just around the corner.

"Wait here," he said. He left the motor running.

I watched him walk up to the parking lot. When he disappeared around the front of the store, I let out a deep sigh. I could feel my shoulders slump.

I'd let myself hope Stan would act like a decent human being for once, that he would save Del and I would get my friend back. Now I didn't see how that was going to happen. I turned and looked back at Del. With his pale gray skin and bloody lips, he looked like a clown from a bad horror movie. His breathing had quieted, so shallow now that it didn't seem enough to keep him alive.

I was just turning back when Rex yanked open the door and jumped in. He didn't say a word, just jammed the accelerator hard. His seat rocked back and he almost lost control of the car.

"What are you doing?" I said as he regained control.

"How's he holding up?" he asked, ignoring my question and glancing back at Del.

"I don't know," I said quietly. But I did know. He was dying.

We drove in silence for a few minutes as I chewed on my thumb and tried to figure out what to do. Even if I could get in touch with my mom, I couldn't see her giving me a thousand dollars to take Del to some sketchy garage somewhere or wherever this fixer was. She'd insist on taking Del to the hospital, for sure. I thought about asking Aunt Trudy. She seemed like the kind of person who might, but for all I knew, she was aware I'd been out all last night and had been freaking out, wondering where I was since morning. She could have a kitchen full of police and my mom, all frantically trying to figure out where I was and if I was okay.

I felt a sudden jolt of anger at Del. I knew he was suffering, and with Stan and everything I knew he'd been suffering long before the splice. But this all happened because he'd been an inconsiderate jerk. That whole thing with the cop, and now with the splice itself. He wasn't just hurting himself, he was hurting other people. He was hurting me, that was for sure. And he was making me hurt other people too.

I took a deep, guilty breath and put those thoughts aside. There would be plenty of time to be mad at Del later. Right now, I needed to make sure he survived.

It occurred to me that Nina Tanaka might have access to the kind of money we needed. I was trying to sort through the massive jumble of reasons why that wouldn't work, or at least not in time, when we crossed the Avenue out of the city again. A few blocks later, we pulled into the parking lot of an abandoned strip mall on a narrow triangle of land halfway between my house and Aunt Trudy's.

It looked deserted, except for a faint light spilling from a back room in one store. "What are we doing here?"

Rex unfolded himself from the car and lifted Del out of the backseat. This time, he was totally slack.

"What are we doing?" I asked.

Rex didn't reply, just started walking Del across the parking lot. I hurried to keep up with him.

"Rex, what are we doing?" I said again.

"We're trying to save your friend, okay? We're trying to get his splice fixed."

We were approaching the storefront with the light in the back. Rex pulled the door open and called, "Doctor Guzman?"

He waited a second, listening, then called louder, "Doc?"

I heard a soft shuffling sound and saw movement in the light coming from the back. I thought about Simon, and my imagination conjured up a huge, horrible, misshapen creature.

A thin voice called out weakly, "Is that Rex?"

"Here for a favor, Doc," Rex replied. "I think time is a bit of an issue."

Guzman was a tiny man with large glasses and thinning, disheveled hair. He wore a lab coat over scrubs, but it looked like a bathrobe over pajamas. He waved us back, and we followed him through a ratty seating area with half a dozen chimeras, some looking sick, none looking happy. Everyone ignored us except for a girl with cheetah spots in her hair and a cluster of inflamed, painful-looking whiskers growing out of her face. She looked up at us, somehow both bored and anxious. The room reeked of regret.

We kept going, into another room in the way-back, this one bigger, with high ceilings, like a warehouse. There was a row of barber chairs, as well as old-looking medical machines and other equipment. A second-floor loft looked out over the whole thing.

Rex slid Del into one of the barber chairs.

"Eesh," said Guzman, pushing his glasses up his nose and wrinkling his face at Del. "Who did this?"

"Malcolm," Rex replied. His voice was thick with disdain.

Guzman looked up and poked a finger at Rex. "He's a menace, that guy. He shouldn't be allowed to practice." He looked in Del's eyes, felt his pulse. "I mean, what is this? What is this supposed to be?"

"A salamander," I said softly.

He looked at me now, as if seeing me for the first time. "A salamander? Who the hell wants to be a salamander? And where does Malcolm get off thinking he's ready for something like that? He can barely do birds, for Pete's sake."

He pulled open one of the drawers and started rooting around in it. "I can give you the friends-and-family discount, Rex, you know that, but I can't do this for free anymore. You know that too, right?"

Rex nodded and pulled a wad of cash out of his pocket.

"Where did you get that?" I whispered.

Guzman turned and paused, like he was waiting to see what the answer was.

Rex scowled and wouldn't look at me. "I called in a debt."

"Thanks," I said quietly.

Guzman took the money. He gave it a good look, roughly counting it, then he put it in his pocket and turned back to the drawer. He put a series of vials on the counter, then a handful of plastic-wrapped syringes.

"How long has it been?" he asked.

"Thirty-six hours," Rex said. "Give or take."

Guzman paused and gave him a disapproving look, then he shook his head. He stripped open one of the syringes, poked it into one of the vials, and held it up as he pulled the plunger.

"This is just a little cocktail of vitamins, stimulants, a few other things, wake him up a bit and give him enough strength so he'll survive the rest of it—I hope."

He tapped the syringe and wiped Del's arm with an alcohol swab, then jabbed the needle in and pushed down the plunger.

Del took a deep breath that seemed to inflate his entire body. He raised his eyebrows and shook his head, like he'd sniffed smelling salts. But he didn't open his eyes.

Guzman stood over him, looking concerned. Then took his pulse and looked at his eyes again. "This one's in bad shape. You're getting a great price," he said as he crossed the room. "Better than friends-and-family." He hit a switch on the wall and looked up at the loft, where a rectangular platform the size of a bed had begun to descend, gently swaying on its chains. As it got lower, I could see it had a clear plastic bubble over it.

"What is that?" Rex asked.

"Just got it," Guzman said. "Lucky for your friend over there. It's a hyperbaric bed."

"A what?"

"For oxygen therapy?" I said.

He pointed at me. "Exactly. Very smart. Some of these poor schmucks are so weak, they don't have the strength to change back. Like your friend here. Fifteen minutes in here can make all the difference."

When the platform reached the floor, Guzman opened the clear plastic bubble top and motioned for Rex to put Del inside. Rex glanced at me as he did so, and I shrugged.

Guzman closed the lid over Del, then hit the same switch. The platform shuddered slightly with the added weight, creaking as it rose back up to the loft. Guzman climbed a metal ladder, reaching the top the same time Del did. He had to extend his arms through the metal railing to attach a pair of hoses to the side of the unit. He flicked a couple of switches on a panel on the wall and the hoses jumped and stiffened, filling with oxygen.

Guzman checked a couple dials, then shrugged and climbed back down.

"So what now?" Rex asked.

"I'll give him twenty in there, I guess. Then we'll see if we can get started." He turned to me. "You want a magazine or anything?"

I shook my head.

"Suit yourself. I have other patients to take care of, if you two want to make yourselves comfortable in the waiting area."

I couldn't imagine possibly feeling comfortable in that waiting area. Just then there was a banging at the front door and Guzman paused, his head tilted as he listened.

He craned his head to look down the hallway to the front. Flashing red and blue lights reflected along the walls.

"Aw, nuts," he said, turning to us. "This will only take a moment."

Rex looked at the back door, and then at me. "We'll wait out back."

THIRTY

Guzman hooked an arm around each of us and propelled us out the back exit.

Rex was looking over his shoulder as we hustled. It was the first time I'd seen anything remotely like fear in his eyes. That was frightening in and of itself.

"What's going on?" I asked.

"It's just the police," Guzman said. "Shouldn't be a problem. Maybe the check bounced. Just give me a few minutes to clear it up."

He opened the back door, and then we were outside in a dark alley. The door closed behind us. The flashing lights from out front reflected on the treetops at either end of the alley.

I felt trapped. "I don't like this," I said.

I expected Rex to tell me it was nothing. Instead, he said, "Me neither." At one end of the alley, across the street, a cluster of evergreens crowded around a dilapidated garage. "Let's wait over there," he said. "Just in case."

We hurried down the alley toward a stand of trees, and just as we pushed our way into the dense evergreens, a police cruiser roared up the alleyway, followed by a van. A pair of cops jumped out of each, right where we had been standing. One of the cops looked familiar— even from where we crouched I could see the scar across his nose and the WellPlant over his eye.

"That's Cantrell," I said. "The one who shocked Ruth and Pell. The one Del attacked."

Rex's face darkened, and I could feel him tense, but he stayed where he was.

The cops ran up to the back door and a rectangle of yellow light spilled out as they entered the building.

From our vantage point, we could see the police car parked out front, as well. None of them still had their flashing lights on.

"What are they doing?" I whispered to Rex.

"Don't know. Fixing's not technically illegal. I've never heard of fixers getting busted. Even the ones with Dumpsters full of . . . errors."

I felt sick at the thought that Del could end up in the back of a trash truck somewhere. Rex seemed to read my expression.

He shook his head. "Don't worry. Guzman doesn't look like much, but he's one of the best."

A couple of seconds later, the cheetah from the waiting room sprinted out the back door with another girl. They were fast, but not fast enough. Cantrell came out a half second behind them, a stun gun in his hand. He fired twice and they both dropped, hitting the ground hard, their arms at their sides instead of extended to break their falls. As Cantrell cuffed their hands and feet with plastic ties, I felt a burning in my chest as I realized I was partly responsible for this. I tried not to think about how different things would be if I had just left him in the creek.

One of the other cops came out and opened the back of the van. Cantrell hauled in the cheetah girl and her friend. A moment later, a third cop walked Guzman out in cuffs, his glasses bent and a trickle of blood coming down the side of his face.

They put him in the back of the patrol car. Then they marched out the chimeras from the waiting room. Some looked unsteady as they were loaded into the back of the police van, like they'd been shocked.

The patrol car with Guzman in it started moving, coming down the alley straight toward us.

"Get down," Rex said, his voice quiet but urgent.

As we ducked down into the brush, the headlights lit up the branches above our heads. The approaching patrol car sounded like it was going to drive right into the trees and run us over, but at the last second, the headlights swept to the left as the car turned and sped away.

We got back up and saw the remaining cops still standing around, joking and laughing.

They closed the front and back doors and put crime-scene tape across both. Then the van drove away, and the cruiser out front did too.

I turned to Rex. "Where's Del?"

He shook his head. "They must have missed him."

"We need to get him out of there. I mean, we need to find someone else to help him, but also he was only supposed to be in that chamber for twenty minutes. I don't know what'll happen if he stays in too long."

"Wait here," he said as he got up. But I needed to know Del was okay. Rex gave me a dubious look as I followed him out of the bushes, but he didn't try to stop me.

We slowed as we approached the place, looking around warily, listening for any approaching police vehicles. Our eyes met as we reached the back door, now sealed with police tape. Rex tried the knob anyway, but it was locked. He checked the front, but that was locked and taped too.

That left the rusty fire escape in the back. The ladder hung eight feet off the ground. Rex reached above his head and pulled it down with a screech of tortured metal. When he stepped on the first rung, it let out an ominous groan. I gently pushed him out of the way and started up.

It held my weight, but it still creaked. I looked down, wondering how hard I'd hit if the thing collapsed. At the top I climbed onto a small sub roof. There was a window, open about an inch.

I looked down at Rex, so far away he appeared almost normal-sized. He gave me a thumbs-up, and I returned it halfheartedly.

The window opened easily at first but got stuck a third of the way up and wouldn't budge after that. I took a deep breath and then exhaled, making myself as small as possible. Then I wriggled my shoulders through and slid the rest of the way, tumbling onto the floor inside.

I was in a small office. As my eyes adjusted, I could make out the outline of a door. I pushed it open and found myself standing on the loft overlooking the room with the barber chairs, where Guzman had given Del the injection. A lantern was still lit downstairs, and in the light coming up from it, I could see the hyperbaric bed gently swaying on its chains beside the loft.

The plastic bubble was clouded with condensation. I reached for it through the railing, but my hands were sweaty and frantic, and the more I fumbled with the lid, the worse the swaying grew. Finally, I got the thing open. But it was empty.

THIRTY-ONE

How could it be empty?" Rex asked when I opened the back door and told him what I'd found.

"I don't know, but it is. Del's not in the chamber, and I don't see him anywhere else. Maybe between the injection and the hyperbaric bed, he regained enough strength to escape."

Rex shook his head. "We would have seen him."

"Maybe the police got him."

"We would have seen that too."

We searched the place again more thoroughly, the three rooms on the first floor, the loft, the office, and a tiny out-of-order bathroom upstairs. We discovered a half-hidden door to a basement, which was pretty creepy, but all we found was a bunch of dirt and a battery generator with cables running upstairs.

With each empty hiding place, I could feel myself getting more and more frantic. I'd gone through so much to find Del, to save him. I'd come too close to have him snatched away again. But the longer we searched, the more that reality became undeniable. Del was gone.

━━ ━━ ━━

"So what do we do now?" I demanded, after we had double-checked everywhere. We were standing outside the front door, both of us looking around, as if maybe we would just find him lying on the pavement out there.

Rex shook his head. "I don't know. I'll ask around—"

"Ask around? Rex, he's dying! We need to find him *now*."

He held up his hands as if to defend himself. He opened his mouth to speak, but instead let out an empty sigh that deflated us both.

There'd been so much action and excitement and tension, all of it focused on saving Del, and now he was gone. It wasn't just that I didn't know what to do—after losing him, finding him, and now losing him again, I didn't know what to think or feel, either. I was exhausted.

"Sorry," I said. "I appreciate everything you've done. It's more than anyone could ask."

"It's not that," he said. "I just . . . I don't know what to do next." He looked around the parking lot again, as if checking one last time. Then he looked back at me. "Maybe we should go back to his dad. He's a cop; he might have some pull."

"No," I said. "He wouldn't help before, and he's not going to help now. He said Del was dead to him. I don't think those were just words. Besides, the police are already looking for Del because of what happened the other morning. Knowing he needs their help isn't going to make them look any harder."

Rex closed his eyes and took a deep breath.

"Do you know any other fixers we could take him to?" I asked. "Like Guzman?"

He let out a sigh. "I know of a couple. I could try to get in touch with them, but it'll take some doing. And it's not going to do any good if we don't have Del."

"I'll find him."

"How?"

"I'll start checking the hospitals. The way he looked, that's where he's going to end up. Either the police will take him there or someone else will. If the police took him, they might not even know who he is. He could just be some John Doe."

"What are you going to do if you find him?"

"*When* I find him, we'll get him out and bring him to another fixer."

Rex nodded slowly, like he was willing to go along but he didn't for a moment think it would work. "Okay. I'll reach out to the fixers I know. But Jimi, it's all I can do for now. I have to find Ryan and Ruth too."

"I know." I stepped up close and put my arms around him, as far as they would go, and I squeezed as tight as I could, giving him the hug I wanted for myself. Then I felt his big arms wrap around me.

I still wanted to cry, but now it was because, just for a moment, I could remember that feeling that everything might turn out all right. I didn't want to let go, but I didn't want it to get awkward, either.

"Sorry," I said, stepping back.

"Don't be sorry," he said quietly. He opened the car door.

"I need to start calling the hospitals. How will I let you know if I've found him?"

"New Ground Coffee Shop. Leave a message there. And if I find a fixer willing to take him on, I know where to find you."

"Okay. Good luck with Ruth and Ryan." I looked at my watch. It seemed a pointless gesture, considering I barely knew what day it was. But then I saw it was eleven forty-five. "Crap, I need to go," I said. "My aunt gets home in fifteen minutes."

With everything that had just happened, the mountain of family trouble I'd made for myself seemed almost inconsequential. But if there was a chance to get home before things got even worse, I had to try.

THIRTY-TWO

The white-knuckle terror of Rex's driving helped me keep it together on the way home. But when we pulled up at Aunt Trudy's house and I saw that her car was still gone, the tension that had been holding me together dissipated. I felt like I would turn into a puddle on the floor. Rex was confused that after rushing to get home, I didn't hurry inside. But I couldn't.

He leaned forward to look at my face. "You okay?"

I didn't answer.

"We'll find him," he said. "And he'll be fine. Don't worry."

I laughed and he looked confused. Del was missing, dying, maybe dead, and here I was, momentarily paralyzed by the prospect of plunging back into the reality my family life had become in the last couple of days.

"What is it?" Rex asked.

"Nothing," I said. Without thinking about it, I leaned over and kissed him on the cheek. "Thanks."

I got out and slammed the door before he could reply. As I ran up to the gate, I was grateful it opened automatically, so I could keep running all the way to the front door.

I didn't turn around until I got inside, but I watched through the window. Rex sat there for close to a minute before he drove off.

Moments later another set of headlights appeared in the darkness.

It was 11:58. Aunt Trudy was home.

I was sitting on the sofa, pretending to be half asleep and watching an old movie when she came in, carrying a small grocery bag.

"You're here," she said as she put the bag on the kitchen counter. "What did you do all day?"

"Mostly this," I said with a yawn. "Read for a while, did some homework. How did it go with the exhibit?"

She sat in the armchair and studied my face. "I knew you would lie to me, but I wondered if you'd be any good at it."

I could feel my cheeks burning. "How'd I do?" I asked quietly.

She plopped a hand on my knee. "Frankly, you need to work on it."

She took a pint of ice cream out of the bag and put it on the coffee table. "This is for me," she said. "But if you go get some spoons, you can have some." Then she gave me a look that was almost stern. "We need to talk."

— — —

"You have to promise not to tell my mom," I said as we dug into the ice cream.

"Fine." We both knew it was a promise she would almost certainly break, but I was hopeful it would give me enough leverage that maybe she would tone down the most incriminating parts.

I got the impression when I started that she was just waiting for me to finish so she could tell me how I had behaved badly, how disappointed she was, and how there were going to have to be consequences. But she was about as good at the stern look as I was at lying. By the time I got to the part about Del's bad splice and Ruth and Ryan going missing, she was squeezing my hand in sympathy. When I told her about Stan's reaction, and then what happened at Guzman's place, her eyes were moist.

When I finished, she sat there for a minute, thinking long and hard. I knew she was dying to come up with a solution to all my troubles, but I also knew there wasn't one. She'd gotten a pretty good start with the ice cream. I think she ate more of it than she intended to. Maybe because she knew that once she stopped she'd be expected to come up with some sound, adult advice.

Finally, she gave in. "Well, I don't know what to tell you," she said, putting down her spoon and looking vaguely queasy.

"Not much to say." I kept eating. When it comes to ice cream, I'm a pro. And I had barely eaten all day.

"Obviously, you shouldn't have lied to me. Things would have gone better if you had told me the truth from the beginning."

I kept eating, unwilling to concede the point.

"Do you want me to call Del's father?" she asked.

"No!" I said sharply. "Sorry, but no. I don't trust him. He already refused to help. He's hurt Del before, and I don't trust him not to do it again. Del doesn't, either. Or didn't." I looked down, my eyes getting wet again.

Trudy patted my knee. "Is there anything else I can do?"

"I need to start calling hospitals, see if Del has turned up at any of them." I didn't tell her that I was going to try to bust him out if I could find him.

She nodded. "Okay, but not right now. Even if he's at one of the hospitals, they probably wouldn't have processed him yet. You look exhausted. Get some sleep, and we'll get started early in the morning."

She looked exhausted, too, and I felt bad. She'd probably been stressed all day because of me, and she had to work on top of it all.

I nodded and gave her a fake yawn, then we both went to bed.

Once she was snoring, I took the phone into the breakfast room and started making calls.

THIRTY-THREE

My first call was to the police station nearest to Guzman's clinic. I'd been trying not to think about it, because the idea freaked me out, but it was possible that they had Del and they hadn't taken him to get medical treatment.

"Montgomery County Police Department," said a bored and official-sounding woman. "What's your emergency?"

"It's not an emergency," I said, my voice cracking midsentence. I told myself to calm down and lowered my voice, more like an adult. "I believe my son may have been arrested."

"Is he a minor?"

I didn't know what she was talking about at first. "Is he . . . Oh yes, he is. Seventeen years old."

"I'm sorry, ma'am, but we cannot give out information about minors over the phone. You'll need to come in to the station with valid identification before we can release any information about him."

"Really?" I said, the word coming out almost like a sob.

There was a sigh on the other end. "When do you think your son might have been arrested?"

"I don't know. Maybe two hours ago?"

"Well, I can't tell you about any individuals, but I can tell you it's been a slow night. We haven't brought in any minors tonight. He might have gotten off with a warning."

"Thank you," I said, for some reason adding, "He's . . . He's a chimera." Maybe I just wanted to tell someone, and here was a faceless, anonymous stranger.

She let out a different sigh, a combination of sympathy and revulsion. "Well, we didn't bring in any of them, either."

"You didn't?" I said, but she was gone.

I thought that was odd—I saw the bust. But like she said, maybe they let everyone go with a warning. It didn't seem like they'd been doing anything worth arresting them for, anyway.

After speaking with the police, calling the hospitals seemed less intimidating. But it still wasn't easy. There were dozens of them in and around the city, and even more when you added the urgent care facilities and trauma centers.

It took a while, but after half a dozen calls, I got my spiel down: "Hello, I'm trying to locate my nephew, a seventeen-year-old male named Del Grainger, five-foot-eleven, with dark hair. He went missing yesterday after a chimera splice that went . . . wrong . . . and I'm helping my sister try to find him. Can you tell me if you've admitted any unidentified patients who might fit that description?"

A couple of hospitals had possible matches, but each time it turned out they had already been identified, and their families located.

I was halfway through the list when I was put on hold for a particularly long time. I woke up forty minutes later, startled and confused, the call long since ended. Furious with myself for nodding off, I hit redial, and this time managed to stay awake while they made sure they didn't have anyone who might be Del.

The same thing happened an hour later, but I slept a lot longer. When I woke up, it was starting to get light out. My eyes were crusty and my sinuses felt raw, like I was getting sick.

I had five numbers left and the sun had fully risen when a woman at the Wayne Medical Center responded, "Actually, yes, we did admit a young man last night who fits that description, the poor thing. Acute chimeric maladjustment syndrome."

The persona I had adopted for the calls crumbled, my throat constricted, my eyes welled up. Images flooded my brain, Del swollen and misshapen, his breathing even worse, lying in a hospital bed, hooked up to machines trying futilely to keep him alive. Or hooked up to nothing, just lying there dying.

"Let me just double-check that we don't have an ID on him," the woman said, putting me on hold. This time, I stayed very much awake.

I allowed myself a minute to cry. I knew what I had to do. It might already be too late to get Del fixed. But if I could get to Wayne, at least he wouldn't have to be alone. And maybe I could shame them into doing whatever it took to keep him alive, liability insurance be damned. I wiped my eyes and shook my head, trying to reassume my fake, businesslike demeanor.

After several minutes the woman came back on. "Ma'am? We definitely don't have an ID on him." Through the ringing in my ears, I heard myself asking what room he was in, the pen in my hand hovering over the pad next to the words *Wayne Medical Center* and *acute chimeric maladjustment syndrome*.

"I'm afraid I can't give that information out over the phone," the woman said.

My polite voice thanked her for her help, and said I would just come in.

Then I ended the call.

That's when the police arrived.

THIRTY-FOUR

I didn't recognize the sound when the door buzzed, otherwise I might have answered it myself. Instead I just sat there in a daze as Trudy walked by on her way to the intercom panel by the front door.

She did a double take, frowning at me. "Have you been up all night?" she asked, but without waiting for an answer, she pressed a button on the intercom and said, "Hello?" She released it and held up a finger, telling me to wait, as she listened for a response.

I heard a voice with the unmistakable tone of officialdom saying something about just asking a few questions, and Trudy pointing out that it was Sunday morning. The voice said it was important and it would just take a moment.

After having spent two hours in an interrogation room, the thought of "a few questions" filled me with dread. I wondered if this had anything to do with what I had done to that guy Dietrich, and I seriously considered making a break for it, getting the hell out of there and making my way to the Wayne Medical Center. But if the police had information about Del, I needed to know it.

Trudy looked at me, her "wait a moment" finger still raised, as she buzzed the gate open and went out onto the porch. When I got to the front door, she was explaining to two men in suits that, no, she was not my mother, she was my aunt, and that she didn't feel comfortable letting them talk to me without my mother present.

"How did you get this address?" she demanded.

"A neighbor of the Corcorans in Oakton directed us here, ma'am." I felt a stab of fear that Stan knew where I was, then let out a sigh of relief when he said, "A Mrs. Edwards?"

"Well, I'm going to have to talk to Jimi's mother before I let you ask her—"

"It's okay," I said, peeking out from behind her. She paused and turned to look back at me, vaguely annoyed that I was undermining her efforts to protect me.

"You don't have to talk to them if you don't want to," she said.

"No, it's okay."

Trudy leaned close and whispered, "If they ask you about anything that could get you into trouble, say you need to talk to me in private, and you tell me before you tell them."

I nodded.

"Okay," she told them, stepping back so they could come in. "But I'm going to be right here the whole time. And if I don't like where this is going, I'm putting a stop to it."

The detectives were young. One of them was handsome, with light brown skin, a scattering of dark freckles, and a playful smile. The other one had hooded eyes and what looked like a permanent scowl. I wondered if they'd decided who was going to play good cop or bad cop based on how they looked, or if over time they just started to look like the roles they played.

"It's really just a few simple questions," the mean-looking one said. "Nothing to worry about."

"Good morning, Ms. Corcoran," said the handsome one. He turned the smile up a notch, and I wondered how much mileage he usually got out of that. "I'm Detective Washington of the Pennsylvania Bureau of Criminal Investigation. This is Detective Salvatore." They both held up badges. "We'd just like to ask you a couple questions, if that's okay."

"Am I in trouble?"

He smiled again. I was starting to think I liked the mean-looking one better. "Not at all. Our questions concern a friend of yours."

I nodded, trying to decide how much I should tell them about what Del had been up to over the last few days. I wondered how much worse trouble he could possibly be in, and whether any of it would help them find him. Or if they already had him in custody and were just building a case against him.

"But first, how old are you, Ms. Corcoran?"

"Sixteen."

"And where do you go to school?"

Trudy let out an exasperated sigh. "You're using up your questions awful quick."

Washington gave her his charming smile. "We just need some background info."

I told him.

"And when was the last time you saw Leo Byron?"

"What?" I was stunned by the question. I hadn't seen Leo since I was a kid.

"Aren't you going to ask me about Del Grainger?"

The detectives looked at each other. "Who's Del Grainger?" Salvatore asked.

"Leo Byron?" Trudy cut in. "Isn't that your friend, the boy who had a crush on you when you were little?"

"What? No . . . I mean, yes. But he didn't have a crush on me. I haven't seen him in years."

"You haven't seen him in years?"

"Not since he moved away."

"So, you haven't—"

"Okay, gentlemen," Trudy said, clapping her hands. "It's obvious that was the question you wanted to ask. You've asked it twice. You have your answer. Now I'm going to have to ask you to leave."

I was still shocked. I totally hadn't expected a question about Leo.

The detectives stiffly thanked us for our help and Salvatore gave Trudy a business card.

"If you see or hear from Leo, it's important that you give us a call," he said.

Trudy gave him a big fake smile. "We surely will."

She had them halfway out the door by the time I snapped out of it enough to call out, "Is Leo okay?"

Washington stopped, one hand on the door frame. "Actually, he could be in serious trouble. If you see him, you'd be doing him a favor by letting us know."

— — —

"You didn't need to talk to them," Trudy said when she came back inside. "In fact, I wish you hadn't. Here I am supposed to be taking care of you, and I let you speak to the police like that, after what happened with that chimera house the other day and without a lawyer present or your mom or anything."

"Sorry, I just wanted to know if they knew anything about Del."

She let out a deep sigh and eyed the breakfast nook. "Have you been calling hospitals all night?"

I nodded.

"Well, I have to go into work, but I'll be back in a few hours. If you get any leads, I can drive you wherever you want when I'm done." I was about to tell her that I needed to go now, as soon as possible, that we were running out of time. But then she added, "After we call Del's dad, of course."

"His dad?"

"Absolutely. I know you're not crazy about him, but if we find Del in a hospital somewhere, we have to let his father know."

It was as if she hadn't been listening to half of what I told her the night before. I was speechless.

"So, did you have any luck with the phone calls?" she asked. "Is there anybody out there who could be Del?"

I knew Trudy was trying hard to be a good temporary parent, to figure out the right thing to do. But she was getting it wrong on this one.

"No," I said. "Not one."

THIRTY-FIVE

Wayne was on the other side of the city, ten miles outside it, but it had a Levline stop and the medical center wasn't far from it. Trudy had taken so long getting ready for work, I started to suspect she'd caught me in another lie and was messing with me. By the time she finally left, I had fifteen minutes before the next train. I watched her drive away, waited five minutes, then ran to the station. I got there with time to spare.

The train took me past the Oakton stop, then the one I'd be getting off for school. Two stops after that was Silver Garden, where New Ground Coffee Shop was. It was a neighborhood of industrial buildings and row homes—one of the few neighborhoods in the city where artists and chimeras could still afford to live.

Three stops after that was Temple University, where Del and I were supposed to be planning to go to college. It was an express train, so we didn't stop. The campus's tall modern buildings with the bold red *T* logos rose quickly in front of us, and then shrank away to nothing.

Just before we plunged underground, Center City appeared ahead, a forest of tall glass towers. The majority of them were pharmaceutical and wet-tech companies. The largest by far was Wells Tower, the plain glass box that housed WellPlant's global headquarters.

Three underground stops later, we reemerged into the daylight, the towers behind us as we headed south, away from the city.

As we approached Wayne, I noticed the zurbs were in much better shape than around Perkins Park. The towns seemed to be doing okay on their own with plenty of solar and wind, and the few homes out between them were huge, well maintained, and covered with solar collectors.

Wayne Station was right inside the town, which didn't seem to have a fence or a gate. I studied a faded map posted on the platform to orient myself, then walked down the metal steps.

The medical center was half a mile up the road, past a quaint commercial district of small brick storefronts. It was a beautiful day. It was a cute little town. It was freaking me out. Nothing should be this perfect when things were otherwise so screwed up.

The hospital itself was a mash-up of colonial-looking brick buildings with modern glass and steel additions grafted onto them. When I saw it, I paused, my throat tight as I considered what I expected to find inside, what I hoped and what I feared.

But I kept walking, through the entrance and toward the front desk. The woman behind it was in her early sixties, looking friendly but decidedly no-nonsense. I realized nonsense had been the extent of my plan—telling her some story about my mother parking the car and me not wanting to wait. When she looked up at me, I knew immediately she was not going to fall for anything I was ready to pull.

Above the desk was a sign with arrows pointing in a handful of directions: medical imaging this way, medical offices that way, emergency downstairs, gift shop to the right, next to the elevators. Patient rooms were upstairs.

I angled away from the front desk, toward the elevators. I could sense the receptionist watching me, about to call out. I made for the gift shop instead. When I glanced back, I saw her turn away to help an elderly couple just walking in.

The elevator doors opened and a couple in their forties stepped off, crying and leaning against each other. For a moment I was so struck by the rawness of their suffering, I just stood there. But as the doors began to close, I slipped onto the elevator and darted to the side, out of the receptionist's line of sight.

I pressed the button for the second floor and the doors closed.

When they opened again, I was across from a wide circular desk bustling with nurses and other attendants. A sign overhead said

NEUROLOGY and CARDIOLOGY, with arrows pointing in either direction. A screen on the wall listed room numbers—A01 to A20—names and abbreviated diagnoses. None of them said JOHN DOE or UNIDENTIFIED or anything like that.

As I scanned the board, two of the nurses looked at me with tentative smiles. The doors started to close behind me, and I said "Sorry," stepping back through them.

On the third floor the doors opened onto an identical setup, but the sign said OBSTETRICS AND GYNECOLOGY. I quickly tapped DOOR CLOSE. On the fourth floor the sign over the desk said TRAUMA and GENERAL CARE. My eyes swept the patient board until they hit room C17, JOHN DOE, diagnosis code ACMS. Acute chimeric maladjustment syndrome.

Del.

━━ ━━ ━━

For a moment I couldn't move. Then the guy behind the desk glanced over at me and I looked away and started walking, like I'd been there before and I totally belonged.

Room C17 was just a few doors down. A small whiteboard on the door said JOHN DOE in black marker.

Lying on the bed, under a mass of tubes and wires, was a bloated pink lump with a horribly misshapen nose. Before I could stop myself, I gasped, and the poor thing turned its balding head to look at me. His eyes were gummy and vacant.

I stepped back.

"You're not the one who called, are you?"

The voice startled me. I leaned forward and saw a woman in green scrubs standing in the corner of the room. Her name tag said G. FORRESTER, NP. She had a kind face, but there was something blank in her eyes. Unaffected. Like she'd seen this too many times.

"My mother's parking the car," I said.

She frowned and shrugged, like she wasn't surprised the rules were being flouted. "Well, like I told your mother on the phone, our John Doe is male, adolescent, dark hair, suffering from acute chimeric maladjustment syndrome."

"That's not Del," I said. I wanted to turn and run.

"Are you sure?" she said. "These changes can be quite dramatic."

The face was horrific, the eyes tragic, but I stepped closer, trying to see if there was anything of Del in there. I shook my head and closed my eyes, overwhelmed—with despair that Del was still out there, maybe dead, maybe dying—but relief as well, that at least he wasn't this. I also felt the tragedy of *this*, of whoever it was, lying there on that bed.

"I'm sure," I said, trying to keep it together. "Thanks." I ducked out into the hallway and ran back to the elevator, jabbing the buttons frantically.

Forrester came up behind me. "We suspect someone intentionally spiked this kid's splice, added some faulty pig DNA, maybe as revenge for something. But we're just not sure."

I stared at her in horror.

"The liability department won't let us do much for these kids, even when we know who they are and what they were spliced with," she said. "Cases like this, though . . ." She shook her head. "There's nothing we could do for him, even if our hands weren't tied. Other than try to make him comfortable."

The elevator doors opened and I got on and hit the button for the lobby. Forrester got on with me and kept talking as the elevator started down.

"People talk about the risk of disease from chimeras, that they could act as a bridge for viruses to jump from birds or monkeys to humans. It's theoretically possible, I guess, but there's no indication it's ever happened—not like those intensive farming operations, packed with the cows or pigs or chickens. They've proven to be much more dangerous in that regard. Anyway, this stuff with the splices that go wrong . . ." She let out a long sigh. "If people are going to insist on getting spliced, I just wish it could be aboveboard and regulated, so these kinds of things wouldn't happen."

Between the buzzing in my ears and the effort of trying not to cry, I could barely hear what she was saying.

When the door finally opened, she said, "Anyway, good luck finding your cousin."

"Thanks," I said. Then I ran through the lobby and onto the street, and finally let the tears come.

As glad as I was that it hadn't been Del in that hospital bed, I knew this was the end of the line for me.

I needed to leave word for Rex at the coffee shop, like I promised. After that I needed to move on—try to salvage things with Trudy and Mom, start repairing some of the damage.

And figure out what my life was going to be like without Del in it.

THIRTY-SIX

New Ground Coffee Shop was a couple blocks from the Silver Garden Levline station, a crappy storefront with plywood paneling instead of a front window.

A hand-painted sign over the door said NEW GROUND with a picture of a small seedling breaking through bare soil. The plywood was covered with posters, including one for a chimera punk fusion band called Katz and Dogs and one for something called "Earth for Everyone," its E4E logo clearly riffing off H4H.

It didn't look any better inside than out, but it smelled incredible—coffee, spiced tea, and baked goods—making it warm and welcoming. The place was half full and seemed to be evenly divided between chimeras and not.

There was one table of girls around my age, chatting and laughing. Their nice clothes and hair and manicures made me feel grubby and self-conscious. I wondered what they were doing at a place like New Ground—as if I had any more right to be there than they did. Then I noticed that one of the girls sitting with her back to me had her hair pulled up into a messy bun, showing off a sprinkle of leopard spots on the back of her neck. Well, that explained it.

A table in the corner was covered with Earth for Everyone posters. A girl with orange tabby stripes and a little button nose was sitting there with another girl who seemed unspliced, a clipboard and a stack of brochures in front of them. Both wore Earth for Everyone T-shirts.

Pell was behind the counter, loudly making some kind of coffee drink. Her face was ashy and drawn.

The chimera girl at the E4E table held up her clipboard at me. "Can you sign our petition to protect chimeras?"

"We're asking the governor not to sign the Genetic Heritage Act," said her friend.

"Sure," I said, adding my name.

"Would you care to make a donation?" she asked with a big smile. "The owner here says he'll match whatever we raise."

"Sorry," I said. "Not right now."

The smile dimmed, and when I was done signing she pulled the clipboard back and looked away.

I went up to the counter. "Hey, Pell."

"Jimi!" she said, surprised. The smile she gave me was tired, but genuine. "What are you doing here?" She leaned forward over the counter. "Rex told me what happened with your friend Del. Any word?"

I shook my head. "No. I checked all the hospitals but there's no sign of him. I came here to let Rex know."

She grimaced and shook her head. "I'm sorry. Rex has been asking around, though, I know that. He may turn something up yet. You know—"

"Anything from Ruth or Ryan?" I interrupted quietly.

She slowly closed her eyes and shook her head again. Her eyes were wet when she opened them.

A gravelly voice grunted behind her, and she glanced over her shoulder into the kitchen at a guy in his forties wearing a sleeveless T-shirt and an apron. He had a bolt through his nose and tiny pointed studs across one eyebrow. His arms, neck, and scalp were covered in tattoos of leafy vines and small animals. From the scowl he was giving her, I figured he was her boss.

"Can I get you a drink? Maybe a pastry?" She arched her eyebrows in his direction.

"Sure," I said, looking at the menu board. "You know what? I'll have an orange juice. And a toasted poppy seed bagel with butter."

Pell popped a bagel in the toaster, and the guy in the back

disappeared. Then she rang me up with an awkward smile. "I never thanked you for saving Ruth, from that cop and all." She seemed shy all of a sudden. "So . . . thanks."

"Of course," I said. "And thanks for helping take care of Del."

"Sure." She handed me my change, then my orange juice. "I think Ruth and Ryan are both okay. I do." She nodded, like she was trying to convince herself. It must have been a hard sell, after having been so sure the mysterious "poachers" had abducted them. Then she added softly, "I know there's a lot of crazy stuff going on these days, the H4H loonies and their protests, the Genetic Heritage stuff and whatever else they're doing. Maybe that's why, but Ruth and Ryan, they'd been talking about Chimerica. I think they found it, Jimi. I think that's where they are."

"Chimerica?" I said, trying hard not to sound dubious.

"Yes," she said, leaning forward like she was letting me in on a secret, and as if the more she told me about it, the more she would believe it herself. "It's a place where chimeras can go and be safe, but it's all hush-hush."

"Um, cool. . . . And where exactly is it?"

"No one knows. It has to be a secret, so the H4Hers can't find it."

I didn't say anything.

"It wouldn't have been easy for Ruth to go without me," she said with a shrug. "But she probably got a lead and had to go fast. She'll get word to me soon, though. I'm sure of that."

I nodded, pretending to agree.

"Del's okay too, Jimi. He probably got up and walked out of Guzman's clinic on his own power. Between the shot and that oxygen tank or whatever it was Rex said, that stuff probably gave him the strength to bust out of there." She laughed. "He probably took out a few more of those cops on the way out too."

She leaned back, looking like she was waiting for me to congratulate her on how smart she was. I didn't have the heart to tell her we were watching the entire time and that was not how it happened.

"So, when did you talk to Rex?" I asked.

"First thing this morning."

"Does he live around here?"

"Not far." She squinted at me, then smiled. "You like him, don't you?"

"What? No, I don't."

She laughed. "No need to be shy about it. Rex is awesome."

"I'm sure he is, but no. Really. No."

"If you say so." She turned and got my bagel from the toaster, smeared it with butter, put it on a plate, and handed it over.

"Thanks."

"Of course. Enjoy. I should stop talking, though, or else Jerry'll be on my back. He's a good guy, but he can still be a pain in the ass."

"Okay," I said. "When you see Rex, can you tell him what I said? About not finding Del in any of the hospitals?"

"Sure thing, yeah. Hey, it was good to see you, Jimi."

"You too," I said, wondering if I'd ever see her again.

THIRTY-SEVEN

I was sitting in the corner, finishing my bagel and wondering when the next train was to Perkins Park, when I noticed one of the girls from the chatty table standing in front of me, the one with the leopard spots.

She was so totally out of place, her makeup was different, and her hair was up. It took me a second to recognize her.

"Nina?" I said incredulously.

She smiled. "Hey, Jimi."

Nina was a chimera.

I tried to cover my shock with the apology I owed her. "Nina, I'm so sorry about Friday," I said. "I was such a jerk."

She sat down next to me. "Don't worry about it. I didn't mean to be nosy. I just . . . It seems like you've really been going through it."

I laughed. "I *have* been going through it." I could have elaborated, but we barely knew each other anymore.

She smiled, and her teeth were dazzlingly white. "Well, you *look* great."

I was wearing old jeans and a faded T-shirt. "You too," I said. She, of course, actually did. Everything was perfect, right down to the way her tiny gold necklace and burgundy sweater offset the leopard spots on her neck.

"You also look like something's weighing you down," Nina said carefully.

What the hell. Maybe elaborating wouldn't be so bad. "It's Del."

"Is he okay?"

"I don't know."

"Oh, God. It's his dad, isn't it?" She lowered her voice and leaned closer. "He always creeped me out."

"Well, Stan's part of it, I guess. But . . . Del got spliced."

"Del's a chimera?"

I nodded.

"Well, not the best timing with all this H4H stuff going on, but it's no big deal. I got spliced too, a few months ago." She turned around and ran her fingertips over the back of her neck.

"I saw. Your folks let you do that?"

"My mom did. We both got them when we were in Belize over the summer. My dad doesn't know about it, but I only see him one weekend a month."

I pictured her and her mom in white hotel robes with cucumber slices over their eyes, sipping elaborate fruit drinks with little umbrellas as they got their IVs hooked up. I had a feeling that with little cosmetic splices like Nina's, the "sweating out" was probably more like a light perspiration than what Del went through.

"Aren't you worried about GHA?" I asked.

She wrinkled her nose. "My mom says it'll never happen. So what's the issue with Del? Second thoughts?"

"There was a problem," I said. "He got a bad splice."

"Ouch. If it's new he can go to a fixer and get it reversed." She lowered her voice. "Danielle Wrabley got a splice she didn't like, so she went to this guy, Doctor Guzman, and he changed it back."

Danielle Wrabley was one of the richest, most uptight people in the entire school.

"That's who we took Del to see." I shook my head. "I'm having a hard time picturing Danielle Wrabley going to Guzman's scuzzy storefront."

Nina waved that notion away. "She paid him, like, triple to do it in private, at his house." She gave me a wry smile. "Although she said his house was even scuzzier than his clinic."

If I wasn't so depressed I would have gotten a kick out of the rich girl dishing about the super-rich girl. "The police raided the place while we were there," I told her. "They arrested Guzman and took away everyone else. Del just kind of disappeared."

"Oh my God, I heard about that raid. You were there?"

I nodded.

She sat back, looking confused. "It's so weird that the cops did that. But, you know Guzman's out, right? The police let him go."

If I'd been drinking my OJ, I would have spit it out. "They *did*?"

"That's what I heard. This morning."

Guzman might know where Del was! I wondered if Rex knew about his release.

"Thanks, Nina." I said. "Listen, I'm sorry to cut this short, but—"

"No worries," Nina said, pushing back her chair.

Pell's boss, Jerry, was standing close by, but I ran over to her anyway. "Pell, have you heard anything about the police letting Guzman go?"

Pell glanced back at Jerry, then looked at me with a shrug and a shake of her head.

"I just heard they released him this morning," I told her.

"Don't know anything about it. Sorry."

"That's okay," I said quickly. I had one last chance to find Del after all, and there was no time to lose.

As I headed for the door, Nina turned from her table and called out, "It's good to see you, Jimi. I miss you."

I smiled at her. "You too." Then a thought occurred to me. "Hey, Nina," I said.

She turned again.

"Do you ever see Leo Byron?"

She smiled sadly and shook her head. "Not in years."

THIRTY-EIGHT

Guzman's clinic was two miles from the Levline stop, just before Perkins Park. I ran the whole way. I wasn't wearing my running shoes, but I was in a hurry and I needed to clear my head.

The joy I felt at moving dissipated when the strip mall with Guzman's clinic came into view. The crime scene tape was still on the front door.

I realized it was ridiculous, but I had kind of hoped the place would be open, that Guzman would be back in business already, with cheerful but broken chimeras lined up to be fixed. And Del would be lying peacefully in that hyperbaric bed, already turned back into his old self.

Instead, the place looked deserted.

To be sure, I walked around to the alley, but the back door was still taped as well. The fire escape was down, just as Rex and I had left it.

I looked around to make sure I was alone. Then I grabbed the ladder and started climbing. I crawled in through the same partially open window as before. Daylight now illuminated the dirty and cluttered office. I hurried through the doorway to the loft. The hyperbaric bed was swaying slightly in the breeze from the open window. But that was the only movement.

I hurried down the metal steps to the first floor and checked the waiting area, even the basement. Nothing. I returned to the main room and looked up at the hyperbaric bed, the last place I'd seen Del.

Frustration and sadness and anger boiled up in me, and I clenched my fists and let out a long, loud scream. It echoed through the empty building, maybe through the whole empty neighborhood. When I was done, I felt a tiny bit better, but all that had really changed was that

Del was gone that much longer and was that much less likely to ever come back, or even to survive.

I climbed back up the stairs to the upper-level office. The desk was piled with papers. I flicked through them, a meaningless jumble of receipts, menus, magazines. The more I looked, the less any of it meant. I could feel the frustration building again, and this time a scream was not going to relieve it. I was on the verge of throwing it all out the window when I noticed a white envelope with a blue bar across the top and bold white letters that said JURY SUMMONS.

I didn't see Guzman as the type to comply with something like that, but he had received it nonetheless. It was addressed to him at 2702 Lorber Street, just south of Silver Garden.

I had his home address.

THIRTY-NINE

As I ran back to the Levline, I reminded myself not to get too excited. It was Sunday afternoon. Del had been spliced Friday morning. The splice was a done deal, and at this point, all I could hope for was that Guzman knew where Del was—and that Del was getting the medical care he needed.

Sitting on the Levline train, I fidgeted all the way to Silver Garden, then got off and ran some more.

I was approaching Broad Street, halfway to Dr. Guzman's, when I first suspected something was up.

Broad Street had become totally revitalized over the years and was one of the busiest streets in the city, with mile after mile of stores and businesses, and relentless traffic of cars, buses, pedestrians, and even drones buzzing overhead. But the side streets were residential, and it seemed odd that they were so congested too.

As I got closer, I could see that even though the traffic lights were changing, the cars waiting to cross Broad Street weren't moving. They weren't even honking. Then I realized no cars were driving along it, either.

Instead, there were people on foot. Thousands of them. Some were marching and more were lining the sidewalk. Some were clapping and singing, others looked on in horror.

A girl my age had her hand over her mouth as tears silently streamed down her face. I was about to ask her what was going on when I noticed that the marchers and most of the people cheering and clapping were wearing H4H buttons and T-shirts. I realized we were in front of Church of the Eternal Truth, the mega church where Stan Grainger spent all his time. H4H central.

There was a huge electronic sign out front. It usually made some obscure reference to scripture, but sometimes it condemned homosexuals, immigrants, or other groups. This time it said PROTECT OUR GENETIC HERITAGE—SUPPORT THE GENETIC HERITAGE ACT!

Under the billboard, workers were adjusting microphones and cords on a temporary stage. Next to the stage, at the center of a thick knot of men in suits, was a tanned, handsome, and now familiar face, with straight white teeth and a shiny trademark WellPlant. Howard Wells, yet again. His entourage had grown since the march a few days ago, and each of their faces was embedded with a WellPlant.

Right behind Wells, a small man with thinning blond hair was tapping one finger against his lips as he scanned the crowd, like he was counting the people. I wondered if the lip-tapping was some sort of WellPlant thing.

In front of the stage was a line of men holding banners, and there was Stan Grainger, holding the same banner as before. The little guy counting the crowd gave Stan a dirty look and motioned for him to hold the banner higher.

I saw another familiar face up front, Officer Cantrell, holding a sign that read ALTERED IS NOT EQUAL.

As Wells took the stage, the cheers were deafening. He waved and pointed at people and held his hands over his head, working the crowd into an even bigger frenzy, then patted the air in front of him to calm them, as if he hadn't just riled them up.

He stepped up to the podium with a warm smile. "The human genome is the most amazing and miraculous creation God has placed on Earth," he said. "It is our heritage as humans, and together, we are going to preserve it."

The crowd roared, and the last few marchers hurried to make sure they didn't miss a word. One of Wells's entourage dragged a goat onto the stage, and Wells reached over without looking and grabbed the goat's tether.

"This is a very special goat," he said, ruffling the animal's neck in a fond, absentminded way. "It has been genetically modified to grow organs that can be transplanted into young people in need, saving human lives. Now, I have nothing against scientists engineering these goats with human genes for something like that. I think that's great. But I don't want to let this goat vote, do you?"

The crowd roared, "No!"

"I don't want to let him drive a car, or own a gun, or be president of these United States, do you?"

Again, the crowd roared, "No!"

Wells smiled and patted the goat on the head, handing the tether back to his helper. "Of course not," he said, lowering his voice and bringing the crowd down with him. "And I'm sure no one else is saying that, either. That goat is obviously not human. But what is? The point is, you have to draw the line somewhere, right?"

"Yeah!" said the crowd, slightly more subdued.

He nodded. "Of course. And what I'm saying—what *we're* saying— is that the natural place to draw the line is the place it's naturally drawn. The place God has already drawn the line. Human is human. And goat is goat. But something in between? Well, I don't know what it is, to be honest. But it's not a person, is it?"

"No!"

Wells continued, his voice rising. "No, it's not. And I am very pleased to tell you that our governor agrees with us on that."

The crowd swelled with cheers and applause.

"And I'm even more pleased to report that today, he has proven it. The governor just announced that he has signed the Genetic Heritage Act into law in the great state of Pennsylvania."

FORTY

The Genetic Heritage Act had become law. Chimeras were no longer legally people. And the frantic urge I had to get to Dr. Guzman's exploded into overdrive as this new threat sank in. But there were thousands of people between me and where I needed to go.

Wells left the stage and got in a limousine, his motorcade disappearing up Broad Street with a police escort. The crowd parted to let him go by, mostly cheering and waving to him, but a few people cursed him or flipped him off. A half a sandwich sailed through the air in a gentle trajectory that ended with a splat on the limousine's back window. Immediately, the crowd surged toward the source of that trajectory.

Another speaker took the stage, a dull voice reading a statement about how people could help get a national Genetic Heritage law passed. The crowd was probably with him on that, but they weren't paying attention.

I could feel a ragged energy, like the crowd had become a mob.

I tried to push my way through, hoping to slip across Broad Street. But the wall of H4Hers was dense, and unmoving. A couple of them scowled at me, and I realized I was wearing the chimera pin Ruth had given me. I reached up to take it off, but then I thought to hell with these people. They were wrong, and I shouldn't be afraid to say it. I still had doubts about the whole chimera thing, and I was devastated that my best friend had become one, but H4H wasn't about protecting people from bad choices or saving them from dangerous splices. It was about legalizing discrimination, and capitalizing on hatred and fear, to attract new H4H members and to further Wells's political ambitions.

Looking around at them, I realized that, deep down, they probably didn't even care about chimeras. They probably didn't know any. They might dress up their motivations in Howard Wells's fancy words, but really, they just needed someone to hate. Someone different.

That's what this was about.

I pushed in again but bumped into a wall of flannel. A mean-looking face turned and glared down at me. His eyes locked on my pin and his face got even meaner.

"Nice button," he said. "So I guess you think goats should be able to vote and own guns?"

For a moment I thought he was having a psychotic episode, then I realized he was referencing Wells's speech.

A guy standing next to him, dressed identically but three-fourths the size, said, "If mixies aren't people anymore, what does that make mixie-lovers?"

I looked up at the pair of them, feeling rage and hatred boiling up inside me. I wanted to tell them to go to hell, that they were the ones who were subhuman, not the chimeras. Luckily, in addition to the rage and the hatred, I was smart enough to also feel fear.

I ran. I put all my anger and hatred into my feet, and I took off. They sprinted after me for twenty yards or so, enough to boost my adrenaline. Then they stopped, laughing and shouting that I'd *better* run, shouting all the awful things they would do to me if they caught me.

━━━ ━━━ ━━━

As I made my way out of the Broad Street district and entered Silver Garden, the sky turned a dark gray, and the vibe felt even more dangerous. The area was more run-down, but that wasn't all of it. It was also filled with people, many still wearing their H4H T-shirts and hats. I realized a lot of them weren't just drunk on righteous victory; more and more, there seemed to be alcohol involved as well.

When I reached Guzman's block, I slowed reluctantly. A dozen men were hanging out across from his house.

A couple of them looked over at me and I slowed even more. They were drinking and laughing too much and too loud. I was three doors away from Guzman's house when I saw someone else approaching from the opposite direction.

She was small and frail and very, very pretty. She was a chimera, some kind of feline, with large gray-green eyes and a spray of spots from her forehead into her hairline. She looked at the men, then at me, then at Guzman's house. She slowed too, but she didn't stop.

A few of the men noticed her, then they all turned to look. She glanced at me again. Then she locked her eyes on Guzman's house and walked toward it.

A couple of the men stepped out into the street, blocking her way. I could suddenly see things turning very bad very fast. I thought about running up to the door and banging on it, slipping inside as soon as it opened. But as the men began to encircle the girl, I knew I couldn't leave her there.

The largest of them said something to her and she stepped back, bumping into the guy behind her. The rest of them laughed, and I saw she was crying. The circle was three-quarters closed.

"Hey!" I called out. They stopped and turned to look at me. "What are you guys doing?"

The biggest one let out a harsh laugh. "I beg your pardon?"

"You're grown men," I said. "Stop messing with her!"

They watched as I stepped into the street. A few of them stepped toward me.

"She's a mixie," he said, as if that explained it.

"A cute mixie," said one of the others, earning him some laughs and backslaps.

"Yeah," said a third. "There's no law against it."

"So?" I said. I was trying to keep them turned to face me, moving so the gap in their circle would be behind her. So she could escape. "What are you guys, perverts?"

"Who the hell are you?" said the big one.

They were all still looking at me, but they were now positioned exactly as I'd hoped.

I caught her eye, then looked deliberately past her, at the open space behind her. She was confused at first, but then she glanced behind her. I gave her a tiny nod.

"Who am I? Who are you? The League of Extraordinarily Gross Gentlemen?" I took a step toward them as I said it, and they moved toward me.

I stepped back now, trying to look scared—which was easy, since I was terrified.

The entire group came toward me, all smiling the same smug, evil smile, and I heard the rapid tap of tiny footsteps receding.

"Damn, she got away," one of them said.

"Forget her," said the leader, his eyes locked on me.

I started to shake. But I reminded myself that they were a bunch of drunk, middle-aged idiots. And I was a runner. As long as I stayed on my feet, I'd be okay.

I took a quick look around, making sure there was nothing to trip over. I stepped backward once again. Then they came at me for real.

FORTY-ONE

I let them stay close the first block or two, so they'd keep chasing me and not go back for the other girl. But I'd been running a lot, and I could feel it in my legs. A cramp right now would be the end of me.

Halfway back to Broad Street, I spotted more idiots up ahead. I turned right and sprinted to the next block, then ducked around the next corner. Distant sirens seemed to come from every direction, all of them getting closer.

From my hiding place, I saw my pursuers stumble into the intersection like they were ready to pass out. Half of them doubled over, hands on their knees, trying to catch their breath. One threw up in the gutter.

They stood there for a minute in the middle of the intersection, laughing and insulting each other. Then they kept on walking toward Broad Street.

When I was sure they were gone, I took a different route back to Guzman's house. I paused a block away, nervous and scared, but the street was quiet and empty.

I went up the three front steps and knocked on the door. There was movement in the dim light inside. But no answer. I knocked again.

A rumble of thunder joined the sirens, like they were trying to out-ominous each other. I knocked again, harder.

A voice inside said, "Go away."

"I need to see Doctor Guzman," I said, my voice urgent, even though I was trying to stay quiet.

"Go away before I call the police."

"I'm not going away." I pounded on the door again.

The door jerked open six inches. Behind a security chain, an older woman squinted out at me. "Are you one of them mixies?"

I bristled, but said, "No."

"I'm sick of them coming around here, looking for him. Drawing attention." Her eyes scanned the street. She was scared, and I didn't blame her. I was too.

"Is Guzman here?"

"He hasn't lived here in over a year. I don't know where he lives, so tell those goddamned mixies to stop coming here looking for him, and tell those goddamned H4Hers he ain't here, either. Now go away, before I call the police."

With that, she slammed the door.

I stood there for a moment, staring at the door. I had no idea what to do next, and turning around would mean confronting that fact.

I almost jumped out of my skin when a voice behind me called quietly, "Are you looking for the doctor?"

I spun around and saw two big eyes peering at me from the shadowy gap between the row homes across the street.

It was the girl the men had been harassing, the chimera.

She flinched and stepped back when I looked at her. As I crossed the street toward her, she stepped back even farther. But she didn't run away.

"I am," I said.

"He's not there?"

I shook my head.

"Is he coming back?" She was younger than me. Maybe fifteen.

"The woman inside said he hasn't lived there in over a year."

She looked down, then back up, her eyes now wet. "They gave me two addresses," she said.

"Who did?"

"My friends. The ones who told me he could change me back. They said he moves a lot." The skin around her big eyes and her feline nose was pink and raw. Her eyes were slightly red too, although the green irises were crystal clear.

"You have another address?"

"7649 Willow Road."

"Where's that?"

"About a mile. Still in Silver Garden. Do you want to come?"

She said it hopefully, trying to convince me. She didn't want to go alone.

Once again, it was the only lead I had. "Sure."

She glanced down the street, fear flashing across her face. Then she looked up at me with a brave smile and nodded. "I'm Claudia," she said.

"I'm Jimi."

— — —

"I made a mistake," she said, scurrying to keep up as we walked. She was so beautiful, it was difficult to feel sorry for her. Maybe she had been even prettier before the splice. "I'm not ready for this. Especially not now."

I thought about all the feelings running through me because of Del getting spliced. I couldn't imagine if I had done it to myself.

Suddenly an orange flash lit up the sky, accompanied by a raucous cheer nearby.

Two blocks to our left, halfway to Broad Street, a car lay burning upside down in the middle of the street, its charging port emitting blue sparks and orange flames that reflected off the buildings under billowing black smoke.

"What's going on?" Claudia asked, her cat eyes comically large.

"They're rioting," I said, my anger mixing with fear as we hurried across the street. "It's how morons celebrate."

Her face hardened into a bitter scowl. "This is them celebrating the Genetic Heritage Act?"

As if in reply, we heard a loud crunching sound and a crash—another car being rolled—followed by the *whumf* of a fireball not too far away.

Our fast walk to Willow Road became a jog. Two blocks later, we heard a ragged chant of "Nix the mixies, nix the mixies!" and a mob of about fifty angry people turned the corner toward us. The chant disintegrated into hoots and catcalls when they saw us, and someone yelled, "Hey, there's that mixie!"

I grabbed Claudia and we ran down the cross street and into an alley, the harsh voices close behind. We found a house that looked empty, but it had a steel door, reinforced windows, and a security panel. The voices were getting closer. I looked on, stunned, as Claudia jammed a house key under the security panel and pried it open. As the display started flashing and counting down from fifteen, she pulled several wires and calmly reconnected them. The countdown stopped at eight and the door clicked open.

The house was furnished but dark and uninhabited. We went upstairs, so we wouldn't be seen from outside, and found a bed by the front window. Claudia's face was blank as we watched the rising smoke and flashing lights around us.

"Why are they doing this?" she asked.

"Because they're idiots."

"Why do they hate chimeras so much, anyway?"

"I don't know. Some people are so filled with fear or hatred, they have to direct it at someone. I guess chimeras are an easy target."

A helicopter swung by, its searchlight momentarily illuminating the street.

"How long's it been since you got spliced?" I asked.

"Last night," she said, looking dazed. "I guess twenty hours now."

"You're doing pretty good."

"It was a mistake."

I nodded, not knowing what to say about it.

"My boyfriend and I," she said, "—my *ex*-boyfriend—we were supposed to do it together. I'd already started. Then he backed out. He ran home and left me sweating it out on my own." She paused to gently wipe her eyes. "I was just coming out of it when I found out they actually passed it, the Genetic Heritage Act." She shook her head, and tears rolled down her face. "Now they're saying I'm not even a person anymore."

"Well, for what it's worth, you look very beautiful," I told her. It was shallow and inadequate, but it was true. I didn't know what else to say.

She laughed through her tears. "Thanks. I guess it is kind of cool. It's weird, though. I look into a mirror and it's not me looking back. I can't keep it. Not with all these psychos out here. I shouldn't have done it in the first place, but now with all this . . . I need to get it fixed."

"It'll calm down soon," I said.

"Thanks for saving me back there."

"Of course. Are you okay?"

"Thanks to you." She bit her lip for a second. "You're not a chimera."

"No," I said quietly.

"So . . . why are you looking for the fixer?"

"For a friend. My best friend." Saying it out loud brought it all back to me. I had to swallow hard to keep it together. "He got spliced, but . . . it went wrong. He got really sick. We took him to Guzman's clinic, but then the police raided the place and took everyone away. Actually, they didn't seem to take my friend, but he disappeared."

"He got away?"

"I don't know. I was hoping Guzman could tell me."

"When did he get spliced?"

"Friday morning."

"So . . . too late for a fixer, right?"

"At this point I'm just trying to find out if he's alive. And if he is, do what I can to keep him that way."

She was quiet after that, and so was I.

We found some yogurt and granola bars in the kitchen. Claudia pinned some money to the refrigerator with a magnet. "On me," she said with a weak little smile.

We ate our fill and sat back on the bed, looking out the window for hours, waiting. Things showed no sign of calming down until the sky exploded in thunder and lightning and wind, and the heavy clouds finally released their payload.

By the time the rain let up an hour later, the streets were deserted. "Time to go," I said.

When we slipped out the back door, my nose was assaulted by the strange mixture of smells—wet ash, burnt plastic, the ozone smell of the electrical fires, and behind all of it, the fresh scent of rain.

As we hurried over to Willow Road, Claudia and I kept silent. So much was riding on whether or not Guzman was there, what he could or couldn't tell us or do for us.

We found the house, but it seemed somehow darker than the houses around it. Emptier. As we approached the door, my heart sank with each step. I knocked even though I knew there would be no answer.

Through the front windows, I could see bare floors, bare walls, no rugs, no furniture. Mail was piled on the floor behind the front door, envelopes stuffed in the mail slot. I pulled some out, yellow and weathered, addressed to occupant or one of several names that weren't Guzman.

I knocked again, then tried the doorknob. The door swung open. We went inside, hoping against hope. But the place was empty. Guzman didn't live here. No one lived here.

I looked back at Claudia. She was staring at her watch, calculating how screwed she was. "That's it, then," she said. Tears rolled down either side of her face. "This is me. This is what I am."

I wanted desperately to say or do something, to somehow make her feel better. Then I had an idea.

FORTY-TWO

I had never been the first kid to school in the morning before, but that was the least part of why it felt so strange. My hair was disheveled and my clothes rumpled from a few hours of fitful sleep in some strange house. Also, I had no intention of going inside.

Standing on the school steps, I felt guilty to have disappeared on Trudy's watch again. It was Monday morning, so I hadn't seen her in twenty-four hours. She'd be angry and hurt by how I'd deceived her.

This would make things even harder between her and my mom, I realized. And the way my screwups were starting to accumulate could do actual, lasting damage to my own relationship with my mom as well. It hit me then how I'd been so worried about Del blowing off school and not getting into college, giving him such a hard time, and now here I was, doing the exact same thing. Latenesses, absences, being picked up by the police. Temple would look at my application and laugh. If I even sent one in.

When the other kids started showing up, I felt both conspicuous and invisible. Each of them slipped past me without a glance, deliberately looking away from me. None of them were my friends, but some were kids I knew. They weren't talking to each other, either. Maybe because it was Monday morning, or maybe they were shell-shocked from the Broad Street riots, from the new law. I knew I was.

It wasn't like I wanted to talk to any of them, either. Except for Danielle Wrabley.

She was our last hope of finding Guzman.

When the buses arrived, the stream of nonfriends became a deluge of faces slipping past me on either side. A few minutes later, the first bell rang and the torrent of students slowed to a trickle. I looked up the block to where Claudia was hiding and gave a helpless shrug, conceding defeat. But as I placed my foot on the next step down, a black luxury sedan pulled up, and Danielle stepped out.

She came up the steps fast—not as fast as I would have been moving if I was that late—but hurrying nonetheless. She kept her head down and moved to step around me. When I stepped in front of her she looked up, surprised and annoyed, the first person to look me in the face since I got there.

"Danielle?" I said.

"I'm late," she said, stepping around me again.

I moved in front of her again. "I need to find Doctor Guzman."

Her eyes widened and she looked back at the car that had dropped her off, but it was already gone. "I don't know who that is," she said.

"I know you were at his house, and I need to find him."

She tried to go around me but I stayed in front of her. Someone was walking toward us from the football field. Mr. Sciorra, talking into his radio.

The buses pulled away and the second bell rang.

"I just need an address," I said.

She shook her head. "He told me not to tell anyone." She tried to step around me, but I blocked her way again.

"Please."

"Hey!" Sciorra called out. "It's late! You need to get inside."

Danielle scowled at me. Then her face relaxed. "Whatever." She pulled out a secure web phone and thumbed through it. "He's in Silver Garden. 7823 Hampton Road. But don't tell anyone I told you."

She slipped around me and ran up the steps.

Sciorra shouted after me, "Jimi? Is that you?" But I was already running.

— — —

The house on Hampton Road was similar to the one on Lorber. Next door, a massively obese guy was sitting on the steps, drinking from a bottle of lemonade-flavored vodka.

Claudia had stayed close to me the entire way there, checking her watch every five minutes. When we finally climbed the steps onto the porch, I saw a light on inside and felt a wave of relief so intense it made me nauseous. Claudia looked like she was going to faint. I knocked on the door with one hand as she squeezed the other. Half a minute later, we both let out breaths I don't think either of us knew we'd been holding. I leaned over to look through the window. A reading light was on next to an armchair. An old-fashioned paperback book lay open, facedown on the table. A dozen more were stacked on the floor.

"This is his house," I whispered. "This is where he lives. I'm sure of it."

Claudia's nails dug into my hand. "Then where is he?" she whispered, her voice shaking.

I knocked again, then turned to the neighbor. He didn't look friendly, but he didn't seem like he was a threat. "Excuse me," I called out. He turned his head halfway in our direction. "Do you know where Doctor Guzman is?"

He gave a slight shrug, then looked away.

As I stepped away from the door, Claudia said, "But . . ."

"Let's check the back."

The narrow yard that wrapped around the house was pocked with puddles of muddy water. Next to the back door, there was a bundle of rags on a plastic chair. When we got closer, I saw it was a person.

Claudia started to scream, but I held up a hand and it came out as a stifled squeal.

"Is it Guzman?" she whispered, her lips trembling.

The body wasn't quite normal, spindly legs tapering to painfully thin ankles that disappeared into a pair of red sneakers. "It's a chimera."

Then I realized the sneakers were red because they were soaked in blood. There was a pool of blood between them.

"He's hurt," I said, running over even though I had no idea what to do. He'd been shot or stabbed. The fact that the blood was still dripping gave me hope that he was still alive, but I didn't know how badly he was injured, and I didn't want to risk making things worse.

I tapped his shoulder gently. "Are you okay?" As soon as I said it, I felt stupid. Unconscious and bleeding out, he was obviously not okay. But somehow, "Hey, are you alive?" seemed inappropriate.

The chimera looked up at me, wincing in pain. Recognition registered in his eyes at the same moment it registered in mine.

"Jimi," he said with a smile. "What are you doing here?"

FORTY-THREE

Jesus, Ryan, what happened?" I said.

"You know him?" Claudia said.

I ignored her. I wondered if this was how things would be with the new law, if this was someone's idea of preserving our genetic heritage. "Who did this to you? Did it happen in the riot?" I thought back to what Ruth had said—if this is what human is, maybe I didn't want to be one, either.

He looked at me cross-eyed, struggling to focus. "What riot?"

"Never mind. Where were you? What happened?"

He smiled again and mumbled something, then said, "They're going to Chimerica."

"What?"

"They're going to Chimerica."

"What are you talking about? Who?"

"Ruth and Del."

"*Del's okay?*" The relief was so intense, my legs almost gave out underneath me. I grabbed Claudia's arm for support as tears sprang to my eyes. "Where, Ryan? Where is he?"

"The poachers got us, then these other people rescued us. They took us to a safe place called Haven." He lowered his voice. "It's a secret, but I came back anyway, to tell Sly and Pell and Rex about it. And to say good-bye to my mom. It's dangerous to get there," he said. Then he looked down at his midsection. "Dangerous to come back, too." He let out a laugh that turned into a cough. Then his head sagged onto his chest.

"Where's the doctor? Where's Guzman?" Claudia demanded.

Ryan snickered, then winced again in pain. "I was kind of hoping he'd be here. But I guess he's out." His eyes looked heavy.

Claudia let out a soft whimper.

"Where is Haven?" I said. "What is it? Are Del and Ruth still there?"

"Not for long," he said with a smile. "They're going to Chimerica. . . ." Then he sighed and closed his eyes.

I gave him a gentle shake, but he was out of it. He was going to die unless I could think quickly, and at that moment, I could barely think at all.

I looked up at Claudia. "The coffee shop," I said. "It's not too far. If we can get him there, they can help him."

She stood frozen for a moment, and I realized how devastated she was. She wasn't quite out of time, but if Guzman wasn't here, she was pretty much out of chances, out of hope.

Then she looked down at Ryan, and when she looked up, there was compassion mixed with the tears in her eyes. "I got this side," she said with a quick nod as she put her shoulder under one of Ryan's arms.

I took the other side and we stood him up, revealing a puddle of blood on the chair where he'd been sitting. His legs tried feebly to participate as we maneuvered him to the front of the house. The neighbor was gone—not that I expected him to help us anyway.

"It's just a few blocks," I said. "Past the Lev station."

Claudia nodded again and we started walking.

The first couple of blocks weren't bad, especially where the street dipped down under the Lev station. Climbing back up on the other side was a different story.

A handful of commuters walked past us, avoiding eye contact as they headed for the train.

A small woman stopped right in front of us with a sweet smile. For a moment I thought she was going to help.

"Whatever happened to that thing," she said, pointing at Ryan, "he brought it on himself."

She had an H4H pin on her sweater.

I tried to think of something smart to say, something deep and noble and cutting that would make her stop and think. But I came up empty. I stuck out my tongue. It felt juvenile and inadequate, but I had to do something.

She cringed and her face pinched into a scowl. For a second I thought, *I guess I told her,* then I saw Ryan's middle finger raised in a salute.

I laughed as the woman hurried off, but the laughter died in my throat as Ryan went slack and I looked up at the hill, still rising in front of us. The gentle slope now seemed like a steep climb.

The train came and went, and suddenly the street was deserted—no cars, no pedestrians, just the sheer brick walls of warehouses on either side of the street. We passed a blackened spot on the asphalt where a car had been torched.

Tears of frustration burned in my eyes, and I wondered if we'd made a terrible mistake, if we should have left Ryan at Guzman's, called the police, gotten him to the hospital, and hoped for the best. Maybe they wouldn't know what to do for him, but they might be able to keep him stable for a while—long enough to give us information.

Ryan's head fell forward, limp. He was dying. And with him, maybe, any chance of finding Del.

"We need to carry him," Claudia said.

She was such a little thing, I didn't know how strong she could possibly be, but we each put an arm under his knees and lifted him. He was tiny, but we were exhausted by then, and we staggered under his slight weight.

Finally, the street leveled out and I spotted the sign for the coffee shop, half a block away. I was still wondering if we would make it when the door opened and Pell walked out.

FORTY-FOUR

P ell!" I cried feebly.

She did a double take, then sprinted over.

"Jesus, is that Ryan?" she said as she got behind him. She put her hands under his arms so Claudia and I could take his legs. "What happened? Where's he been? Where's Ruth?"

I shook my head, not yet able to speak.

The front door of the coffee shop opened, and Pell's boss came out scowling, probably coming to tell Pell to get back to work. When he saw us carrying Ryan, his face turned even darker.

"No," he said, slicing his hand through the air for emphasis.

Pell kept right on going, so we went along with her.

"Come on, Jerry," she said, "don't be a jerk. He's hurt."

Jerry trembled for a second, like he was exerting a great force of will. Then he sagged and sighed and said, "Okay, whatever. Take him around the back."

He stepped out of the way as we hustled down a narrow alley. Pell yanked open the wooden screen door and we carried Ryan inside, through a utility room and down a short hallway. Just before the kitchen, Pell steered us into a cramped office.

Jerry was already there, clearing off his desk. He threw a stained tablecloth over it and we laid Ryan down on it.

"Is that Ryan?" he said, looking closer. "What happened?"

I dropped into a chair against the wall, unable to speak. Purple and yellow splotches danced in my vision.

Before Pell could say anything, Jerry peeled back Ryan's jacket and looked at the bloody hole in his shirt. "For Christ's sake, he's been shot." He looked over at us. "Why the hell did you bring him here?"

"Didn't know where else," I said, closing my eyes, still catching my breath.

Pell darted out of the room.

"Was this from the Broad Street riot?" Jerry asked.

I shook my head. "He said no. We found him at Doctor Guzman's house."

"You were at Guzman's house?"

I nodded, glancing at Claudia, who had shrunk back into the corner of the room, looking tiny. "Do you know where he is?"

He stared at me, squinting, like he was trying to place me. "Who are you?"

"Jimi," I said. "I'm friends with Pell. And Rex."

He looked at Claudia. "Who's she?"

"She needs a fixer. I met her while looking for Guzman. She helped me carry Ryan."

He nodded and left the room without a word. For several minutes Claudia and I sat there, watching Ryan's chest slowly rise and fall. Each time, I felt a tiny rush of anxiety, hoping he would take another breath, feeling each second tick by, seconds we had tried so hard to save.

In those quiet moments of inactivity, I could feel the exhaustion seeping into my bones.

My eyes were drifting closed when the door burst open. Pell and Jerry came through and stepped to the side, out of the way. Guzman came in after them.

"Doctor Guzman," I said, and Claudia shot to her feet, her eyes round.

Guzman placed an old-fashioned black doctor's bag on a cabinet behind the desk and pulled out a stethoscope, a pair of scissors, and a bundle of other instruments wrapped in white cloth. He started cutting through Ryan's shirt. Then he paused and said, "The bullet went clean through him. Doesn't look like it hit anything vital, but he's lost a lot of blood. Looks like he was wounded some time ago." He turned to me and said, "Do you know when he was shot?"

I shook my head. "At least a few hours ago."

Guzman's eyes stayed on me, like he was seeing me for the first time since he walked into the room. "You again, huh? Trouble seems to follow you, doesn't it?"

"What happened to Del?"

He squinted, like he was trying to figure out what I was talking about.

"My friend Del?" I said. "He was in the hyperbaric bed when the police came. We haven't seen him since."

"No idea. I assumed the police got him." He looked past me, at Claudia. "Who's she?"

"She needs a fixer," I said.

"Shame," he said. "Looks like a good splice. But these are interesting times. How long has it been?"

"Yesterday morning," she said. "Around eleven, I think."

"Cutting it close," he said, studying her for half a second. "You got any money?"

To my surprise, she nodded and said, "A thousand dollars, right?"

She held out the money, and he took it. "You know the change back is as bad as the change," he said. "Sometimes worse."

She nodded and he put down the scissors, motioning for her to come forward while he reached into his bag with the other hand and took out a syringe.

"You'll be fine," he said as he swabbed her arm and gave her an injection. He rested a hand on her forehead, gentle and reassuring, just for a second. "Find her someplace quiet," he said to no one in particular. "I'll be with her when I'm done here."

Pell led Claudia toward the door. Before she left, Claudia wrapped an arm around my neck and said, "Thanks."

I thanked her back, and then she was gone.

Guzman resumed cutting Ryan's clothes.

"Ryan said Del was okay," I told him. "Before he passed out. But I need to find him."

"Afraid I can't help you," he said, not looking up at me. "But I'm glad to hear he's okay."

A minute later Pell came back, and I reached out for her hand. "Pell," I said. "Ryan told me he was at a place called Haven, a safe place. He said Ruth and Del were there too."

She put a hand against the wall to steady herself. "Oh, thank God. Where?"

I shook my head. "He passed out before he could tell me. Have you ever heard of it? Either of you?"

Pell shook her head. "No," she said desperately, turning to look at Ryan, lying there unconscious and bleeding, the only one who knew where Ruth was. She stared at him hard, as if willing him to wake up.

Guzman cut away Ryan's shirt and jacket, revealing a round chest and slender abdomen, skinny but muscled and covered with a sheen of striped gray hair that was matted with blood on one side. As the garments fell to the floor, I saw a piece of paper sticking out of the inside pocket of Ryan's ruined jacket.

"Sounds like one of those imaginary places people make up to feel better about things," Guzman said. "Like Chimerica."

I looked up. "He mentioned Chimerica too."

Guzman snorted and shook his head.

Pell ignored him. "Are you serious?"

"He said they wouldn't be at Haven for long," I told her. "He said they were going to Chimerica."

FORTY-FIVE

Chimerica!" Pell said with a squeal. "I knew it! We have to find them. We have to tell Rex!"

"What you have to do is clear out and let me do my work," Guzman said as he cleaned Ryan's wound.

"Come on," Pell said, pulling me out of my chair. I scooped up Ryan's clothes before we left.

She turned to me as she closed the door. "Poor Ryan," she said, "but I *knew* it." Her eyes flashed. "I told you they'd been talking about Chimerica."

She looked over my shoulder and made a tutting sound at the small line waiting impatiently at the counter. "Be right back."

As she went behind the counter and started taking orders and bustling around, I sat at a table and pulled the paper out of Ryan's shredded jacket. A Levline ticket stub came out with it, punched for Carston, PA, to Zone One, Center City, Philadelphia.

All I knew about Carston was that it was a tiny city upstate.

The larger paper was smudged with bloody fingerprints. It was the top half of a flyer or poster, torn and folded in thirds. The printed side was covered in red and blue lettering. GAME DAY! was the headline, and underneath it, "Pitman's traditional festival of fun is back, with old-fashioned entertainment and new surprises, too! Pregame Fair brought to you by Mayor Charles Randolph and the Pitman Chamber of Commerce."

The other side was covered with pen marks—lines, squiggles, zig-zags, circles, arrows, and a couple of *X*'s. In the middle of it, next to the horseshoe curve of a river or stream, was a star. One of the *X*'s said PITMAN, the other said CARSTON.

Pell returned with two coffees and a peanut butter and banana sandwich. The coffee she put in front of me had a smiley face in the foam. When I looked up at her, she was doing her best to produce the same expression.

"You look like you could use it," she said, her big eyes blinking. I didn't know if she meant the coffee and the sandwich, or the smile. Truth was, I needed them all.

"Thanks," I said, tearing into the sandwich.

"What's that?" she said, looking at the paper.

"It was in Ryan's pocket," I said, washing down a bite with a sip of coffee. "I think he drew a map. It's on the back of a flyer from a place called Pitman." I looked up at her. "There's also a train ticket from Carston, up north. According to the map, it's not far from Pitman." When I said it out loud, Pitman sounded familiar, but I couldn't think of where I'd heard of it. "I think this star might be where Ruth and Del are." I put the map on the table, flattening it out with my hands. "Do you have an actual map of Pennsylvania?"

"Let me see," she said. She disappeared for a moment and returned with an old road map. She put it on the table and got back to work.

I unfolded the map and found the Carston station on the Levline, forty miles north of Philadelphia. Pitman was about ten miles west of it. I folded the map down to a manageable size and put it on the table next to Ryan's hand-drawn scribbles.

I was still studying it when a shadow passed over the table and I heard Pell say, "Rex!"

My eyes shot up to find him already staring at me. Before I could say anything he eased himself onto the chair across from me. "Were you out there last night?"

I nodded.

"Are you okay? I couldn't find you. I was worried."

"You were looking for me?"

"I was."

"Rex, it was a lot more dangerous out there for you than it was for me."

He looked down. "Jimi, about Del . . . I couldn't find Guzman, or any of the other fixers. I think they're are all lying low after what happened to Guzman, and everything else."

"Guzman's here," I told him.

"What?"

"Out back. Ryan's been shot," Pell said, now standing over us. "Guzman's working on him."

"*What?* Was he shot in the riot?"

I shook my head. "We found him at Guzman's house. He didn't know about the riot."

"He said he'd been with Ruth and Del," Pell told him. "He said they're okay!"

Rex looked back and forth between us, stunned. "Where are they?"

"You tell the rest, Jimi," said Pell. "Jerry's giving me the evil eye."

As Pell got back to work, Sly showed up, and I told him and Rex what happened since we found Ryan. "He said they're at a place called Haven."

"Haven," Rex said. "Where's that?"

I slid the ticket and the hand-drawn map toward the middle of the table. "I found these in Ryan's pocket. The train ticket is from Carston."

Sly looked up. "Carston? That's a hike."

Rex pulled the paper closer. "What's this?"

"I think it's a map." I flipped it over. "On the back is some kind of flyer from a town called Pitman, west of Carston."

He turned it back over. "A map of what?"

I put the printed map next to it. "This *X* is Pitman and this *X* is Carston. I think this line is the creek, here, and this line is the old highway, right?"

"What's the star?"

I looked up at him. "I think that's Haven. Where Del and Ruth are."

"For the moment," Pell said, hovering nearer again. "Ryan said they're going to Chimerica."

Rex snorted. "There's no such thing as Chimerica. That's a fantasy made up by lonely kids who think getting a splice is going to solve all their problems but find out it creates a whole bunch of others."

I didn't want to agree with him in front of Sly and Pell. "Maybe, but that's what Ryan said."

He nodded, thinking for a second, then put his hand on the blood-smeared map. "Okay, I'm going out there," he said, pulling it toward him. "And I'm going alone."

I slapped my hand down on it as well. "Actually, *I'm* going out there. But you all can come with me if you want."

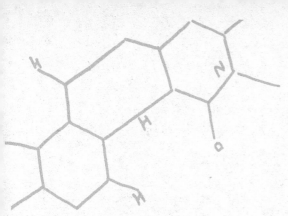

PART TWO

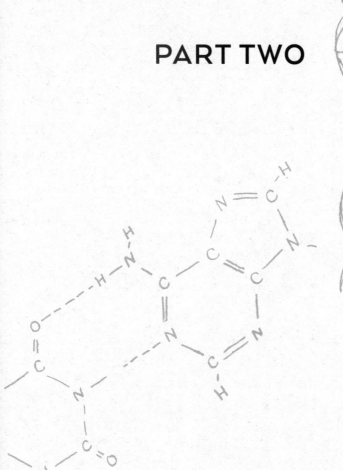

FORTY-SIX

When we first arrived at the Levline station, we were the only ones there. But after a few minutes, a trio of thirty-something men arrived, wearing rumpled khakis, scuffed shoes with thick soles, and matching bright blue polo shirts with a logo from some big-box store. They were the kind of guys Del said he didn't ever want to become, and sure enough, they looked miserable to be heading off to work. But as they stared at Sly and Pell and Rex, you could tell they wouldn't trade places in a million years.

"So, what's our plan?" Pell asked. "Once we get on the train?"

I couldn't tell if she was oblivious to the stares she was getting or so used to them she didn't care.

"Plan?" Rex shook his head. "Well, *my* plan was for me to go out there on my own, sneak around, see if I could find Ruth and Del, and figure out what's going on. Now I don't know."

"Well," said Sly, "that wasn't much of a plan anyway."

Rex gave him a dirty look and continued. "Then I guess *we* get out there and try to figure out what's going on. Take it from there. . . . And try not to get killed by nut-jobs on the way."

"Sounds good," said Pell. "Everybody have passes?"

Everyone nodded.

"We have to change trains in Alder," Rex said, "to get to Carston."

The thought of waiting for a connection with a bunch of chimeras in the middle of nowhere brought back a twinge of anxiety, but before it could turn into anything more than that, the train appeared in the distance, a tiny glint of sunlight rocketing toward us.

As we got on, the three guys in the blue shirts made a point of get-ting on a different car.

We took the wide bench seats by the rear door, and sat with our backpacks between our knees. Jerry had packed them for us. He hadn't wanted any of us to go, or at least not Rex and Sly and Pell, not after the riot, not with the new law. But once he knew we weren't going to listen to him, he gave us some money and some backpacks from the coffee shop's lost and found. He filled three of them with bottled water and day-old muffins, and in the fourth he put binoculars, a compass, and a heavy-duty flashlight.

I had been fully aware the trip could be dangerous—I'd seen what happened to Ryan—but until I saw Jerry filling that last pack, I'd been thinking, *We just take the train to the place, get our friends, and come home.*

Jerry had noticed me watching him. "Just in case, right? Who knows what's going on out there with these H4H whack jobs." Then he had leaned closer and said, "Be careful, Jimi. And be careful with Rex and them, too. You're not spliced, but they are. The world's a dangerous place, but it's especially dangerous for chimeras right now." He got choked up as he told us all to be careful and that we needed to make sure we didn't get hurt, too. Then he seemed embarrassed about it and acted cranky, following us out onto the street to remind Pell that she had a shift on Thursday.

I smiled at the memory, then looked around me. Midmorning, headed away from the city, there were only a dozen other people in the car. The closest one was an old woman in a green hat with fake leaves on it. She got up and sat several rows farther away. The next closest passenger was a man in a suit. He got up and moved as well.

Rex caught my eye and raised an eyebrow. *See?*

I nodded and looked away from him, my face turning red. These people thought chimeras were weird or strange or gross. Not that long ago, I'd felt kind of the same way—not in an H4H-crazy-hatred, they're-not-people way. But they made me uncomfortable. Maybe they still did in a way, but they definitely weren't *revolting*, for God's sake. And they definitely *were* people. They were good people. They were my friends.

I looked out the window just in time to see my school pass by. It looked alien and unfamiliar, like a part of someone else's life.

Two stops after that was Perkins Park. I sank lower in my seat, half expecting Trudy to get on—maybe my mom as well—and drag me off the train and ground me for the rest of my life. Something like that would be coming at some point, but as the train pulled away from the Perkins Park station, I relaxed, knowing it wouldn't be now.

Before long, I was thinking about Del, who was never *not* on my mind. Positive thoughts, I told myself. I imagined how relieved I'd be when I found him and he was doing just fine. Punching him in the shoulder for making me so worried. Hugging him tight, seeing with my own eyes that finally he was okay.

Over the next several stops, more people got on, filling in the empty seats at the far end of the train.

Outside the city the stops were farther apart and the train could pick up even more speed, the vibrant small towns and abandoned zurbs all blurring together. After a while, the air traffic increased. A lot of copters and drones were headed to or from a large tower on the horizon.

"What's that?" Sly said, pointing at it.

Rex was studying the folded map. "That's City View Tower," he said, looking up from the paper. "A luxury super high-rise. It's on the Levline, but it's set up so that people mostly copter in and out."

Sly laughed. "City View? We're nowhere near the city."

"A hundred and forty stories tall," Rex said. "Supposedly, from the top you can see both Philadelphia and New York. But you're right. We're nowhere near either city. If that's City View, then we're almost at Alder."

Five minutes later we were there. No one else got off at Alder. The other passengers either watched us leave or deliberately didn't, but I could feel their relief that we were leaving.

As the train pulled away, the old lady in the hat stared at us through the window, slowly shaking her head.

The station was just outside town. From the platform we could see a tall fence surrounding a community of big houses and a ritzy commercial district. City View Tower was massive but still distant. There were rolling hills to the east, and mountains beyond them. To the west, low on the horizon, there was a dark line of clouds.

The connecting train was due in ten minutes. The first five passed, quiet and uneventful. We were the only ones there. Then we heard footsteps, a single set coming up the metal stairs. Pell and Sly were oblivious, but Rex met my gaze. His face was impassive, but there was no reassuring smile, just blank acknowledgment that someone was coming.

The kid who joined us on the platform was about my age, maybe a little older. He wasn't bad looking, with pale skin and pink cheeks, but his eyes looked almost as lifeless as the WellPlant just above them. He had on an expensive Nanoma jacket, its colors slowly shifting and swirling, probably controlled by the WellPlant. He looked surprised to see us, but then an ugly smirk spread over his face. He snickered and shook his head.

He had an H4H pin on his jacket.

A few minutes later, another set of footsteps came up the stairs. Another jackass, dressed almost the same, down to the WellPlant and the H4H pin. They looked like they could have been brothers. The second one gave us the same smirk, then caught the first one's eye and they shared an eye roll.

"What's up, Petey?" said the second one.

"Hey, Theo," the first one replied. "How's it hanging?"

Theo looked over at us. "When did the circus come to town?" He said it loud, obviously for our benefit.

Petey laughed. "I don't know, just got here and there it was."

"Kinda ballsy, don't you think? Coming out here the day after GHA gets passed?"

"Ballsy or stupid."

They both thought that was hilarious.

The train was due in three minutes, but I was anxious. I wasn't exactly afraid. We outnumbered them. Hell, Rex outnumbered them. But they were obviously trouble.

We heard a third set of footsteps, but this time lighter and faster. A young woman appeared at the top of the stairway. She wore heavy boots, torn jeans, and a variety of piercings. She wasn't spliced, but she seemed like a different species from the jackass twins.

She smiled slightly when she saw us, nodding her head in approval. She walked straight up to us.

"Hey," she said.

Rex looked on warily.

Sly stepped forward. "Hey," he replied.

"Chimeras," she said. "That's awesome."

Sly nodded.

"Sorry about all that Genetic Heritage crap." She jerked her head at the two boys. "These H4H idiots. It's messed up."

"So, with the new law, can we just do whatever we want with them?" Theo said loudly.

Petey nodded thoughtfully. "You mean like, can we put them on leashes, like dogs?" He looked straight at Rex. "Or cages, like birds?" He looked at Pell.

Sly stepped forward and Rex stood straighter, showing his full height.

Petey and Theo laughed hard, slapping each other on the back.

The girl with the piercings rolled her eyes and mouthed the words, "Such A-holes."

Suddenly, Theo turned toward us and said, "Dudes!"

It took me a moment to realize he was addressing someone behind us, and I turned to see four more idiots walking up the platform, including one kid about twelve years old.

The six of them huddled up, talking quietly and snickering, then they all laughed as the twelve-year-old turned and ran down the stairs.

"So, guys," Theo started up again, his voice loud. "Obviously, chimeras aren't people now—we all get that—but are they animals? I mean, sure they're gross, but some of them are kind of cute, too."

Petey laughed hysterically. "Dude, you're a pervert!"

"No, I'm serious," Theo said. "Can we just tap some chimera whenever we want? Just grab it off the street? Hell, can I take it home and keep it in my basement?"

Rex was clenching his fists. "Careful," I whispered. "They're just trying to get a rise out of you."

He stepped toward them and Theo glared at him. "Bad dog!" he snapped. "Down, boy!"

They all shrieked with laughter. Theo's cheeks and ears turned red from the exertion.

The twelve-year-old returned up the steps, followed by a weary-looking guy in a Levline uniform.

"Oh good," said Theo. "Martin's here."

The twelve-year-old rejoined the group.

The Levline guy, Martin, looked at them and hung his head, like he had dealt with these guys before. "What is it now?" he asked.

"Just need to clarify something," Theo said. "That sign over there, at the top of the steps. What's the third item on it?"

Martin took a deep breath and squinted. "No dogs or other pets allowed, except for service animals."

Theo nodded while the others snickered. "That's what I thought."

Martin pinched the bridge of his nose. "Why?"

In the distance I could hear the whoosh of the approaching Lev train.

"I just wanted a ruling," Theo said. "As of yesterday, those chimeras over there are not people, not that they really were before. My train's going to be here any minute, and I don't want any animals getting on it." He looked past Martin, right at me. "Excuse me, miss. That's quite a zoo you have there. Is that your service dog? Are you, like, blind or something?"

As the train approached, Martin turned and looked at us. There was no sympathy, no apology, no feeling one way or another.

I smiled at Theo. "No, I'm not blind. If I was, I wouldn't be able to see what a pathetic little creep you are, and I wouldn't be able to see those ridiculous ears of yours turning red when you get embarrassed, which I'd imagine happens a lot." They lit up, right on cue. "Yup, there they go. If you're so proud that your DNA is human, you might want to try acting like one. And no, he's not a service animal, he's my friend. And he's more of a man than you'll ever be."

The train slid up to the platform and the doors opened.

The redness had taken over Theo's entire head. His eyes had narrowed to a malevolent squint, but the rest of the group was laughing at him.

Martin stepped forward, between us and the doors. "Sorry," he said, holding his arms out from his sides, barring our way.

"Theo, you're an ass," said the girl with the piercings. "Sorry," she said to us, then she turned and got on the train through the next set of doors.

Theo and his friends stared at us and laughed as they filed onto the train. Then the doors closed and it pulled away. In seconds, it was gone, snaking across the countryside.

Martin turned and headed back down the steps.

"Excuse me," I called out.

His shoulders slumped and he stopped. "Yes?"

"What time is the next train to Carston?"

He thought for a moment. "The express doesn't stop here, so the next train would be in three hours."

"And will we be allowed on it?"

He shrugged. "If no one complains, I guess. Otherwise, I guess not."

FORTY-SEVEN

We stood in stunned silence for a moment. Then Rex mumbled, "Let's go." We followed him down the stairs. Sly and Pell were visibly upset. I'm sure I was, too, but I was mostly concerned about Rex. His jaw was clenched so tight I thought his head was going to crack.

I knew it was different for them. I wasn't one of them. I saw injustice and hatred and evil, but they experienced it directly, felt it aimed at them. And I could see how each insult or injury or legal travesty would make them want to distance themselves that much more from the "people" responsible.

At the bottom of the steps, there was a vast parking lot. Beyond that was a road, a broken mess to our right, where it headed east, but nicely paved to the west as far as the eye could see. On the far side of the road was a sign that said ALDER ENERGY PARK in front of a tall chain-link fence surrounding a massive expanse of solar panels, miles and miles of them. Beyond them a cluster of wind turbines turned lazily in the distance.

On the near side of the road, a similar fence surrounded the town itself. A pair of guards eyed us warily from a gatehouse. They were absolutely not chimeras, but they still reminded me of the guys Malcolm had guarding the house where Del got spliced.

A sign on the road by the gate said NOW ENTERING ALDER.

Rex took out the compass, then pointed down the nicely paved road that ran between the town and the energy park. "This way should take us in the right direction. Even walking the rest of the way, we should still get there before the next train."

"Through the town?" Sly said, his voice dubious.

"Between the town and the energy park, not through it," Rex said.

"Otherwise we have to go around the town or the energy park. Either one adds hours to the trip."

The guards in the guardhouse watched us closely as we left the parking lot and started down the road. As we passed the NOW ENTERING ALDER sign, I looked behind us. On the back it said NOW LEAVING ALDER. PROCEED WITH CAUTION. UNSAFE ROAD CONDITIONS.

Rex walked right next to me. "Thanks," he said quietly. "For back there. For stopping me. Especially now, if I had done anything, that could have been big trouble."

I nodded. "Well, it's not like they wouldn't have deserved it."

"And thanks for what you said."

"I meant it."

As we walked, Pell and Sly lagged back a few steps, giving Rex and me a chance to talk.

"What do you think happened to Ryan?" I said.

He let out a sigh that sounded like it came from an old man. "I don't know what Ryan was up to. I mean, I guess he went out to Pitman or Carston or whatever, did whatever he did, saw whatever he saw, maybe he decided to come back to tell us, and he ran into some of these H4Hers." He shook his head. "He wouldn't be the first chimera shot by those maniacs. I'm sure he won't be the last. Especially now that GHA has actually passed."

"Hard to believe it really did."

"Yup." He shook his head. "I honestly didn't think it would."

"Me neither. I'm still not sure what it means. How they're going to enforce it."

He laughed. "No one knows."

Pell and Sly quickened their pace, listening in.

"Earth for Everyone had lawyers analyzing it," Rex continued. "They said it's a mess. It's evil and discriminatory and whatever else, but they said it's also terribly written. That's part of the reason no one thought it would pass. I mean, if chimeras aren't people, what are we?

Are we animals? Things? Nothing at all? It doesn't say. And it doesn't say how you determine who is a chimera and who isn't."

"Wait, I thought that part was clear," Pell said. "Anyone whose DNA isn't one hundred percent human isn't a person."

Sly snickered. "You know there's a lot of rich kids' parents talking to lawyers right now, saying, 'It's just a few little cat whiskers or whatever. Surely that doesn't count.' "

I thought about Nina. I could totally picture her dad pulling strings, but then again, he didn't know.

"No." Pell shook her head. "Chimeras are chimeras, right? You really think they'd try to say, 'I'm a chimera, but just a little bit'?"

"I'm sure some of them would," Rex said. "Besides, who gets to decide what the standard human genome is, anyway? And how can you tell who's a chimera and who isn't?"

"If it looks like a mixie, it's a mixie," Sly said, doing an old-man voice.

Pell laughed.

Rex shook his head. "For a lot of us it's obvious, but what about the rich kids hiding splices under their hair or their clothes?"

"A blood test would be definitive," I said.

"Right," he said. "So anytime someone is buying something, working, driving, getting arrested, or a hundred other things we haven't thought of yet, they need a blood test to prove they're human?" He laughed. "It's insane."

"All these rich kids getting their little fashion splices is probably what caused the GHA in the first place," said Sly. "It's one thing if a bunch of loser kids are getting spliced, but when the one-percent kids start doing it, Mumsy and Dadsy have to put a stop to it."

Sly did a hilarious snobby voice for the last bit. Pell cracked up and Rex let out a snort.

I considered telling them about Nina's mom, but I was pretty sure a mumsy with a splice was an exception to the rule.

Overall, what Sly was saying made a certain amount of sense. In the end, though, I had my doubts. Maybe cracking down on genies wouldn't work, because that's not where the rich kids were getting spliced. And making splices illegal would make the rich chimeras criminals along with the rest of them. But robbing them of their legal personhood didn't address any of that. It didn't protect them or prevent them from getting spliced; it just threw them all into the same legal limbo. Maybe it was really just about religion after all.

I kept my thoughts about it to myself, though. I didn't know how well my nonchimera opinions would go over.

Everyone else stayed quiet, too, deep in thought.

After a few minutes, Rex let out another laugh, quiet and bitter. "I'll tell you one thing I do know for sure. Judging from the evil that humans do when they stop thinking of each other as people, it's going to get pretty damned ugly now they've got the law telling them they're right."

"I'm so sorry," I said. I felt guilt by association as a nonchimera.

Rex angled closer and put his hand on my shoulder. "Don't be silly. You have nothing to be sorry about."

We were quiet after that, walking down the center of the road. There was no surface traffic, just lots of copters and drones. We'd gone a quarter mile when Rex looked up and said, "Uh-oh."

A police drone zipped past overhead, then came back slowly, hovered above us, and zipped off again.

Minutes later a twinkling red-and-blue light appeared ahead of us in the distance, growing quickly. Fifty yards away, it slowed to a crawl, then stopped. A police van.

As we got closer, the driver's-side window slid down. The cop was young and jacked. He looked at us and laughed, shaking his head, then beckoned us with his fingers to come over to the car.

As we did, he looked me up and down. "Sweetheart, what are you doing, hanging out with this mixie trash?"

"These are my friends," I said evenly.

"Friends? Don't you know they're not even people?" He laughed again. "So, what, are you taking them for a walk?"

"That's right," I said. "We're going for a walk."

"Yeah? Well, not in Alder, you're not." He flicked a switch on the dashboard and the doors at the back of the van slowly swung open. "Get in the back."

Rex said, "We're not doing anything wrong."

"I'm not talking to you, dogface," he snapped, then turned back to me. "For your information, miss, this is a motorway. No pedestrians allowed. So, for your safety, I cannot let you continue to walk on this road."

We hadn't seen a single car other than his. But I figured it would be best to keep that to myself.

He fingered the shock baton next to him, like he wanted to use it. "I'm going to say it one more time, and then I'm going to consider you to be resisting an official directive. Get. In."

I looked at the others. I didn't see that we had a choice.

We walked around to the back and climbed in. Rex had to fold himself in half to fit through the door. Inside, there was a bench on either side with handcuffs bolted every couple of feet. *Could be worse*, I thought.

Rex and I sat on one side, Pell and Sly on the other. Pell was trembling, and Sly put his arm around her. We had barely sat down when the van took off fast, sliding us all to the back. It stopped abruptly and we fell forward; then it took off again, swerving violently, tires screeching as it fishtailed and straightened out.

The guy was shaking us around on purpose, roughing us up without laying a hand on us. I didn't know where we were headed, but Rex was seething and I was worried about what was going to happen when we got out.

We drove that way for no more than five minutes; then the van braked hard and we all slammed against the front. After a hard, nine-point turn, we took off in reverse before coming to a sudden stop that slammed us against the back. A moment later the doors opened.

We tumbled out onto the road in front of another sign that said NOW LEAVING ALDER. PROCEED WITH CAUTION. UNSAFE ROAD CONDITIONS.

We were on the other side of town.

The doors closed and the van backed up next to us. The cop smiled down at us, still in a heap on the ground.

"This isn't a taxi service," he said. "Next time I pick you up, I'm not taking you where you're headed. Understand?"

Rex tensed and I put my hand on his arm and whispered, "We need to keep moving." Then I turned to the cop. "We understand."

He sped off, his flashing lights shrinking to a twinkling point before they disappeared altogether.

FORTY-EIGHT

Half a mile outside town, a pickup truck roared past us, hurling obscenities, insults, and a large soft drink that splashed at our feet.

Sly gave them the finger with both hands, doing a little dance in the middle of the road as he did.

"Morons," Pell called out. She was trying not to let it bother her, but I could see she was upset.

Rex was seething. I didn't know how much more of it he could take without responding. Or how much I could take without responding, either.

"We need to get off the road," I said.

Sly shook his head. "Bullshit. We have every right to be here."

Rex scowled at the idea, but Pell nodded.

I turned to Rex. "Can I see the map, the real one?"

He handed it over and I studied it for a moment. "There's a trail up ahead, over these hills instead of around them. It's a more direct route, right past Pitman to where Haven is supposed to be. We can get off the road and still get there quicker, probably be there by nightfall."

Rex looked dubious and Sly picked up on it, copying him.

"Look," I said, "we need to get where we're going. We need to find Del and Ruth, right?"

"And Chimerica," Pell added.

"Sure," I said. "But each time we run into trouble, it's going to slow us down." Rex and Sly were listening but they looked unconvinced. "As far as we know, this is where Ryan was shot. We need to take that seriously. We need to be safe."

Rex took the map back and studied it for a moment before he nodded and let out a sigh. "Makes sense."

The entrance to the trail was hidden by vines, but once we got past the first twenty yards, it was clearer.

The trail itself was rougher than I expected, but it was still better hiking through nature than navigating the perils of people.

We walked in silence as a thin layer of clouds replaced the blue sky. I tried picturing Del again, tried to steer my imagination toward a positive place. Instead, I plunged into the now-familiar mix of hope and fear, anxiety and resignation.

I almost welcomed the diversion when Pell and Sly started talking about Chimerica, wondering what it could be, where it could be, who would be there.

"Ruth said she pictured it on a lake in Canada," Pell said solemnly. "She said it would be controlled by chimeras, and they'd grow their own food, bake their own bread and everything. It wouldn't be totally built up, like a city, but it would have plenty of energy for lights and stuff. And other people could be there, too, but they'd have to promise to be nice to the chimeras and not make fun of them or anything, and if they did, they'd have to leave." Sly listened intently, as if Ruth's suppositions now had some great authority.

I was still pretty sure the place wasn't real, and I turned to Rex. But he was listening intently too. I wondered if things had gotten so bad in the real world, he'd decided it made sense to believe in Chimerica after all.

At the bottom of a hill, we crossed an access road carved into the woods. On the other side of it, the brush had turned scraggly and brown, with brittle-looking grasses and dead, twisted trees.

When we crested the next hill, a small tower appeared up ahead, surrounded by a cluster of small buildings and a fence. All of it was rusted and falling apart.

"What's that?" Pell asked, looking around us.

"I think it's a drill," I said.

Rex looked at me. "Oil?"

"Or liquefied coal. Del's dad used to help build these, before he became a cop. When the oil and gas started running out, some people started pumping more and more chemicals into the ground to get the last few drops out. Sometimes the chemicals seeped back to the surface."

"God, it killed everything," Pell said breathlessly, looking at the devastation that surrounded us.

"And that's just a tiny one," I said. "Del told me about some places that had giant operations, with these huge dead zones around them."

"I can't believe they're allowed to do that," she said.

"Oh, it's totally illegal. But no one does much to stop it. Doesn't look like this one has been used in ages."

"I guess the damage is already done," she said.

Sly cleared his throat. "This is all very fascinating, but how about we hurry up and get out of here before it kills us, too?"

We quickened our pace up the next hill, and by the time we had reached the top, the grass had recovered somewhat, then the trees.

The thickening clouds parted for a moment, bathing everything in a golden light that seemed unnaturally bright and cheerful after the brown and gray around the drilling installation. Then the light faded as the sun disappeared once more.

Rex looked at the sky. "Might be some rain headed our way."

As we walked on, I stepped closer to him. "Do you think we'll make it by nightfall?"

He shrugged. "I hope so. But I don't like the looks of those clouds."

A chilly breeze picked up. Rex checked his compass and we angled to the right, along the access road.

Half a mile later, it let us out onto another road, once paved but now mostly rubble. A sign confirmed that we were headed toward Pitman, but the distance had been obliterated by rust.

Down the road a hundred yards was another metal structure. I thought it might be another drilling installation, but as we got closer, I saw it was a sign.

I could make out the words VILLAGE MALL, although several letters were missing.

Rex glanced at his map. "We're not far from Pitman, but still a ways off from Haven."

Lightning flickered and the ground shook with thunder. It was still late afternoon, but the clouds overhead were darkening dramatically. The wind swirled, picking up grit and bits of debris.

Rex pointed at the sign. "If there's an old mall, we could shelter in it."

We crossed the road, relieved finally to have a destination. Sly put his hand at the small of Pell's back, helping to propel her along.

Other than the sign, there didn't seem to be any hint of a mall or anything else, but as the trees swayed in the wind, we could see metal light posts, spaced out evenly among them. It was an old parking lot. Beyond it was the mall itself. "There," I said, pointing at a darkened jumble of glass, chrome, and concrete.

The clouds lit up with lightning and we all flinched as the thunder echoed around in the valley. Then the rain came down.

FORTY-NINE

The parking lot was covered in mud and leaves. We were soaked in seconds, and halfway across the lot, the water was already ankle deep, cascading down the steep hills surrounding the mall.

One wall of the glass atrium at the entrance had been shattered, and we picked our way past the shards that littered the pavement, making our way inside.

A flash of lightning lit up the first twenty yards of the dark, musty, cavernous interior. A pair of benches faced each other, flanked by escalators on either side leading up to the next level.

We stood there for a moment, dripping, then simultaneously dropped our backpacks and collapsed onto the benches.

Pell and Sly were sitting together, and I wondered if there was something between them. Then I noticed Pell smiling at Rex and me, like she was assuming the same thing about us. She winked at me, then looked away.

I opened my backpack for something to eat, but all that was in it was the flashlight and the binoculars. I was about to ask the others to pass around some food, but a noise made me pause. Behind the roar of the wind and the rain pounding on the roof, I heard a low rumble. A crash echoed through the mall, followed by the sound of moving furniture and a barely audible whoosh.

"What is that?" I whispered.

Rex gave his head a tiny shake. "I don't know."

We were all staring into the dark interior of the mall when lightning flashed and I saw it, just at the edge of where the light reached.

I grabbed my backpack and yelled, "Run!"

A river of mud was surging through the building, dark and dangerous, glittering with broken glass, pushing large chunks of debris as it came at us fast.

Between the mud and the rain and the mold covering everything, I could barely get any traction, running in place like a cartoon character. But I was still the first one moving, straight toward the way we came in.

I opened my mouth to tell everyone to grab their stuff, but it was too late—the backpacks disappeared as the mud picked up the benches we had just been sitting on, snapping them into pieces and tumbling them toward us.

Rex was just a few steps behind me and the others right behind him, when Pell tripped and let out a squeal of pain, grabbing her leg. Rex reached past Sly and yanked Pell by the jacket, jerking her away from the onrushing mud.

As we stumbled back out into the rain, the mud exploded through the atrium, shattering more windows, twisting the metal skeleton. The roof groaned and sagged, raining more glass. The mud poured out into the parking lot, then it stopped.

The rain slowed to a drizzle and the mud settled as we stood there stunned, trying to catch our breath. It was almost dark outside, but I could see the brown scar of exposed earth on the hillside behind the mall, where the mudslide had come from. The building shuddered. Some unseen section of roof collapsed with a crash, pushing out a gust of damp, moldy air, like a dying breath.

I looked at the others, soaking wet and wide-eyed with shock—even Rex. I'm sure I looked just as shaken. "Is everyone okay?" I called out over the sound of the wind and rain.

"Mostly," said Pell.

"She cut her leg," Sly said. He looked worried.

"It's not too bad," Pell said.

Sly put his arm around her.

I knelt down beside her and gingerly lifted her pant leg. It was a nasty gash, but it would probably be fine if we could get it cleaned and bandaged.

"No, not too bad," I repeated.

Rex met my eye, a look that said he agreed with my unspoken assessment more than the one I'd said out loud. Then he stepped closer to me. "How about you? Are you okay?" His rumbling voice reverberated through my body.

"Yeah," I said. "I'm fine."

Soon the rain stopped entirely, and the evening sky started to clear. The air was turning crisp and dry, refreshing at first but with a slight chill. The thunderstorm had been intense, and it seemed like a cold front was coming through behind it.

We were drenched and exhausted. We had nothing to eat and nowhere to stay. Pell needed medical attention.

"So, now what?" Sly asked, pulling his jacket tighter around him. "I'm freaking starving."

I was, too.

We all looked at Rex, and he actually took a step back. I felt bad for him. He hadn't wanted us to come with him. He might have been fine on his own, just camping out in the woods.

I looked around, at the mall we had just escaped, at the low, puffy clouds, drifting by under the rising moon and stars. As the clouds passed behind the hilltops, they glowed briefly, as if lit from below.

"What's that?" I said, pointing.

Rex and Sly turned to look.

Sly turned back. "I don't see anything."

Rex squinted. "What, you mean the light?"

"Yeah. Under the clouds."

"I don't know. Actually, it could be Pitman. We're pretty close."

"We still have our money, right?" I said. "Maybe we can get some food and supplies there."

All three of them looked at me like I was crazy and stupid. Rex shook his head sadly. "It's not safe. Chimeras can't just walk into a town in the middle of nowhere, definitely not these days."

"I know that," I said. "But I can."

FIFTY

Rex was against the idea, but he had to admit it made sense. I don't think Sly or Pell were crazy about it, either, but they were hungry and thirsty and we were all worried about Pell's leg.

The plan was that I would go into town, buy food and water, some bandages and first aid cream, and bring it all back out to where they were waiting. It would still be a cold, uncomfortable night, but at least we'd have the essentials and we could take care of Pell.

"Let's get a little closer to the town, and reassess," said Rex, apparently still unconvinced. "Maybe there'll be a better option."

Pell's limp was getting worse, probably aggravated by the steep incline we were climbing.

"Is this a hill or a mountain?" Sly asked, breathing hard.

"It would be a very small mountain," Rex said.

"Yeah, well, it's a big-ass hill."

From the top of the hill, Pitman was clearly visible—a tall fence surrounding an irregular grid, all bathed in the soft blue glow of super-efficiency streetlights, with a few brighter orange and yellow lights sprinkled in. On the far side of town was a jumble of industrial buildings lit up in white and a tower topped off with an orange flame. Behind that was a patch of inky black.

"It's pretty," Pell said. "Especially the flame."

"I guess," said Sly. "What is that?"

"It looks like a coal well," I said. "Like that old one we saw. That flare burns off excess gases and impurities. It looks like they're still operating it." I turned to Rex. "But they couldn't be, right?"

Rex shook his head. "They shouldn't be."

Below us a shattered road curved past an open gate set in the tall fence. Another road split off it and went through the gate, and the part inside looked newly paved.

As we watched, a car came out through the gate, tiny in the distance. It turned away from us and sped off down the bumpy road in the opposite direction, disappearing quickly over the next hilltop.

Rex grunted. "That way is probably the closest Smart-route."

We descended the hill but stayed in the woods, keeping our distance from the road. The trees were bare, except for the ones draped in vines, but they were dense enough that twenty feet in, they gave us some cover.

We huddled behind a thick mat of kudzu.

"I don't like this," Rex said. "I don't know what happened to Ryan, but this could be where it happened. I don't think you should go in there."

"I don't, either," Pell said, putting her hand on my arm. "I'll be fine until tomorrow."

Sly was quiet. I got the sense he shared their concerns, but he was worried about Pell, too.

I patted Rex on the shoulder. "I'll be okay," I said. "I'll go in, find the store, and get out fast. I'm more worried about you guys. You need to make sure you aren't seen."

"You need a story," Sly said.

"What do you mean?" I asked.

"It's a small town. They're going to know you're from the outside. You need a story as to why you're there, alone at night."

"What do I say, I was out hiking and I got lost?"

"The storm," Sly said. "Tell them you lost your stuff in the storm. In a gully washer or whatever."

I nodded.

"I still don't like it," Rex said. Even in the darkness, I could see the worry in his eyes.

"I'll be fine," I said. I gave Rex the flashlight and the binoculars but kept the backpack with me, so I could fill it with food and medical supplies. "I'll be back before you know it."

I gave them a smile, then turned and left the woods.

FIFTY-ONE

As I crossed the road, I looked through the gate and saw people walking this way and that. A sign on the fence said WELCOME TO PIT-MAN, and below it were rules and regulations, a history of the town, and a list of things to do. I couldn't imagine there was much since the place was tiny, but I wasn't planning on staying anyway, so I didn't read it.

The streetlights were dimmer than the ones in the city, but after so long in the darkness, I could see just fine.

The guardhouse by the gate was empty. Past it was a street lined with small, neat houses with little patches of grass out front, and fenced-in yards out back. A couple of larger homes were mixed in, too. Apart from the constant flame visible in the sky behind the houses, it was a lot like some of the neighborhoods near my house.

I had expected it to be weirder.

I seemed to be on the main street going straight through the heart of town. The utility poles had posters for Game Day, just like the one on the back of Ryan's map. Several blocks ahead, the lights were brighter. I could see signs and storefronts and figured that must be the commercial district. There were plenty of people on the sidewalks, all headed toward the center of town.

To be safe, I took off the pin Ruth had given me and slipped it in my back pocket. As I did, an older couple came out of the house I was walking past. They both looked at me.

I smiled, and so did the woman. The man tipped his head and said, "Evening."

"Evening," I said, thinking, *This is going to be easier than I'd thought.*

I took a few more steps, and then the man called out, "Excuse me, young lady?"

Or maybe not. I turned and smiled sweetly. "Yes?"

"I believe you dropped this," he said, holding up my pin.

I realized I must have dropped it when I tried to put it in my pocket.

"It's very pretty," said the woman. "You wouldn't want to lose that."

Both of their faces were open and sweet and seemed to be utterly devoid of suspicion or ill will. Either they didn't realize it was a pro-chimera pin or they didn't care.

"Thank you," I said, taking the pin and putting it in my backpack.

"You'll want to be careful," he said conspiratorially. "Even in a nice town like this, not everyone is as honest as we are."

They both laughed as if he'd said something hilarious.

I thanked them again, and we exchanged good-nights.

Half a block after that I heard a screen door slam and seconds later a small voice behind me said, "Who are you?"

I took a deep breath and turned, rehearsing my lines in my head. A little boy about seven years old was squinting up at me, like he was trying to place me and wondering why he couldn't.

"My name's Jimi. Who are you?"

"I'm Sam. Jimmy's a boy's name."

I nodded. "Usually it is, but not always, because I'm a girl."

"You're not from Pitman, are you?"

"Nope. Just visiting."

"Are you here for the Pregame Fair?"

"No, I'm not."

"We haven't had a Game Day since I was a baby. They're saying this year's is going to be the best one yet."

"Wow. That sounds like fun. I'm actually looking for a store. Do you know where there's a store?"

"Sure," he said. "Pratt's Market is up there." He pointed in the direction everyone was headed. "We missed the beginning of the fair because my mom said we had to do our chores."

"Okay, thanks," I said. "Well, see you later." I started walking, but so did he.

"So where do you live?"

"In Philadelphia," I said.

He stopped, wide-eyed. "I never been to the city."

"Well, I'd never been to Pitman before now," I said over my shoulder.

He ran to catch up with me. "What are you going to get at the store?"

Then another voice behind us called out, "Sammy, what are you doing? I told you to wait on the steps."

Sammy turned and shrugged. "You took too long." Then he looked up at me and said apologetically, "That's my brother, Andrew."

"Who are you?" Andrew asked, scanning me up and down. I felt suddenly self-conscious about the mud on my pants, my mussed-up hair.

He was about my age. Big and athletic. Actually kind of cute, except for the way he seemed to be judging the state of my clothes.

"I beg your pardon?" I said, putting a little ice on it.

"Sorry," he said, smiling now as he looked closer at me. "I'm Andrew. I hope this one isn't bothering you."

"No, *he's* fine," I said. I turned and started walking again.

"This is Jimi. She's from the city," Sammy said, walking alongside me again. I got the sense he was bragging, since he had discovered me.

Andrew caught up with us, eyes almost as wide as Sammy's had been. "Are you really?"

I was starting to regret having engaged the little guy. Things were getting a bit too involved. "Yes."

He laughed. "What are you doing here?" Then he looked at me, vaguely confused. "Are you here for Game Day? The storm mostly missed us, so the fair's still on tonight."

"No, I'm just looking for the market."

"Really?" Now he looked really confused. "Well, here it is." We were approaching a tiny storefront. PRATT'S MARKET was painted on the window. The lights were on, and inside I could see food, a first aid section, even some camping supplies. A sign said OPEN TILL ELEVEN, but there was a piece of paper taped to the door, with big letters: CLOSED FOR THE FAIR. BACK AT 9:30.

"We're headed to the fair," Andrew said, pointing down the street. Most of the lights I had thought were coming from the retail district were actually from the football field down the block. Now that I was closer, I could hear live music and the murmur of a crowd. I could also smell food cooking.

"Everybody's there, even Pratt," he said, a wry smile twisting his lips. "Why don't you come along and then you can buy your stuff afterward, when he reopens."

"Um . . ." I looked at my watch. It was a quarter to nine. I looked back at the gate, thinking I should let the others know what was going on, but worried it would look suspicious if I left and came back. And it seemed like I would generate more attention if I was the only person in town not at the fair than if I just went and blended in.

"Come on," he said. "It's just up the block."

"Okay, I guess."

"Yay!" Sammy clapped his hands.

Andrew stepped up on my other side. Close. He smelled of soap and aftershave. "So, what in the world brings you to Pitman?"

"It's a long story."

He flashed a smile that was artificially shy, but somehow still charming. I felt myself blushing. "I bet it's fascinating," he said. "I'd love to hear it."

Sammy looked up at him, like, *What the heck are you guys talking about?*

I just smiled. Then we were there.

FIFTY-TWO

The football field had a stage at one end and food stands and carnival games around the edges. The center was filled with adults talking over the music and laughing, while little kids chased around their parents' legs. The field was damp from the rain.

The band on stage was playing classic rock standards, and Andrew tapped my arm and pointed. "With any luck, we might have missed the boring part—the speakers!"

Sammy tugged at my shirt. "Our dad is the mayor!"

"Wow," I said, suddenly concerned but trying to sound impressed.

Andrew put his hand at the small of my back. "Can I buy you a chili dog?" he asked, gently steering me toward the food tables.

My stomach practically grumbled the words: *Yes, feed me something!*

I thought about Rex and Pell and Sly, out there in the woods—cold, wet, and hungry. I felt guilty, but my not eating wasn't going to make them any less hungry.

"Sure," I said. "That'd be great."

He ordered two chili dogs and two sodas, then turned to look at me.

I smiled and he smiled back, letting it linger. I couldn't look away, but the more I stared back at him, the more I seemed to be saying something I didn't mean to be saying.

He finally turned away when the food was ready.

"Thanks," I said as he handed me mine, careful not to meet his gaze.

"The pleasure is all mine," he replied. His attempt at sounding suave was torpedoed by Sammy's voice whining, "Andrew, where's *my* chili dog?"

Andrew's eyes flashed with anger for an instant, then he ruffled

Sammy's hair and turned back to the vendor to order another chili dog. He handed it over with a syrupy smile. "Here you go, buddy," he said.

Sammy took a big bite, then ran off, leaving a trail of chili as he joined a group of other kids his age chasing each other across the field.

Andrew and I walked and listened to the band as we ate our chili dogs. He said hello to about half the people we passed and tried to introduce me, but I just smiled tightly and looked away, concentrating on finishing my chili dog without spilling any on my shirt. I was still hungry when I was done, but I didn't want to spend any money, and I definitely didn't want to ask Andrew to buy me another one.

The crowd was festive, and there was a warm, small-town friendliness, old-fashioned and reassuring. It made me feel somehow nostalgic, even though nothing from my life had been anything like it. It was like something from a past that I wished I'd had.

Even the flare burning in the sky seemed somehow comforting, at least until a whiff of sulfur and ammonia reminded me that it wasn't a hearth or a campfire; it was an illegal coal-well rig, unsafe and unsound.

I looked at my watch and felt a sudden wave of anxiety. It was a quarter past nine. I'd been in Pitman for forty-five minutes. I was so close to where Del was supposed to be, and instead of making progress, I was eating a chili dog at a town fair. I felt even guiltier as I thought about the others, waiting out in the woods.

I relaxed a little when the band announced they were going to play one last song after a few words from the head of the chamber of commerce. As a smart-looking older woman in a suit took the stage and began talking, a couple in their late forties approached us. They had an oddly artificial polish, like successful Realtors or TV newspeople, or like local politicians. I realized it was Andrew's mom and dad, the mayor and his wife.

The man had a WellPlant, so they weren't hurting for money, even in this little town. The woman didn't have one, for what that was worth. Their focus was on Andrew, but they were giving me sidelong glances, making it plain they were wondering who I was.

"There you are," the man said to Andrew. "I assume the dishes are done?"

Andrew rolled his eyes. "Yes, Dad. And the trash is out."

"And Sammy dried the knives and forks?" the woman asked.

"And he put away his toys. He's running around somewhere."

Onstage, the woman from the chamber of commerce was talking about Pitman's bright future.

Andrew said, "This is Jimi." Then he turned to me. "This is my mom and dad."

"Nice to meet you," I said.

The mom looked me up and down again, staring for a moment at my muddy pants.

"I haven't seen you around before," said his dad.

"No," I said. "I'm just visiting." It was then that I noticed a tiny H4H pin on his lapel, and a similar one on his wife's cardigan.

He opened his mouth for a follow-up question. Fortunately, I was saved when the woman onstage gave a big shout-out to Pitman's wonderful mayor. Andrew's dad stopped and turned, waving to the crowd. Then the band started up again, louder than before, and no one could hear a word.

Looking around, I spotted at least a dozen more of those tiny H4H pins. I needed to get what I came for and get out of there, back to my friends. Things would be wrapping up soon and the store would be reopening.

"Thanks for the chili dog," I said, moving my head close to Andrew's so he could hear me. "The store will be open in a minute, so I should get over there."

Andrew shook his head with a smug smile and put his hand

around my waist as he leaned even closer. "Pratt's not leaving until this is over, so you might as well wait. Besides, what's your hurry?"

We were standing by the entrance to the park. I could see the store, see the note still on the front door.

"Just don't want it to get too late," I said, stepping away from his grasp.

He was cute, but he was a bit much.

Then the band finished anyway. The singer said, "Good night, everybody. Have a great Game Day this Thursday!" Then the stage lights went out and the crowd starting edging toward the exits.

"Okay," I said, stepping toward the exit, too. "Well, thanks again for everything."

He drew close again and said, "I'll come with you."

FIFTY-THREE

I didn't want to be mean or ungrateful. I didn't want to string him along. And I really didn't want to complicate my exit. I'd managed to avoid telling my made-up story, and I wanted to keep it that way. But he seemed determined to come with me.

I figured I'd put off the awkward farewell until after I left the market. I'd do it quick, abrupt, and if his feelings were hurt, that would be on him.

We walked along with the crowd, and as we approached the store, I saw an older man climbing the steps to the front door with a key in his hand.

"Evening, Mr. Pratt," Andrew said loudly as we approached.

The old man turned with a start, then smiled. "Evening, Andrew."

He did a double take when he saw me, squinting and frowning.

"This is my friend Jimi," Andrew said.

"Oh. Hello," Pratt said with a smile as he opened the door.

The place was quaint but vaguely creepy, like it had been stuck in time for fifty years. But it seemed to have everything I needed.

Andrew and Pratt talked about the weather and various people they knew while I picked up a basket and filled it with four self-heating cans of soup, four bottles of water, four chocolate chip cookies, and a bag of bread. Then I grabbed some gauze, numbing spray, first aid cream, and large adhesive bandages. They even had a cheap foil emergency blanket. I threw that in as well.

There was a sign taped to the register: THIS STORE IS FOR HUMANS. WE RESERVE THE RIGHT TO DENY SERVICE TO MIXIES. Another one, behind the counter, said NO DOGS ALLOWED, with the words OR MIXIES added with thick black marker.

Pratt stared at me staring at them. "Will that be all?"

I nodded and gave him my most innocent smile.

Pratt totaled it all up, and Andrew watched as I put it in my backpack, as if noticing my purchases for the first time. He looked up at me with an odd expression. "Are you hurt?"

"Nope," I said cheerfully. "Just stocking up."

I paid, thanked Mr. Pratt, and headed for the door.

As Andrew walked me down the steps, I steeled myself, trying to figure out how I was going to play this, how I was going to shake him and get away.

If worse came to worse, I could just stomp on his foot and run. But when we got down to the sidewalk, we practically bumped into his parents.

"Hello there!" Andrew's mother said brightly.

"Did you enjoy the fair?" the mayor asked, perfectly nice but still weirding me out.

"Yes," I said. "It was great."

As we stood there, each person that walked by said, "Evening, Mayor Randolph." They were all wearing H4H pins.

"Well, I should get going," I said. I took a step away from them, hoping Andrew would get stuck in conversation with his parents and I could slip away.

"I'll walk you home," he said.

"No, that's okay. It was nice meeting you."

"You're just visiting, right?" Mayor Randolph said. "Where are you staying?"

And there it was.

I wondered which would be easier, starting down the road of lies and explanations, or just running for the gate.

"Outside of town."

All three of their brows immediately furrowed, like I had just said I was staying on Mars.

"Outside of . . ." The mayor tilted his head, confused. "But . . . where?"

"I'm backpacking," I said lightly. "Camping out."

Mrs. Randolph looked genuinely alarmed. "In the *woods*?"

I nodded and smiled and turned to go.

"So, where are you going now?" the mayor asked.

I tried to maintain the smile as I turned back. "Just getting on my way," I said.

Andrew looked down at my stuffed backpack. "You're bringing all that just for you?"

I didn't want to get into who I was or wasn't traveling with. Before I had to, the mayor said, "The gate's closed for the night."

"I beg your pardon?"

"The gate's closed. We're not in the city. We close the gate every night. For security reasons."

"Well, can we open it?"

"Sure thing." He smiled. "In the morning."

FIFTY-FOUR

For a moment I just stood there, staring at Mayor Randolph and trying to keep the panic rising within me from showing on my face.

"So I'm locked in here?" I said, trying to sound casual.

"Well, yes, if you put it like that," the mayor said. "But more to the point, undesirable elements are locked out. Even if the gate wasn't locked, I couldn't let you go out there on your own at night. There's all sorts of creatures out there."

I knew he was lying about that. Between the climate and the mining and drilling, the entire state was just about devoid of wildlife. Unless he was talking about chimeras, which would make sense according to Ryan's map.

He looked at me appraisingly. "How old are you, anyway?"

"Nineteen."

Andrew snorted and looked away. The mayor didn't seem like he was buying it, either.

Mrs. Randolph put her hand on my arm. "We couldn't just let you go out there on your own at night," she said. "You can stay in our guesthouse."

"Unless you've got friends with you," Andrew said.

The mayor's face looked suddenly hard. "Are there?"

"No," I heard myself saying.

"Then it's settled," Mrs. Randolph said, smiling broadly. "You can leave in the morning if you want to."

The mayor smiled but his face was still stern. "Or we can drive you to the Levline, if you come to your senses."

Sammy was over the moon that I was staying with them, nattering on all the way back to their house about his toys, his friends, and his comic book collection.

Andrew seemed pretty upbeat, too, practically biting his cheek to keep the smile off his face.

I was in shock. As we walked down the road, I could see the gate up ahead, now closed. I felt claustrophobic. I wanted to run over and try to open it or climb over it, or at least shout into the woods that I was okay and I'd be back in the morning.

I wondered if my friends were all right, especially Pell. I wondered what would happen if they gave up and went on without me, or if they came to get me and ran into this horde of chimera-haters. I wondered if the hours I was wasting here would be the difference between reaching Del in time or never seeing him again.

The Randolphs lived in a large single home. It was neat and comfortable, nice but strangely old-fashioned. As soon as we walked in, Mrs. Randolph went straight back to the kitchen, the mayor stopped in the dining room and poured himself a drink, and Sammy ran upstairs to get ready for bed.

Andrew invited me to sit on the sofa. Then he did, too. Close. I slid away from him.

Mrs. Randolph came in from the dining room with a smile. "Well, I've set up the guesthouse for you. You'll have some privacy there. I'd be happy to wash those clothes for you."

Before he could hide it, a flash of interest crossed Andrew's face. Mr. Randolph walked up behind his wife, putting a hand on her waist. The other hand held a cut-glass tumbler with brown liquor in it.

"No, I'm fine," I said. "Thank you, though. You're very gracious."

"I'm not crazy about the idea of you hiking around out there on your own," the mayor said, sipping his drink.

"I'll be fine," I said with a smile. "I do it all the time."

"Well, we can talk about it some more in the morning."

"Just let me know when you want to go to bed," Mrs. Randolph said. "Everything is ready."

"That's great," I said, faking a yawn that became real halfway through. "I should probably go to bed now."

Andrew sat forward. "Already?"

I stood up. "It's been a long day." Images of it flashed through my mind, leaving me even more exhausted. I yawned again.

Mrs. Randolph called upstairs, "Sammy, come say good night to our guest!"

Sammy scrambled down the steps sounding like a herd of tiny buffaloes. Mrs. Randolph winced as he hit the floor running. He was wearing footie pajamas with a cowboy motif, and his feet slid across the floor as he scampered. When he finally got traction, he took off like a shot in my direction, arms out wide for a midsection hug that was more like a tackle.

"You're going to bed?" he said, his arms wrapped around me. "I'm going to bed now, too. I got to stay up late because of the fair. Are you staying for Game Day?" He stopped and looked up at me.

"No, I don't think so."

He looked disappointed for a fraction of a second, then said, "Are you going to eat breakfast in the morning?"

"Um . . . I guess so. Probably."

"Good!" he said, letting me go. "My teacher says breakfast is the most important meal of the day." He turned and ran back upstairs. "Good night!" he shouted down.

"Good night!" I shouted back.

Mrs. Randolph said, "He seems pretty smitten."

I smiled. "He's a cutie."

"He's a handful," she said. "Come on. I'll show you to the guesthouse."

I nodded and looked over at Andrew, still sitting on the couch. "Good night," I said.

He smiled. "See you later."

FIFTY-FIVE

The guesthouse was a small cabin behind the main house, one room with a bed, a side table and a chair, and a tiny bathroom off to the side. It was rustic, with exposed wood and baseboard heaters.

Mrs. Randolph showed me the towels in a cupboard.

"Thanks for your hospitality," I said. What I really wanted was to be out in the woods with my friends, to give them their food, to take care of Pell's leg, and to help them stay warm. But I was still touched by her kindness. It didn't seem to add up: the whole H4H thing and the willingness to welcome a complete stranger.

"Of course, honey," she said. She looked at me a moment longer, her eyes lingering just for a second, like she was trying to pick up clues about who I was, or like she was sending me a message. There was something sad in her eyes. I wondered if she was thinking about me leaving there in the morning, maybe wishing she could leave with me. "Sleep well, okay?"

Then she closed the door and I was alone. I paced the room for a moment, running through my options. It didn't take long. I wanted to run away, to escape and go to my friends. I wanted to communicate with them somehow, but without drawing attention to them, or endangering them. I wanted to let them know what was happening, that I was okay, and that they were right next to H4H central. But the more I tried to think of a way to make that happen, the more confident I was that it wasn't possible.

I needed to stay where I was until morning, say my gracious good-byes, and hope Rex and Pell and Sly were okay and waiting for me when I got out. And if they weren't, I'd cross that bridge when I came to it.

I sat on the bed and took off my boots and my socks. My feet were damp, white, and wrinkled. It felt so good to wiggle my toes in the air. I lay back onto the crisp sheets. They smelled clean, but not freshly washed, like they had just come out of a cedar chest. It was oddly comforting.

I turned off the bedside lamp and in seconds could feel my eyes closing in relief. But the rest of me felt clammy. I knew I'd be a lot happier in the morning if I laid my damp clothes out to dry.

I turned the light on again, then slid off my pants and draped them over the back of the chair. I was lifting my shirt to pull it over my head when there was a tap at the door. Then it opened.

I clutched my shirt back down as Andrew stepped into the cabin.

"What are you doing here?" I demanded, for some reason keeping my voice to a terse whisper.

He smiled that charming smile. "Sorry. I just wanted to check and see if you were okay." He closed the door behind him.

His eyes glinted as he looked me up and down again.

"You need to go," I said.

"Come on, I just got here." He stepped closer. "Are you really leaving tomorrow?"

"Yes. Now get out of here."

"You hanging out with some mixies out there? Is that who all the soup is for?"

I didn't say anything and he smiled.

"I thought so," he said. "I saw that mixie pin in your backpack. I guess you're a bit of a free-thinker, huh?" Another step. Another smile. "You're also gorgeous, you know that?"

His smell was stronger now, that aftershave or body spray. This close it was overpowering, revolting.

"Back off," I said, shocked by the fear in my voice. Because what I mostly felt was anger.

"Come on," he said, cocking an eyebrow. "We could have a lot of fun."

His body was inches away from mine, and he reached out and touched my hair.

I twisted, just enough to give me some torque. Then I brought up my knee as hard as I could, right between his legs. His face twisted and he let out a breath that came from so deep it smelled of chili dog.

He folded and staggered back into the corner, between the door and the wall, one hand over his crotch, the other hand bracing himself so he didn't fall. His face was purple and twisted in pain and fury.

I wanted to run, to take my chances outside, but he was leaning against the door. And I wasn't wearing pants.

"You bitch," he hissed.

I threw my backpack and jeans over my shoulder and grabbed my boots. I went for the door, but he was blocking my way. He pulled something from his waistband and unfolded it. A large pocketknife.

"Are you serious? Don't be insane," I said. "Do you know how much trouble you'll be in for threatening me?"

He waved the knife in the air, slowly, almost gracefully. "I'm a Randolph," he said, creeping closer. "We don't get in trouble."

I wished I hadn't taken off my pants and my boots—especially my boots. But boots could be helpful, even if they weren't on my feet.

"Well, at least one of us is still going to have fun," he said, waving that blade back and forth, like he was trying to mesmerize me. I waited until the knife was pointed away from me, then I swung my boots as hard as I could at his elbow. I was hoping to hit his funny bone and send the knife clattering across the floor. Instead, I heard a sharp whimpering sound. His mouth was a perfect O, like an old-fashioned porcelain Christmas caroler. His hand still gripped the knife, but the blade was embedded in his other arm. Blood started dripping off his elbow.

I had hurt him, but I needed to get out of there. He was still in front of the door, and he still had a knife. When he came to his senses he was going to be angrier than ever. I drew the boots back and was about to swing them again, flashing back to Dietrich and aiming for his head this time. But then the door burst open with a bang and a spray of splinters. Andrew disappeared behind it.

Rex filled the doorway, his chest heaving and his fists clenched, ready for action. His eyes smoldered as he scanned the room, but his expression became increasingly confused.

I pointed at the door behind him, and he peered around it.

"Oh," he said, looking down at Andrew, crumpled and unconscious. Then he turned to me again. "You're okay?" he said as we held each other's gaze.

I nodded, and he nodded back. Then he looked away. "Finish getting dressed. We need to go."

I wriggled into my jeans and pulled on my boots, then stuffed my socks into my pocket and grabbed the backpack. "Ready."

We paused at the door, peeking out each way. A window lit up on the second floor of the main house, then another.

"Which way?" I said.

Rex pointed into the darkness and we took off running, pausing behind a cluster of scraggly bushes. I grabbed his shirt and pulled him close. "Careful," I said. "This place is full of H4Hers."

He nodded, then took my hand and guided me through the shadows. We darted across a street under the dim blue lights, then plunged back into darkness. As we cut through backyards, I heard yelling and some kind of commotion behind us.

The ammonia-sulfur smell grew stronger, and the fire in the sky loomed over us. I could see the tower between two houses, and just beyond it, the waste pit. It was an expanse of absolute black, the toxic by-products left over from liquefying the coal and bringing it to the surface. The houses here were more run-down, the yards mostly packed dirt. We had cut across four blocks when we slipped through a backyard and came to the edge of town. There was a metal swing set just a few feet from the outer fence.

Rex didn't slow down. Letting go of my hand, he swung himself onto the swing set, wrapped one leg and one arm around the top, and then reached down with the other hand. I grabbed it and he swung me to the top of the outer fence. Then he hung from both arms and swung himself out as well. The fence shook and rattled when he hit it.

We both climbed over and dropped into the shadows at the base. A hundred yards to our right, the town gate was opening. *Oh sure,* I thought, *now you open it.* Flashing blue-and-red police lights reflected off the trees, and sirens started in the distance.

We exchanged a quick nod, then darted across the street and scrambled into the woods.

Halfway up the hill, we heard rustling in the brush straight ahead and a pair of eyes flashed in the moonlight. Sly's voice whispered, "It's okay—it's us."

Then I saw Pell, the moonlight playing off the feathers on her head. Even in the darkness, I could see she was hurting.

As the sirens rose in the town below, Sly grinned, showing his teeth. "Whatever you guys did down there, you sure shook them up."

FIFTY-SIX

At the top of the hill, we turned and looked back toward Pitman. Police vehicles were speeding away from the gate in both directions. A dozen flashlight beams slashed back and forth in the night, crossing the road toward us and then spreading out.

In front of us, the far side of the hill dropped away, a steep, rocky descent to a wide stream below. Moonlight highlighted the undulating hills, extending to the dark horizon. In the distance a bright snake of light cut across the night. The Levline.

If Ryan's map was accurate and we were reading it right, the star he drew between Carston and Pitman—Haven—was on the other side of the next big hill, just a couple miles away.

Rex pointed to a small bridge, a few planks, really, that crossed the creek where it narrowed.

We started down, sliding and stumbling as fast as we could. Rex was practically carrying Pell, but it was still hard for Sly and me to keep pace with him. Behind us, half a dozen of the flashlight beams speared the misty air like searchlights as our pursuers came up the other side of the hill. They stopped where we'd just been standing, at the top of the hill, then one by one their beams sliced down as they headed down the hill after us.

At the bottom of the hill, we paused at the footbridge to look back at the lights making their way down the hillside. A thick fog was rolling in. To the north and south, more beams crested the hill, joining the jagged line of searchers already angling down the slope after us.

The bridge groaned as we crossed it and the shouts behind us grew louder. The scattered beams began to reassemble as the search party headed for the bridge.

We plunged into the scraggly brush on the other side. Rex checked the compass, then we angled along the creek, toward a different peak to the south.

We were maybe a half a mile away when the first flashlights crossed the bridge behind us. But they kept going straight and headed right up the hill in front of them, instead of coming toward us.

I sighed with relief.

"We've got to keep moving," Rex rumbled softly. He put Pell down and she kept up okay. Forty minutes later we reached the top of the next hill. The lights of Pitman were visible behind us, but there was no sign of our pursuers. On the far side of the hill, just a little ways down from the top, there was a massive boulder next to a hollow left by a fallen tree, shielded from sight by its massive roots. We all stopped, an unspoken unanimous agreement that this was where we would camp.

Rex walked a quick circle around us, sniffing the air and checking our surroundings. Sly helped Pell get comfortable as I unpacked my purchases, putting aside the soup, water, and blanket and focusing on the medical supplies.

"Let's look at that leg," I said, kneeling in front of Pell.

She shook her head. "Let's eat first. I think I might starve to death before any infection gets me."

We sat in a circle, and I passed around the soup, the cookies, and the bottled water. We each pushed the buttons on the bottoms of our soup cans, then shook them to heat them up quicker.

Even after eating that chili dog, I was starving. The others must have been ravenous. No one waited the full two minutes for the cans to heat, and just a few minutes later we were all done, tapping the last drops of soup into our mouths, licking the cookie wrappers.

Rex said he was going to check out our surroundings more thoroughly.

I turned to Pell. "You ready?"

She nodded.

I set up the flashlight and lifted her pant leg. She stiffened and gasped, but didn't cry out. The wound was nasty, about three inches long and covered with dirt and mud.

"I have numbing spray, but it's still going to sting. You probably need stitches, but you're not going to get them tonight."

Sly held her hand as I got to work with the numbing and cleaning. Luckily, it didn't look infected.

"So, what happened down there?" she asked, wincing.

I glanced up at her and saw Sly staring down at me as well, waiting. I sighed, embarrassed to talk about it.

"The town was shut down for some kind of fair, so I had to wait until it was over for the store to reopen. By the time it reopened, they had locked the gate. The town was closed for the night."

"Yeah, we know that part," Sly said.

I looked up at him, and he shrugged.

"Rex had the binoculars." He snickered. "He was getting pretty annoyed until we figured out what was going on."

"Anyway," I said, "there was this guy, Andrew. His dad is the mayor. His folks insisted I stay at their guesthouse. They were nice enough, I guess, although the whole town was, like, H4H headquarters."

"What happened?" Pell asked quietly.

I kept my eyes down. "Andrew paid me a visit," I said. "I think he's a bit of a hotshot in town, God's-gift-to-women type. I said no. He didn't like it. It got nasty."

"Are you okay?" she whispered.

"I am," I said, looking up at them. "Andrew's not. He pulled a knife. Somehow it ended up stuck in his arm. Then Rex broke in the door and flattened him."

Sly laughed. "Damn right."

Pell said, "Jesus, Jimi, that's really scary."

I nodded. It *was* scary.

When I was done, Pell's face looked rough, but the wound

looked much better, slathered with antibiotic cream and wrapped with gauze.

"Thanks," she said quietly as I pulled her pant leg back down. I smiled at her, and so did Sly. She closed her eyes and her breathing fell into a gentle, steady rhythm. Just like that, she was asleep.

I took out the foil blanket and spread it over her.

Rex returned and pulled me aside. "How's she doing?"

Sly followed us, listening intently.

I shrugged. "She seems okay, I guess. It's a nasty cut, and it was filthy. I'm hoping the cream will prevent any infection before it gets started."

Rex nodded, looking over at her. "Okay. Well, Pell's got the right idea. We need to rest up. No idea what tomorrow will bring. Sly, can you take the first watch?"

Sly nodded and Rex slapped his shoulder, towering over his small friend. Then Rex turned to me and gestured toward Pell, asleep under the blanket. "It's going to be a chilly night. We should huddle up to help keep her warm."

An image flashed through my mind of us lying under the blanket, side by side. My heart jumped, catching me by surprise, before I realized we'd be keeping Pell warm by lying on either side of her.

"What?" he asked, a half smile on his face as he tried to read my expression.

"Nothing," I said.

We lay down on either side of Pell and pulled the foil blanket over us.

Rex looked at me over Pell's head and smiled.

Even with Pell between us, there was something intimate about lying under the blanket with Rex. I wondered if maybe Pell was right, and I liked him in a way I hadn't realized. Then I thought of Del. And his kiss. And suddenly it seemed like I was torn between a half dog and a half salamander. I blushed in the darkness, ashamed of myself for thinking of them that way. I still didn't know what had become of Del, but I was getting to know Rex pretty damn well. He wasn't half anything, or point-zero-five, or whatever. He was just Rex. They were just people. Although, to be honest, they weren't exactly normal people.

So why can't you find a normal boy? I asked myself. Then it occurred to me that if Andrew was a normal boy, maybe normal wasn't what I wanted after all.

Rex's breathing fell into a steady rhythm, a counterpoint to Pell's. Then so did mine, and I slipped into a fitful sleep, puzzled that I was suddenly trying to find a boy at all.

FIFTY-SEVEN

When Rex woke me for my turn on watch, the sky was a slate blue.

"It's almost light out," I said, whispering so as not to awaken the others. Sly was asleep next to Pell, where Rex had been earlier. "You should have woken me earlier," I said, stretching out my limbs. "You're going to be exhausted."

Rex smiled. "I'll be okay. I slept earlier."

With that he crawled under the portion of foil blanket I had just vacated. It barely covered half of him.

I shook my head and walked a tight circle around the camp, more to get my blood moving than to monitor the perimeter. That boulder was less than fifteen yards from the camp. When I climbed up onto it, I could clearly see the camp and the area around it.

In the distance a Lev train zipped across the horizon like a shooting star. As the sky slowly lightened, hilltops rose out of the thick fog, like sea serpents undulating across the ocean.

I smiled, thinking Del would like that, wishing he could see it, wondering if maybe he was on one of those hilltops. I tried to picture him again, to conjure him safe and warm and comfortable, but once more I had a hard time bringing him into focus.

So instead I thought of home, and the trouble waiting for me there. With the clarity of early morning, I was more certain than ever that I was doing the right thing. But I also knew I was going to pay a price for it.

I tried to think about something else—anything else—something positive and good, and just as the sun appeared, a sliver of red on the horizon, I heard a twig breaking behind me and I turned to see Rex approaching. He smiled and climbed effortlessly up onto the rock next to me.

"Is this okay?" he said, looking out at the sunrise, the landscape below.

"Of course," I said. "But you should be sleeping."

"I'd rather be here."

I looked at him, and he smiled again. "Any sign of our friends from Pitman?"

I smiled back. "Nothing."

He nodded. "Good." Then his expression turned serious. "They could still be out there, though. We need to stay alert." He looked over at me. "You cold?"

"A little."

He moved a couple of inches closer, and leaned back on his hands, his arm behind me but not around me. Almost touching me, but not quite. I eased back, just enough so that I was barely leaning against his upper arm. It would have felt like a tree trunk if not for the warmth coming off it.

We sat there for several minutes, silently enjoying the view and each other's presence. The sun grew into a fiery red ball, still muted by the haze on the horizon.

"I was worried about you," he said without looking at me. "Down there last night."

"I was okay," I said softly.

"I know. You took care of yourself. That's good."

"I heard you were watching me through the binoculars."

He grunted. "I was worried and scared."

A few more minutes passed. The sun had burned through enough of the mist that it now illuminated the rest, a golden glow that filled the space between the pink-and-orange sky above and the blues, greens, and purples of the hills below.

"Can I ask you a question?" I said. I could feel him stiffen.

"Okay."

"Why did you do it? Why did you decide to become a chimera?"

He laughed and looked away, maybe slightly embarrassed. "It's not the easiest thing to explain. For me, it was more about becoming a part *of* something, instead of apart *from* something, you know? I never meant to leave humanity, and I don't think I did—never mind what Wells and the H4Hers say. To me, being a chimera is about more fully joining the rest of the world, not about being any less of a human. And it's about being able to choose who and what you want to be."

He shifted slightly and I settled in closer. "I do think that humankind has lost some of its best self, though," he said. "Some of its humanity, in the way it's become so separate from the natural world or the animal world, so destructive of it. For a lot of us, this is partly a movement to reclaim that, to embrace the natural world by becoming part of it."

"Why did you choose a dog?"

"That's a long story. That involves a different lifetime." He looked at me intently. "Some other time, okay?"

I nodded, but I wasn't done. "Do you ever regret it?"

"Hardly ever." He took a breath, and I could feel him holding it in. "Do you think I'm . . . repulsive?" he asked.

I whipped my head around to face him, but his eyes were straight ahead, not looking at me. I was going to say *of course not* or *don't be ridiculous*, just to be polite, to be nice. But it was not a ridiculous question. When I'd first met him, I'd definitely been struck by how different he looked. Now I barely noticed it. His frame was unusually large, true. But it was lithe and strong. His face was still striking, for sure—not entirely human. But it was also noble. Dignified. Handsome, even. And when I really thought about it, the most arresting thing about him was his kindness. His intelligence. His *humanity*.

"No," I said, my voice suddenly hoarse. "Not at all."

Now he turned to look at me. "I like you," he said.

"I like you, too," I said.

His lips parted slightly and I pictured myself kissing them. I might have been moving closer to do just that when a crashing sound nearby made us both jump.

Sly emerged from the bushes, rubbing his eyes with one hand and scratching his crotch with the other. He stumbled past us, behind another bush, and let out a groan as he relieved himself.

I moved away from Rex, just a couple inches, and he shook his head and laughed.

When Sly appeared again, he was slightly more awake. "Oh, you're up," he said, yawning as he approached. "What are you guys looking at?"

I looked out at the pastel pink clouds in the orange sky, the soft blue-green of the mist-shrouded hills, and the flecks of gold the sun cast over everything. It was beautiful.

But before I could point that out, Rex said, "Now that the sun's up, I'm looking at that creek."

Below us in the morning light was a meandering creek, much like the one we'd crossed the night before. But this one doubled back on itself in a distinct horseshoe curve, before winding toward a red covered bridge a couple miles away. Rex took out Ryan's map and held it up. The curve of the creek below clearly matched the horseshoe curve next to the star on the map.

"That's where we're headed," he said, pointing at the hill rising up on the other side of the creek. "That's where we'll find Haven."

FIFTY-EIGHT

We woke Pell, and after a quick breakfast of bread, we packed up what little stuff we had. Pell looked rough, but so did the rest of us. Her leg was sore, and she had a noticeable limp, but there was no sign of fever or infection.

Before we set off down the hill, Rex pointed to the boulder where we'd been sitting. "This outcrop has a good view of the surroundings, and it's big enough that it should be visible and easy to find, even from a distance. Those searchers could still be looking for us. If anything bad happens or we get separated, meet back here, okay?"

As we descended into the valley, still filled with shadows and mist, I imagined all sorts of dangers lurking in it. But as the sun rose over the next hill, its rays inched down to meet us, and by the time we reached the bottom, the fog had burned away.

I tried to let the sunlight cheer me. Still, with each step closer to Haven, I felt increasingly anxious about finding Del. Even though Ryan said he was okay, part of me was prepared for the worst. And even if Del *was* at a safe place beyond the next hill, the absolute best-case scenario was that he was happily adjusting to the "new him." The Del I knew was gone.

As I stepped over rocks and roots, I thought about what had happened over the last few days. The last few months. Maybe even the last year. I considered the possibility that the Del I knew had been gone for some time. The Del I used to know wouldn't have been so eager to skip school. He wouldn't have assaulted that cop. He wouldn't have gone off and gotten a tattoo without telling me, much less gotten spliced. He had changed already.

Things between us had changed, too, even before we kissed.

Maybe we'd been drifting farther apart, and I just hadn't realized it. I guess I was probably different, too.

Lost in thought, I'd been lagging behind the others. I rushed to catch up.

"Yeah, it's a stupid law," Sly was saying. "But what do you expect? The idiots who wrote it didn't think any of it through. But the sleaze-bag politicians who latched on and supported it because it was popular, now *they've* thought it through."

"What are you talking about?" I asked.

"Voting," he said. "And how chimeras don't do it, even the ones who are old enough. That's why the politicians don't care about them. The sad fact is that most of the A-holes supporting the Genetic Heritage Act know it's riddled with gaps and contradictions, and they probably don't care about chimeras one way or another. But the H4Hers, they all vote. And Wells tells them who to vote for. That's why the politicians are lining up to make him happy. If chimeras voted, they'd care what we thought, too, but we don't vote, so they don't care."

As he kicked a rock off into the woods, he noticed me staring at him. "What?" he said defensively. "I read the news."

"Well, the chimeras will vote now for sure, right?" Pell said. "I mean, all the ones I know are mad as hell."

Sly tilted his head at her, then looked away and laughed, shaking his head.

"What?" she demanded defensively.

"It's a little late for that," he said bitterly. "The law says we're legally not 'persons.' Only people can vote."

We walked in silence for a few minutes, each of us reflecting on how messed up it all was.

"So what about Chimerica?" Pell asked after a minute. "What do you think of that?"

Sly scratched his chin, thinking. "A year ago I'd have said it was BS. But now I believe."

"Why?" Rex asked, like he didn't believe in it but he wanted to, badly.

"You mean apart from the fact that Ryan said they were going there?" Sly shrugged. "Things are getting bad for chimeras around here. And not just the punks like us. It's dicey for the chimeras out there who are doing okay for themselves. They're smart—I'm sure some of them saw this coming and made sure there was a safe place somewhere for them and their money. And their friends." He shrugged. "Seems like the closer the H4Hers got to passing that damn law, the more chimeras started disappearing. I know there's poachers—Ryan said that's who got them, right? But someone rescued them, too, and they're taking them to Chimerica."

"Where do you think it is?" Pell asked.

"North," Sly said, with great certainty. "South and west are even more H4H than around here. Maybe somewhere like New York State, where there's lots of empty land, and not so many H4Hers."

"They've got enough. They might be passing the same law."

"Maybe Canada, then."

Rex laughed. "Canada practically *is* Chimerica—no H4H or stupid laws. They treat chimeras okay up there."

"They treat *Canadian* chimeras okay up there," Sly corrected him. "Lots of countries treat chimeras okay, but they don't allow new ones in."

"We could sneak in," Rex replied.

"Yeah, but where would we stay?" Sly replied.

"Chimerica?" Pell said.

"Exactly."

She wrapped her arms around herself and shivered. "I hope it's not in Canada—so cold up there."

Sly smiled sagely. "Not as cold as it used to be."

We were just coming over a slight rise when we saw a fence cutting through the woods ahead of us. It was eight feet tall, chain-link with razor wire coiled on top and barbs embedded everywhere else. From top to bottom, every four inches, a jagged twist of metal jutted out. It looked serious and brutal, and it filled me with apprehension.

"Jesus," Pell said, touching one of the barbs, then snatching her hand away.

"Not very welcoming," Rex said quietly.

The fence stretched off in either direction, as far as the eye could see. We all looked back the way we had come, feeling suddenly trapped between the searchers, if they were still coming, and this fence, which could be our destination or an obstacle to it. Maybe it was part of Haven and there to protect the chimeras. Or, maybe it was what it looked like: something very, very bad.

Rex looked left and right. "Which way?"

Pell and Sly shrugged.

I pointed south, to our right, farther away from Pitman. "All things equal, might as well move away from the angry mob."

We pushed through the brush and after ten minutes came to a spot where the fence was closely flanked by two trees, a tall evergreen on our side, and a maple on the far side. Each trunk was barely six feet from the fence, their thick branches intertwined in the air just a few feet above the razor wire.

Just beyond them, twenty yards inside the fence, we saw a girl, a chimera, with striking markings, like a panda. We stopped without a word and tried to duck behind the evergreen tree. Rex was too big to hide, so I whispered in his ear, "Say hi," and I pushed him back out.

The girl seemed oblivious until Rex said, "Hello?"

She froze and then turned to stare at him.

"Sorry," he said, trying to be heard without being loud. "I'm looking for some friends of mine. Chimeras. One is named Ruth, and the other is Del."

She stared at him for a moment, then she turned and disappeared into the woods.

Sly stepped out and slapped Rex on the back. "Well, that went well."

Rex frowned. "I guess they'll be expecting us."

"She was a chimera," Pell said hopefully. "She seemed more scared of what's out here than anything in there."

She had a point, and it made us less apprehensive as we resumed walking.

The fence curved away from us, and as we followed it, the monotony lulled us into a bored complacency.

It was quite a shock when a voice on the other side of the fence called out, "Jimi?"

It was even more of a shock when I turned and saw that the voice belonged to Del.

FIFTY-NINE

D el!" I screamed, running to the fence, and stopping just short of impaling myself on a hundred little spikes. "Oh, my God! Del! You're alive!"

"Of course I'm alive!" he said, smiling wide as he came up to the other side.

He was more than alive. He was bursting with vitality.

When he spotted the others, his smile became a grin. "Sly! Pell! And Rex. This is so great!"

The others hurried up behind me.

"Is Ruth here?" Pell asked, coming as close to the fence as she dared.

Del nodded. "Absolutely."

"And she's okay?"

"She's great."

Pell almost collapsed with relief, tears rolling down her cheeks. Sly put an arm around her, supporting her. "Damn, Del," he said. "Somebody fixed you up good."

Sly was right. I'd been so shocked, so happy to see him, I hadn't taken it all in at first, but he looked better than he ever had. He was taller, and even through his shirt, I could see that his chest and his arms were broad and sculpted. His face had changed as well. The deep brow and the green tinge from the salamander splice were still there, but his other features had now grown, matured. There was a feline quality to them. He had a sheen of fur, and his cheeks, throat, and forehead were streaked with tiger stripes.

Del threw back his head and laughed, a strange, hearty laugh, revealing an impressive set of sharp teeth. "Yeah," he said, his eyes twinkling. "They fixed me up good, all right. Come on. The gate's up here," he said, walking along the fence in the direction we had been headed. He looked back over his shoulder, his eyes scanning the woods. "So, I guess Ryan told you where to find us. How's he doing?" No one said anything and Del just kept talking. "Did he talk to his mom? Did he say when he was coming back?" Del shook his head. "I told him, he might not get another chance back in here, especially if he left once, but he insisted on going." Finally, he noticed our silence and looked over at us. "What is it? Is he okay?"

"Ryan was shot," I said softly.

"*What?* What happened?"

We continued on as I told him what we knew. As I spoke, Del's face darkened and he clenched his fists.

"I bet it was those savages from Pitman," he said, with a sudden rage that made me almost glad there was a fence between us. "I'd like to kill them all!"

Rex and I exchanged a look. Del picked up on it. "What?" he demanded.

He was already so angry I didn't want to add to it. "Nothing," I said, hoping Rex wouldn't mention what had happened there.

"Poor Ryan," Del said. "I hope he's okay."

"Also, the governor signed the Genetic Heritage Act," Sly told him. "I don't know if you heard."

Del nodded. "Yeah, I heard. Idiots. Looks like this place will be getting a lot busier."

"What is this place, anyway?" Rex asked. "It's got a hell of a fence."

Del laughed again, not quite as loud, but still with a decidedly strange, un-Del-like quality to it. "This is Haven," he said. "It's a refuge for chimeras like us. This fence helps protect us from evil, like those H4H crazies."

I was trying to listen to his words, but waves of emotion were washing over me, obscuring them, obscuring everything else. For days I had been trying to prepare myself for Del being dead or damaged, had barely allowed myself to hope that he'd be alive and well.

But this? He was better than well, brimming with vigor and energy, a happiness I'd never seen in him before. I wasn't ready for that. Despite my efforts, my eyes filled with tears.

"Del, what happened to you?" I said, my voice cracking. "I thought you were dead."

He turned and tried to come closer to me, his fingers hooking through the fence despite the barbs. "I'm okay, Jimi," he said softly. "Everything's okay."

I closed my fingers over his, holding his hands through the fence. There were claws under his fingernails. I could feel them retracting under my hands.

No, everything was definitely not okay. "You've been gone four days," I said, as anger crowded out my other emotions. "I've been looking for you for four days."

"And I'm okay," he repeated with a smile that made me even angrier. He pulled his hands away.

"Yeah, well I'm not!" I said, my voice rising. I could feel the fence's barbs cutting into my hands as I clenched my fingers. "I've been through riots, I've been threatened, I've trudged for miles through the woods, the whole time getting myself into deeper and deeper trouble, all to find you. I've been scared out of my mind, Del! Scared for myself, but mostly for *you*! Why didn't you tell me you were okay? Why didn't you just let me know?"

The others hung back a step, listening but giving us space.

"I couldn't," he said softly.

"Why not?"

"Come on. The gate's not much farther. We can talk inside."

"No, tell me now," I said. "I need to know what happened *now*."

He nodded and resumed walking. "I don't remember a lot of it," he said, absentmindedly running one of his claws between the rows of barbs on the fence. It made a harsh *click, click, click, click.*

I let go of the fence and followed him, the others falling in behind me.

"I vaguely remember the house where I got the splice, and you and Rex taking me to the fixer. Thanks for that." He looked over his shoulder at Rex. "Both of you. I know it didn't work out how you planned, but you saved my life. Anyway, I remember being in this coffin thing, then I woke up in the back of a big-box truck. I was still in bad shape." He laughed. "The others said they thought I was dead."

"What others?" I asked.

"The other chimeras in the truck," he said. "Some were at the fixer when I was. Some got picked up in other places."

"Picked up by the police?"

He looked grim. "Some of them, yeah. Go figure, right? Apparently, some of the police were working with the poachers."

"So the police got you at Guzman's? How? We were watching the whole time."

"We ducked down," Rex said quietly. "Remember? When the headlights were on us. They must have brought him out then."

I started to protest—the police officer I'd spoken to on the phone that night had said no one came in. But of course they hadn't come in, I realized. They hadn't been arrested. They'd been *abducted*. "Who are these poachers?" I asked. "What did they want with you?"

"I don't know. I never actually saw them. I woke up in the back of this old truck. Then the team from Haven showed up with guns and bolt-cutters and saved us. They busted us out and brought in a bus to take us all out of there. They got us out fast. I don't even want to think about what might have happened if they hadn't shown up. I was still pretty far out of it when we were driving out, but I remember looking up and seeing a fire burning in the sky."

"Pitman?" I said. "The poachers had taken you to Pitman?"

He nodded. "You can see that fire from on top of the hill here. But Mr. Jasper won't say that's where we were when his people found us. He doesn't want us seeking revenge, or drawing those bastards from Pitman back here."

"Who's Mr. Jasper?" Rex asked, walking closer now.

The gate was up ahead, flanked on either side by a cluster of security equipment. A dirt road ran up to it from the woods and kept going inside.

"He's the guy who runs this place. He saved my life. By the time they got us here, it was too late for me to see a fixer, so he brought in a genie, an actual medical doctor. They stacked an emergency splice on me."

"Another splice?" I said, trying to keep the dismay out of my voice.

He nodded. "Yeah, they said it would, like, overwrite the earlier splice and fix any errors. They used some kind of accelerant, but they gave me sedatives and painkillers, so it was a breeze compared to the first one."

"It's kickass," Sly said. "What is it?"

Del held his arms out in front of himself, admiring the stripes and muscles that covered them. Then he looked over with a big grin. "Bengal tiger."

Pell whooped.

"Damn!" Sly laughed. "That's awesome!"

"They're extinct," I said.

Rex nodded. "Must have cost a fortune."

"I know, right?" Del laughed. "Jasper's the best."

When we reached the gate, Del pressed a button on the security console. He looked up into the camera and said, "Tamil. With three chimeras." He looked at me. "And one guest."

SIXTY

The gate swung open and as soon as we walked through it, Del wrapped me in a big hug. Up close, the changes were even more striking. He towered over me, and his arms and chest were thick and solid—not as big as Rex's, but close. I pulled back, looking up at him and his crazy tiger stripes.

He caught me staring. "Like I told you, I'm fine," he said with a nonchalant grin.

I punched him in the arm. Hard. "You *told* me five minutes ago. You still haven't answered my question. How come you didn't tell me *before*? Let me know somehow?"

He didn't flinch, didn't squirm, didn't react in any way other than to put his hands on my shoulders and say, "I'm sorry. Like I said, I couldn't. This place is a secret. I couldn't exactly send you a mail drone." Then he turned to the others and said, "Come on, let me show you around."

As we walked along the dirt road, the brush seemed greener, the trees healthier. "Did you call yourself 'Tamil'?" I asked. "What's that about?"

He turned and looked at me, a bit condescendingly. "New me, new name. All chimeras take a new name. I didn't get a chance to choose one after my first splice."

Pell nodded, her head bobbing on her neck. Rex looked away.

Del—or Tamil—studied my face and shrugged. "It's what we do," he said simply.

"It's really lush here," Rex remarked, looking around. "Compared to the surrounding countryside, I mean."

Del nodded. "Jasper is detoxifying the land. Those idiots in Pitman, and people like them, like my dad, they were so desperate to get the last bits of carbon out of the ground, they ruined the land doing it."

"They're still doing it," I said.

"I know," he said. "Pitman has an illegal coal well, right in town. Even my dad admitted they weren't safe, and he said Pitman's was one of the worst—no backflow preventers, no basic safety precautions, nothing. I can't believe the government hasn't shut it down. I guess they don't care, out in the middle of nowhere. Too busy harassing chimeras." He turned and looked at me. "You know my dad worked on that thing when I was a kid, right?"

"In Pitman?" Even as I said it, though, I realized that was why the town had sounded familiar.

He nodded. "Remember he used to drag me to all these messed-up little towns and the stupid local kids would tease me all day? Well, that's one of them. I remember at night, I'd lie in bed and look out at those flares through my window—all those different towns, but each of them had a flare; that was the one familiar thing. Then one time Stan pulled me aside, in some horrible town with an especially half-assed rig—might have even been Pitman—and he tells me if I ever see one of those flares go out, I need to run like hell, because it'd take about a minute to build enough pressure to blow up the whole rig, five minutes to blow up the whole town."

"Are you serious?" Sly said.

Del nodded with a laugh, but his eyes showed a glimpse of fear at the memory.

"Sometimes protesters would try to climb the towers, cap the thing, and make it blow. Stan would get so pissed. I saw it once, this young guy scrambling up the side of the rig, all these old farts huffing after him, terrified he was going to blow the rig." He looked far off for a moment. "I was rooting for him, too, that kid."

Rex caught my eye. His face was blank but somehow his eyes made it plain he wondered if Del was a little bit crazy.

"Anyway," Del continued. "That thing is like a time bomb waiting to go off, even apart from the slow-motion death it's leaching into the soil. You tell me what kind of people put something like that in the middle of their town." He shook his head. "Mean, horrible people, in a miserable little town."

They weren't all bad in Pitman, but they had a lot of hate, too, with all their rabid H4Hers. A lot of people were just scared of the unknown, the unfamiliar, but man, anyone who didn't like different sure wouldn't have liked Del.

"You can smell it all the way up here sometimes," he was saying. "The sulfur and ammonia. You see what they've done to the area; you'd think they'd learn." He shook his head. "Anyway, Jasper has restored thousands of acres." We came over a slight rise and there, spread out in front of us, were several acres of green farm fields, being tended by a handful of people. They seemed to be chimeras. "We grow most of our own food here." He pointed to a wind and solar array just visible beyond the trees. "And our power."

Pell looked around, wide-eyed. "It's perfect, just like—"

The bushes behind us rustled, and a high-pitched squeal rang out, instantly doubling in volume and suddenly in stereo as Pell's face split into a huge smile. I turned and saw Ruth running toward her, arms outstretched, screaming. The two of them collided and their arms wrapped around each other. Laughing and crying, they danced in a circle.

Just as it started to get awkward, Ruth let go of Pell and hugged Rex, then Sly, and then me, too.

"What happened to you?" Pell asked, stroking Ruth's feathers. "God, I was so worried."

"It was scary," Ruth said. "I was walking along outside, then suddenly I wasn't. They drugged me somehow, a dart maybe, although I never found a mark. I woke up with a hood over my head, in the back of this big truck. I never saw their faces. There must have been thirty of us in there, all chimeras. They kept us in there for hours and hours. Then we were parked on the side of the road, and these guys with guns came and rescued us, took us here. It was terrifying, pitch-black in that truck. I was in there a few hours before I realized Ryan was with me." She paused and looked around. "So, Ryan didn't come back with you? Did he find his mom? He said he might not come back right away, that he needed to make things right with her."

"They shot him," Del snapped. "Those bastards from Pitman."

"No!" She put her hand over her mouth.

"We don't know where it happened," Rex said.

Del waved him off. "If he got shot anywhere out here, it was someone from Pitman. There's no one else around."

"How is he?" Ruth asked.

"He's alive," Pell said quietly, putting a hand on her shoulder. "But it's bad."

"I was afraid something would happen to him," Ruth said with a sob. "I told him it was dangerous, but he said he needed to see his mom before he left. I was so desperate to get word to you, I thought, if he was going anyway . . . We knew it was against the rules. We're not supposed to leave once we're here, or tell anyone where we are."

I looked at Del, confused.

"I told you before. Jasper doesn't want to risk H4H finding out where we are. He doesn't want them coming after us."

"I helped him draw a map," Ruth said. "So he could get to the Levline, and to help you find us." She started crying.

Rex took out the map and held it up.

Ruth nodded, eyes wide when she saw the bloody fingerprints.

Rex squeezed her shoulder. "He'll be okay."

"Put that away," Del snapped. "And don't let anyone see it or know about it."

Rex cocked an eyebrow as he tucked the map back into his pocket.

"Sorry," Del said, lightening up. "It's just . . . they have to take the secrecy thing seriously here. There's so many crazies out there."

"Okay," Rex rumbled, acknowledging it if not accepting it.

He looked at me as Del turned to continue walking. I shrugged, then followed along.

Pell put her hand on Ruth's cheek, smiling. "It's so good to see you, Ruthie."

━━ ━━ ━━

The dirt road curved briefly through more woods and up a small hill to a wide lawn in front of a massive wooden lodge. It was made of logs and had several sections, each with a peaked roof. Giant windows, decks, balconies, and an immense porch all overlooked the lawn and surrounding woods. Two chimeras were playing Frisbee on the grass.

Sly whistled at the sight of it. "Nice place."

"Pretty impressive," I said.

Del laughed. "I know, right?"

I paused. "So, how long are you planning to stay here?"

Rex and Sly and Pell stopped to hear his answer. Ruth looked down and bit her lip.

"Not long," Del said with a grin, looking at the others. "Soon, we're going to Chimerica."

SIXTY-ONE

Chimerica?" I repeated. "Really?" Despite what Ryan had said, and Sly's theories, I still wasn't buying its existence. I guess I had assumed that when we got here, we'd find out that Ryan had been hallucinating from blood loss or something.

"There's no such thing," Rex said quietly, without much conviction.

But when Pell looked at Ruth, Ruth nodded in confirmation.

Del, still smiling, nodded too. "Yeah, there is. Haven's a temporary refuge. Soon, we're all going to Chimerica."

"Where is it?" I asked.

"That's a bigger secret than this place is."

Something caught his eye and he turned and waved at the house. An older man in a suit was standing at the top of the wide steps, waving at Del.

"I'll tell you more later. That's Jasper," he said. "You're going to love him."

As we approached the lodge, I noticed a copter port in the back, with two quadcopters parked on the platform. A handful of black off-road sedans were parked below it. In the rear was another structure, bigger than the lodge, but modern and simple.

"Those are the dorms," Del said, pointing at it. "There's not enough room for everyone in the lodge, so most of the chimeras are in the dorms. I'm in the lodge, which is great, but the dorms are still pretty cool."

"I see you have company, Tamil," Jasper said. He was in his mid-sixties, and he had a kindly face, like someone's grandfather, but something about him creeped me out. He had a WellPlant in his brow, like lots of rich people, but his eyes were flat, like painted disks, not much more expressive than the WellPlant above them.

Del smiled back at him. "Mr. Jasper, I'd like you to meet my friends—Sly, Pell, and Rex. And this is Jimi."

"Welcome to Haven," he said, his smile so broad it made my cheeks ache. He stared at Rex for a moment. "My, you're a big one, aren't you? How did you all find us?"

Del cleared his throat. "Um . . . Ryan told them."

Jasper's smile faltered. "Ryan, eh?" He frowned. "Did he tell anyone else?"

"No," I said. "I don't think so."

He nodded, thinking. "Well, I am going to have to talk to him. We have rules for a reason. Is he back?"

I shook my head.

"He's been shot," Rex said.

"Good lord," Jasper said. "Is he all right?"

"He's alive," Rex told him. "But it's serious."

"It was those people from Pitman, I know it," Del said, as if the bitterness in his voice was the only thing holding back the rage.

Jasper turned to Rex. "Is this true?"

"We don't know."

"It had to be," Del snapped.

Jasper held up his hands and made a soft shushing sound. "You don't know that, Tamil. These days it could have been anyone, maybe someone from Carston. It could have been a hunting accident."

Del let out a harsh laugh. "There's no one hunting these hills. There's nothing left to hunt."

"Enough," Jasper said sharply. "It doesn't matter, because we're not going to do anything about it. As I've told you before, we can't be leading trouble to our doorstep. I won't allow our residents to be put in danger like that."

Del looked away and nodded begrudgingly.

Jasper turned to us, his smile back in place. "You look like you've had quite a trip. I bet you'd like to freshen up, maybe get something to eat. How does that sound?"

Food and a shower sounded pretty good. But I had serious doubts about this place. It seemed great, maybe too good to be true. I don't know what I'd expected, but this was not it.

As Del led us into the lodge, I kept thinking about that fence, how we weren't just protected, we were trapped. Jasper was weirding me out, too, with the whole secrecy thing and the rules. And his eyes.

I should have been overjoyed that Del was alive and well, and I was. But I was also angrier than ever. Not only had he been happy to leave me out there thinking the worst, he was also planning on leaving forever. Leaving me to deal with the fallout with my mom and his dad. Leaving me to deal with the police. Leaving *me*. I thought about the mess I'd made of my life in trying to find him. He hadn't just thrown away his own future, he was wrecking mine.

And he'd been planning on doing it all without even saying goodbye.

SIXTY-TWO

The dining room had a big wooden table and a chandelier. It was obvious the place had been some kind of resort at one point, and it looked like someone had sunk a lot of money into restoring it. Pell and Sly seemed wowed by it all. To me it felt like the whole place was trying too hard. And the way Rex met my eyes over the table, I think he felt the same way.

They gave us grilled cheese sandwiches and tomato soup. Del talked the whole time we ate, mostly about how great Haven was and how great Jasper was. Maybe it was my imagination, but it seemed to be about how great Del was, too, since he was now a part of it.

He was describing how the table had been restored from some mansion a hundred miles away, how a helicopter had brought it in.

"And what's the point of that?" I asked.

"What do you mean?"

"Seems like a lot of trouble and expense. If what he's really trying to do is save chimeras, why is Jasper spending so much money making the place so grand? It's a bit much, don't you think?"

He looked like I'd slapped him. "No, I don't. I think it's awesome. Why shouldn't it be nice?"

"Well, you're not going to be here long anyway, right?" I could feel myself getting snippy. "Aren't you going to Chimerica?"

"Yeah, so what?"

"I don't know. It's all just weird, that's all. The big fence and the secrets and all that."

"The fence protects us," he said indignantly. "You saw what happened to Ryan."

I could feel the others looking at us, the scene getting tense.

"So, when are we going?" Pell said. "When are we going to

Chimerica?" I think she wanted to know, but she also wanted to change the subject, calm things down.

Del sat back and gave her a knowing smile. "Soon," he said.

I went back to my sandwich.

When we were done, Ruth took Pell to the infirmary and Del brought the rest of us to our rooms. Sly was in a room next to Ruth and Pell's, right off the lobby. Rex's room was at the end of the hall.

Rex paused in the doorway, glancing at Del, then looking back at me, before he went in and closed the door.

Then it was just Del and me.

We stood there for an awkward moment. Then he said, "Your room is this way."

We walked around the bend and down the next hallway. He was quiet, the quietest he'd been since we got there.

"I appreciate you trying to help me, Jimi. And I would have let you know somehow. Eventually." He stopped, opening the door to a bedroom.

I nodded, not sure I believed him. "I haven't even told you half of what I've been through. The cops picked me up when you ran off that day. My mom freaked out, so now I'm living at Trudy's."

He grimaced. "Crazy Aunt Trudy?"

"She's okay. But I've barely been there because I've been sneaking out searching for you." Bits and pieces of all I'd been through the past few days ran through my mind, including my run-ins with Stan. I wanted to tell Del about it, but I knew it would only hurt him. Tears started spilling down my face, and I found I couldn't speak. I was still so angry at him, but then he came over and put his arms around me, and for one moment, that was all I wanted.

He stroked my hair and when my tears subsided, he finally said, "I'm sorry."

I pushed him away. "You should be sorry. My life has turned to crap. And while I've been out of my mind worrying, you've been . . . here."

He put his hands on my shoulders. "Jimi, I'm sorry," he said. "I never meant to hurt you, you know that, right?"

I nodded, too tired and too upset to explain to him how little difference there was between intending to hurt someone and letting them get hurt because you didn't bother to think about them.

"Look, I have to go. There's a big banquet tomorrow for the people who are paying for this place, and Jasper asked me to help with the preparations. Why don't you get some rest and wash up, and I'll come get you when we're done?"

I nodded again, almost in a daze. I had come so far and worked so hard to find him; it seemed bizarre to be just going our separate ways because he had a meeting about a party. But it wasn't like Del had been busting his butt trying to find me. I looked up, expecting him to say more, realizing he wasn't going to. I decided that him getting out of my sight wouldn't be the worst thing that could happen just then. I went inside and turned to look back at him.

"I'll see you soon, okay?" He said it with an oblivious smile.

I closed the door, wondering what the hell I was doing there, if I had misunderstood everything about the world. Wondering if *I* was the crazy one.

I'd have to think about that.

The room was small but nice. The bed beckoned, but I was too dirty to get in it. First, I took a bath.

I'd always been more of a shower person, but this was exquisite. I washed my gross hair and scrubbed my mud-caked arms and legs, then drained the tub and refilled it with clean, hot water, just to soak in. In no time, I drifted into a shallow sleep filled with vague dreams.

Someone I knew was holding me. His hands were large and comforting. I couldn't tell if it was Del or Rex, or some combination of the two of them. The atmosphere was different. Then it dawned on me that I was different, too, and I realized with a jolt that I was a chimera. In my dream, I looked down at my body, but before any details could register, I awoke with a start, my face flushed and my skin tingling.

The water was lukewarm and someone was knocking at the door.

"Just a second," I called. I stumbled out of the tub and raced to the mirror, checking to make sure I was all me, even as the reality of the dream faded away. I dried off with a big bath towel, then wrapped myself in it. There was no peephole in the door. "Who is it?" I asked, my hand on the knob.

"Tamil," came the reply. Then, lower, "It's Del."

I pulled the towel tight and opened the door.

His eyes swept over me, a quick flicker that I almost didn't notice. His once-brown irises were now flecked with gold, making the pupils seem somehow blacker than before.

"Hey," he said quietly.

"Hey," I said back.

"Jasper wants to talk to you," he said. "When you're ready, of course."

"What does he want?" I felt like I was being called into the principal's office, only it was a secret school that was surrounded by razor wire.

"It's nothing, I'm sure. He probably just wants to make sure you're doing okay."

Jasper was creepy, and I dreaded the thought of meeting with him, but part of me liked the idea of getting a closer look. "Okay," I said. "I'll be out in a minute."

SIXTY-THREE

My clothes felt even dirtier as I put them back onto my clean body. I eyed the bed longingly, but only for a second. Then I opened the door.

Del was waiting in the hallway. "It's this way," he said, leading me down a side hallway with burgundy carpet, deep green walls, and dark wood doors.

"How long have you actually been here?" I asked. For someone who had been an outcast at school, he sure seemed to be fitting in.

"Just a couple days, really, and I was out of it the first day. But in a way, it feels like I was born here."

I stared at the side of his head, wondering if he could even hear himself, but he seemed oblivious. We doubled back through the lobby and down a set of stairs to another hallway.

There were a hundred questions I wanted to ask, but before I got past that first one, Del stopped in front of a heavy wooden door and knocked.

A voice on the other side said, "Come in," and Del opened the door for me.

Jasper was sitting behind a large desk, smiling broadly behind steepled fingers. The office was huge but not as luxurious as I expected. The desk was big. It had an old-fashioned corded phone, and the rest of it was covered with papers, as if he was using every square inch.

He gestured to a chair next to the desk. "Have a seat, Ms. Corcoran." Then he looked up at Del. "Thanks, Tamil."

Del backed out the door, flashing me a small, reassuring look.

"So, what do you think of Haven so far?" Jasper asked with a smile that did not extend to his eyes. I found myself looking into his

WellPlant instead, as if I might have better luck trying to read something from it.

"Seems great," I said.

He nodded, waiting, like he expected more, like it was a test and I hadn't passed it yet. But I didn't feel like giving him any more than that. I nodded back at him until he continued.

"It is," he said. "It's a wonderful place. There's a lot of bad out there in the world. It's gotten quite dangerous." He looked at me. "Especially for young people. And chimeras, of course."

From what I'd heard about the old days, kids weren't much safer then. But he had a point about the chimeras, so I nodded again.

He leaned forward, lowering his voice. "I don't know what's going to happen with the Genetic Heritage Act. It might be overturned; it might spread to other states. It might become federal law, or even part of the Constitution, like some people want. But right now, it is state law." He shook his head. "Things have always been hard on chimera kids. But this is a whole new level." He punctuated that last sentence by firmly patting the desk. "And that means it's a dangerous world for those who try to protect them, too. There are people who don't approve, who'd like to stop us. That's why it's so important that our location remains a secret. Do you understand?"

I nodded.

"Those people in Pitman have no idea what we're doing here. We need to keep it that way." He shook his head. "Ryan knew he wasn't supposed to go back. I told him so myself. 'If you want to help your friends,' I said, 'we can go and get them. Bring them to safety.' But he snuck off on his own. And look what happened to him." He leaned back in his chair, studying me. "You put us in an awkward spot, Ms. Corcoran."

"How's that?"

"Haven is for chimeras. We have a hard enough time taking care of them. We have strict rules that only chimeras can stay here."

"Okay." I had no intention of staying there.

"But we also have rules against folks leaving. For security purposes. Surely you understand how important it is that our location remains a secret."

I nodded, my mouth suddenly dry. He was starting to freak me out. "Your secret is safe with me."

He leaned forward, his eyes somehow both intense and blank. "I hope it is." He stared at me like that for a moment, then leaned back again. "We've worked too hard, invested too much. We have too many chimeras to save to risk losing that."

"Well, you don't have to worry about me." I wondered what was happening here, what he was getting at. I was also wondering if the door behind me was locked, if I could get through it before Jasper could come around that desk to stop me. I found myself wondering if Del would help me once I did.

I took a deep breath to calm myself. I was getting ahead of myself. I wasn't a prisoner or anything, not yet.

"How old are you, Ms. Corcoran?" Jasper asked, bringing me back.

I hesitated, and he said, "You are sixteen. You are a minor. That means you are here illegally, without a guardian. Many of our chimera guests are, too, but no one is looking for them. Frankly, they have been discarded. If not for us, they would have no one." He smiled. "I imagine someone will be looking for you. So already, you put us at risk."

He slid the phone across the desk toward me. "This line is secure and untraceable. I would like you to call your parents and tell them you're safe. But you must not tell them where you are. Say you're at a friend's house, whatever you want, but you cannot tell them you are here. Do you understand?"

I nodded. "I live with my aunt."

"Yes," he said. "Del told me. In Perkins Park, if recall. So call your aunt and tell her you'll be home tomorrow."

"I don't know if she'll be home. She might be at work, or—"

"Then leave a message." He wasn't smiling anymore.

I picked up the phone and punched in Trudy's number, hoping she wouldn't pick up. She did.

"Hello?" she said, sounding tentative and scared.

"H-hi, Aunt Trudy." I could hear the tremor in my voice, feel it spreading through my body. The sudden connection to Trudy—warm and caring, and yes, normal—it was like shining a light on the bizarreness of the last few days.

"Jimi, thank God! Are you okay? Where are you?"

"I'm okay."

"Where are you?"

I wanted to tell her that I was sitting in this crazy lodge in the middle of a fenced-in compound filled with disappeared chimeras who were being rescued to the Promised Land by some kindly old rich guy with the dead-eyed stare of a sociopath and a computer implant that seemed to have more personality than he did.

Instead, I looked at Jasper, who was staring at me. "I can't say. I'll be home tomorrow."

"*You'll be home tomorrow?* What do you mean? Where are you? Do you know how worried we've been? You going missing with all these riots going on? I've been worried sick. Your mother's worried sick."

I felt my insides twisting with guilt. "It's all right. Tell her I'm okay."

"Tell me where you are. I'm coming to get you."

I almost did. Trudy could probably make it out there in an hour. I could be home in two. I'd be in massive trouble, but I'd be away from here, back at Trudy's or even in my own home. Grounded for life, maybe, but so what? At this point, I just wanted to crawl into my own bed and stay there anyway.

"Jimi, are you there?" Trudy said. "Tell me where you are right now."

As Jasper stared at me intently across the desk, I saw something pass through his eyes. It wasn't an emotion—there was no sign of that. More like a calculation. I felt a chill.

"I have to go now, Aunt Trudy," I said quietly. "I'll see you tomorrow, okay?"

"*What?* No, Jimi, it's not okay!" Her voice was getting screechy and loud. "Tell me right now. *Where are you?*"

"I love you, Aunt Trudy," I told her. And I hung up.

SIXTY-FOUR

I felt a wave of sadness after I put down the phone, and regret, too, like I'd had this tenuous link to normalcy, a chance to return to it, and I had let it go. These feelings turned to fear when I realized Jasper was still staring at me.

There was a long moment before he spoke.

"I'm trusting you," he said. "You realize how important this is. Your friends' lives depend on it."

Well, I'm not trusting you, I thought. What I said was, "I told you, I won't tell anyone." I tried to make it sound as convincing as possible.

"All right," he said, after another brief pause. "For now you're welcome to stay, enjoy the grounds, spend some time with your friends. Tomorrow we'll send you home. We might be out in the middle of nowhere, but we're not too far from the Levline in Carston. There's a train every other hour on the hour. We'll get you on the ten o'clock train. You'll be home by noon and you'll never say a word about what you saw here, or where we are, or what our plans are."

I nodded.

It seemed as though we were done. Then he smiled again, all nice and charming, and leaned back in his chair. "So, Ms. Jimi Corcoran. It's a rather interesting name for a young lady, 'Jimi.' Is it short for something? Jemma? Jemima maybe?"

I felt trapped in his office, trapped in the compound, trapped in a world that had gotten out of kilter. I wanted to get away from him, but it seemed like we had to have a friendly chat first so our meeting wasn't all business.

"It's a nickname. My real name is Dymphna," I said.

The muscles in his face didn't move, but in his eyes I saw a flicker of true emotion. It was so out of place I didn't recognize it at first, but it looked vaguely like fear.

"Dymphna Corcoran?"

"I'm named after—" I was about to say after my aunt, but for some reason I decided not to. "An Irish saint."

His head tilted as he stared at me, long enough that I was starting to feel even more uncomfortable—which I wouldn't have thought possible. The phone rang and I jumped, but he kept on staring.

I cleared my throat. "Are we done?"

"Yes, we are," he said absently, ignoring the phone as he came out from behind the desk and opened the door.

Del had been sitting in a chair in the hallway, but he shot to his feet when I came out. Jasper closed the door without another word, and a second later the phone finally stopped ringing.

"You okay?" Del asked, looking both concerned and relieved.

"I'm fine," I said. "Why, what did you expect?"

"Nothing. What did Jasper say?"

"Just that I can't stay, and how important it is that I don't tell anyone where this place is."

"So . . . when are you leaving?"

"Tomorrow."

I saw a familiar mixture of pain and vulnerability in his eyes—like the old Del. It looked out of place in his face now.

"I have more stuff I have to do for the sponsors' banquet," he said. "But I have some time right now. How about I show you around the place?"

"Sure," I said, suddenly choked up. "I'd like that."

SIXTY-FIVE

We walked in silence through the lobby, now filled with chimeras of all types. Several seemed to have splices from species that were endangered or extinct, including one hulking brute with a rhino horn growing out of his face. He nodded at Del as we walked by,

It was strange and unfamiliar to me, but it was Del's world now.

By the time we stepped out onto the porch, tears were falling down my face. As we descended the steps onto the wide lawn, Del put his arm around my shoulder.

I rested my head against him and let myself cry. I was a little embarrassed, but no matter what, Del was still my oldest and closest friend. Besides, it didn't matter what he saw, what he thought. Soon he'd leave, and I'd never see him again. The finality of it hung over me as we walked, a dark echo of when I thought he was dead.

The grounds were huge and the day was beautiful. Del pointed out the solar arrays, the different crops in the fields, the maple trees and the sugar house where the sap was processed. Mostly, though, we just walked, picking up a steep trail that wound up into the woods.

"Are you sure you want to do this?" I asked.

"It'll level out in a minute."

"I don't mean the terrain," I said. "I mean all of this. This, you, Chimerica, the whole thing. Are you sure about all this?" Again, my question didn't come out the way I wanted it to. I still had my doubts about whether Chimerica even existed, but I wasn't asking what he believed. I was asking what he felt, what he wanted. I was asking one last time if he fully intended to abandon the world he had always known, to abandon the world that I was a part of. And to abandon me, for something so unknown. At least if he lived in the zurbs somewhere, I'd know where he was. Maybe Jerry would even give him a job.

Del stayed quiet, thinking about my question or something else, I didn't know. The trail took us past a broad ledge that looked out over miles of green and brown ripples of land extending into the hazy blue distance. I was too distracted to appreciate the view.

I was worried about Del, but I worried about myself, too, about being left behind in a world where I had no friends, where I had lost my oldest friend and my new ones, too. I hadn't realized it until right then, but it looked like Ruth and Pell and Sly would be disappearing from my life, as well. I had only known them for a short time, but the thought upset me deeply.

And what about Rex? He hadn't said anything about his plans, but I knew the loyalty he felt toward his friends. Surely, he'd be going with them. I didn't even know what Rex meant to me, but I was totally unprepared for the possibility of losing him. The realization left me unsteady on my feet.

Del wasn't just leaving my world; he was destroying it, taking all the good parts to some secret place where I wasn't welcome, where I could never go. Once again, anger flared inside me. Just as it was about to explode, Del leaned over and kissed the top of my head.

I moved away and looked back at him, stunned. I knew he probably meant to comfort me, but it was such an odd, patronizing gesture, like an adult comforting a child.

"I'll be back," he said softly. "You know I will."

It might not have been fair, but in the midst of my revelation of my feelings about Rex and the likelihood of him disappearing from my life, it seemed outrageously presumptuous to assume I was only upset about Del.

"Don't lie to me, Del, or *Tamil*, or whatever your name is. Whoever you are. You're not coming back. Hell, you're already gone. You left me when you got spliced without telling me. I've been doing everything I could to save your life, but there's nothing I can do to save *us*. Our friendship. Or whatever this is."

"Jimi, don't say that."

"Not saying it won't make it any less true, Del." I shook my head and let out a ragged laugh as the words I'd been thinking since I'd arrived at Haven suddenly bubbled to the surface. "I can't believe I was so worried about you. So upset, while you were here the whole time, fine, planning on leaving forever without looking back, without even saying goodbye." The tears started falling again, and I was angry at them, too. "And you're not just leaving me, you're leaving me alone. I'm not just losing you, I'm—"

I was about to say, *I'm losing Rex, too,* but before I could, Del leaned toward me, like he was going to kiss me.

"No!" I said, pushing him away. "No, Del. You don't get to do that."

He took a step back, looking hurt. "I'm sorry."

In an instant my fury was gone, replaced by sadness. "Let's just go," I said quietly as I started back down the trail. "You'll need to get back."

We walked in silence for a few minutes. I was just passing the ledge with the view when something caught my eye and I paused.

In a gap between two of the surrounding hills, I could see Pitman, the pinpoint of orange flame above the coal well, and on the hillside directly across from us, the rock where I had sat with Rex.

"What is it?" Del asked, coming up beside me.

"That's where we camped last night," I said, pointing across the valley. My voice sounded strained, but I was making an effort to move on from what had just happened. "Right by that rock there."

"That's Pinecone Rock. At least, that's what some of us call it." It was awkward, but he was making an effort, too. Then he turned to me, surprised. "Wait, were you sitting there this morning?"

"Yeah, why?"

He laughed. "I saw you over there when I was up here this morning." A couple of other chimera hikers passed us. Del nodded at them, then turned to me, his brow furrowed. "Were you with someone?"

"Part of the time, yeah." I felt suddenly self-conscious about it, but defiant as well. "Rex was with me."

Del's eyes narrowed and his nostrils flared. I could see the predator in him and a momentary tingle of fear passed through me. Then it was gone and he was Del again. I wondered if he was jealous. Then I wondered if I cared.

"He's a good guy, that Rex," Del said.

"Yes. He is," I said. Then I turned back toward the rock, and thought about Rex's instructions from that morning. "Del, listen. If anything . . . bad happens, that's where we're going to meet. At Pinecone Rock."

He laughed. "What do you mean?"

"I hope you're right about Jasper, and this place. But something about it bothers me." Another hiker came by, a girl with huge lemur eyes. I waited until she had passed, then lowered my voice. "If anything bad happens, meet me there, at that rock."

"Don't be silly. Nothing bad is going to happen. Besides . . ." He trailed off, as if he had thought better about finishing that sentence: *Besides, you're leaving tomorrow.* "Look, Jasper's working hard to save chimeras," he continued. "He rescued me from those poachers. He saved my life, remember?" He stretched out his arms and flexed his muscles. "He paid for this incredible splice to overwrite the one Malcolm botched." He pointed at the flare atop the coal well. "If you want to worry about someone, worry about those savages in Pitman. That entire town should be wiped off the face of the Earth."

Once again I was struck by the intensity of his hatred. "Wiped off the face of the Earth?"

"They're evil," he said. "I've been there. I know. And look at the devastation to the land around them, everything green turned to brown. It even looks like a cancer."

He was right about that. The brown tinge of death emanating from the town was starkly visible from up where we stood. "That's what humans do, what they've always done. They can't help themselves. Even now. They've seen what happens, but they can't stop." He shook his head. "Look at that half-assed coal well. They're happy to risk their lives—their kids' lives—just to bring up more stuff to burn, so they can keep killing a world that's already halfway dead."

"There are good people down there, too."

"I doubt it," he said. Then his head whipped around. "Wait, how do *you* know?"

"I stopped there on our way here."

"For God's sake, why? The whole town's full of extreme H4Hers. Jimi, you need to watch where you go out there."

"I know a lot of the things those people say and do are toxic, but deep down, most of the people themselves aren't evil." I suppressed a shudder thinking of Andrew, but then I thought of Sammy and the other little kids, and the old couple who found my chimera pin. "Definitely not all of them, anyway."

Del stared at me. "Did something happen down there?"

"It was nothing."

He grabbed me by the arm, hard. I could feel the tips of his claws. "Tell me."

"Let go, you're hurting me." I twisted out of his grip.

"Sorry," he said, "I just . . ." He struggled to find the right words.

I looked down at my arm, at the red scratch marks left by his claws. "Jesus, Del," I said, taking another step back away from him. He was still searching, but the words hadn't come to him. I turned and hurried down the trail without him.

SIXTY-SIX

Del caught up with me quickly, but he had enough sense not to say anything until we emerged from the woods.

"Look, I have to go," he said with a lame forced smile, as if that was some kind of apology. "I'll see you at dinner in a couple hours, okay?"

I nodded but didn't say anything. Then he turned and sprinted across the grass with a stride that was impossibly fast and seemingly effortless. He curved around the front of the lodge, and within a few seconds he had disappeared behind it.

I stood at the edge of the lawn, feeling the sun on my face, and inside, an urge to find Rex.

Before I could act on it, someone called my name and I turned to see Ruth, waving as she approached. "I've been looking for you," she said. Then she tilted her head, studying my face. "Are you okay?"

I shrugged.

"What's the matter? I thought you'd be happy. You found Del, and he's safe and sound and headed out of harm's way, away from all this GHA craziness." Her brow creased. "Did you hear something about Ryan?"

"No, it's nothing like that." I smiled, but I wasn't feeling it. "I'm so glad you're all okay, I am. It's just . . . Del's my oldest friend, and he's leaving, going for good. You guys, too. I'm going to miss you and Pell and Sly . . . . And Rex."

She put her arm around my shoulder. "Yeah," she said softly. "Pell told me about you and Rex."

"We're just friends," I said, pulling away from her. "But I guess we won't be for long, since you're all leaving."

"You could come with us, you know."

"No, I can't. I can't even stay here. Jasper made that pretty clear. Chimerica, or wherever it is you're going, that's just for chimeras."

"You could get a splice," she said quietly. "Come with us, then."

I took a deep breath. The dream I'd had in the bathtub still felt vaguely real, and I wrapped my arms around myself to reassure myself it wasn't. But . . . it hadn't felt all bad, being different in that dream. For a moment I wondered if it was a legitimate idea. Maybe the things I'd get to keep meant more to me than the things I'd give up. And there was definitely something to be said for skipping the massive pile of trouble waiting for me at home. The world was getting more and more cruel, for chimeras, especially. In a weird way, that felt more like a reason to do it—get a splice just to show the H4Hers what I thought of them.

But I knew it wasn't for me. Even apart from what it would do to my mom. The future seemed a lot murkier than it had just a few days ago, but even if Temple University ended up being out of the picture, I knew I still had a better future as a human than I would if I got spliced.

It was scary, how fast things were changing, but I had been changing, too. The things I'd done in the last few days would have been inconceivable to me just a week ago. I was pretty sure I wasn't done changing, either. Maybe I never would be, and maybe that was a good thing. But I didn't feel like I needed a splice to alter myself even more.

I hadn't thought much about it, but I realized I actually liked the person I was.

"No," I said, before I could think about it anymore. "At least, not right now."

She nodded, accepting that. "Are you angry at Del?"

"What makes you say that?"

She shrugged, her large eyes blinking. "Just a vibe."

"I'm upset at him for leaving me. For not telling me he was getting spliced, and then not letting me know he was okay."

"It's only been a few days," she said. "They spliced him super-fast, the fastest I've ever seen. But he was still out of it at first. He couldn't contact you then."

"He could have afterward. I know it's not allowed, but he could have found a way if he wanted to." Ruth nodded but didn't say anything, so I went on. "I'm also having a hard time getting used to some of his changes. He has even more anger now than before." I told her about Pinecone Rock, how he had seen Rex and me and his reaction when I told him I'd been in Pitman.

"He hates Pitman. Pell told me you went in there," she said. "Was it awful?"

I didn't know what to say. "Parts of it were. In ways it was like any other place. But they were all H4Hers."

"When Jasper's team rescued us, we were right outside it. Some of the chimeras here said it was people from Pitman that abducted them. They're horrible."

"Some of them are, I guess."

"I think about what happened to Ryan and I feel sick. I hope he's okay."

"Yeah, me too."

"I don't know why it is they want to hurt us. I've never heard of a chimera hurting a regular person."

"I have, actually," I said. "When I was first looking for Del, a chimera named Simon tried to hurt me. Rex saved me. That's how I met him."

"I've heard of Simon," she said, nodding slowly as she considered it. "And yeah, I've heard he's bad news."

"And those guys working for Malcolm weren't all sweetness and light, either."

She laughed. "I think they're just for show, but I see your point."

"Becoming a chimera doesn't mean you're suddenly good, does it?" I asked her.

"No, I guess not." She sighed.

"But you're right, I'm sure chimeras are no more likely to hurt anyone than other people."

"Then why?"

"I don't know," I said, thinking of what I'd told Claudia. "People can be afraid of what's new and different, and for some of those people, the only way they can show their fear is through hatred and violence."

She laughed. "You think they're scared of *me*?"

I laughed, too. I couldn't think of anyone less scary than Ruth. "Not really, but I think part of that fear is like how I'm scared of losing Del."

"You don't have to lose us," she said. "The only reason we're going anywhere is because of the H4Hers and all this Genetic Heritage nonsense."

"It's not just about going away, it's about the change itself. You don't die when you become a chimera, or go away, necessarily, but you *do* change. People are afraid of losing the person they knew before."

"You really think Howard Wells and his type have lots of friends who have gotten spliced?"

"No, probably not. But for them, they don't miss the people who have changed, they miss the world that's changed."

She let out an impatient huff. "Everybody changes. The world changes. It happens every day."

"You're right. You're absolutely right. So, how about your folks?" I said, changing the subject. "Do you think they miss you?"

She shook her head. "My mom died when I was little. I doubt my dad's even noticed I'm gone, much less that I got spliced. How about you?"

I told her about my dad, and about Kevin. "Sometimes it seems like my mom doesn't notice I'm there. But I'm sure she's noticed that I'm gone. She'd miss me if I didn't come back."

Ruth nodded. She lay back on the grass, and I lay next to her, just looking up at the clouds. I saw one that looked like a fish, and she spotted a bird. Then I spotted a snake with a lion's head, and she saw a penguin with rabbit ears. We started getting giggly after that, and she pointed at a cloud that didn't look like anything.

"Look," she said, "it's a chipmunk-turtle-jellyfish." Chimera humor, I guess, but we both thought it was hilarious, and we laughed for a good five minutes. Best laugh I'd had in ages.

When we stopped, I thought again about how much I was going to miss her.

We lay there a little longer, talking more about our families and telling stories about our childhoods. We talked about the zurbs, and she told me how scary they could be for chimeras. I told her about Rockland, about being attacked on the playground there when I was a kid.

Her shining black eyes widened. "I can't tell you how many stories I've heard like that. It even happened to Rex when he was a kid, too," she said. "He got beat up out in the zurbs."

"Really?" I hadn't realized that kind of thing was so common.

She nodded, then looked over toward the lodge and waved. Sly was coming over.

"He doesn't like to talk about it," she went on. "I think it was pretty bad. He was out in some neighborhood that was starting to fall apart. It's amazing how quickly the world can change like that. One day it's a nice neighborhood, then it's bad, then it's not even a neighborhood at all. Just a bunch of empty houses and a few bad people left over." She laughed. "And maybe some chimeras."

"Hey," said Sly, suddenly looking down at us.

Ruth looked up at him, shielding her eyes from the setting sun. "Have you seen Rex?"

I got the feeling she was asking for my benefit.

"He's asleep," Sly said, crouching down on his haunches to talk to us. "He only got a couple hours in last night. He relieved me way too early."

"And he woke me up late," I said. "Then got up early to sit with me."

Ruth gave me a knowing smile, but I ignored her.

"Sometimes he seems to think he's indestructible," Sly said. "Anyway, he better be up soon, because dinner's in ten minutes. I was just coming to let you folks know."

We thanked him for the info and watched as he trotted back to the lodge, but veered over to a small group of girls sitting under a tree. One of them was a fox chimera, too.

Ruth turned to me and studied my face. "We should get ready for dinner. Are you going to be okay?"

It was a big question, but I knew what she meant. I gave her a brave smile. "I'll be fine."

SIXTY-SEVEN

The banquet hall was huge, and it was packed with by far the most chimeras I'd ever seen in one place, and the most exotic ones, too.

Apart from Del, there were several other felines, including a boy with a lion's mane; a girl who looked part panther, with flashing yellow eyes and a thick black coat; and a handful of tigers. The kid with the rhino horn sat in the corner, with the panda girl and a stunningly beautiful woman with a long neck and a pattern on her skin like a giraffe. There were two zebras and a variety of antelopes, gazelles, and ibexes, with all sorts of horns and antlers. The more exotic chimeras were the centers of attention. The rest included some dogs, wolves, and foxes; a couple bears; and lots of birds of all different types. In the corner was a table of reptiles, who seemed to be mostly keeping to themselves. The sound was deafening, and I thought it was exactly what you'd expect a hall full of wild animals to sound like. Then I realized it was also exactly like the lunchroom at school.

I was at a table with Pell, Ruth, and Sly. They were talking about Ryan, worrying and hoping he was okay. There were two empty chairs, presumably for Del and Rex.

Del was across the room, chatting with a table of girls. One of them was part cheetah. I wondered if it was the girl from Doc Guzman's. She looked completely recovered.

Del was laughing broadly and grinning, flashing his teeth, like he was trying to charm them. Sly watched him, looking envious. The girls seemed to be falling for it, too, smiling a lot and laughing whenever Del did.

I scanned the room, looking for Rex. I was just starting to worry when he walked in, pausing at the entrance. He looked less haggard and his color had returned.

A couple of the girls Del was talking to looked over at Rex, but he didn't appear to notice. His eyes swept the room from right to left. When he saw me, he smiled and came over.

I smiled, too.

"You're alive," I said. He still looked sleepy.

"I am now. Guess I was more tired than I realized."

"You slept the whole time?"

"Just about." He nodded, looking around. "Man, that's a lot of chimeras."

I could hear snatches of conversation from the tables around us. Mostly it seemed to be musings on what Chimerica would be like when they got there. Lots of "I think it's going to be . . ." and "I bet it'll be like . . ." and "I wonder if it'll have . . ."

Jasper was sitting with two other men at a table in the front. On one side of him was a brutish-looking man, heavyset, with a nose that looked like maybe it had been broken a few times. On the other side was a small, vaguely familiar-looking man with wispy blond hair holding his finger to his lips, like he wanted to shush the crowd. They both had WellPlants, like matching moles over their eyebrows.

I leaned over to Ruth. "Who's that little guy sitting with Jasper?"

"His name is Timms," she said. "Why?"

"He looks familiar."

She shrugged. "I'd never seen him before I got here."

I stared hard at Timms, still trying to place him. But then Jasper stood and started tapping his glass with his butter knife, demanding attention. The tone penetrated the din, and everyone quieted down. Del made his way to our table, saying hi to almost everyone he passed. He sat next to me so I was between him and Rex.

"I'd like you all to welcome some new additions to Haven," Jasper said when everyone was quiet. He gestured toward our table. "Pell and Sly and Rex. Plus their friend Jimi, who is our guest."

The chimeras sitting around us gave a polite round of applause.

"Before we eat, I would like to make a few announcements," he said. "As you all know, we will be leaving here soon, leaving the state for somewhere more welcoming, where you will all be appreciated for the diversity you represent."

Someone shouted out "Chimerica!" and the crowd burst into cheers and applause.

Jasper smiled and held up his hands, calming the crowd down. Once the cheers died out, he continued. "Tomorrow night is our sponsors' banquet, in honor of those whose contributions make Haven possible. Prior to that, we will have an athletic exhibition, to help you show them how truly remarkable you all are. I hope you will all participate to the fullest, give it your best effort, and enjoy a wonderful dinner, thanks to their generosity." He raised his glass in a toast. "To Haven, and to Chimerica."

The room erupted in a ragged chant, repeating Jasper's toast, "To Haven, and to Chimerica!"

The doors from the kitchen opened and staff came out pushing carts piled high with food. They weren't chimeras—they seemed to be mostly Vietnamese and Filipino, probably sea-rise refugees. I hadn't seen any of them before.

"The food here is great," Del said, his eyes flashing as he eagerly unfolded his napkin.

The server brought us a big bowl of salad and a platter of pasta with spinach and veggie protein. Del heaped both onto his plate. He shoveled it into his mouth like a little kid, like he had done for all the years I'd known him. I suddenly felt sad, this one unchanged thing making all the other differences that much more pronounced. He looked around the table as he chewed. When he got to me, he swallowed. "What?"

"Nothing," I said. I ate quietly. Everybody did, except Del, who talked through the whole meal, reducing the rest of us to the occasional exchange of awkward glances. He started out talking about how great Haven was, and then how exciting the banquet would be. But he seemed to hit his stride talking about Chimerica, reciting theories, guesses, and conjectures as if they were somehow new information. "I can't wait to be in a place where chimeras don't have to be fearful," he said, "where we can't be mistreated or discriminated against, where we aren't less than people."

At that point, I'd had just about enough. "Tell me," I said, "have you suffered a lot of discrimination in the four days since you became a chimera?"

"What?" He was surprised at first. Then he realized it was a dig. "Yeah, you know what? I have. I've seen my friends shocked and beaten. I've been abducted. I've seen a lot of it, and I can't wait to get away." His voice rose with every word.

Jasper got up and started making his way toward our table. He was still smiling, but he didn't look happy.

"Yeah, just leave it all behind," I said. "I'm sure there's not a single thing you'll miss, is there?"

Del lowered his voice. "Jimi, come on. You know it's not like that. You know I had to get away. From my dad, from all that. Of course I'm going to miss you. But . . ." He opened his hands as if to say, *What can you do?*

Jasper and his smile leaned between us. "You need to calm down and lower your voices," he said.

I ignored him. I could feel myself starting to lose it, and I knew I had to get out of there, but there was one last thing I had to say to Del. "I thought you were my best friend, and that was great," I said quietly. "But I realize now you were just my only friend. And that's sad."

Del looked stricken.

I turned to the table, mustering a smile I didn't feel. "Mr. Jasper will be taking me to the ten o'clock train from Carston tomorrow," I said. "In case I don't see you, I wish you all the best. I'll always remember you."

I looked at them one by one. "Ruth. Pell. Sly." Ruth and Pell were already crying. Sly shifted uncomfortably. When I got to Rex, his big dark eyes seemed to be swimming with sorrow and regret, and something else. Longing.

I tried to say goodbye, or even just to say his name, struggling to find that one syllable and not lose it entirely.

I failed. I heard a sob ring out in the now-silent hall. It came from me. I turned away as a handful of voices called out, "Jimi!"

I don't know if any of them was Del's, but I definitely heard Rex's voice rumbling underneath the others.

I clamped a hand over my mouth to prevent another sob and I ran, trying to get out of there before the tears caught up with me.

SIXTY-EIGHT

I was up the next morning before five. The Levline station was ten miles away. I figured, to be safe, I'd give myself three hours to walk it. Jasper said he'd put me on the ten o'clock train. I planned to be on the eight.

The night before, I'd cried on my bed until I was exhausted. Several times someone knocked on my door, but I didn't answer. I couldn't. By the time I fell asleep, I knew I needed to get away from there as fast as I could. I had said the goodbyes I needed to say.

Except for Rex.

But that couldn't be helped. He was leaving, and I understood that. And I needed to leave, too, to get back to my life, or what was left of it. Start figuring out what the rest of it was going to be.

So when I opened the door and quietly pulled it closed behind me, I was surprised to hear a quiet rumble saying, "I thought you frowned on leaving without saying goodbye."

I knew it was Rex, but I jumped anyway.

"Jesus, you scared me," I whispered. "What are you doing out here?"

"Waiting for you," he said. "I knew you wouldn't let Jasper drive you to the ten o'clock. After last night, I figured you'd probably want to make a clean getaway, catch the eight o'clock." He shrugged. "It's a three-hour walk. So here I am."

I didn't know what to say. I threw my arms around him and tried to stay quiet as his arms went around me, too.

"Del doesn't deserve a ... friend ... like you," he said.

I was going to say I didn't deserve a friend like Rex, but the truth was, I did. I just wasn't going to get to keep one.

I held on to him anyway. Tight.

My eyes were almost dry when he cleared his throat and said, "We'd better get going."

Tiny night-lights burned in the hallways and the lobby, but apart from that, the place was dark and still. We slipped out onto the front porch, into the predawn chill. The moon was close to full, but it still took a moment for our eyes to adjust.

Rex pointed off to the left. I followed his finger to a gap in the trees. Two figures walked side by side, carrying rifles. We watched as they moved out of sight, then we looked at each other and headed off in the other direction.

Once we had crossed the lawn and entered the trees, I breathed a little easier.

I took the lead. I was happy to have Rex along, but I knew where I was headed. We followed the dirt road a few hundred yards, then angled off to the right, through the brush.

Rex followed without question or complaint. I was pretty sure he knew where we were headed, too. When we came to the fence, we followed it for a quarter mile, until we came to the place where the two trees grew on either side of it, their limbs intertwined overhead. From this side they seemed to be reaching out to each other, like they were trying to embrace but were kept apart by the fence between them.

Rex looked at me with something like pride. He cocked an eyebrow at me and nodded, as if to say, *Proceed*.

I hugged the maple tree and shimmied up a couple of feet so I could grab the lowest branch. After that it was easy to climb up to a thick branch that stretched over the fence. Holding smaller branches for balance, I walked out and stepped onto a similarly thick branch growing from the evergreen tree outside the fence. It swayed, but not too badly. I waited until it stopped, then made my way toward the trunk, grabbing two other branches for support. I dropped to the next branch down, and from there to the ground.

Rex grinned in the darkness. Then he started climbing.

"Wait!" I whispered. "What are you doing?"

"I'm coming with you," he said as he clambered effortlessly up the maple tree.

"You can't! It's not safe out here for you."

He paused, standing on the branch, which swayed even more under his massive weight. It let out a loud splintering sound. I tensed, expecting it to break.

Rex laughed softly, inching along the maple branch and stepping onto the evergreen bough, which swayed even more. "No place is safe for anybody."

"But what about Chimerica? If you leave Haven, they won't let you back in. All your friends are going there."

He bent his knees and stepped off, flexing them again as he landed on the ground next me.

"Not all of them," he said with a wink. "Besides . . ." He tilted his head back at the tree he'd just jumped from. "I can always sneak back in."

SIXTY-NINE

At the bottom of the hill there was an old covered bridge. A chewed-up road passed through it heading east, toward Carston. We set off walking through the woods alongside it, staying clear of the road, but not far from it.

For much of the walk, we talked about nothing, and for the rest of it, we didn't talk at all. Rex asked me what I liked to do when I wasn't trying to save my friends.

"I like to read," I said.

"Me too," he replied.

"I like to watch Holovid movies."

"Yup."

"Most of all, I love to run."

He turned to me with a gasp of mock surprise. "*I* love to run, too."

That made me laugh. Neither of us had the right shoes or clothes, but I don't think he cared, and neither did I. "I'd hate to miss my train," I said.

We ran flat out, or at least I did. I got the sense Rex could have easily left me in the dust, but he paced me perfectly.

As always, the run cleared my head, and helped me forget for a little while how messed up my life was. The sun even came up, as if it were making a point.

Part of me wanted to run all the way to the station, and maybe keep going after that. But my feet were complaining from within my boots that if I wanted to be able to walk, it was time to stop.

"That was fun," I said as we slowed to a stroll and caught our breath.

Rex smiled. "We'll have to make sure we do it again sometime."

We were quiet after that, and soon we were approaching Carston.

We moved a little farther away from the road, just in case. The town looked too much like Pitman for comfort, with the fence-enclosed grid of streets and a similar mix of houses. It had a solar and wind farm instead of an illegal coal-well rig, but so did Alder, and that hadn't been the friendliest place, either.

The Levline station was just outside of town. It was similar to all the others I'd seen: twenty feet above ground level, constructed of glass and concrete and steel, with dense metal mesh enclosing the track. But the parking area was so huge it had its own little tram, a miniature Lev train running from each parking area to the station.

We sat on a rock at the edge of the woods, barely touching, looking down at the cars filing into the parking lot. At a quarter to eight, I said, "I guess I should get down there."

Rex nodded.

I turned and looked up at him. "Be careful, okay? Going back. And afterward."

He nodded again. "You be careful, too."

I got to my feet and so did he. "I hope Chimerica is everything you want it to be." I tried to keep it light, nonchalant, like I didn't care one way or another. The truth was, I cared both ways. I didn't want him *not* to go—definitely not because of me—but I didn't want him to go, either.

"Who said I was going to Chimerica?"

"Well . . . aren't you?"

He smiled and scratched under his chin, thinking. "I still don't know if I believe it's real. If it is, I guess there's plenty of reasons why I should." His eyes met mine. "But there are some pretty big reasons not to, too."

I felt a wave of relief, like a little bit of something bright just returned to my life.

Rex cleared his throat. "Plus, there's something about Jasper and his pals I'm not sure about. But whatever happens, you'll see me again, okay?"

I nodded. "Okay. Until then."

He smiled. "Until then."

I felt like I wanted to say something else, and I had plenty to say, but I couldn't put it into words. Instead I put my arms around him again. I held him and he held me, too.

But then that wasn't enough, either. I went up on my toes and gave him a deep kiss that sent shivers through me.

I don't know what effect it had on Rex, but when I turned and ran, my legs were still wobbly.

The station was fifty yards away, and I didn't look back until I was up on the platform. When I did, he was gone.

I was still looking for him when I heard the familiar *shush* of the Lev train coming. When I turned to watch its approach, I noticed a poster on the partition next to the ticket machine. GAME DAY, it said, in red and blue letters. I read it from top to bottom and smiled. After all this, I still didn't know what the heck Game Day even was.

I glanced back the way I'd come one more time, and saw a black off-road sedan approaching across the parking lot, moving fast. The windows were tinted, and I couldn't see the driver. It looked like one of the cars I'd seen parked behind the lodge at Haven.

The train arrived and the doors opened. Something about the car made me hurry onto it, and made me will the train to pull out in a hurry, too.

As the doors closed, the car skidded up to the bottom of the steps to the platform. The car doors flew open and three men got out. The two in the front were bigger. The one in back was small, with thin blond hair and a WellPlant. He looked like Timms, the guy who had been sitting at Jasper's table.

They looked angry, watching the train leave and unable to do anything about it. People miss trains all the time, and they're usually angry about it, so maybe I was being paranoid, but I had a feeling those men were there for me. Maybe Jasper was angry that I had left early, and without saying goodbye. I smiled at that thought, but shuddered as well, wondering what would have happened if they'd arrived a few minutes earlier. I was glad Rex was safely off in the woods.

SEVENTY

After having trekked for so long to get out to Haven, it was bizarre to be back in Perkins Park in less than an hour. And it was strange to find myself on a train full of commuters in the middle of the morning rush.

My clothes were filthy, and my fellow riders stared at me without making eye contact. I wondered how much worse it must have been for Ryan, bleeding and legally less than a person. Ryan hadn't been far from my thoughts since I'd found him at Guzman's house, but with all that had been going on, he hadn't been front and center, either. I was anxious to see how he was doing, but apprehensive as well, afraid of what I would find out.

The first two stops were towns similar to Carston. The third stop was Alder. City View Tower rose up ahead, immense and impressive when you got up close to it. I half expected to see an unfriendly policeman waiting to make sure I didn't get off the train in his town.

The stations after that were more like Perkins Park: less imposing, with smaller parking lots and fewer quadcopters. The landscape between the stations looked more familiar, too—stretches of green, the occasional enclave along a Smart-route, and wide swaths of abandoned zurbs. We passed the swampy, dilapidated streets of Rockland. And then we pulled into Perkins Park.

I was the only one who stood to get off. Everyone else was headed into the city.

It was a Wednesday morning. A school day. Part of me thought about just going to school. I wouldn't even be that late. I laughed at the thought as the doors opened. Hard to believe I'd only missed two days.

It struck me again how much trouble I was in. Trudy was surely freaking out. My mom was probably there, freaking out even more. There'd be counselors and school shrinks and meetings. There'd be consequences. There were always consequences.

But after all I'd been through in the past few days, I could handle whatever they threw at me. And there really wasn't much they could do to me anyway. Grounded? Fine, I had nowhere to go. Chores? Extra schoolwork? Sure, I had nothing else to do. Can't see my friends? Well, most of my friends were gone anyway. Except Rex, maybe.

Thinking of him made me feel better, actually.

I looked up at the train schedule. There was a train headed back out to Carston at four ten. For a second, I thought about it—go back out there, get a splice, and go off with my friends to Chimerica.

But that wasn't the answer. Not for me.

I took a deep breath and stepped off the train, almost ready to face the music.

But not quite.

As the doors began to close, I got back onto the train.

SEVENTY-ONE

New Ground Coffee Shop was almost empty, and Jerry was behind the counter. He looked up when I walked in, twitching his eyebrows in greeting. I wondered if the scant crowd was because of his customer-service skills, but then I realized there were no chimeras in there at all.

"Where is everybody?"

He shrugged. "Some split, some are laying low with all this crazy GHA stuff going on. As for the rest, you tell me. Where's Rex?"

"I'm not sure," I said truthfully. "But we found Ruth and Del."

"For real?"

I nodded and lowered my voice. "That place Ryan mentioned, Haven, we found them there."

"No kidding."

"They also say they're going to Chimerica."

He threw back his head and laughed, drawing looks from the few patrons in the place. "You mean cloud cuckooland. What are you talking about, Chimerica?"

I shrugged. "They think it's real and they said they're going there. A secret place, somewhere out of state or in Canada or something."

He snorted. "Even Rex?"

"I don't know," I said. "He's still trying to figure out if he believes it, and if he's going."

"You're kidding me. I wouldn't have thought Rex would fall for that stuff. And where's this Haven place?"

"It's totally hush-hush, like a big secret. The guy running the place made me swear I wouldn't tell anyone where it is."

He snorted again. "Well, don't worry about that. Rex showed me the map before you guys left. It's the place out near Pitman, right?"

I didn't say anything.

He laughed and shook his head. "That's crazy, but smart too, right? Nothing out there but some old coal wells and a bunch of redneck H4Hers."

"Yeah, well, that's probably who shot Ryan." I tensed myself before I asked. "So . . . how is he, anyway?"

Jerry's laughter died instantly. He looked down and gave his head a little shake. "Guzman got him stabilized. We took him to a hospital, but the poor guy had already lost too much blood."

"He's dead?" I felt it like a punch. I staggered and bit my lip, trying not to cry, trying not to feel. It seemed like I'd been doing so much of both.

Jerry nodded and put his hand over mine on the counter. "You did what you could, kid. It was heroic, you two carrying him like that."

I nodded, hearing him if not agreeing.

Ryan was dead. I hadn't known him well, but I'd glimpsed the type of person he was the night when Del was changing. He was kind to that girl, talking her out of getting spliced. He was kind to me, too, reaching out, reassuring me, inviting me to walk with him.

Images of him came to me—staring at me from the driveway the first time I saw him, laughing outside of Genaro's, his eyes flashing in the darkness that night at Malcolm's. Bleeding in my arms.

In all of them, he was alive. And now he wasn't.

I thought about all those chimeras at Haven, feasting and having the time of their lives, preparing to go to Chimerica, not knowing their friend was dead.

I realized Jerry was still staring at me, concerned.

"Is there going to be a service or anything?"

Jerry shook his head. "His folks came and got him. The mom was a mess, but the dad was a jerk. Actually made a crack about burying him in the backyard. I wanted to smack him."

"What about Claudia?" I asked. "Is she okay?"

"Yeah, she's good. Guzman fixed her up. She sweated it out okay, and now she's home with her folks." He smiled faintly. "She's a smart kid. Reprogrammed the memory function on my espresso system before she left. That thing's been out of whack for years."

I smiled, too. At least there was that.

"Earth for Everyone filed a couple of lawsuits, trying to get GHA overturned." He shrugged. "It's only been a couple days, but hopefully the courts will step in, put a stop to all this craziness before it spreads across the country. But H4H, man, they got a lot of money. The forces of evil got a lot of influence in this state."

"But the forces of good have you, right? You're still working to fight it?"

"Hell yeah, man. It's wrong. Earth for Everyone, right? We're still gonna meet here Tuesday nights. You should come by."

I nodded. "If I'm not grounded for the rest of my life, maybe I will."

SEVENTY-TWO

As I walked up to Trudy's house, a gentle breeze swayed the trees and the dappled sunlight that filtered through them. I was overwhelmed by how quaint and homey it felt. Just a few days earlier, it had seemed so strange and unfamiliar.

The gate opened as I approached, and almost immediately the front door opened as well. Trudy burst through it, running toward me. Her face was wet and she was clutching a handkerchief.

"Jimi!" she cried, running up to me. Her face was contorted by a mixture of anger and fear and pain, but there was relief as well. "Thank God you're okay!"

"Hi, Aunt Trudy."

She wrapped me in a tight hug.

I felt the tears rise in me, but they didn't spill out; maybe I was done crying for a little while. Trudy's anger seemed to dissipate before she'd even shown it. "Are you okay? We were so worried about you," she said, her voice quivering as she held me tight.

I patted her on the back. "I'm okay."

She seemed to believe me, because some of the anger came back. She gave me a tiny shake, growling through gritted teeth. "Do you realize what you put me through? Put your mom through? We've had the police looking for you and everything."

"Is she here?"

"She'll be back soon. She's a basket case, you know. Especially since she missed your call yesterday. She came back here and left Kevin on his own when you disappeared, down at the University of Delaware. When you said you were coming home today, she drove down to get him this morning."

Just as she said it, the gate opened again and my mom's car came in. It lurched to a stop just inside, and my mom jumped out and ran toward me. She practically tackled me, squeezing me tight. Then she held me at arm's length for a moment, her eyes furious. "Don't you *ever* do that again!" she said. "Do you know how worried we've been? You're out there with those chimeras and with all these anti-chimera riots going on? We've been terrified!" She looked down at my dirty clothes and shook her head. Then she pulled me close and started crying again.

Over her shoulder, I could see Kevin in the passenger seat, asleep.

"I know things haven't been easy for you lately," my mom said into my ear. "But this has to stop. Disappearing like that, without telling anyone, it's unacceptable. And I have to say, very seriously, you need to stop looking for Del, you need to let it go—"

"I found him."

"You're never going to— You what?"

"I found him, Mom. That's where I was."

"Where?"

Trudy put out her arms, one hand on each of our shoulders, and said, "Let's get her inside. Then she can tell us everything."

As Trudy steered us toward the door, I looked over my shoulder back at the car.

"What about Kevin?" I said. He hadn't moved since they got back.

"He'll be fine," my mother said, hurrying to get inside so she could grill me.

My mom sat on the sofa and pointed to the seat next to her. "Start talking."

Trudy went into the kitchen, listening in as she made tea. I think she wanted to make sure she didn't get in the way.

I told them most of it. I started with finding Ryan and what he said, the map he had on him. And about how we took the Levline and then walked, out past Pitman.

"Pitman?" My mom wrinkled up her face. "That's forty miles

away. Why would anyone go out *there*? There's nothing. Even when people used to go hunting around there, everyone said it was an awful little town. I'm shocked it still exists."

"Well, the town's definitely still there. I went through it." I left out what happened with the cop in Alder, and with Andrew in Pitman. I just said I bought some supplies there and it was really lame. Then I told her about hiking through the woods and finding Haven and finding Del, and how he'd been spliced a second time.

"Okay," Mom said, holding up her hand. "Go back a minute. Where is this Haven place, *exactly*? Because if that's where Del is, we need to tell Stan."

"I told you, it's out in the woods somewhere. I couldn't find it again," I said, lying. "But Mom, even if I could, Stan doesn't care about Del. He really, really doesn't." I explained how Rex and I tried to take Del home, when he was dying from the bad splice, and how Stan would barely look at his son, let alone help. How he threatened to call the cops on us.

She shook her head, disgusted. "Well, the police could have helped him," she said.

I gave her a look appropriate to such an idiotic suggestion. "Really, Mom?"

She closed her eyes and nodded. "Okay, okay, I get it. So then what?"

I shared a little more about Haven, and about how the chimeras all said they were going to Chimerica.

"Chimerica?" she said, in the tone of voice you'd use with a child. "Sweetie, there's no such thing as Chimerica. Even I know that."

I tried not to be annoyed. "That's what I thought, too."

"Thought?"

"Think," I said. "I don't know. They all think it's for real. Or most of them do."

My mom cupped my cheek, lovingly but condescendingly, like she was prepared to let me believe that even though it wasn't true.

I didn't know if I believed it or not, but for the first time, I realized I *wanted* there to be a Chimerica. I had chimeras in my life whom I cared about—deeply—and I desperately wanted there to be a place where they'd be safe.

SEVENTY-THREE

By the time I'd finished talking, I was exhausted. Recounting it all felt a little like reliving it, and even leaving out big chunks, I realized, I really had been through a lot.

The last thing I told them about was Ryan's death, which left us all quiet and sad.

"Let's get you home," Mom said after a moment, and I felt a pang of whatever it is that you feel when you're homesick and you get to go home.

It only took a few minutes to get my stuff together, mostly still packed in the totes I'd brought with me. From the bedroom, I could hear Trudy tearfully apologizing to my mom for letting me disappear and my mom tearfully apologizing back for dumping me on Trudy right when I was in the middle of such a difficult phase. If I wasn't so tired, I would have been angrier—*Yes, there's nothing terrible happening; it's just Jimi overreacting because she's going through a phase.*

When I came back out, I cleared my throat to give them time to stop talking about me.

My mom smiled. "Got everything?"

I nodded.

Trudy gave me another hug, holding on like she didn't want to let me go. "Don't be a stranger, all right?"

"I won't," I said quietly, thinking maybe I hadn't used up all my sadness after all. We hadn't spent much time together, but I was going to miss her, too.

She smiled, and as we stepped out onto the porch, I thought, now that all my friends were gone, maybe Trudy could be my first new one.

My mom gave her a hug, too. A real one.

Kevin woke up as we put my stuff in the trunk.

"Hey," he said as I got in the backseat.

"Hey," I replied.

"Doofus," he said. Then he went back to sleep.

I gave Trudy a little wave as we drove off, watching her house receding behind me, another leg of this journey that was taking me farther and farther away from Del, separating my life from his.

The "athletic demonstration" was probably going on at Haven at that moment. I knew Del would be showing off his new abilities for his new friends, and making Jasper and all those Haven sponsors happy. I wondered if Rex and the others were, too.

I tried to imagine Del thinking about me, missing me, feeling the pain of someone leaving and not saying goodbye. Maybe it wasn't fair, but I couldn't. I saw him laughing and smiling, thinking about his future, his new life.

I tried to push him out of my mind. The void was instantly filled by thoughts of Rex, but I pushed him out, too. I'd think about him and everything else later.

It had been less than a week since I'd moved into Trudy's house, but it felt like months had gone by. The blooms had faded in my mom's garden, and the big sycamore tree out front was dropping bark and leaves. The chill in the air was more than a hint. The sun was setting earlier. My sense of time was out of whack, and so was my sense of place.

My mom parked on the charging pad in the driveway, and Kevin woke up again, looking around, bleary-eyed and confused. As my mom got out and opened the trunk, he looked back and gave me a nod. "You okay?"

"Yeah," I said. "I'm okay."

When we went in through the kitchen door, the place had an odd smell, like a vacation house that had been closed up, or a house that had been empty for a vacation. Clean, but stale. The smell of a house without people or activity.

I brought my stuff upstairs to my room and sat on the bed, looking around. There were pictures of ponies and rainbows and bands

I didn't like anymore, things I'd slowly outgrown. I couldn't find a single item that didn't seem like it was from a different lifetime. The effect was so complete, it was like the *things* weren't out of place, *I* was.

I looked up to see my mom peeking through the door, smiling. "Did you miss all this?"

I hadn't, not for a moment. But I said, "Sure did."

She smiled again. "It's good to see you, Jimi. I missed you."

I smiled back. "You too, Mom." And that much, at least, was true.

"You know we're going to have to talk about all this, right? What happened, and what's going to happen from now on?"

I nodded.

"Maybe we'll get takeout tonight? I imagine Kevin will be at Malik's house, so it'll be just you and me."

"Sure," I said. "Sounds good."

"If you've got laundry, bring it downstairs. I'm about to do a load."

I nodded, fully intending to ignore that last bit, but I was feeling antsy, and my clothes were filthy. So were my boots.

I changed out of them and carried it all downstairs, passing Kevin on the steps.

"Twerp," he said affably.

"Dolt," I replied.

As I put my clothes in the washer, I could hear Mom on the phone with the police, explaining how I was fine and it had all just been a misunderstanding.

I took my boots outside to scrape off the dried mud. When I stepped out the back door, I froze at the sight of Stan Grainger's Jeep parked in the driveway.

I hadn't actually considered the fact that I'd still be living next door to that nutcase. It creeped me out.

The back of the Jeep was loaded up. When I squinted I could make out a couple of duffel bags and a stack of rifle cases. A fluorescent orange vest lay on the backseat.

The Graingers' screen door slammed and I jumped. Looking up, I saw Stan staring at me from the other side of the Jeep.

"What the hell are you snooping around for?"

He looked different. Older and feebler, maybe crazier. But somehow, even with a rifle in his hand, he didn't seem as scary as he did before. I wondered if losing Del hit him harder than he'd expected.

"Del's okay, Mr. Grainger," I said. I figured, apart from anything else, he was still Del's dad. He deserved to know.

He snorted. "The hell he is. He's a goddamned freak."

He was dressed in camouflage pants and jacket, but under the jacket he was wearing his black "Humans for Humanity" T-shirt—the same one he'd been wearing at the march we got stuck behind, when he was holding that stupid banner. I fought a smirk as I remembered Stan not holding it high enough, getting scolded by Howard Wells's minion, standing on the stage—

Something clicked in my mind.

Timms. Jasper's assistant. I suddenly realized where I recognized him from. *He* was the guy at the Wells rally, counting the crowd and scolding Stan. But what was he doing with Jasper at Haven if he was also working with Wells and H4H? It didn't make sense. Not unless the whole scenario was total bullshit.

"Wait—" I heard myself say, but Stan silenced me with a scowl as he opened the car door and put the rifle behind the seats, on top of the other cases. That's when I saw the flyer sitting on the front seat: red and blue lettering across the top. On top of it was a piece of paper that said GAME DAY VIP, and underneath it ADMIT ONE. THE PITMAN EXOTIC GAME PRESERVE WELCOMES YOU TO A VERY SPECIAL GAME DAY. It was stamped PAID.

Stan got in and slid the papers out of view, still glaring at me as he started up the car and backed out of the driveway.

But I'd already seen it. I'd already read it. And now I knew what it meant.

They were hunting chimeras.

SEVENTY-FOUR

Running in the back door, I almost leveled Kevin, who was busy emptying his pockets onto the dryer and cramming his laundry into the washing machine. The top of the dryer was piled with old receipts, crumpled bills, gum wrappers, and car keys.

"Kevin, I need you to drive me somewhere."

He rolled his eyes and slumped his shoulders. "Dude, I just spent five *hours* in that car. Why? Where do you need to go?"

I looked at the clock over his shoulder. It was three fifty-nine. If we left right then, we'd get to the train station in time for that four ten train to Carston. I could be back there by five.

"The Levline."

He cocked his head to one side. "Why?"

"I can't tell you."

He snorted and shook his head, then looked over his shoulder to make sure Mom wasn't in earshot. "Aren't you in enough trouble? If this is more of that crazy chimera crap, you need to let it go. Seriously. Before you get yourself in even deeper trouble than you're already in."

Then he turned and walked away.

I stood there, shaking with anger and frustration, with fear and with anguish.

I peeked through the kitchen door to make sure neither Kevin nor my mom was nearby. Then I picked up the phone, got the number for the coffee shop, and placed the call.

Jerry answered, "Higher Ground."

"Jerry, it's Jimi, Rex's friend."

"What's up?"

"Listen, there's something terrible going on in Pitman."

In the next ten seconds, I told him what I knew, and what I

suspected, and what I planned. Then I hung up and grabbed Kevin's car keys. I took his money, too.

The car had only been parked on the charger pad for half an hour, but I just needed to get to the Levline station. I'd taken enough lessons to know how to do it, but I was flustered and frantic and I forgot to disengage the charger the first two tries.

By the time I was barreling down the driveway in reverse, Kevin was outside pointing at me and laughing in disbelief. By the time I swerved out into the street, my mom was running down the driveway after me, screaming, "Jimi! No!"

I was so freaked out, I couldn't remember how to set the autodrive, so I kept it under manual control until I thought it was safe to pull over four blocks later, take a deep breath, and figure it out.

I called up Perkins Park Station on the nav console and said "Yes" when the display showed the name and the map. The car surged underneath me. It was a strange sensation, sitting in the driver's seat with autodrive on. As a passenger, it didn't make much difference whether it was my mom driving or autodrive, other than the vague awareness in the back of my mind that I was much less likely to die with autodrive. Sitting in the driver's seat, though, it felt weird.

The station was a couple miles away, and I was just a few blocks away from it when the hazard lights started blinking extra fast. I flicked the switch on and off, but it had no effect. I was just starting to suspect something was up when the car drifted to the side of the road and the motor shut off.

The lights inside the car started flashing, too, and a computer voice said, "This vehicle has been reported stolen. Please remain by this vehicle until police arrive. Failure to do so may result in additional criminal charges. Thank you for your cooperation."

At least, I'm pretty sure that's what the last bit was. I was already running down the street by that point, grateful that my mom had only sprung for the bronze theft deterrent package. If she had silver or gold, I would have been autodriving back home, locked inside the car.

I was halfway up the block when the police lights appeared behind me. I ran up a driveway and covered the rest of the distance to the station cutting through backyards and jumping over fences. I was a lot better at it than I would have been a week earlier. I smiled, thinking Rex would be proud. Then my throat cinched tight as I thought about what could happen to him if I didn't warn him in time.

When I got to the station, I ran up the metal steps to the platform and waited. I couldn't see the police cars, but the flashing red and blue lights were reflecting in the trees.

Then I heard the familiar *shush* of the Levline. The train appeared around the bend and slowed to a stop right in front of me.

SEVENTY-FIVE

The zurbs were a blur as the Lev train sliced across the landscape, but sitting in my seat, I felt like I wasn't moving at all. And that was driving me nuts.

The train was half-full. I wasn't covered with mud, and I wasn't traveling with chimeras, but people were still staring at me, still keeping their distance. Maybe they could read something on my face.

As I thought about what I was going to tell the others, the terrible reality of it played through my brain. I tried to come up with another explanation, one that wasn't so . . . evil.

But I couldn't. Haven wasn't a refuge, protecting chimeras from the world outside until they could be moved to some mythical out-of-state paradise. It wasn't protecting my friends from the H4H nut-jobs in Pitman and beyond. It was the Pitman Exotic Game Preserve, a murderous fraud, lining them up for the slaughter.

And Game Day wasn't some quaint family fun day. It was a hunt, and my friends and the other chimeras—many of them spliced with creatures that were exotic or even extinct—were the prey. It would be mass murder.

There had been a lot about Jasper and his whole Haven setup that hadn't seemed right from the start—the fence, the secrecy, the vibe. But as I sat on that train, more pieces came together in my mind. Pitman was a screwed-up little town with a lot of past and not much future. And that past was based on two things: coal and hunting. When the easy-to-find coal ran out, they'd started liquefying it to get the last little bits, pumping more and more chemicals into the ground. The climate had wiped out most of whatever animals there were to hunt, and the chemicals from the coal wells took care of the rest. The hunters stopped coming when the game died out.

It horrified me to even think it, but having exhausted the natural resources they once had, the people in Pitman found a new one; and now, thanks to the Genetic Heritage Act, it was even legal. The posters in town said GAME DAY IS BACK. Now that chimeras were no longer legally people, as far as the H4Hers and the people in Pitman were concerned, they were animals. Animals to be hunted.

Unless I could stop it.

SEVENTY-SIX

I t was just after five o'clock when I got off the train with the throng of commuters at Carston Station. They quickly dispersed through the parking lot, and as I stood alone on the platform, watching the train pull away, I realized I was no closer to a real plan of action than I had been when I'd grabbed Kevin's car keys and took off. I supposed I was going to try to sneak into Haven, tell everyone what was going on, and get back out again, hoping that Jerry and his friends at Earth for Everyone could somehow help keep us all from being killed.

As impossible as it seemed, I knew that maybe the hardest part would be convincing Del to leave. His zeal for Haven had been creepy even when I thought the place was legit. Knowing what was really going on made it infinitely creepier.

And what I was going to tell him was so bizarre, so horrifying, I couldn't see him just taking my word for it. But I had to try.

A tiny, spiteful part of me might have found some satisfaction that this thing he was abandoning me for was so different from what he'd thought it was. But apart from the horror of what was actually going on, I knew what this would do to him, and I felt pity for him. He'd been acting like a jerk, but at least he'd seemed happy in his new world, happier than I'd seen him in a long time. It was going to tear him apart to find out it was all a lie. And it was going to hurt me to tell him.

Minutes ticked by while I tried to figure out my next step. The posters said Game Day wasn't supposed to start until tomorrow, so conceivably, I could start hiking. But I felt like I needed to get there as soon as possible if I was going to save my friends.

As I stood there, a car drove up to the parking kiosk at the bottom of the steps. The driver got out, tapped some buttons on the keypad, and swiped his card. The machine spit out his parking voucher, and he got back in and drove off to find a parking spot. He'd left the car door open and the motor running the whole time.

At the far end of the parking lot, another car entered and drove toward the kiosk. I watched for a moment, letting it get closer. Then I started down the steps, timing my stride so I was walking past the kiosk just as the car pulled up. The guy who got out was in his late forties. He stared at me with a sleazy smile as he crossed over to the kiosk. I glared at him until he looked away, embarrassed.

Then I got in his car and drove away.

I could hear him yelling behind me, but I didn't look back, trying not to think of the mounting pile of serious trouble I was getting myself into. My mother probably wouldn't press charges against me for stealing her car, but I doubted this guy would be as forgiving.

I zigged and zagged until I spotted the exit, and I was turning toward it when the owner of the car jumped out in front of me. He wasn't smiling anymore. I swerved around him, terrified I was going to hit one of the parked cars. He punched the back of the car, hard. The sound made me jump, and almost made me lose control of the car. As I skidded through the exit and onto the road, he flung himself at the back of the car, but missed. I looked back and saw him on his knees in the middle of the road, yelling at me.

For the first couple of miles, I drove with the window down and my elbow outside it, in case he had a better security plan than my mom did. But apparently, he didn't. His next car probably would.

There were a lot of other cars on the road at first, and I squeezed the wheel tightly, terrified I was going to hit one. But when the traffic died away, I felt nervous and conspicuous. If anyone was coming after me, they'd have no problem finding me.

I knew I was heading in the right general direction, but that was about it. I was hoping to get as close as I could by car, then go the rest of the way on foot. But I had only the vaguest idea where close was.

Within a couple miles, I could feel the road deteriorating under my tires.

I was starting to panic that I was lost. A police car passed me going the other direction, slowing as it disappeared around a curve. I couldn't see what town it was from.

I kept an eye on the rearview, waiting for the cop to reappear behind me. But as the road straightened, I spotted the covered bridge off to my right up ahead, and I exhaled.

It spanned a small creek with gentle, rocky banks. I didn't want to damage the guy's car any more than I already had, but I also didn't want to get caught before I got to Haven. Besides, the banks of the creek weren't much bumpier than the road itself. I drove slowly onto the shoulder, then down the gentle incline toward the stream. When I was confident the car was no longer visible from the road, I got out and started running.

SEVENTY-SEVEN

I reached the top of the first hill just in time to see the sun setting. I paused for a brief second, feeling its warmth on my skin. I knew it was the last I would see of the sun that day, and it crossed my mind that I might never see it again.

Haven was big, but I didn't know how big. I knew it covered much of the far side of the hill in front of me, but I had no idea how much of this side it included as well.

A quadcopter buzzed past overhead, and I ducked under a bush. It didn't seem like it was searching, just going from one place to another, but I tried to stick to the more densely wooded areas, just in case.

A stream ran through the valley between the two hills. I paused when I reached it, then started up the other side. A few more quadcopters went by, but I ignored them and they ignored me. Two-thirds of the way up the hill, I came to the barbed fence.

It seemed even more sinister now. I gave it some distance, maybe forty yards, and followed it as quietly as I could. After a quarter mile, I heard footsteps and I froze, squinting through the trees at the fence, at the trees on the other side of it.

Then I saw them: two guards with shock rifles. They looked like hunters, and something like vertigo passed through me as I was reminded of what I was trying to prevent.

The guards were moving in the opposite direction, so a few minutes after they passed me, I continued on. Half a mile later, I saw the dirt road cutting through the woods in front of me. It was getting dark for real now, but following it with my eyes, I could just see the gate. I moved closer to the fence and followed it until I found what I was looking for: the trees Rex and I had crossed over that morning.

The one on the outside was easier to climb. I jumped up to grab the lowest branch and swung myself up, ascending until I was higher than the razor wire on top of the fence. Then I stepped from one branch to the other, and climbed down the trunk on the other side.

I felt slightly protected by the gathering darkness, but increasingly afraid I might stumble across a guard. I circled through the woods, staying clear of the lawn as I made my way to the overlook where Del had taken me that afternoon, hoping to get there before the banquet, hoping the banquet would be later than the simple dinner the night before. By the time I got there, it was getting seriously dark. Down the trail, I could see people making their way across the lawn toward the lodge, and I worried I was too late.

"Better hurry," a voice said behind me. "They already rang the bell."

I turned to see the small girl with huge lemur eyes, blinking at me in the darkness.

She tilted her head. "Oh. I thought you left."

I felt a strong compulsion to warn her, tell her to run away. Instead I smiled. "Not yet. Do you know if Rex is still here?"

She smiled back. "The big cute guy? Sure he is. Why?"

"I have to show him something up here before I leave. Can you ask him to come meet me here?" I smiled even more, trying to keep it light.

"Um . . . I guess," she said. She walked down the path, looking back at me over her shoulder.

I moved into the trees on the side of the trail, but I realized immediately that I couldn't rely on some stranger to tell Rex to come and find me in the dark. I was about to step out onto the trail and go find him, when I noticed a dull red glow on the leaves and branches around me. Then I realized it was the reflection from the bright red dot blazing on my chest.

A voice in the darkness said, "Move a muscle and I'll shoot."

SEVENTY-EIGHT

For a second I considered jumping off the outcrop, into the woods below. But before I could figure out how badly I would shatter my legs, a second red dot appeared on my midsection. Another figure appeared on the trail in front of me and said, "Hands in the air."

I raised my hands. "I didn't do anything," I said.

The figure on the trail came up to me, his gun on me the whole time. "You're under arrest for trespassing," he said as he moved behind me.

They whispered back and forth for a second. Then one of them said, "Walk," poking me in the back with his weapon. I turned around and looked down at it, surprised to see it was a shock rifle.

"Don't get any ideas," he said. "You get hit with one of these, you'll be begging for a bullet."

As I started walking, the other guard muttered something about how ridiculous it was that they only had stun guns. For a moment, I thought maybe I had it all wrong, they didn't want to hurt anybody. Then the other guard replied, "Rich bastards are paying good money to hunt. The last thing Jasper wants is mugs like us shooting the game for free."

My blood ran cold.

The lawn was dark and empty. As the guards marched me around the edge of the trees, toward the back of the lodge, another passenger quadcopter approached, a halo of lights slowly turning as it descended over the landing area, which was now crowded with copters.

As we walked down the slope toward the rear of the lodge, a service entrance in the lower level came into view. When we reached it, one of the guards stayed outside as the other one opened the heavy door and walked me down a long, brightly lit, tile-and-concrete corridor.

We passed doors marked UTILITY, CATERING, LAUNDRY, BOILER, and several that weren't marked at all. Finally, we stopped at a heavy door marked SECURITY.

The guard reached around me to swipe his card through a reader and pull the door open, then we entered a similar corridor with doors spaced along the left-hand side. The door we had just come through began to close slowly behind us.

The first door on the left was open, revealing a small room with a heavy, gray-haired man sitting in front of a dozen small security screens. He looked up at me, then nodded to the guy behind me. Then he went back to watching his screens.

Just past that, another door opened onto a small room with a bench on either side. The guard shoved me inside it. It was the first time I got a good look at him. He looked stupid and slow, more like a thug than a cop, even a dirty cop. "Wait here," he said with a glare.

Then he took three steps farther down the hallway and I heard his voice, muffled, saying, "Hey, you got any cuffs? I forgot mine."

Another voice said, "Jesus, Frank, you need to get a proper belt."

In the background I heard a sound—*creak, creak, creak*. I peeked my head out the door. To my left I could see the back of the guard, leaning his head and shoulders into the next room. To my right, past the room with the video screens, was the door we had just come through, still slowly closing.

Once it clicked shut, once the guard came back with handcuffs, I'd be stuck.

I made a dash for it. I don't think the guy in the video room even looked up, but he'd see me on the cameras soon enough.

I got to the door just as it was about to close, got my fingers into the tiny gap just in time for the door to crush them. But I gritted my teeth against the pain and I put my shoulder against the door. It swung open, slowly, and I skidded out into the corridor.

I knew I had only seconds as I looked over the labeled doors. The closest one said CATERING. I didn't have time to be picky, so I opened it just enough to slip inside, then pulled it shut behind me.

As soon as it clicked, I turned and ran down a dingy passageway. The walls and floor were unpainted concrete. A row of bare bulbs ran down the ceiling. Cases of produce and big cans of cooking oil and tomatoes were stacked against the wall. I hurried down the passageway toward another one that ran perpendicular to it. As I approached the turn, a small man rounded the corner, struggling with a large trash bag. I slipped around him at the last second, and he turned to look at me. His eyes were kind and wise and sad, and he said something, but I couldn't understand. I kept running until I came to a set of steps leading up to a wooden door.

Just as I reached the top of the steps, I heard the door to the corridor opening behind me downstairs, then footsteps running on concrete. I tore open the door at the top of the steps and burst into a bustling kitchen. I recognized the staffers who had served dinner the night before, but working among them were chimeras, who all seemed damaged somehow, with withered arms or legs, or other deformities. Not good enough to hunt.

Some of them looked up at me as I burst through, unalarmed, unconcerned, just vaguely defeated as they went back to their work. I couldn't tell what the chimeras had been spliced with. The last one to look away from me appeared to be a cat chimera, except for her arms, which seemed vaguely reptilian. She was peeling carrots with a gnarled hand.

I went up to her and said, "Do you know Rex, the really big dog chimera?" I held my hand high above my head to indicate his height.

She shook her head.

"How do I get out of here?" I didn't know where I needed to go, I just needed to get away from whoever was chasing me.

The far wall had two doors. She pointed her peeler at the one on the right.

"Thanks," I said.

As I turned to go, I saw a knife rack in front of her. I put my hand on the largest knife and looked at her. She cocked an eyebrow and shrugged, showing a hint of a smile. I took the knife and darted out the door.

The hallway I stepped into was like a different world. The walls were the same warm tones as the dining hall, and the floor had the same plush carpeting. I could hear the muffled approach of heavy footsteps. Directly across from me were three doors, evenly spaced twenty feet apart. I felt like a contestant on an old television game show. But this was no game, and I had to make a decision, fast.

I ran to the door to the right, flung it open, and dashed through.

In my mind I heard a game show buzzer: *WRONG!*

SEVENTY-NINE

I was standing near the front of an enormous ballroom, much bigger than the dining hall. There must have been thirty tables, each with at least six people. Most of the tables were occupied by chimeras, but the ones at the far side appeared to be rich, old white men. All of them had WellPlants. They were surrounded by a cadre of servants, standing behind them. Some had stacks of luggage as well, as if they had just arrived or were just leaving. I knew they were supposed to be the sponsors of this place, but a chill ran through me as I considered why they were really there.

To my right, at the front of the room, was a stage in front of a massive set of windows. Jasper was on stage with Del, one hand on his shoulder, the other holding a microphone. His mouth was open, like he'd been in the middle of addressing the crowd.

But he wasn't speaking now. And they weren't looking at him. They were looking at me, wondering what I was going to do.

I was wondering the same thing.

Seconds ticked by as I scanned the crowd. I spotted Rex sitting toward the back, staring at me intently, his muscles tensed, ready to act on what I said. Pell and Ruth and Sly were with him, their faces startled and concerned, the remnants of smiles slowly fading from their faces.

I was almost starting to doubt myself, wondering if I had somehow gotten it all wrong, when I spotted Mayor Randolph from Pitman sitting with the funders, glaring at me. He wasn't wearing his H4H pin.

Then I saw Timms, staring at me, tapping his lips.

"Jimi, what are you doing here?" Del said, exasperated, annoyed I had messed up his party, almost like he was disappointed in me. He had no idea.

I looked around the room. Things were going to explode into chaos and mayhem when I said what I'd come to say.

I looked right at Del. "Pinecone Rock, remember?"

"Yeah, but . . . what about it?" He looked embarrassed.

I looked at Ruth and Rex, making sure they'd heard. Rex nodded.

"Ms. Corcoran," Jasper said, "we're in the middle of our sponsors' banquet. The generous people who fund our mission have traveled a long way to meet the brave young chimeras that they are helping bring to Chimerica."

He nodded at the back of the room, and a pair of guards began edging toward me.

"There's no such thing as Chimerica," I said.

A murmur ran through the room. If I didn't have all the chimeras' attention before, I had it now.

"These men aren't here to save you," I said, my voice rising above the buzz. "They're here to hunt you."

Jasper laughed. "Ms. Corcoran, that's preposterous." Even as he said it, he was flicking his hand at the guards, gesturing for them to hurry up.

"Is it?" I said, backing away from them. "Then why is the mayor of Pitman here?" I looked at Mayor Randolph. "I notice you're not wearing your H4H pin. Here in disguise, huh?" Then I turned back to Jasper, pointing at Timms. "And why is Timms here? Howard Wells's right-hand man?" I looked at Timms. "Did H4H give you the day off?"

The chimeras all gasped. It was a strange amalgam of sounds, all those different species and splices and mixtures, all exclaiming involuntarily.

Now I looked at Del. "It wasn't until I got home that I remembered where I recognized him from—marching with Wells, and with your dad, Del. The day after you disappeared, Timms was at a rally with these hatemongers. Practically *running* it."

The guards were getting closer, and I backed away from them, toward the middle of the room. The chimeras backed away from me, unsure and not wanting to get caught up in whatever trouble I was causing. I held up the knife and waved it through the air, making the guards step back, too.

"Jasper isn't here to protect you from the people of Pitman. He's packaging you up for them. For Game Day. It's a tradition in Pitman, isn't it, Mr. Mayor? The pride of your town. Or at least it used to be, until there was nothing left to hunt. But now it's back, right? I'll bet you've got people coming from all over, don't you? Probably paying some good money."

"Jimi, what are you talking about?" Del said, his voice weak, confused. But he already understood. He just couldn't wrap his mind around it.

"Now that chimeras aren't legally people, there's plenty to hunt," I said. "And not just squirrels and raccoons—for the right price, you can hunt giraffes, leopards . . . even a Bengal tiger, if you don't mind a little human mixed in."

I looked out at the room full of chimeras. "You call this place Haven. They call it the Pitman Exotic Game Preserve," I said. "And you chimeras are the exotic game." Then I lowered my voice. "Just like Ryan was." I felt a tear roll down my cheek, and I looked over at Rex and Ruth and Pell and Sly. "He didn't make it."

There was a moment of absolute quiet. Then Del turned to Jasper. "Is this true?" His voice cracked, his face crumbling.

Every eye in the place turned to watch them, including mine.

Jasper shook his head, almost bashful. He looked at his feet, then out at the sponsors' tables.

He stepped away from Del. "Frederick," he said, calling to the far side of the room. "Maybe you should explain." He followed that up with a solemn nod.

One of the men sitting with the funders stood with a shrug and said, "A little unorthodox, Jasper, but what the hell." He turned and whispered to the servant standing behind him. Then a gasp ran through the crowd and everyone ducked as he turned back with a hunting rifle in his hands, and he brought it up to aim.

Without thinking, I threw the knife at him. I'd never thrown a knife, and we weren't that close. It didn't spin through the air and sink into his chest. It tumbled, almost lazily. I was worried it might not even reach his table, much less hit him, but the handle hit his arm and it bounced up and sliced his chin.

I was trying to disrupt his aim, make him miss Del, and I succeeded. The gun went off with a bang and a hole appeared in the massive window behind Del and Jasper. Cracks radiated out from the bullet hole, turning the entire thing cloudy. It hung in place for an instant, then it dissolved, raining down in a million little pieces.

The chimeras scrambled in sudden pandemonium. Frederick screamed, "You bitch!" and turned the gun toward me. The two guards closed on me, and as I dove for the floor, one of them screamed with a bullet in his thigh. A bullet meant for me.

I scrambled for the door. Rex and the others were lost in the crowd. I could smell the electricity, hear the sound of guards shocking the chimeras. I was almost at the door when Del let out a roar. I turned and saw him towering over Jasper, who was cringing in fear. Del swiped one hand across Jasper's face. Four deep gashes appeared, one almost severing his nose.

Del turned to the room and roared again, louder. His voice thundered, *"I'll kill you all!"* He turned and leaped through the smashed window, disappearing into the night.

EIGHTY

When I got back to the door I had come through, I found it locked behind me. They were all locked. I fought a moment of panic as the guard pushed his way toward me, using his shock batons to cut a path through the mass of terrified chimeras jammed up against the other doors. I caught a glimpse of Rex slamming into one of those doors. It buckled and gave way, and chimeras began streaming out through it.

But the guard coming after me was blocking my way to that door, so I decided to go the same way Del had, up onto the stage and out the window. I didn't know what to expect, but as I got closer, in the light spilling out, I was relieved to see a small deck about six feet below the window, and the lawn maybe eight feet under that.

I jumped through the window and onto the deck, swung over the railing, and lowered myself as far as I could before dropping the last few feet. A lot of the others began doing the same. When I looked up from where I'd landed, I could see chimeras leaping through the air above me, illuminated by the light coming from inside. Some stuck the landing and some hit hard, but they all took off running, streaming across the lawn in every direction.

I heard a crackling, sizzling sound as a guard and a chimera tumbled through the air over my head, the guard shocking the chimera with his baton in midair. The chimera screeched and they both landed awkwardly, with a sickening snap. The baton landed several feet away.

The chimera rolled away, shaking her head, dazed from the charge. The guard got up, too, one arm dangling bent and useless. His good hand reached for the baton, but I got to it just before he did, snatching it away as his hand closed on empty space. He turned and looked at me with a face twisted in pain and anger and hatred. I jabbed him in the belly with the baton. His eyes rolled up as the rest of him dropped down. I gave him a few seconds for good measure, understanding now the urge to hold it there like Del had. I could feel the rage in me, compelling my arm to push that baton hard into his gut and keep it there until he was dead.

But I didn't. I let go and left him moaning and coughing on the ground. Then I ran off, trying to figure out what to do next. I wished I had Rex to help me figure it out, and for a moment I felt a blast of devastating fear and sadness at the thought he might not be okay. But I pushed that aside. I had to think.

Game Day wasn't until tomorrow, but fenced in the way we were, it might as well have been Game Day right then. If the hunters had night-vision goggles, it would be like shooting fish in a barrel, and that's really what those sick bastards were paying for.

As I headed toward the trees, headlights swung out from behind the lodge, sweeping across the lawn. Looking back, I saw a pickup truck with half a dozen guards in the back. One of them reached out and shocked a chimera, then jumped out to handcuff him. Almost immediately, another guard did the same.

The woods were alive with blue sparks. It looked almost like fireflies, but I knew they were chimeras being shocked in the darkness.

Unless I did something about the fence, they would eventually get all of them. All of *us*. And in a couple of days, we'd all be dead.

I looked back at the truck as yet another of the guards shocked a chimera and jumped off to immobilize him.

The pickup bounced violently as it crossed the dirt road, almost pitching the two men still in the back. Then it curved around, heading in my direction. They'd seen me.

The driver's window was open. It gave me an idea.

I held my baton close to my body and ran slowly, veering to the left so the truck would come up on my right. I could see the headlights streaming around me, hear the motor noise getting louder, closer.

It took every ounce of willpower to maintain my pace and not turn around. From the corner of my eye I saw the front of the truck just pulling even with me. When I saw the side mirror, I turned and threw myself at the driver's window.

One of the guys in the back of the truck lunged forward, his baton spearing the air where I had just been.

I dove through the window, jamming the tip of my baton under the driver's ear. He clenched the wheel tight and his foot must have jammed down hard against the brake, because we slammed to a stop.

My ribs smashed painfully against the window frame. The guy who had tried to shock me flew over the front of the truck, tumbling through the air and landing in a heap twenty yards away, lit up by the headlights. The guy still in the back slammed hard against the cab and crumpled to the bottom of the truck's bed.

I kept my baton jammed under the driver's ear. His eyes were rolling up, and his mouth was foaming, but I wasn't taking any chances. I didn't pull the baton away until I had the door open. The truck started rolling forward again, and I grabbed him by the shoulder and threw him to the ground.

He wasn't wearing a seat belt.

As I got in, I made sure to buckle up before I jammed my foot on the accelerator and drove down the dirt road, toward the gate.

A couple of chimeras darted through the beams of my headlights, but mostly I just caught glimpses of them in the darkened woods.

I was hurtling down the dirt road, barely keeping the truck under control, when a hand reached through the window and grabbed my hair. I'd been so intent on not running anyone over, I'd forgotten about the bad guy in the back of the truck.

I screamed and reflexively turned the wheel in his direction. A series of large branches smacked against him, forcing him to let go. I looked behind me and saw him standing in the back of the truck with a large sliver of wood sticking out of his upper arm, glistening with blood. He touched the tip of it, then glared in my direction. I jammed the accelerator down as hard and fast as I could. He staggered back against the tailgate, but he didn't go over.

Then I slammed on the brakes. He crashed into the cab once more, his face smushed up against the glass, but he was still there. I waited until he got to his feet, then hit the accelerator once more. Again, he staggered to the back but didn't go over. I was terrified for my life, but I was also starting to get annoyed. I slowed the truck to a moderate speed, then gradually accelerated, watching in the mirror as he made his way toward the cab.

I grabbed the wheel as hard as I could with my left hand, bracing myself against what I knew was coming. When his big arm reached in once again to grab me, I jabbed him with the baton, holding it in place for a good three seconds. Then I pulled it away and slammed the brakes at the same time.

I don't think he even hit the cab as he flew overhead, his limbs completely limp. He disappeared into the darkened woods with a sound of cracking branches and a loud thud.

I turned back onto the dirt road and floored the accelerator. I didn't know how much farther I had to go, but I knew I needed to build up some speed. I honked the horn and flipped the lights on and off as I went.

The gate appeared thirty feet in front of me. Two chimeras were climbing on it and I blasted the horn at them. They both turned, their eyes wide, and jumped off, rolling into the bushes.

Then I blasted through the gate, sending the two sections cart-wheeling into the darkness in opposite directions.

A bunch of chimeras ran for the opening, but two guards with batons ran to head them off. It wouldn't be long before reinforcements showed up, with more potent weapons, too.

I realized they could easily cover a single gap in the fence.

I held down the accelerator, the tires skidding on leaves and dirt as I weaved through the trees and curved back around. Fifty yards to the right I punched back through the fence, this time tearing out a thirty-foot section. The second time was more fun and less scary. I may have laughed out loud, even as the front tires blew out from the fence barbs.

In the darkness I could see chimeras streaming through the second hole behind me. I was back inside the fence, though, and that made me nervous. Plowing through the brush and bouncing over the rough terrain, I could feel the wear and tear on the truck.

My plan was to punch one more hole in the fence, then keep going, drive the truck as close as I could get to Pinecone Rock and go the rest of the way on foot. I'd meet up with the others, and then we'd be gone.

I found another gap in the trees, and I was just turning the wheel to aim the truck at the fence when out of the corner of my eye I saw a figure emerge from the trees to my left.

The air filled with blue sparks and every muscle in my body went rigid. My mind screamed, "What the hell is going on?"

But I knew I had been shocked. My neck burned where the baton had connected. I lost control of the truck. Luckily it swerved to my right, pulling me away from the baton, but I was seriously dazed from the brief contact.

I was just coming out of it when the truck hit a tree stump and went up on two wheels. I braced myself, waiting for it to slam back down, but it teetered for a second and came to a rest on the driver's-side door.

Through the back window, in the darkness, I saw an evil grin coming closer, a sinister blue flicker getting brighter as he approached, fingering the trigger of his shock baton.

I fumbled with my seat belt, finally releasing it. Then I pulled the handle on the passenger-side door and pushed. It opened a couple inches, but it was heavy and I didn't have the leverage to get it open. I put my feet on the steering column, climbing up and pushing myself between the door and the metal frame of the truck. When I finally got out, he was almost on me. I jumped, hitting the ground hard. Then I took off running into the black night.

EIGHTY-ONE

Running through the woods in absolute darkness with the sound of my pursuer behind me was like something out of a nightmare. I was disoriented and terrified. I had no idea where I was or where I was going, no idea if I was about to slam into a tree or come face-to-face with that evil grin.

The adrenaline had me running flat out. Luckily I was tired and flat out was slow enough that when I saw a cloud of tiny specks of light glinting in front of me, I skidded to a stop just in time, my face inches from the fence's razor-sharp barbs.

Panic welled up inside me. Now I was trapped. I still had my baton, and I thought about trying to get behind my pursuer, to shock him before he could shock me. But I didn't like my chances. Then I realized the fence wasn't just a barrier, it was also a landmark, something to guide me so I wasn't running in circles.

I heard footsteps and heavy breathing in the brush behind me, so doubling back toward the holes in the fence wasn't an option. The only way I could go was forward. But at least now I knew where forward was.

The clouds parted briefly, and in the moonlight, I could see once more the barbs glinting on my left. Then the light was gone and I was moving again through darkness. I had to slow down, but as I did, I could hear the footsteps, the breathing, growing louder behind me.

I was inching along when I bumped into something solid. A tree, growing right next to the fence.

It was the maple tree I'd used to cross over earlier. I squinted intently through the links, just making out the trunk of the evergreen on the other side.

Jamming the baton through my belt, I shimmied up the tree. I reached around in the darkness until I found the first branch, then lifted myself into the tangle of tree limbs above. Part of me wanted to just hide, but the longer the others were waiting for me at Pinecone Rock, the more likely someone else would find them.

I felt around with my hands and feet until I found the thick sturdy branch that extended over the razor wire. Grabbing the smaller branches for support, I stood and inched my way out.

When I was almost halfway across, the branch I was standing on let out a loud splintering sound. At the same time, the clouds parted and the moonlight shone on me like a spotlight on a tightrope-walker.

It also lit up my pursuer, staring up at me.

With the added light, I could move more quickly, but so could he. He was already swinging up into the tree, clambering toward me with surprising speed, considering his injury.

I had made it past the razor wire when the branch shook and cracked loudly. I turned back to see my pursuer taking his foot off it. He had tried to come after me, but he knew it wouldn't hold both of us. As I moved toward the evergreen bough, he extended his foot. He was waiting until I stepped off, then he would come at me.

I hesitated, then went ahead and moved onto the evergreen limb. As soon as I heard that maple limb creaking, I turned. He smiled, coming toward me, almost at the fence.

I crouched down and wrapped my hands as tightly as I could around the branch he was balancing on, and I jumped.

The maple branch lurched violently, but I held my grip and he kept his balance, his arms waving spastically in the air. Then the lurching subsided.

I don't know if he had figured out what I was trying to pull, but I'm pretty sure he could tell it hadn't worked.

For a second, he looked at me with that evil smile. Then the branch snapped completely.

He grabbed for it and we both held on, even as the branch hit the top of the fence with a jolt. He was just inside the fence, and I was a couple of feet outside it. We teetered there for a moment. He must have outweighed me by a hundred pounds, but I had much more of the branch on my side. It was a lever, and I had the leverage.

He was confused at first, but not alarmed, as I slowly sank and he slowly rose. Then the entire branch abruptly slid in my direction, pulling him straight toward the fence. I dropped to the dirt. He tried to let go, too, but not in time. His arms plunged into the razor wire and his body slammed against the barbs. He struggled, gasping and grunting, thrashing around, his boots dangling two feet off the ground.

His hands were trying to grab on to something—anything—to relieve the pressure and ease the pain. His boots scraped at the fence, trying to find a foothold. The barbs on the fence were tearing at his knees and elbows.

In the moonlight, I could see red dripping down the fence.

I stood on the ground, frozen, relieved and repulsed and wondering what to do next. He was working his arms free of the razor wire. Looking at me through the fence, through the pain, his mouth spread in a bloody grin.

"We're going to kill you all," he said. "You know that, right? And when you're dead, we'll stock up with more mixies, and we'll kill them, too."

I stared at him in horror, and he laughed.

I knew I had to get moving, but I also knew before long he'd pull free and come after me. Then I saw something on his belt, glinting in the moonlight. Right next to where his baton would have been.

Handcuffs.

His jacket had bunched up, so the closer I got, the less he could see of me. I reached my fingers between the barbs and grabbed the cuffs out of their holder, pulling them through the fence. "What are you doing?" he said, sounding suddenly unsure.

Crouching down, I poked one of the cuffs back through the fence and clamped it around his ankle.

As soon as he heard the click, he started thrashing around, kicking his feet, pulling my hand against the fence. The barbs cut into my skin and I almost let go of the other end of the cuffs, but I held on. He was much stronger than me, but he had no leverage. I pulled the chain toward me and clamped the cuff onto the fence, locking him in place.

He started screaming at me, horrible names, horrible things he would do to me. I grabbed the handcuff chain and jerked it hard, jamming him against the barbs of the fence. His curses died out, replaced with a pathetic groan.

I was just about to leave when I had a thought. I reached through the fence one last time, and plucked the key to the handcuffs from his belt.

EIGHTY-TWO

By the time I got to Pinecone Rock, I was a wreck. I don't know how long it took me, stumbling through the blackness, jumping at every sound, second-guessing every turn. But when I finally saw Rex through the trees, and then Pell and Ruth and Sly, I almost wept.

Rex was saying, "Anywhere is safer than here. We can lay low in the city or camp out in the zurbs, decide if we want to leave the state, or the country."

Sly shrugged. "Close enough to a plan for now."

When I stepped through the bushes, Rex said, "*Jimi!* Thank God." He came over and wrapped his arms around me, lifting me off the ground. I looked into his eyes, saw the intensity of feeling there, and I knew I felt the same way. I didn't know what to think about that, but I also knew now wasn't the time. "Are you okay?" he said, looking me up and down.

"I'm fine."

Pell slapped my back. "You had us worried, there, girl."

Rex let out a brief laugh. "That was you in that truck, right? Driving through the fence. That was brilliant."

"You saved our lives back there," Ruth said. "Thanks."

"Yeah, seriously, kid," Sly said. "We owe you." Then he spotted the shock baton shoved through my belt, and he laughed. "Holy crap, you took one of their shock batons? You're such a badass."

I looked down, embarrassed, then Sly clapped his hands and rubbed them together. "Seriously, though, now it's time to get the hell out of here."

"Where's Del?" I asked. "Did he make it out?"

Rex looked away. "I don't know."

Sly shrugged. "Probably. But he's not here. We shouldn't be, either."

"I told him to meet us here," I said. "He's supposed to be here."

Sly snorted. "Well, he didn't and he's not."

I looked at him. "Are you mad at him? What's that about?"

"A lot of us had doubts about Jasper from the beginning," Ruth said. "Del wouldn't listen to any of it. Jasper got him that super-expensive splice, and Del thought he was the best thing ever." She looked down. "It got so he would, like, intimidate anyone who said anything bad about Jasper. And if anyone asked questions about Haven or who these sponsors were, he would attack them for being ungrateful. Yesterday, he went off on me for like five minutes."

Sly cocked an eyebrow. "And in the end, he damn near got us all killed."

A few days earlier, I would have been unable to picture Del as the type to intimidate anyone. But before then, he'd never been in a position where he could. The self-centeredness, though, the stubbornness—he'd been getting more like that even before the splice. I was quiet. There was nothing I could say in his defense.

Then Rex said, "We can't stay much longer."

"We can't just leave him here," I said.

Sly stepped forward. "He almost got us all killed once. I don't want to let him do it again. We need to get going."

"Not me," I said, shaking my head. "I've been trying to save him since before I even knew you guys, maybe trying to save him from himself. I can't give up on him now."

"We're running out of time," Rex said. "We need to go."

"Then I'm staying."

Rex ground his jaw for a second, fuming. "Come here," he said, turning and stomping off into the woods.

"What?"

He stopped and looked back at me. "I need to show you something."

I followed him up to the crest of the hill.

"I pulled these off a guard back in Haven," he said, handing me a pair of binoculars. "Take a look. It isn't pretty."

What I saw chilled me to the bone. Pitman and the road leading up to it were clogged with traffic. Half a mile of it, at least. Pickup trucks, SUVs, RVs, a hundred of them, all waiting to turn inside the gate to Pitman. For Game Day.

Up in the sky, three or four quadcopters were approaching to land. A handful of blinking lights behind them indicated more on the way.

Rex looked on, his face blank but his eyes brimming with sorrow, as if he tried and tried and tried to give people the benefit of the doubt, to hope they would come through, and every time they let him down.

I wanted to say something to comfort him, to make him feel better about humanity, about me. But I had nothing.

I looked at the line of traffic, trucks with rifle racks and trailers, hard-looking men at the wheel, and women, too.

"This isn't some small thing," Rex said. "This is huge. It's open season on chimeras. Literally. We can't take the Levline back to the city. We're moving on foot, and we have to move fast, because they're going to be coming after us. Including you. Maybe especially you."

I was moving the binoculars down the line of vehicles, studying the faces of the people who wanted to kill my friends. There were so many of them. So much hate.

"I need to get my friends to safety," Rex said quietly.

"I understand," I said, keeping the binoculars up to my eyes, as if somehow they protected me. Even as they made those hunters appear closer, they made the reality of it farther away. "You need to go do that."

He put his hand on my shoulder, making sure I was paying attention even though I wasn't looking at him. "That means you, too. You're one of them."

"I'm staying here," I said quietly.

"I can't let you do that. It's too dangerous."

"I'm waiting for Del."

He gently pushed the binoculars down, away from my face. "He wouldn't wait for you. You know that, don't you?"

"He's my friend."

"He doesn't deserve to be."

I put the binoculars back up to my face.

"I can't let you sacrifice your life for him. He's not worth it, Jimi."

"You don't even know him," I said. I could hardly see as my eyes clouded with tears.

"Do you?"

I could feel the tears rolling down my cheeks.

"Come on," he said softly.

"I'm staying."

"You're not."

"What are you going to do, carry me?"

"If I have to, yes."

I was just lowering the binoculars to tell him I had made up my mind when something caught my eye, and I lifted them back up.

"What is it?" Rex asked as I swept the side of the road, trying to find it again.

"It's Del," I said, confused, wondering why he was down there, hiding in the bushes. He could have come past Pinecone Rock on his way down there.

"Are you sure? What's he doing down there?"

As I watched, Del emerged from the trees below us, bounding down the side of the road with a stride that was not entirely human. Once he was past the line of cars, he crossed the road and disappeared into the trees along the fence. I caught a last glimpse of him, inside the town of Pitman, running toward the town center.

Suddenly, I knew where he was headed, and what he was going to do. What I didn't know was whether I could get there in time to stop him.

EIGHTY-THREE

grabbed Rex's arm and ran back to where Ruth, Pell, and Sly were gathered. I told them what I'd seen. "You guys go on. It's not safe for you down there. I'm going to get Del."

Ruth and Pell and Sly didn't protest. They knew I'd made up my mind. We shared quick hugs and I headed back up to the top of the hill. But Rex followed me, whispering forcefully that it wasn't safe for me, either, down there, and that most of the people I was trying to save would kill me without a second thought.

But I thought about the elderly couple and I thought about the kids, about Sammy and his friends. And as wrong as their parents might be, as filled with hate, killing them was wrong, too.

"Get them to safety," I told him. "And yourself, too."

He started to protest, but I silenced him with a kiss. Then I turned and plunged down the hillside.

My legs were moving as fast as they could, but gravity was doing most of the work. I was just trying not to lose my balance or slam into a tree.

My plan was to intercept Del, talk to him, get him out of there before he got himself killed. I had hoped more details would come to me on the way down, but the bottom of the hill was coming at me fast, and I didn't even know how I'd get through the gate.

The baton was still wedged into my belt, slapping against my thigh with every step. It gave me an idea.

As I approached the edge of the woods, I angled toward the last truck in the line. The driver was alone, and his window was open.

I pulled the baton out of my belt and ran straight for him. I was almost there before he looked over and did a double take. By then it was too late.

The baton hit him in the throat, just under the chin. I felt bad assaulting a stranger, but he was there to slaughter my friends, so I didn't feel bad enough to stop. Just like before, I held the baton in place as I opened the door and dumped him on the road.

By now, people in front of us had seen me. They were yelling and honking their horns.

I put the truck into reverse and backed up about forty yards, then put it back in drive and jammed the accelerator hard. Two old men in the truck in front of me got out and ran, thinking I was going to ram them.

But I jerked the wheel hard to the right and plowed through yet another fence, dragging a twenty-foot section of it behind me. I cut across a couple of lawns and leveled a signpost, which snagged the fencing and tore it free. I was getting good at this.

Half a dozen men were running after me, but I quickly lost them. As I shot through an intersection, I saw flashing police lights a quarter of a mile to my left, still headed back out toward the gate.

To my right the flare was burning in the sky. I knew that's where Del was headed. I zigzagged through town, keeping the fire in front of me until I arrived at the entrance, another fence, another locked gate. A cluster of police lights appeared in my rearview, this time coming after me. Fast.

I jammed down the accelerator, punching through one more fence, and bouncing across the dirt lot that surrounded the coal well facility. Pipes, hoses, and ductwork crisscrossed the ground. I tensed myself for an explosion, but somehow managed to not hit any of it.

By the time I got out of the truck, a crowd was gathering in a circle around me. The police were closing fast. I looked up at the tower and paused.

There was Del, climbing the metal scaffold.

A hand grabbed my arm, and I turned to see Mayor Randolph glaring down at me. "You!" he said, his jaw clenched. "What the hell are you doing here?"

Jasper was standing behind him, his face patched together with medical tape, his eyes fluorescing with anger and hatred.

"Let go," I said, pulling my arm free. "I'm trying to save your town."

Del reached the top of the tower and a moment later the flame went out. A gasp swept throughout the gathering crowd, then an ominous silence.

"He shut down the pressure relief valve," said a small man in overalls and a hardhat now standing behind the mayor. "There's no backflow preventers. In five minutes the entire system will be hyper-pressurized."

The mayor turned to him. "And?"

"The whole town could go up."

EIGHTY-FOUR

Searchlights from the police cars sliced through the sky before converging on Del, standing at the top of the tower.

"What the hell is that thing?" asked a voice in the crowd.

"Some kind of mixie tiger," said another.

I ran to the base of the tower and looked back at the crowd growing behind me. I spotted Cantrell, the H4H cop, staring up at Del with murder in his eyes. I wondered if he was a paying customer. Then I thought about him rounding up chimeras, and I realized he was part of the whole thing. He was in on it.

But I put that out of my mind for the moment.

A pair of workers in hardhats and coveralls started climbing the tower, but Del called out, "Get back, or the whole town goes up. I swear to God, I'll do it."

"Del!" I called out. One of the spotlights swung around to illuminate me.

Del looked down, squinting into the searchlights. "Jimi?"

The quadcopters that had been dots on the horizon a few moments earlier were now loud and close. Some were news copters, hovering in the sky with spotlights and cameras. Others were landing in nearby open spaces. I did a double take when I saw Jerry from the coffee shop and a dozen other people climbing out of one of the larger copters with an "Earth for Everyone" banner.

"Don't do this, Del!" I said. "Please! Just come down from there, and we'll figure this all out."

"You already figured it out, Jimi. You were right. They tricked us. They made a fool out of me. These evil bastards were going to hunt us down and kill us all. I can't let them get away with that."

Behind me, the engineer said to the mayor, "You've got four minutes before the whole town is at risk."

"You can't kill innocent people!" I screamed. "Then you're as bad as they are!"

He let out a crazed bark of a laugh. "There's no innocent people down there, Jimi. Only you." Even at that distance, and in the harsh glare from the searchlights, I could see his face looking at me with sad fondness. "You need to get out of here, Jimi. You need to go home."

Before I could say anything else, a familiar voice boomed right next to me, making me jump.

"I see some things about you haven't changed a bit, have they? You're still a pathetic little freak!"

Stan Grainger had appeared next to me, holding a bullhorn to his face.

Del shielded his eyes from the light. "Dad?" He laughed that crazed laugh again. "What are you doing here?"

"I was supposed to go hunting. But looks like you messed up my plans as bad as you messed up your own self. I can't even figure out what it is you're supposed to be, other than a blasphemy against God."

"You never could. But you never cared, either. Not about me, not about Mom."

"You leave your mother out of this," Stan said, any trace of teasing or sarcasm replaced by a murderous cold. "I'm just glad she's not here to see what you've done to yourself."

The engineer was frantic. "We're almost out of time," he hissed, his hand clenching a fistful of the mayor's shirt. "You need to get him down from there and open that valve, or you need to start evacuating this town and getting these tourists out of here."

Del was laughing at his father's words, but even at a distance, I could see tears running down his cheeks. "Yeah? Then I guess it's a good thing you drove her to kill herself, you miserable—"

"Del!" I called out. I shoved Stan out of the way, hard. He smelled of stale beer and cigarettes. "Look at me, Del!" I called out, and he did. "You kissed me, Del, before you got spliced, before any of this. Remember that? What did that even mean?"

"Jimi," he said, softly, sadly. ". . . It meant goodbye."

As he said it, I was startled by a loud crack right next to my ear.

The whole crowd turned to see Stan holding his hunting rifle up to his eye. Then we looked at Del, a red spot in the middle of his chest glowing bright in the glare of the searchlights, spreading as we watched. His eyes were wide with surprise and shock. Blood bubbled at his mouth.

"Del!" I screamed.

Then Stan's rifle cracked again.

The bullet sparked off the valve by Del's hand, shattering it and sending chunks of metal spinning off into the air. Del looked right at me, as if for confirmation that this was really happening. Then, with a deep, throaty *whumpf*, the top of the tower erupted in a massive fireball.

I screamed again.

The fireball churned in place for a long moment before fading into a cloud of black smoke that rolled up into the sky. Leaving Del behind, fully engulfed in flame. He teetered for a moment, then pitched backward off the tower, trailing fire as he fell through the darkness until he disappeared with a splash and a sizzle into the depthless black of the waste pit below.

"Del!" I screamed, running toward him.

Behind me, I could hear voices yelling, "Get back! Get back!" and "It's going to blow!"

The ground rumbled beneath my feet.

Something solid slammed into me, wrapped around me.

Then the world erupted into flame.

EIGHTY-FIVE

I didn't lose consciousness. Not entirely. I remember the blast and the heat. I remember being carried away from it, held safe in strong arms even as flaming debris rained down from the sky.

At some point, I was lying on a stretcher, an oxygen mask over my face. I remember struggling to get up, telling the paramedic holding me down that I was fine. Maybe he believed me, or maybe he was just too busy helping other people, but soon after that I was up, running through the area surrounding the coal well. The town had been spared, but the coal well was half gone. Sirens and flashing lights shredded the night. People were running in every direction. My ears were still ringing from the blast, my senses still dull. But my mind was clearing.

The place was crawling with agents wearing windbreakers from a handful of state and federal agencies, grouped by the letters on their backs—FBI, EPA, ICE, LAND MANAGEMENT—arguing with each other and with the Pitman police. Stan Grainger was in the middle of a group with Mayor Randolph, who was praising him as a hero for having saved the town. The engineer was saying he had destroyed public property. And someone with the federal government was saying he was a murderer.

A state police car arrived, squeezing between the official vehicles already parked there and the fire hoses crisscrossing the ground. The two plainclothes cops who got out were immediately swallowed up by all the commotion.

A contingent from Humans for Humanity was holding up banners, chanting and singing. Jerry and the Earth for Everyone protestors chanted right back, outnumbered but not outmatched. A couple of them wore T-shirts with the same design as the button Ruth had given me, with the stylized chimera icon. A few others had the E4E logo. Jerry caught my eye and nodded without pausing his chants.

A fire crew and a bunch of workers in hardhats and overalls were busily working on the coal-well rig.

Half a dozen news broadcasters already had lights and cameras set up, each trying to find a camera angle that contained as much action and destruction as possible without showing their competitors' cameras or logos.

Running past them, I could hear snatches of what they were saying: "... not apparent if any laws were broken" ... "violating at least sixteen environmental and health and safety statutes" ... "a long history of animal cruelty allegations" ... "from hunting without a license to animal cruelty to murder ..."

I desperately wanted to listen to what they were saying—to understand. But there was something I wanted even more. I kept running until I got to the edge of the waste pit. Rescue workers were probing the depths with long hooked poles, sloshing the oily black liquid as they searched for Del.

One of the rescue workers, a woman, came up and said, "Don't worry, we'll find him." She put a hand on my shoulder to comfort me.

I nodded, but turned away. I realized I didn't want to be there when they recovered what was left of him. I didn't want that sight to be my last memory of him.

"Hey," I heard the rescue worker call gently. But I started walking. There was nothing she could say to comfort me. There was only one person who could. And I knew he was there, somewhere. I turned and looked around, then plunged back into the pandemonium, searching until I spotted him in the shadows.

I ran back through the knots of arguing humans. One of the reporters called Stan Grainger a hero for saving the town. Jerry interrupted her, pointing at me, saying, "That's the hero. You want to know who saved this town? That young lady, there. She not only thwarted this town's sick plan, but she saved these people from the vengeance they had coming to them."

Some of the cameras and lights turned away and started following me, the reporters taking turns shoving microphones in my face, peppering me with questions: What do I think of Humans for Humanity or the Genetic Heritage Act? Why did my friend try to blow up the town? And again and again, was I a chimera, too?

I ignored them, making my way toward the shadows.

I knew Rex didn't want to be part of the spotlight, ever. And I knew it made sense for him to stay hidden. But I needed to see him, and I had a feeling he knew that. I had a feeling he needed to see me, too.

The glare from the television lights preceded me, lighting him up in the shadows like it was daylight. A buzz ran through the crowd behind me, people saying, "He's one of them, a chimera."

Rex stood up straighter, glancing nervously over my shoulder at the crowd behind me. Then he looked at me and he smiled.

I hadn't seen him smile like that before. There was no reserve, nothing held back. It thrilled me to know that smile was for me.

I walked right up to him and pressed my body against his. Then I grabbed his head, running my fingers through his hair, and I pushed my lips against his.

His arms wrapped me up tight, holding me upright even as his kiss made me weak. I could hear cameras snapping pictures, video cameras whirring. Some people cheered and others groaned in disgust.

But none of that mattered. Nothing else mattered.

I felt a closeness with Rex that I'd never felt with anyone, not even Del. It was like I had known him all my life, and I knew this was supposed to be.

We were still kissing when the crowd went silent.

Our lips finally parted, and Rex put me gently down onto the ground.

I noticed two men standing next to us, rigid and upright. I

recognized them as the detectives who had come to Trudy's house, Washington and Salvatore.

Salvatore was standing farther back with his hand resting on his holster.

Washington, the handsome one, stepped closer, holding up a piece of paper.

He cleared his throat, looked at Rex, and said, "Leo Byron, you are under arrest."

EIGHTY-SIX

I stood there, immobilized by the detectives' words as they reverberated in my skull. "Leo Byron?" I said breathlessly, when I was able to speak. But by then they were leading him away in handcuffs.

"Leo?!" I called out as I ran after them. A dozen thoughts and reactions tried to elbow past each other to be first out of my mouth. When I caught up with them, running alongside as the police marched him toward the squad car, the best I could come up with was, "Are you kidding me?"

Rex closed his eyes and took a deep breath as he walked. "Sorry," he said. "I was going to tell you." He looked at me, his dark eyes anguished. "I wasn't trying to hide it from you."

It was still sinking in that this massive chimera I had fallen in love with was little Leo Byron.

"Of course you were," I said, still too shocked to be angry.

"I changed my name," he said with a shrug. "We all do."

I walked a couple of steps, my head spinning. When it stopped, I said the first coherent thing that came to mind. "How did you get to be so big?"

He laughed and shook his head. "My parents and doctors had me on all these growth treatments when I was a kid. They didn't work then, but somehow they all kicked in when I got spliced. Apparently, I had some sort of genetic disorder that the splice fixed." He gave me a crooked smile. "Someday I'll tell you about *my* sweating out."

It was too much to comprehend, too much to reconcile. I needed to focus on more immediate issues. I turned to the cops marching him along and said, "Wait a second, with all the crazy stuff going on here, *he's* the one you're arresting? What's he being arrested for?"

"Robbery," said Washington. "He held up Genaro's Deli in the city last week. We have security video, plain as day."

I remembered sitting in that Volkswagen around the corner from Genaro's while Rex ran in. Right before he mysteriously came up with the money to pay Guzman to help Del.

"There's got to be some sort of mistake," I said, because that's what you say, even when you know there isn't.

Detective Salvatore smiled at me sadly.

I leaned my head close to Rex's and whispered, "Is this why they raided Guzman's?"

He shook his head. "Doc said they didn't even ask him about it."

The reporters and camera crews trailed behind us, shouting questions at me and at Rex and at the state police. Now they were focused on crime among chimeras. Did I know Rex was a criminal? Could Rex be arrested if he wasn't legally a person?

I lagged behind for a moment as we approached the police vehicle, parked right up next to one of the fire trucks. For a moment, I was grateful to be outside the focus of attention, so I could think about what to do next. I thrust my hands into my pockets and felt something in there. I looked up as Salvatore opened the back door to the squad car and squeezed Rex inside.

Rex looked at me, his eye twitching, and I gave him a smile. Then I covered my face with my hands and ran away. A few reporters called out, asking if I wanted to make a statement, but I ignored them. Other people watched me go, some murmuring sympathetically, some laughing spitefully. But no one came after me.

When I got past the fire trucks, I doubled around and came back behind the state police car. I could see the back of Rex's head, looking out in the direction I had run off. The state police had been drawn into the arguments with the feds and the local cops.

When I opened the back door to the police car, Rex jerked his head around in surprise.

"I can't believe you never told me you were Leo," I whispered, kneeling on the floor of the car.

"What are you *doing*?" he whispered back.

The cuffs they'd put on Rex looked identical to the ones I'd put on that guy back in Haven. I still had the key I'd taken from him, and I took it out of my pocket and pulled Rex's hands toward me. Holding my breath, I slid the key into the slot in one of the cuffs and turned. It fell open. Without a moment to celebrate or thank the gods or anything else, I quickly unlocked the other one, as well.

Rex looked at his hands, suddenly unshackled. Then he looked at me, one eyebrow raised.

"I'll tell you about it later," I said, and put the key in his hand. "Here. In case you need it again. Wait a few minutes, then get out of here. And be careful out there."

I leaned in farther and kissed him again.

As I backed out the door, he called out in a whisper, "Jimi!" When I looked up, he smiled and said, "Thanks."

"You're still in trouble, *Leo*," I said. "But we'll talk about that later, too."

Then I slipped out, leaving the car door open behind me.

EIGHTY-SEVEN

The pandemonium was dying down, and at least one of the television crews had turned their lights off. The cops were still arguing jurisdiction as I walked into the middle of the throng and said loudly, "I have a statement I'd like to make."

There were grumbles from the people who had obviously decided that whatever this story was, it had been adequately covered. But the television lights that had been turned off came back on, and that seemed to be a signal to the others to pay closer attention.

I stood away from the police car, so the cameras and everyone else were looking away from Rex.

Then I cleared my throat and realized I had no idea what I was going to say.

"I'm not a chimera," I said. "But a lot of my friends are. They're good people, some of the best I've ever known. Smart, kind, generous. There are those who think chimeras shouldn't have rights as people, that they're less than human. Across the country, there are efforts to strip chimeras of their rights. And in our own state, I'm ashamed to say, they've succeeded." Some of the people from Pitman cheered, while Jerry and the E4E crowd booed. "But look what has happened. Look what they've accomplished. In less than a week since the passage of the Genetic Heritage Act, those same people have tried to use this law to justify mass murder. They tried to kill my friends in cold blood, for their own sick amusement. Well, I say no."

The E4E crowd cheered loudly at this. Everyone was getting louder as I went on, and truth be told, I was getting caught up in the moment as well.

"This is *wrong*," I thundered. "We have to make sure no more of these laws are passed anywhere else in this country and that this law doesn't stand in our state. Howard Wells asks why chimeras have turned their backs on humanity. Well, they haven't, and he knows that. But the more he and his organization poison our society with hatred and bigotry, the more some might be justified in saying, 'If that's what human is, then why would I want to be human, anyway?'"

The crowd was evenly divided between those cheering and those booing. As I looked out over their heads and their waving arms, I saw the dome light of the police car was off. The back door was closed. Rex was gone.

"But humanity isn't about DNA," I said. "It's about kindness and decency and treating others with compassion. And the chimeras I know are some of the best humans I've ever met. It's time to stop bickering about who is a person, who qualifies as human," I said, "and remember what it means to be human at all."

EIGHTY-EIGHT

The next few days were a blur. I was battered and bruised, exhausted and dehydrated. There were interviews with local, state, and federal authorities from various jurisdictions and agencies.

There were press inquiries as well. Video clips had gotten out: me trying to talk Del down; me kissing Rex (Someone made up T-shirts with our silhouettes and the caption "Dog Meets Girl"); and of course, me babbling on trying to create a diversion so Rex could escape. Little did I know my impromptu speech would become some kind of chimera manifesto.

It was embarrassing. I stood by everything I said, for sure, but if I'd known it was going to be a big deal, I would have written an outline first and tried not to ramble so much.

In between all the interviews with the police and the media, there was a seemingly endless series of "interviews" with my mom, as well. She made good on her promise to "really talk about all this" with me, and then some.

I told her everything this time, and our conversations alternated between two extremes of, "You're so brave; I'm so proud of you" and "How could you be so stupid; you're lucky you didn't get yourself killed."

Kevin was busy with school and sports, but we had a couple of heart-to-hearts that were oddly similar to the conversations with my mom. He told me he had been worried about me, too, and he was glad I was okay. He said he was proud of what I did, but he also called me an idiot for doing it. But when my mom would have given me a hug, Kevin would flick my ear, like he used to when we were little.

On my second day back, late in the afternoon, my mom was pretty heavily into get-on-my-case mode when I interrupted her to ask why she had never told me about my aunt Dymphna.

The question stopped her in her tracks. "Don't change the subject," she finally said, but it was clear she was on the defensive.

"I'm not changing the subject. We've been talking about the same thing for two days: *me*. I think I have a right to know who it is that *I* am named after."

She went silent after that. Then she said quietly, "That was your father's decision, not to tell you about her. I was just respecting his wishes."

I looked at her, waiting for more. But she just stood and said, "We'll talk about it later." Then she left me alone.

I couldn't believe it. I really did want to know about Aunt Dymphna, but for several days after that, whenever she started riding me too bad, I brought up Aunt Dymphna and she would back off. It was like annoying-mom Kryptonite. I figured I'd milk it for as long as it was useful. And then, if she still wasn't ready to talk, I'd go back to Trudy. I had a feeling she'd tell me straight. Especially after all this.

▬ ▬ ▬

A few days later, things began to settle down and I had more time and head space to think about Del, and about Rex.

They never found Del's body. I don't know how hard they searched, really. It was a nasty environment to be looking in. The gunshot probably killed him before the fire, before the fall. Whatever was left would have been devastated by the toxic pool. Dark images crossed my mind, of him down there, alone forever. I pictured future anthropologists uncovering his remains and trying to make the case for some newly discovered branch of evolution.

The pain of knowing he was gone was a constant physical thing, a void in my life, in the universe, made even worse by the betrayals that had led up to it, and the pain that had pushed Del down that path.

All of me was sad, but only part of me was shocked. I had lost him so many times, by the time he was really gone, I was almost ready for it.

Maybe that made it even sadder.

Rex wasn't dead, but he was gone, and I was *not* prepared for that. I wasn't prepared for him to be Leo Byron, either. In some ways it made me feel even closer to him. He wasn't just my newest friend. He was one of my oldest, too.

I could understand why he didn't want to tell me. And I believed he had his reasons. But there was a lie stretching between us now. Until we got some time together, to talk about it and figure it out, the fact of that lie was going to stay between us. Between me and knowing what to think about it all.

I missed two weeks of school. In part to heal, in part to make time for all the interviews and examinations and depositions. They told me the process could drag on for months, but by the end of the first week, the worst of it was over.

They said it would be even longer before they knew if anyone was going to jail for what had happened. Jasper was a good bet to do time, although he was rich, and that counted, unfortunately. It came out that Cantrell, the cop, was Jasper's partner, his main source of chimeras. Cantrell and his pals would round them up. Then Jasper's men would "rescue" them, take them to Haven, where they could heal and have a great time and wait to be transported to Chimerica. Game Day would have been the first "legal" hunt, and by far the biggest, but although there was no evidence, some suspected there may have been smaller chimera hunts previously, even before GHA. It was horrifying to think about, and even more chilling to think about what could have happened if they had gone through with Game Day and it had become a regular event.

Cantrell was charged with a variety of crimes, including kidnapping, but only for the abductions before GHA was passed. After that, it might not have even been illegal.

Mayor Randolph was indicted for operating an illegal coal well and cited for dozens of violations. He had numerous ties to Jasper, including kickbacks from the long-term lease he'd given Jasper on the land Haven sat on. He had also been in on the hunt—the whole town had been—but it wasn't clear if any of them would be charged in connection with that. He might have cut a deal to testify against Jasper.

Andrew Randolph would recover fully from the injuries Rex and I had inflicted on him back in Pitman. But they said it would take a while. That was fine with me.

Stan Grainger became a hero to certain factions in H4H. Other people, myself among them, thought he was a morally repugnant scumbag of the worst kind. He was wanted for questioning and faced possible charges, but he disappeared after that night and no one had seen him since.

Timms disappeared as well.

Howard Wells came out of it all unscathed. It was decided that he was legitimately uninvolved in what was going on in Pitman. He condemned Jasper's whole operation vehemently—almost convincingly—but he never said he thought it was wrong. He only talked about how it undermined the broader Humans for Humanity movement.

And he was right about that. The whole thing gave H4H a big black eye, stalling efforts across the country.

Eventually, Earth for Everyone got an injunction overturning the state's Genetic Heritage Act. The fight wasn't over yet, not by a long shot. But it was an important early victory. For the time being, chimeras were as safe as they had always been. Which was to say, not very.

By the end of the two weeks, the pain of losing Del had lessened just enough to let me know it might one day lessen some more. But my fear and anxiety about Rex intensified. I wondered constantly where he was, what had become of him. Deep down, I was confident he was okay. But I wondered if maybe that was just because I couldn't bear the thought of him not being okay.

I worried about Ruth and Pell and Sly, as well. They'd gotten away safely that night, but I hadn't heard from them since. Frankly, I worried about all the chimeras.

And when I was done thinking about everyone else, I worried about me, about my future, about what damage I had done to it and what enemies I'd made.

I hardly slept most nights, my mind racing with all the usual anxieties plus a thousand new ones. When I closed my eyes, sometimes I saw things—evil faces with bloody grins leering at me through razor wire, or Del, looking in my eyes as the flames covered his body and he disappeared into the muck.

I started running again in the evenings. I used to run to clear my head; now I did it to tire myself out as well, so I'd have a fighting chance at sleep. Maybe also because I was still looking for something.

Sunday night before my first day back at school, I knew sleep really would not come easily. I needed to be extra tired, so I planned an extra-long run.

As I did my stretches on the grass between my house and Del's, I wondered what the next morning would be like, going to school without Del. When the time came, would I be able to leave without him, or would I feel compelled to keep waiting, as if somehow I could conjure the sound of his screen door slapping, the sight of him bounding down his back steps?

I thought about missing the bus in Del's honor, one last time, and walking to school the way we had done just a few weeks earlier, in a previous lifetime.

But if I was going to get my life back together, I needed to start by making the bus. Del had been my excuse for missing it, and Del was gone.

So, instead of missing the bus and walking the next morning, I ran the route that night.

I took it slow at first, a light jog past the Devon Street Bridge, which was still out. Then I headed toward North Avenue and the city line.

I saw Del everywhere I looked, remembering most particularly our last walk around here. Memories of him showing me his tattoo, walking backward and teasing me, trying to convince me to ditch school with him that day.

I wondered what would have happened if I had. There was no way of knowing, no point in wondering, but it was a thought I couldn't unthink, and it stayed with me.

I was approaching the Avenue and was still a ways off when the pedestrian light turned green. I put on every bit of speed I had and made it, stepping onto the far side just as the light turned red.

It was dark and I was outside the city, but I was completely unafraid. I was already running fast, so I kept on going, past the squat where I'd first met the chimeras, where Del had almost killed Officer Cantrell. That was still a question—what would have happened if I had left him in the creek, how differently might things have turned out? But I knew that wasn't something I could have done.

I kept running, picturing Ruth and Pell on the steps, poor Ryan standing in the driveway, Rex lurking in the doorway, tall and brooding and mysterious, strong and handsome.

I passed the empty house where he had saved me from Simon. I shook my head as the thought crossed my mind, as it had done so many times the past two weeks: Leo goddamned Byron.

Crossing back into the city, I sprinted all the way to my school. It looked smaller than I remembered it, but still imposing in its way. I thought back to the last time I'd been there, a visitor, running away while the rest of the students went in to class. I jogged up and down the steps a handful of times, letting the place know I wasn't intimidated.

On my way back, I looped past Genaro's Deli. And when I could run no farther, I headed home.

Coming up the driveway between Del's house and mine still felt weird, for so many reasons.

As I paused to stretch once more, I saw a figure in the shadows.

For an instant I thought it was Del. But of course it wasn't.

It was Rex.

He caught me before I landed. He kissed me before I screamed. He held me for a long, long time. When he finally he put me down, we stared into each other's eyes.

"I missed you," he said.

I reached up to touch his face, making sure he was really real. "I missed you, too, Leo Byron," I said with a wry smile. "But you've still got some explaining to do."

He smiled back. "I know."

I glanced over at the warm light spilling out through our kitchen window. Inside, I could see my mom at the sink rinsing recyclables. Soon she'd be bringing them outside.

"Want to come inside?" I asked. I knew it was a bad idea, and I knew he'd say no.

He took my hand, squeezing it. "Yes, but not right now."

"Are the others okay?"

"They're fine."

"Where have you been?"

"I've been looking for answers," he said. "And I found some."

"What do you mean?"

The back door swung open and my mom came outside carrying the small recycling bin from the kitchen. Standing in the light from the kitchen, she couldn't see us, but she would in a moment.

"What do you mean?" I whispered again, urgently.

"Jimi?" my mom called out, squinting into the night. "Are you out here?"

Rex leaned so close his lips touched my ear, and he said, "Chimerica is real."

"What do you *mean*?"

"I have to go, but I'll be back soon."

"What? You just got here." I couldn't bear the thought of him leaving again.

"Until then," he said, and he kissed me again, longer and deeper.

When we parted, he turned to leave, but I held on to his shirt, not letting him go. "Until *when*?"

He smiled. "Until soon."

Then he kissed me once more, quickly on the cheek, and melted away into the shadows.

Mom came down the steps and emptied the recycling bucket into the bin with a clatter. She squinted at me in the darkness. "Jimi? Are you okay?"

My lips were tingling. My heart was racing. I was smiling, and I realized I couldn't stop. "Yeah, Mom," I said. "I'm great."

She came over and drew me close, putting her arm around my shoulders. "I love you, Jimi."

As we turned to go up the back steps, I said, "Love you, too, Mom."

I followed her up onto the porch, but when she went inside, I paused at the door. Turning, I looked back out into the night and whispered, "Until soon."

ACKNOWLEDGMENTS

Many people helped in many ways to make this book a reality. I'd like to thank all of them but can only thank some. My wife, Elizabeth, makes all things possible and is an inexhaustible source of love and support—and beta reading and story advice. I am especially grateful for her insights as a children's librarian into this book, my first written primarily for young adults.

Stacia Decker, my agent and close friend, is smart, energetic, creative, and endlessly (so far) patient. She believed in this book from the moment I called her, breathlessly excited, to tell her the idea—long before her editorial brilliance helped shape it into the book it was supposed to be. I also thank her for finding the book a home with the wonderful people at Holiday House. My editor, Kelly Loughman, has been wise, thoughtful, and thorough, an incredibly supportive creative partner, and a lot of fun to work with as we took this book the final mile (okay, several miles). I'd also like to thank Terry Borzumato, Emily Mannon, Emily Campisano, and the entire team at Holiday House, whose enthusiastic support for this book has been both humbling and inspiring.

As always, I am incredibly grateful for the help and support of the amazing community of writers that I call my friends. Some, like Jonathan Maberry and Joelle Charbonneau, were indispensible as I wrote this book. There are also many others who might not have helped with this book specifically but without whose help along the way I would never have gotten to this point. So, special thanks to everyone in the Liars Club, the extended Writers Coffeehouse community, and my friends at Mystery Writers of America and International Thriller Writers.

Finally, I'd like to thank the world's librarians and booksellers. Being married to a librarian, I have a special insight into how fabulous they are, and as an author and a reader I have the utmost appreciation for those who connect books to the people who love them and make this whole thing possible.

Read on for a sneak peek at

SPLINTERED,

where Jimi Corcoran's
chilling adventures continue. . . .

Before he could finish his sentence, the door opened and Ruth and Pell burst back inside with a third person propped up between them. I didn't recognize him. He had some kind of bird splice, but different from Ruth and Pell. More colorful. The feathers that framed his head were bright yellow, but they were also matted and filthy. So were his clothes. His head hung down on his chest.

Rex and I rushed over to them. Doc followed, slower.

"Who's this?" I asked, and Rex said "What happened?" as we both helped them move him to a chair.

"We don't know," Ruth said, out of breath.

"We found him on the train tracks," Pell added.

"The Levline?" Rex said, alarmed.

"No," Pell said, "the freight train."

Doc was already examining him, gently lifting his head. He was young, our age or maybe younger. There was some sort of metal bottle hanging around his neck, with a plastic mask attached by a hose.

Doc looked at it, then up at Ruth and Pell. "What's this?"

"No idea," Ruth said.

Doc looked in the kid's pupils, felt his pulse, and then put an ear to his chest and listened to him breathing. The kid looked terrible.

"Is it a bad splice?" I asked. I'd seen up close how devastating it could be when a splice went wrong.

Doc shook his head. He looked worried. "No, I don't think that's it."

Jerry came around from behind the counter, looking concerned but exasperated. "Should we get him into the back?"

"No," Doc said. "We need to get him to my clinic. Now."

Doc's van was parked out front. Rex and I carried the sick kid out and got into the back with him. Ruth and Pell followed, but when Pell started to get into the van with us, Ruth put a hand on her arm.

"The meeting," Ruth said. "It's important."

Pell paused as Doc started the motor.

"It's okay," I said. "We got it."

What I meant was, Doc had it. Ruth and Pell weren't going to make much difference, and neither was Rex or I. Doc was the only one who really mattered.

Pell nodded. "Keep us posted." Then she stepped back and closed the door.

Doc drove away, fast but not reckless.

The kid was totally out of it, but I held his hand anyway, feeling strangely awkward. I hadn't seen Rex in so long, and now here we were, sitting with an unconscious stranger between us and Doc in the front seat. It didn't feel like the best time to resume our conversation. Not that we'd even really had a chance to start it in the first place.

The kid's sleeve had slid back, revealing a slender, dirty wrist with a white plastic band around it. I leaned in for a closer look in the dim light coming from the windows.

"What's that?" Rex rumbled.

"It looks like a hospital bracelet," I said. The interior of the van lit up as we passed some lights outside.

"A hospital bracelet?"

"Something like that. It says 'Patient name: Cornelius.' No last name. It doesn't say what hospital, either, just some numbers."

Cornelius looked like a nice guy, with a soft brow and a mouth that seemed like it probably smiled a lot. The splice suited him: the colorful feathers nicely offset his bronze skin, and his strong beak-like nose suited the angles of his chin and his cheekbones. Maybe it was the fact that now he had a name, but I felt a pang of intense sadness. He was not well at all. His breathing was shallow and fast, and his face was speckled with nicks and cuts and what looked like burns. His clothes were torn and singed. I had a lot of faith in Doc Guzman's abilities, but I didn't think Cornelius was going to make it.

"He doesn't look good," Rex said softly. Then the back of the van was plunged into darkness, meaning we had left the city and crossed into the zurbs. No municipal electricity, so no streetlights.

"No, he doesn't," I said. "Do you think he needs this?" I held up the grimy metal canister around his neck.

"We'll be there any minute. We should let Doc decide."

A moment later, the van lurched and came to an abrupt stop. Rex opened the back door, and together we carried Cornelius out.

Doc was already unlocking the front door to the clinic, which sat in the middle of an abandoned strip mall in the zurbs, a half mile outside the city. The only light came from the van's headlights, but they were bright enough to light up the entire row of stores.

As Doc opened the door, a figure stepped out from around the farthest store. I could barely make him out in the darkness, but he looked like trouble.

"We have company," I said to Rex.

He nodded. "Hey, Doc," he called out, just loud enough to be heard. "Is this your friend from earlier?"

Doc turned to us, then saw the guy approaching. His shoulders slumped and he nodded. "Brian Kurtz."

Kurtz stepped into the light, looking drunk and disheveled, with manic eyes set deep in a pale, freckled face under a blond buzz cut. He did look belligerent, but he also looked scared and confused. Like a little boy only slightly hidden under a thin veneer of whatever he thought a man was supposed to be.

"Look, kid," Doc told him. "Like I said before, I don't know where your friend is. But even if I did, I couldn't tell you."

"Right. Patient-doctor confidentiality," Kurtz replied with a sneer. His voice sounded even younger than he looked. "Like a real doctor would be set up in a crappy place like this out in the zurbs."

Rex met my eyes and whispered, "Put him down."

I slowly lowered Cornelius's feet to the ground. Rex moved him upright, handing him off to me so that I could lean him against the van. With his head closer to mine, Cornelius's wheezing sounded even worse. Some of his feathers were bent and broken. Rex stepped slowly away from the van and closer to Doc.

Kurtz froze for a second as he took in Rex's size. The sneer returned, but the fear didn't leave his eyes. "Oh, so you brought your mixie bodyguard to protect you, is that it?"

Cornelius was slipping from my grasp, and as I readjusted my grip, Kurtz looked over at me and laughed. "If that's your friend and he's sick, I'd be careful bringing him to this guy. You might not be happy with the result."

Rex took a step closer and Kurtz whirled on him, pulling a gun from his waistband. The tension in the air skyrocketed and my stomach clenched.

"Okay, now, now let's calm down," Doc said, showing his open hands in a soothing gesture. "That's serious business right there. Deadly business."

Kurtz clenched his eyes for a moment, then opened them as he swung the gun in Doc's direction.

"Doc, look out!" I yelled.

Rex lunged, whipping out his arm with extraordinary speed and snatching the weapon.

Kurtz seemed stunned, staring at his empty hand for several seconds before realizing Rex now held the gun.

"I told you before, son," Doc said gently. "I don't want any trouble."

Kurtz turned to Rex. "You . . . you need to give me that back."

Rex opened the gun's cylinder, shook the bullets into his palm, and flung them into the air. A moment later they pitter-pattered back to Earth in the overgrown, trash-strewn lot across the street.

Rex clicked the cylinder back into place. As he was handing the gun back, an oddly smug, malevolent smile flickered across Kurtz's face. Then I realized why.

"He's got more bullets," I called out.

Kurtz flashed me a murderous glare as his hand moved to his pants pocket. I might have heard a faint *clink* as he did.

Rex snorted and snatched the gun back, then heaved it into the dark sky.

Kurtz tried to track the arc, but it disappeared. "Hey . . . ," he said, pausing as a distant, muffled crash emerged from somewhere in the night, "that was my dad's gun."

Rex took a step closer and loomed over him. "Get out of here."

Kurtz took a step back. "You'll be sorry you did that," he said, his voice jagged with emotion. Then he turned and ran, disappearing around the corner. Rex, Doc, and I exchanged glances as a car door slammed and tires squealed.

Rex and I lifted Cornelius again as Doc opened the door.

"Does that happen a lot?" I asked as we carried Cornelius inside.

"It happens," Doc replied, slapping a switch to turn on the battery-powered lights.

"You shouldn't be out here on your own," Rex said.

Doc avoided Rex's eyes. "Just take him straight back and put him in the chair."

We carried Cornelius through the small waiting area and into the large treatment room in the back.

It felt strange to be at Doc's clinic again. I'd only been there a couple of times, several months earlier, all in the name of helping Del after his splice went bad.

A lot had gone down after that.

And worst of all was that I'd lost Del—again and again, it seemed—until the day he died and I knew nothing would ever be the same.

Being at the clinic was bringing back a lot of memories for me, and Rex seemed to pick up on that. After we laid Cornelius into one of Doc's barbershop examination chairs, Rex put his arms around me and pulled me close.

"You okay?" he said as Doc bustled around Cornelius.

I nodded as we both watched Doc work. His expression seemed to support my grim prognosis. He picked up the canister and looked at it, confused.

"I was wondering if maybe he needed to use that," I said. "To breathe."

Doc glanced at me, then sniffed at the mask. He fiddled with a knob on the valve, then sniffed it again and jerked his head away. "I don't think so," he said, giving it a shake. "It's pretty much empty, but it doesn't seem like it was good air to start with. Maybe that's what made him sick."

He pressed a button on the bottom, and it made a loud, whirring noise.

"What is that?" I asked, as the noise faded out.

Doc turned it around, looking at it from different angles. "It's got a compressor. It's refillable. Probably meant for short-term use, I guess."

He sniffed at it again. "Smells better now." He shrugged and put it aside.

As he checked Cornelius's pulse again, I said, "He's got a bracelet on the other wrist. Like a hospital bracelet. Says his name is Cornelius."

Doc lifted Cornelius's other wrist and studied the bracelet. He nodded to himself, then began cutting off Cornelius's filthy shirt. The skin underneath seemed unaffected by his splice, but it was scratched and bruised. Doc listened with a stethoscope to his heart and lungs, poked his midsection, and thumped it with two fingers, listening to the sound.

"His condition is deteriorating," he said, as he turned to a drawer and took out a vial and a syringe.

I knew what it was: vitamins and stimulants meant to boost Cornelius's strength, keep him going while Doc figured out how to help him.

As Doc wiped Cornelius's arm with an alcohol swab and gave him the injection, I had a vivid memory of him doing the exact same thing to Del.

It hadn't worked then, and it didn't seem to work now.

Doc attached an oxygen monitor to Cornelius's finger, a glowing plastic clip connected to a machine the size of a toaster on a tall metal stand. When the digital displays on the monitor flickered to life and started cycling through numbers, Doc started drawing vials of blood. He took four of them, and put them into four slots on top of an ancient-looking white plastic apparatus that said DIAGNOSTICOMP. He flicked a switch on it, adjusted a couple of knobs, keyed in some numbers on a keypad, and then stood back as it began to whir and hum.

Apparently satisfied, he turned back to the oxygen monitor and frowned. He readjusted the clip on Cornelius's finger, then smacked the monitor itself. His frown deepened as he removed the clip.

"Either this thing is broken or his blood oxygen level is totally out of whack."

Rex gestured with his thumb toward the corner of the room and said, "What about the hyperbaric thingy you used on Del?"

Doc and I both followed his gaze to the hyperbaric bed, a rectangular platform covered with a plastic bubble that was supposed to help people heal using super-oxygenated air. It was connected to a bunch of hoses that snaked up to the loft upstairs. It used to be suspended from the ceiling up there. I was relieved to see it was now firmly attached to the floor.

"I doubt it'll help," Doc said. "But I suppose it couldn't hurt. We won't know much more until the blood tests are done."

Doc opened the lid and turned to Rex. "Would you mind?"

Rex lifted Cornelius's limp body out of the chair and laid him down in the bed.

Doc gently closed the lids and hit a few switches. The hoses stiffened, filling with pressurized oxygen, and the plastic bubble clouded up.

Doc walked stiffly over to the blood analyzer, suddenly looking tired and old. "We'll give him five minutes and see if that helps."

"Did you see his bracelet?" I asked. "It said he was a patient somewhere."

Doc tweaked a knob on the unit before nodding. "That bracelet is from an OmniCare hospital. I recognize the code."

OmniCare sounded vaguely familiar, a chain of for-profit hospitals. Except a hospital of any kind didn't make sense. "I thought hospitals wouldn't treat chimeras," I said.

"OmniCare's one of the rare ones," Doc said. "They just started to a couple of months ago. Their medical director made a big deal about it on the news."

"Wait," Rex said. "Charleston or something?"

"Charlesford is his name," Doc said. "He's pretty slick. A bit late to the party, as far as treating chimeras with any respect, but better late than never, I guess."

"Well, maybe we can take Cornelius there," I said hopefully.

Doc shook his head. "There are just a few OmniCare facilities that take chimeras. The only one in Pennsylvania is out near Gellersville."

"That's, like, two hours away," I said.

"Yes. And the state he's in, I doubt the kid would make it halfway." Doc looked at the hyperbaric bed and glanced at his watch.

"What about the cord-blood thing you've been working on?" Rex said. "Any chance that could work?"

Doc shook his head. "That's not close to ready for prime time. Besides, we don't even have this kid's birth name, much less his cord blood. Plus, I don't know if whatever is ailing him has anything to do with his splice. And even if we had the cord blood and were able to fix his splice, there's no way he's strong enough to sweat out a change."

"Then what are we going to do?" I asked.

Doc hooked a thumb at the blood analysis machine. "We're going to wait and see what the blood tells us, and then we'll go from there."

For a moment the only sound was the hiss of the hyperbaric bed and the quiet whir of the blood analyzer.

Then something occurred to me. "Doc," I said. "Is OmniCare one of the places Wells gave all that money to after Pitman?"

Just mentioning Pitman made my skin crawl. That was where Del had died.

Doc nodded.

Rex screwed up his face. "You mean *Howard* Wells?"

Doc nodded again. "Pitman was such a public-relations disaster for Wellplant and H4H, Wells tried to buy his way out of it by giving OmniCare money to help care for chimeras."

I'd seen that on the news: Howard Wells saying he and H4H were *horrified* at what happened in Pitman, and making a big show of funding medical care for chimeras, as if he wasn't personally responsible for putting them in danger in the first place.

Rex shook his head with a bitter snort. "Imagine that. You push through a law that dehumanizes people, and then you claim to be surprised that those people are suddenly treated as less than human. I hate that guy."

I was mildly stunned to hear that. There were plenty of good reasons to hate Howard Wells, but while Rex was big and bad in his way, he wasn't about hate. The word didn't sound right coming from him.

"I hear you," said Doc. "If it makes you feel any better, Howard Wells is getting thumped on a number of fronts."

"What do you mean?"

"As much as he condemns what happened in Pitman, a lot of people don't believe he had nothing to do with it."

"Yeah," said Rex. "I'm one of them. What else?"

"His company might be in trouble, too."

I laughed. "Are you kidding? Wellplant's one of the biggest companies in the world. Did you see their holo-ad right before Christmas? Everyone's talking about how powerful the new upgrade is. The company's got to be growing like crazy right now."

"Maybe too fast," Doc said. "Some people think they're over-extended, that they've taken on too much debt and can't fill their orders."

Rex laughed. "Good."

The blood analyzer dinged and Doc went over and pressed a button to print out the results. His frown returned and he shook his head. "This thing must not be working," he mumbled.

I wasn't surprised. It looked at least thirty years old.

Doc shut off the hyperbaric bed and undid the latches on the plastic bubble. Rex and I gathered behind him as he opened the lid. I didn't need confirmation from Doc to know what I was seeing.

Cornelius was dead.

Doc let out a soft whimper of sorrow and frustration. Rex put his arm around me. We stood there for a moment, quietly looking down at Cornelius's body.

Then the silence was shattered by a sharp bang at the front door. A voice barked out, "Open up! Police!"

All three of us froze as a second bang shook the entire building. Then the door exploded into a thousand shards of glass.

Two cops entered, guns drawn. I didn't recognize either of them, and I was struck by the absurdity that my life had taken such a weird turn over the past few months that I might expect to know them at all.

"Freeze! Right there!" said the first officer, holding his gun in front of him with two hands. His name tag said RETZLAFF. He was the younger of the two, and judging from the deepening flush on his ruddy cheeks and the look in his wild blue eyes, the more excitable.

His partner was older, heavier, and calmer, his eyes half closed. The faint wrinkles on his olive skin made him seem almost grandfatherly—but not quite. His tag said TERASOVIC and his gun was pointed at the floor. He put out a hand and gently pushed Retzlaff's weapon down as well. The younger cop looked annoyed, but he went along with it.

Terasovic looked at Doc. "Is this your place? You're Guzman?"

Retzlaff kept his eyes on Rex. His entire body seemed tense.

Doc took off his glasses and polished them with his shirt. "Yes, that's right."

Terasovic turned toward the front door. "All right," he called. "Come on in here."

We heard footsteps on the broken glass, then Kurtz walked in, looking as messed up, as scared, and as defiant as ever.

Terasovic pointed at Doc. "This is the guy you said, right?"

Kurtz glanced around the room, then down at his feet. "That's him, yeah."

"Mr. Guzman, Mr. Kurtz here says that you kidnaped his fiancée, a Ms. Bembry. Is that right, Mr. Kurtz?"

This time Kurtz didn't even look up. "Yes."

Terasovic looked around the lab, then looked at Doc. "Is it okay with you if we search the place?"

Before Doc could answer, Kurtz said, "She's not here."

"What's that?" Terasovic sounded vaguely perplexed. "I thought you told my partner here that this man abducted your fiancée." He glanced at Retzlaff with a hint of a scowl on his face. Retzlaff looked confused. His hands squirmed around the grip of his gun, like they were sweaty.

"Well, yeah, that's basically what happened," said Kurtz. "She disappeared without a trace, and this guy," he said, pointing, "so-called Doctor Guzman over here, was the last person to see her."

Terasovic took a deep breath. "And when was this?"

"Well, I just found out about that part," Kurtz said.

"When did she disappear?"

"October fifteenth."

Terasovic rolled his eyes, then paused, thinking. "The day of the GHA riots?"

"Yeah, I guess so."

"And this girlfriend of yours—"

"Fiancée."

"This fiancée of yours, did she belong to Humans for Humanity or any related groups?"

"No way," Kurtz snapped. "She was a mixie."

Rex stiffened at the slur and Retzlaff tightened his grip on his gun.

Terasovic turned to Rex and said, "Sorry about that." Then he turned back to Kurtz. "Watch your tone, son. So you're saying your girlfriend was a chimera, and she went missing the day of the riots, and you think her disappearance has something to do with Mr. Guzman here?"

"Well, yeah, she just got spliced the night before and she went to see him to get it fixed, because it was stupid. I never saw her again, and he won't tell me what happened to her."

Terasovic's face was darkening. "Well, that's not exactly what you told my partner right before we came in here breaking down doors." He turned to Doc with a forced smile. "I'm sorry for the misunderstanding, Mr. Guzman. I just have to ask, *do* you have any information on the whereabouts of Ms. Claudia Bembry?"

Doc squinted and tilted his head, like he was trying to remember.

I don't know if it was an act or not, but I sure remembered her. I felt myself staring daggers at Kurtz. I had met Claudia when we were both looking for Doc Guzman. The reason she was trying to get her splice fixed was that her boyfriend—*Kurtz*, I now realized—had been supposed to get spliced alongside her, but once she got her splice, he backed out and ran away, leaving her alone to deal with the huge life change they'd been supposed to go through together, and right as all hell was breaking loose.

"Maybe she just doesn't like you anymore," I said. "Maybe she came to her senses and realized what an asshole you are."

"That's not true!" Kurtz yelled. "She loves me! We were supposed to get married!"

I rolled my eyes. "What are you, like, fifteen?"

Terasovic turned to me and said, "Miss, please. Unless you have information to share, please don't escalate the situation." He turned to Doc. "Mr. Guzman, does the name ring a bell? Do you have any information about Ms. Bembry's whereabouts?"

"No. I met her. I tried to help her but couldn't. As far as I know, she's with her parents."

"Okay, that's all I needed to know. Thanks for your cooperation. And I'm sorry for the inconvenience."

"That's it?" Kurtz practically shrieked. "That's all you're going to do?"

"Mr. Kurtz," Terasovic snapped, "have you even *spoken* to Ms. Bembry's parents?"

Kurtz tried to scowl, but it looked more like a pout. "They don't return my calls."

"Because you're an asshole," I muttered.

Kurtz and Terasovic both glared at me. Terasovic took out a business card and approached Doc. "Like I said, Mr. Guzman, we're sorry for the inconvenience." He looked around the clinic, then handed over his card. "You can file a claim with the county to get that door fixed. Just call the number right here, and make sure you have your deed and your property tax ID number."

He gave Doc a fake smile. It was obvious to all of us that no one was paying taxes on the place. Doc took the card anyway and slipped it into his shirt pocket. "Thank you."

Terasovic turned toward the door, motioning for Retzlaff and Kurtz to precede him, but as he did he stopped.

There was an odd expression on his face. He glanced back at Doc, and it took me a second to realize he was actually looking past him. At the hyperbaric bed. The condensation on the bubble had cleared enough that Cornelius's foot was visible.

"What's that?" Terasovic asked.

Doc didn't answer. Terasovic stepped around him, peered into the bubble, then let out a loud sigh, part sad, part victorious, part weary.

"Hands," he said to Doc, as he pulled out his cuffs.

"Wait, what's going on?" I said, but I knew what was going on. Cornelius was dead, and Doc was about to be blamed.

"Were these two involved?" Terasovic asked Doc as he put the cuffs on him.

"You can't arrest him," Rex said, moving toward them. "He didn't do anything wrong."

Retzlaff pointed his gun in Rex's direction, his hands shaking. Kurtz smiled—a smug, infuriating little smile.

"No, they weren't," Doc said. He looked up at Rex and shook his head, telling him not to interfere.

"Sorry, folks," Terasovic said. "I know you fixers think you're doing the right thing, and maybe sometimes you are. But performing unlicensed medical procedures is unlawful. I generally don't give a crap about that, but if someone dies because of it . . ." He put one hand on Doc's shoulder, the other on his cuffed hands. "Mr. Guzman, you are under arrest. For murder."